BY SUCH A PARTING LIGHT

BY SUCH A

Parting Light

A
NOVEL

BARBARA LALLA

The University of the West Indies Press
Jamaica • Barbados • Trinidad and Tobago

The University of the West Indies Press
7A Gibraltar Hall Road, Mona
Kingston 7, Jamaica
www.uwipress.com

A catalogue record of this book is available from the
National Library of Jamaica.

ISBN: 978-976-640-938-8 (paper)
978-976-640-939-5 (ePub)

Cover and book design by Robert Harris
Set in Bembo 11.5/14 x 27

Printed in the United States of America.

CONTENTS

CONTENTS

PART II

PART I

Promise me
if (one day when you wake up) you hear I'm dead,
you will write my story.
Promise.

1

A TALE-SPINNER'S DILEMMA

PROMISES, TO BREAK OR FULFILL. Each lodges in waiting like a razor blade in the purse. When they fade from mind they float free, slicing invisible through the air. We fumble on over the years heedless of how we breathe them in and out. For what to do? Eventually we are thankful just to breathe at all. Especially now, when disaster lurks in that most basic of all instincts – to inhale.

With the usual tearing of mental muscle, I avert my mind from the worldwide mayhem of stacked coffins and container morgues, and I duck behind the old mask of composure. Straightening the three-inch stack of paper to fit flush with the far-left corner of my desk, I grapple with my predicament while I can, for it is barely light and the children are still asleep. The way ahead forks dark and even the path that led here blurs behind me. A beam slants in between yellow-green joints of bamboo fading on my study drapes and lights up today's page of my diary with its list that I shall never get through.

"Despite those famous time-management skills?" our nephew, Francis, asked a decade or so ago when I complained I wasn't writing as much as I had planned. "Why?"

Perhaps because much ought not take form in words let alone materialize in print. But so many conflicting voices inhabit my head.

"Aria, you write what you need to write." A colleague, Jenine Martin, scoffed at the idea of loyalty to anything but Truth. Only, I must, must get it *right* – "true" yes, but also "correct, fitting, decent". I write to make sense of it, impose order on chaos. Yet now I'm at a standstill. "Writer's block?" Jenine had probed once when it had happened before – God knows how I let it drop. Her tone sounded a nice balance of pity and condescension.

"Perish the thought." I turned it aside rather than word my sense of being in spate with all that my other commitments had stemmed up. Years of academic work had forestalled my storytelling – the teaching, research and student matters, and the drone of endless circular meetings. Not to mention the Roche family life. Let's hitch that on as if it teeters on the periphery rather than churning at the core, and as if regular people (and what others *are* there?) shelter in their private lives immune from larger-than-life events. As if all that is heart-stopping amounts to nothing more than melodramatic invention.

Apart from the horrific nature of some ordinariness, there breaks in every now and then that lightning bolt of the unthinkable – of what would have seemed far-fetched had it even crossed one's mind. Only months back, who could have pictured the widescale scything beyond our shores? A year ago how could I have imagined my own intimate catastrophe? From out that blue sky the outside chance smashes in, skewering private routines with slivers of some alternative reality.

And my routines? I reach for them even in this torrent from which I strive to word life back together. Old loves torn away and new ones to keep afloat even as something faceless and ravening circles outside.

I've spent the past months anchoring routines back in, for sanity's sake.

⋯⁊⫯⫰⋯

Before all this, I'd get to my desk before daylight or tiptoe to my study at ten-thirty when the gecko above the window had shut up and vanished. It should have been the end of the day for me too. Yet there I was, drawing in that deep breath. To write anything that might get out there is to take one's life in one's hands, and there was rarely time for it but *late*.

Joel would have fallen asleep or was pretending so as to salve my conscience while I negotiated between my different selves. Joel knew how tightly I wrapped research and marking around Cynnie's Spanish vocab or her painting, how much I wedged between conversations over supper or forages under the Julie mango tree.

Once, as the smell of turpentine hung heavy around us, Cyn dabbed at the canvas on the easel she had set in front her mirror. "How come I catch the likeness when it comes to other faces, but never my own," she grumbled, and she was right. She captured neither that gleam of mischief nor the sweetness – not that I can summon up that inadequate self-portrait now. And what if our true faces fade from mind as well – if any of us had one true face? What rushes back is her dissatisfied scowl at the *un*likeness. "Am I really that lame looking?"

"You're beautiful, Cynnie Roche."

She cocked her head to the side and studied the mirror appraisingly, not a vain tilt but a survey that was ruthlessly clear-eyed for a teenager. Then she flashed that glance at me, a dark sparkle of her eyes and quiver of barely contained grin. "All the self-portraits I've tried would make a book," she said. "A book of not-portraits. A not-book."

I proferred a blatant lie about her self-portraits coming along, and returned to the script I'd had in hand when I wandered into her room. Francis always insisted I took the scripts too seriously. "Skim through and put the grade, Aunt," he said. "You teachers are nuts or what? You could make the job eat up you whole evening so?" But Francis now – who *was* he? Really, I mean.

Or is it age creeping, disorienting – my own mind bending and deforming the world and everyone I know in it, dredging up those gone, vivid as yesterday, while blurring others vibrant around me? Is it dementia eating my universe away, dislodging trust in those I was so sure of, setting me at odds with the one close to me as my soul, prompting me to give ear to this stranger who, Joel insists, is more dangerous than the contagion itself. "Lock the woman out of your head," he said. But I couldn't brush things away like that, even when I could shut up about them.

I could fix my face to erase clues, though. Who on campus knew what domestic emergencies dogged my career? Big ones like the mad babysitter, let alone tiny day-to-day upsets. Once, I paused in chairing a meeting to accept Cynnie's agonized phone call. The temporary helper had ignored chicken parts left out for her and made pelau with spare ribs that were for Cyn's birthday lunch on Saturday.

"Not a problem," I said briskly into the phone. "We'll replace the essential equipment in time for the function." I rang off with all the composure of one operating well above mundane considerations. All a pose.

My screen of serenity worked because of Joel's connivance and his huge enjoyment of Cyn's adventures. She was six when he announced, "Missis says she wants to keep a diary. Asked me whether she'd have to wait till she could spell." When I stared at him, he grinned. "Put it to me on the maxi this morning." He'd accompanied Cyn on a school field trip, riding with the group in a bone-jarring maxi-taxi, and returned bursting with pride over her eagerness to stroke a young anaconda.

Then, too – so far from feeling threatened or offended by what I was – he bragged about me shamelessly at every opportunity. More readily than he, I absorbed the consequences of a failing fridge, ailing rabbit or unreliable help; but there he crouched beside me on sleepless nights over a feverish child. So my spells of examination scripts or conference calamity passed over us without recrimination on his part, any more than rainy or dry seasons could be cause for blame.

Over the years Joel and I found our way into a saving practice, to re-converge on evenings, picking over the hours spent apart in much the same spirit as we deliberated over our platter of snacks. Slowly these had evolved from deep fried or peppery delicacies like phulouri and pommecythere chow. Now, casting his eyes over a dish of carrot and celery sticks with guacamole, Joel might murmur, "Sauvignon blanc, then," conciliating despite that habitual laconic style. Then we'd lounge, sipping, turning over on our tongues the day that was going down around us and comparing our expectations about those in store. The darkening garden filled with the heady scent of a cereus next door while we talked in a desultory fashion, or avidly, or not at all.

Next morning, I'd awake to the incandescence of his first swift celebratory glance sweeping me as I switched on the lamp and bounded from the bed. "Now what?" His eyes snapped with anticipation as he swung his legs off the mattress. "Aha! High Commission, to entice into funding the visit for what's-his-face? Unpronounceable one."

"Just so."

By then he was sliding the shower door, churning out questions faster than I could answer. The pungent smell of that old-time red soap he clung to softened soon enough to the vanilla and clove of shaving cream. A minty kiss and he was off, up the highway an hour before me. As publisher of a major Caribbean newspaper – juggling staff, PR, budget and quality control; cold-shouldering efforts at censorship, and reining in some freelance reporter to evade a libel suit – Joel was northbound on the Sir Solomon Hochoy Highway by daybreak. By evening, he was skimming files on investments. No fiddling with gadgets or cars for him. We called Mr Farley when a door jammed in rainy season or an appliance sparked.

Joel worked involuntarily, the way one breathes. Files rampant over the dining table, orange extension cords snaking across the floor to an obese ceramic table lamp perched precariously on defunct encyclopedia volumes. Two laptops, for viewing documents side by side, lined up with the downstairs house phone and his mobile. In the midst, cocoa cooled scentless, waiting only to spill across a page.

"Who?" he shouted into the receiver, his habitual amplitude on the phone. "*Hold.*" He snatched his cell. "Right, and elsewhere I might get 90,000," he said. "You living here or not, Mitch?" Back to the landline. "So yes, selling newspapers, but not exploiting rape and murder of a child." Mobile jangling again. "Aha? Which? The one without the lede?" Whatever he did consumed him; so I suppose we reinforced each other's *isms*.

"Wearing yourself out," he of all people rebuked me.

Every now and then it comes back to me – the drive from San Fernando in south Trinidad to St Augustine in the north, day in, year out. Before I was thirty I'd landed the appointment on what was one of three campuses in those days. The university had served the Caribbean from sites in Jamaica, Barbados, and Trinidad and Tobago long before any virtual campus was conceived of. When I was in my last trimester and striving to govern my bladder, the car crawled through gnarled traffic, in at the south entrance to the St Augustine Campus. By the time I'd circled for a parking space and scurried towards my building in torment, I would waddle up two flights of stairs and whisk past my office – once only to find the Ladies locked and to chase downstairs again and across to the library. Years passed before I learnt some women carried spare underwear to work. "All very well now," I complained to Joel. "How was I to know that when I needed to?"

"You have this problem with asking for help."

But didn't he have his own deep pockets of reserve? I had a sense of how much he'd chosen not to confide even in me. His father's confused whispers in the old man's last months came back to me as they so often had, and again I put them resolutely out of mind. Still, Joel's passing assessment of me was spot-on, for I'd been young on the job in those days, and who asks strangers more senior and more published than oneself about personal discomforts? Except on TV – like those ads where chic young women in high heels smell laundry and sniff toilets and cat litter, while the elderly share confidences about constipation, debt, male impotence, female baldness or incontinence. So, no. In my middle-class Caribbean reserve I never had compared notes with colleagues about bathroom emergencies on the highway.

Then, the traffic in those days of *cluster*. Once, decades ago, when disaster seemed imminent along the clogged Hochoy Highway, I swung the wheel to dive off onto a side road for a shortcut that I turned out not to know after all. The narrowing thread of asphalt, then gravel, spun me around till I was hopelessly lost for ten minutes before the mean little road spat me back out onto the highway to wait my turn, all over again, in the line of cars.

Another detour Joel often took in dry season seduced me one November from the highway along a road that dissolved into flooded cane fields. I steered on past cars as shut down and stranded as I expected to be at any moment. A patchy brown and white commondog paddled by bravely, muzzle pointed valiantly aloft, and I took courage from him; but after that I eschewed shortcuts and clung to main roads however long and circuitous. So I never grasped the meshwork of alternative routes from which most drivers can choose at will. I get lost easily.

Yet even those tense commutes I could relieve by leaving South three hours before my first class. The choked highway towards home was another matter. If it was early enough I'd have Cyn to collect, or, later, a flat tire at dusk to lay me at the mercy of strangers – who, as it turned out, treated me with utmost kindness. Then, on the seemingly endless drive home, rain pounded down, refracting the light of oncoming cars and submerging the edges of the street.

Meanwhile Joel grimly scrutinized the glistening black road from our doorway, envisioning the worst till he grew explosive with fear. When I got in, he pounded the door with his fist, eyes squeezed too tight to even look at me, because he had *thought something had happened*. Cell phones lay beyond our ken, so we were not, as they now call it, *connected* – well, not by wireless tendrils, intangible, unrelenting, addictive and cold.

And there was time itself to juggle, steering along the highway while working through the forking routes of one project after the next. The struggle of commuting went forward against the rigour of research. Collaborative studies thrilled with their interplay of ideas and nuanced conclusions, but occasionally there persisted some uneasy fit between disciplines. Or, a faint whiff of resentment about uneven participation rankled unspoken, subtly complicating efforts to complete the book. So, like many of my generation in the Humanities I came late to multi-authored publications after spending most of my working life in the privacy of my own mind. Meanwhile, the diverse streams of academia rushed on simultaneously, sweeping us forward to face wildly disparate students reading or refusing to read Literature.

Pointless saying *when I find time I'll push that novel out.* Unless you shook free of day-to-day demands that took hold as if by invisible suction pads, there was never world nor time enough. Ask Marvell, though he had a vested interest – especially in having his interest doff her vest – for he had a point. We snatch what chance we can at ardour of the flesh or mind. We track the little splinters of light that zigzag arbitrarily or go out leaving us clueless of whether they will flicker on again – like candleflies, but for those thin, keen edges.

Different, perhaps, if I'd lived and worked in some well-healed metropolitan institution with competitive salaries, larger pension, more graduate assistance. Oh, I enjoy a civilized and comfortable existence; but we are not called a developing country for nothing. Still, our size and insularity offer protection of a sort.

Islands within islands. Beyond our shores and far beyond the new silence outside our house there brews a storm of apocalyptic proportions. We have sworn to shelter inside for as long as it takes. But what if in the midst of it I have let in something worse, something intent on devouring all we love most, all we have left. And what if there is no more *we*? And at this stage.

Now I have at last more time in the day and less time left in life for writing fiction, the stories press in, or rather out, pushing and shoving for air, egged on by what I've read over the decades. Some relish of the saltiness of time. Those volumes crowd around – novels, verse and drama of all ages, sixteenth- and seventeenth-century political history, metaphysical poets, a plague diary, Elizabethan theatre, the age of expansion, Beatrice, Faustus, Caliban, Shylock, a Scottish castle, a greenworld, feuding factions. An island full of noises.

My older books – some from my childhood, some my parents' – are mainly hardcover in dark mottled fabric, dried and crumbling, pages splitting, fading print on darkening paper, but impossible to part with. Volumes that I prize above my dukedom, as the man said: my first copy of *Macbeth,* my mother's old *Sonnets,* the *Faerie Queen* she bought with the bravest intentions then begged me to take away before she threw it in the ravine. Yes, yes – all online now, and even long years ago decked anew in brightly coloured paperback covers. Carefully aligned with the old editions, these rub shoulders with their elders and with the newer giants of our own time and space. Rank on rank they press forward, Senior, Naipaul, Walcott, alongside Yeats, Marlowe, Austen. Their smell enfolds me.

The walls flash with posters and mementos from students – a tinkling bookmark from China, a pencil sharpener from Stratford engraved *Sharper than a Serpent's Tooth* – keepsakes from a time one walked arm in arm amidst a huddle of other tourists. Cramming a top shelf are plaques, presented for one award after the next before that vanished vista of densely packed faces in some numbingly air-conditioned auditorium.

From under the couch spreads the frayed mat my dear old Raleigh used to lie on, panting and wagging until I carried her to the clinic and held my arms around her while they put her down, because there was nothing else to be done, and I'd cried silently the whole way there and more uninhibitedly the whole way back, but not at the clinic in front of her to make her feel badly for me. Back in my study, alone, I dissolved onto that mat swearing to myself *never* to get another dog to keep up this string of partings every decade or so – never, never again, even as I felt about for a newspaper with the Classifieds to see what pup might be available to stop the pain.

As I tugged the mat from under the foot of the couch, there was my copy of *Pride and Prejudice* used for "A" Level exams and searched for months ago. I'd thought it lost. So I crouched right there reading and crying until I dried up and a dull thud in my chest faded, and no one else was any the wiser. Then, as now, the skin of things was pulled taut over some hollow space beneath, so the pounding found its way into rhythm.

Fiction is my machine for righting pandemonium. Beyond the world of books, the lines between realism, fantasy, horror, soap and sci-fi have dissolved, and so I shall write as I see fit, gathering mental tools and firing up the engine for transforming perplexity to understanding.

Only, now, this new tale – nothing to do with *us,* Joel insists – unfolds alongside me on that other desk that came to us from Cyn. An elegant writing table, yet chilling and portentous in the new presence it has come to project among us. Between us. For now a marriage of over forty years upends and nothing essential is as it was, although black ash from the fires that break out arbitrarily in dry season floats in as it always has and settles on the page. Lives coming apart, apparently, because of lines on paper, carelessly left upon this other, slim-legged desk – this desk on delicate lines.

Lines. Even more relentlessly than they etch the skin around my eyes and into my brain, they slice their way onto the page. How to stop these unspooling bylines, storylines. Bloodlines.

But also, how to tamper with narratives already underway around one. A day comes when you wake up and wonder: could it all have gone another way? Less waste? Time otherwise distributed? And if you open your eyes in the wee hours, these ponderings set on you savagely, piercing screens you had not seen yourself throw up. Was there blood? A flash and rending metal, and a whiff of scorched flesh before silence and rushing dark? Oh God. To stop my mind plummeting I swerve it onto another path. Stop it crashing through emptiness in a long last plunge into the deep.

I try to block such waking nightmares with thoughts of past years, but as those years return to me they propel the narratives carving their way out. All are reset now against the havoc in the world outside, against the absolute requirement to create a complete world, an adequate universe inside these walls. And looping in and out of all these disparate plots runs the empathy for my only child set off on a journey beyond our reach. What wouldn't I give to intervene in her story and have her locked up too, back here with us.

Most of the tales that entice me are forbidden, and all because I forefeel the pang of wounding the very people most worth writing about. Even the odd exposé of some fraud or injustice that deserves or calls for disclosure, even the most urgent investigation may do someone quite innocent an injury too great to be offset by what little good I achieve in bringing it to light. And one, this latest tale elbowing out the rest: might it destroy the lives of everyone I love – as he insists? And then mine would be worthless. Yes of course, if I could I'd turn aside this onslaught of words, memories, intentions, vows sharpened by years and circumstance. Yet it all keeps hacking its way out.

So here I am, haunted by the books I must not write.

2

DOUBLE EDGE

THIS ONE, THOUGH, THIS COMMISSIONED BOOK started with a phone call from the other side of the planet, not even a year ago. Cyn's voice came through on speaker as if from the next room.

"You sound so nearby," Joel shouted into the phone.

"And shall be – if you can stand putting us up while we find our feet." They planned to move back home to Trinidad, she announced.

It's at a time like that, as your heart starts a drumroll of jubilation thundering in your ears, when you know it is very possible to die of joy. Eventually I could hear her again, saying she would bring the children to Trinidad then go back, finish packing up, and return in a fortnight or so. After months of churning out applications she had a firm job offer at last. Yes, of course. Connor's was almost certain as well, with a backup plan for a position in Grenada. If necessary he'd commute until something else turned up here.

Meanwhile – better not discuss it with anyone else – no, don't even message Con, whose blood pressure was through the roof. Yes, *over-excited* about the plan. She was trying to make the move as smooth as possible for him, and of course, he'd be fine. Just – the less talk the better. She'd fill in details when she saw us in a little while.

We couldn't believe it. After she rang off, we stared at the phone dumbly before falling into each other's arms. It was good news and rebirth at the same time, combining the festive and the sacred like a feast of the Church. I mean, off she had gone to the edge of the world – or left us on the perimeter. Whichever. At any rate, what with the postgrad, and then her marriage, it had been years since we had come to understand (though never quite accept) that our one child would live out her days so far abroad we could only hope to see her a few times more in life. The grandchildren would call forth speculation and longing from the other side of the globe and know us mainly by anecdote or thin exchange on Skype. So it was the wonder of this, that our lives would be refilled. And with that thought we at last allowed ourselves to acknowledge how much had seeped away through Cynnie's absence.

After the call, and another jubilant hug or two, Joel and I left for our sushi with the determination to lighten up on the Shiraz this time in favour of Chardonnay. The planning began at once over the Smoky Dragon and called for that little square side dish of extra ginger. The supposing and perhapsing grew more and more playful as our minds sharpened in anticipation of ongoing contact with the young – not just visiting but taking up residence on the same small land mass. It went to our heads: everything we said, however foolish, morphed into a matter for hilarity. "Sort of night we'd have played The Game with Cynnie," Joel reminisced, "and whatever couple friends she had for sleepover. Those were good days, in that old house down south."

Why South? Joel had begun work as a communications officer in a San Fernando firm, and we'd invested in this fine bit of property overlooking the sea. We'd repaired and rented it out for a year or two but moved in there when Cynnie began to run around. At the time Joel planned to build another house from scratch and rent it out, but an emergency had overtaken that – and the less said about it the better. We stayed south till it came to us with grim finality what it meant for Cyn to take firm root in Sydney. Even then we moved north from San Fernando to St Augustine only when I turned fifty-five. Joel was preparing for pre-retirement leave then and had begun grumbling about the hassle of my driving back and forth to campus through solidifying traffic.

Meanwhile, he'd been finessing our finances. We cashed in life insurance policies now our only child had grown up. We had sound medical plans, decent pensions and rent from a couple townhouses. Moving north meant refurbishing a townhouse in Court Augustine and renting the family home. Once we had relocated students from the larger townhouse, we overhauled it completely – what is it these fellows *do* to bathroom fixtures, to furniture, tiles, doors – and we made ourselves tolerably comfortable. "But did you ever work out that burn mark on the ceiling over the toilet?" Joel asked subsequently, from time to time.

The morning after Cyn's call, he said, "We'll stuff our young people in here for as long as they like, eh?" Then, unexpectedly, he asked, "Ever sorry we moved up and rented out the house?"

"Nope."

"How come? Thought you loved it."

"And still do. But I'd have been cleaning it – bit by bit every day to keep up. Then don't talk about the garden. I wouldn't have gone on loving it."

"Could have taken Tinsel for an extra day a week."

"Leaving aside the question of how to get her down the highway, you'd be griping about Tinsel twice a week rather than once. Not that I can see what you have against her. Well, I can. But the woman works hard, she really does."

"Don't know that. And it's exhausting – finding one's way anywhere in the house without running into her. Immanent – in every room at the same time, directly in one's path. And yak, yak, non-stop."

"Anyway," I responded briskly, "you better come to terms with us having her three days each week the children spend with us, at least till their parents get back here." He stared at me in dismay. "Put in a GPS or something," I concluded rudely and planted a loud kiss on his cheek. I had much to do and bustled off.

He shouted after me. "Where you going?"

"To make lists, for Tru Valu, Massy Stores, PriceSmart. Got to start laying in food that isn't primarily high-fibre or low everything else. Like guava cheese for Cynnie. Then there are those weird disinfecting wipes she likes. You better figure out fun things for the children."

"The Game," he said.

Right. I'd originally called it *Missing Branches*, but Cyn said, "Nah! *Missing Limbs*. Sounds more ghoulish." It was more rhythmic anyway. But we only ever referred to it as *The Game*. It was a sort of dialect of charades, through which to convey a member of some family we all knew. Whoever was *It* acted out the way other family members responded to this *missing limb* and the Elder had the final word on the correct answer. Looking back at The Game with Cynnie got Joel anticipating a succession of boisterous romps.

He began hauling out and rummaging through one dilapidated cardboard box after the next.

"I bet Micah and Melody play chess," I said, digging around for those photos we had printed. Scrabbling through the boxes of albums and loose pictures, we agreed Micah and Melody looked alike, as one would expect of even fraternal twins, but some unsorted photos muddled me. I worked out that one Cyn had sent recently must be Mattie. "The image of Micah as we met him years ago."

"Yup," Joel said as he set off about his own affairs. "Much business appertaining," he cast over his shoulder.

I left the boxes right there and wandered off to my study.

~)|~

The evening of Cyn's call, the TV had been off. Joel found accounts of local violence unsettling at night, and I had wearied of the rhetoric on the US channels, especially a type of boastful power-flaunting verbiage we dismissed as Robber Talk. Besides, fitting truth together from it no longer seemed worth the odd unstudied insult. Some international newscaster might toss out the swaggering claim to his own country's exclusive handle on enlightenment or deliver an inane denial like *this is not America.* Spare us, I agreed when Joel powered off. The house was instantly and blessedly quiet.

I'd been taking it easier than usual, because a week or so before we'd had a mild scare about the possible need for a stent.

I'd dreamt I was running, first modelling my efforts on Joel's exercise routine, but then the treadmill accelerated unexpectedly so I reached out to grab the hand offered me. Then it slipped from mine, and from the corner of my eye, I saw a small form dart for the door. I could only scream, but I was screaming a name I could not hear – not only the hand torn from mine but the name from my lips – a nameless child, a promise denied and age suddenly crushing down on me as I stumbled off the treadmill in pursuit. So burdened I could not keep up, it was all I could do to lumber on, eventually sinking to my knees and, as I was there anyway, gasping an entreaty. *Restore this child slipped from me or finish me at once. I could not live if I mislaid a child*, I sobbed; *strike me dead, strike me dead, please, God*, my chest pounding till Joel's voice brought me out and he got me sitting up in the bed while I tried to suck air into my lungs.

Doctor, tests, usual scenario. All over a stupid dream.

False alarm. But it stirred me to start a proper exercise routine with a specialist in cardiac rehab. When I messaged Cyn about the trainer, she had fired back instantly. *That's the way, Mom. Proud of you.* So we knew I was in good shape, and when she'd called Joel and I had been celebrating with the Shiraz my cardiologist prescribed.

I'd earned it, I decided, after a day on the laptop with only a few paragraphs of incisive prose to show for it. Unveiling the familiar world as a place hitherto unknown and in the end unfathomable was work enough, but it was new terrain as well. Retirement had held out to me what seemed a choice between intellectual limbo or a headlong bolt along untried paths. So I bolted, just at the point when most of one's equipage for radical departure was seizing up. We had begun to feel as if we had been fashioned for older, well-mapped and oft-travelled ways. But I bolted.

That evening of the phone call, I'd tripped over Joel's shoes in the doorway as usual. *Why*, I'd demanded inwardly yet again before righting myself to sit down and preparing to ignore them. The ancient glider on the porch creaked plaintively, and I jotted a mental note to oil it, but we wouldn't be sitting long. Joel took the view that we should make my clean bill of health official by going out to eat, and sushi was not too heavy at night. Joel was prone to acid reflux, though otherwise in fine condition for his mid-seventies, having stayed stubbornly below the border for diabetes over the past decade.

For years I'd witnessed with trepidation his breakneck regime on the treadmill. His feet clobbered the running deck till the cabinet on the other side of the wall vibrated and set china and glassware rattling. On this particular night he had showered and changed in time to turn off the local news as it began. "Last thing we need on a night of festivity," he said, and poured the wine.

Joel's long rectangular face and monosyllabic responses might have cast him, to a stranger, as withdrawn. But his eyes were intense, alight with interest in everything before them. "Chairs, you," he muttered.

We were clinking glasses when the phone rang. With his unwieldy right hand Joel set down one of the crystal stem glasses Jackie and the rest had given us for our fortieth anniversary. I remember how it wobbled, chimed again against mine but steadied, as he turned to snatch up the phone with his left.

Following the night of the call, on the narrow porch of our St Augustine townhouse where Joel and I sat evening after evening, we at last put into words what had gone missing from earlier times. We could say it at last now we had the news.

Our daughter, Cyndra, whom almost everyone called Cyn, had seemed permanently fixed in Australia, where she had gone for her graduate programme in pediatric cardiology. There she had met Connor Firaki – a Trinidadian, despite this surname we'd never heard before. He had left Trinidad for the States as a child with his parents, and she met him when he was rapidly rising in a mental health organization in Sydney where he had landed after a brilliant university performance in clinical psychology. Drop-dead gorgeous, Cynnie had described him to us, his path littered by swooning women. That worried me until I actually met him on the usual unreliable Skype connection, where he turned out to be quiet-mannered and unassuming, though unarguably handsome. Despite a fuzzy, juddering screen and fizzing audio I could make out a sweet steady face along with old-world courtesy.

"But he's charming," I exclaimed to Joel, who looked puzzled.

"Why wouldn't he be?" he demanded. "Cynnie's choice." Which summed it up.

I could hardly believe we weren't at the ceremony, but they'd gone to some registrar's office, calling us on the way in what was – for us – the middle of the night. We leaned into the screen to study the pictures. "You don't find she looks thin?" I asked. But Joel protested she'd put on weight. We both agreed she looked deliriously happy. Connor, too, serious or quietly pleasant in every other shot we had seen, radiated a sort of triumphant delight.

For a while they stayed in Sydney, before relocating to Los Angeles. Then, a few years after having the twins, they moved back to Sydney. "Dr Connor Firaki rejoins his old organization as executive director," Cyn announced with a flourish.

The older children, Micah and Melody, were not quite four when they visited us with their mother in 2014. That was well before Mattie was born. Connor had come with Cynnie eight years earlier to celebrate their first anniversary. "What a visit," I reminded Joel, as I reached for an olive while thinking back to that first meeting. "Lovely young man – vibrant, witty. Since the wedding I've kept thinking – if only he'd relocate to our hemisphere."

"Cheese to chalk," Joel agreed, with a gesture of his hand towards Kevin Cambridge's house, across the way to ours in the complex. Kevin had been soft on Cyn for years, but he was only sixteen years younger than me and fifteen years older than Cyn.

"Decent fellow and local, but dull – stolid as crapaud," Joel concluded. True enough, unkind or not. Well. Not as unattractive as a toad by any means, but Kevin could never have turned Cyn on. She'd always been vivacious as well as meticulous, and she'd found Kevin ponderous and his shirt collars depressingly grubby. Connor, now – he lit her up.

That first visit in '06, at the airport, we strained to see this paragon in the flesh almost as desperately as to lay eyes on Cynnie again. We'd prepared ourselves, warning each other that Cyn was clearly besotted. "Nothing mortal could be as she describes him," Joel said.

"Has to be a good sort, though," I reasoned, "and no doubt easy enough on the eye."

When they came out, his head was turned away, and for a moment all there was to see was a shock of dark, glossy curls, thick and springy. Then she waved madly, pointing at us, and he swung around.

Lord, she was right. Straight from Bollywood, but with neither the babyface nor the dark sultry posing. His was an entirely different glamour to the turbulent, teasingly mysterious: it held you with – I can only say – delight. It was the sort of face you could not look away from – the directness of the glance perhaps, its intensity. There was a glow to it – not just the sheen of perfect skin but of vitality, liveliness of mind and body right there on the surface for anyone to see. She darted forward and I grabbed her first, revelling in her filling my arms again, displacing the aching emptiness of years. When she tore away to fling herself on her father, I turned to Connor and paused, transfixed all over again.

Connor's face was that perfect oval framed by large, well-shaped, long-lobed ears (nibbleable, Cynnie later whispered to me wickedly). They complemented the dramatic down-thrust of his nose and the strong but gently pointed chin that was roughened and softened at once by a faint fur of stubble shading the jaw and upper lip. On anyone else I regarded stubble with disfavour, as untidiness. On Connor, it was strokable.

He lit up with amusement, for, as I saw at once, he was studying me study him, his eyes filled with . . . something. Understanding? Soft brown, long-lashed eyes, keen and direct – the mildly upward curve of those lower lids reshaping that wide-eyed gaze to smiling eyes. And above, eyebrows like spread wings feathered off towards the temples so as never to harden his expression.

And the mouth. My God. Shouldn't be allowed. Full lips but without a hint of spoilbaby pout, the upper curving lushly over the slightly smaller, vulnerable lower lip. The natural upturn at the corners creased to a grin. "Hi there, Cynnie's mom." A surprisingly deep voice with the reassuring timbre one hoped for in any doctor, let alone a psychiatrist, drew me into his hug.

Connor was also an instant hit with Joel's nephew, Francis. "Just as well," Joel said. "Boy has been going through such a rotten patch."

When Joel's younger brother went abroad (as they liked to put it), he had left his son, Francis, a toddler, in the care of a somewhat foolish mother. So from the late '70s on, Joel had been trying as far as possible to be a father to the boy. Even a couple decades later, when a truck smashed into the car that Francis's mother was driving south on the Sir Solomon Hochoy Highway after Jouvert, and killed the poor woman on the spot, it was obvious we would be daily in the hospital till Francis was out of danger. (Yes, he was in the car, but his mother was driving it down the Hochoy because he had had one or two too many. So he was in a state over that too.)

It was after his release, when we brought him home, that I grew closer to him. Francis was a well-trained and versatile officer, who'd been rising fast in the Ministry of National Security. He'd developed a confidence that made him even more attractive in his forties than he had been as a youngster. Fun-loving and never still, he now found himself housebound till his ribcage could heal and the right arm come out of plaster. As time crawled his spirits slid lower, and so it was a relief to see Connor's visit lift him.

Sometimes when Joel and I drove Cynnie and the children out to her old haunts, Francis and Connor wandered off by themselves, Connor driving Francis carefully bolstered by firm cushions. Later, I would smell it as we opened the door – oil, peas and pepper heavy in the air and the lingering tang of chow. They'd confess they had been exploring backroads past Princes Town or had dipped by the little streetside stalls in Debe for aloo pies or sahina. Quite as often, though, they stayed put, playing cards and ordering in some other unwholesome snack.

"I thought Cyn was the only person in the world who put ketchup on pizza," Connor remarked, watching in mock horror as Francis ladled it on.

"Don't think you'll break her of that." Francis grinned.

"I've other methods." Connor waved a hand at the red concoction of tomatoes and herbs churning in the blender. "Though she gets anxious when she sees me start my own. I forgot the blender open once, and it blew up all over my face."

"She must have scrubbed you for weeks."

"You know then. She's kind of hyper about spills and smears." Then, "Guess what! I make a mean salsa as well."

The two stayed in touch afterwards — Facebook and that stuff, I suppose. Meanwhile, here in the void between Cyn's visits, Francis filled an evening or two every couple weeks. He seemed as disappointed as we were five years later when Connor stayed back while Cyn travelled from L.A. with the three-year-old twins. Some family emergency prevented him, and although Cyn folded back into her old life here while Micah and Melody frolicked about on the grass, sticky with mango juice, her mind was far away, the gleam gone out.

Then, just before she called this last time, I had worked myself back into shape, determined to see them all soon – together. We were planning our visit to Sydney at last. But not a word had we breathed of it. And now they were coming home to us Joel and I began to figure out how we'd get everything done and out of the way before they arrived, so as to spend time with the children.

⸺⁓⁓⸺

We had to have our work properly sorted out to be able to function. Over the decades our projects had run separately, though side by side. My earlier research came together in a sixth book, prompted by Raleigh's outburst at the regime in which he operated. I tracked his grievances amidst Britain's expansion to the west parallel to my other work on the rising outcry from early Caribbean writers. Teasing out an unspoken conversation between voices worlds and ages apart, I made that the framework for the book.

Perhaps that should have been enough for me. But all the while I was – on a quite different level – *possessed* (the only term I can fix on) by convolutions of character in fiction. Story after story demanded to be heard, more and more vociferously. Often these evolved from scraps of personal experience and hung on characters unveiling themselves – tales I was not sure I should repeat.

Sometimes in the cacophony of competing demands I missed other, nearer voices and commonplace happenings. A jangling startled me into dropping the new cartridge I was snapping into my printer. It was the first time I was getting to my desk since the call. Our doorbell was ringing over and over as if someone had tried politely then lost patience and decided to pummel it. When I got downstairs I discovered it was Tinsel, delivering, sotto voce, a tirade just loud enough to be overheard.

"After I ring this ting till I tired, and like Ms Lady don't know how outside here does be *heated*."

No one knew why Anastasia Penrose was called Tinsel, or even if she really was Penrose. The husband she complained of seemed so elusive, I wondered if the marriage was wishful thinking on her part and whether she was still Anastasia Ramlochan, but I felt reluctant to open the floodgates of her narrative ability by asking. She was bound to make me feel the enquiry was fast and out of place, even as the explanation bore down.

"Morning, Tinsel," I murmured humbly, holding the door ajar.

She eyed me sternly then eased her way in. After some time she relented. "Yes, good morning to you, Mistress Roche." Only she persistently pronounced me *Roach*, and I had given up trying to correct her.

Tinsel made her stately way to the kitchen and threw around a preliminary glance of scorn before seizing a cloth and elaborately wiping a corner of the counter, where she then rested her purse. "Ms Roach, last night I dream I did flying, so when I wake up I say is a sign go help me win the lottery. I have to check you papers (ent you have *Express*?) and I go see if this dream telling me bout bird or plane or what else – so I go buss the mark, nah." Buss the mark? She must have recognized my unfamiliarity with national lottery jargon. "Pick whatever to win – centipede, corbeau, opium man, fish. Whatever, nah."

Joel burst in unsuspectingly, big with his latest idea for the children's entertainment. "What about a rabbit?"

"Say what?" Tinsel demanded at a pitch that spun him around. "Rabbit whe'?"

I postponed a faint recollection that one of the children was subject to allergies and intervened hastily. "Our grandchildren are coming for a visit, Tinsel. We thinking up things they might enjoy."

"Rabbit meat going to cook in here? In you *pot*?" Her posture conveyed that she for one would never again sully her mouth with anything from that kitchen.

"No, no. He means as a pet."

Tinsel's eyes turned back to Joel, but her tone adjusted from revulsion to ridicule. "Which part of *pet*?" Then with a disdainful turning-away of her face and a lofty tilt of her head she swept her eyes from him and marched off, throwing over her shoulder, "I dunno who cleaning up after *dat*."

"Three days a week?" Joel whispered in anguish.

"If not, I'll spend all my time cleaning and cooking, and get nothing out of the visit at all. Well, of course it's not a visit, more of a prelude to their settling in."

"But it has to be perfect," he agreed. "Children know nothing about the place. Must feel right from the minute they set foot."

That was the thing with Joel. He homed in on the essentials right away. He swept up the pictures he'd left all about, because in no time we'd be surrounded by the real thing. Then he disappeared briefly to return clutching the hand vacuum for the flakes of old plastic bag and crumbling paper.

"I wouldn't rush the rabbit, though," I said. I didn't want to crush the idea (I like rabbits), but we needed to know more about the children. "They'll be all excited about taking it with them to their new house, and how do we know their parents are ready for a pet?"

"He could stay here."

"Who?"

"Rabbit."

"I notice you don't say *she*."

"God forbid. Probably arrive in flourishing condition and put down a litter pronto."

"What we know about the children, though? I say hold on the rabbit for now. Lay in gummy worms."

"OK," he said.

But I picked it up, the merest flicker of his eye, decisive and secretive as a shutter let fall. Having given in on this one, he would henceforward be making his own arrangements without consultation.

My brain churning, I traipsed upstairs after Tinsel, to get down the drapes for washing and to turn out the linen cupboard so as to find out whether the Wonder Woman sheets had survived. I bawled down to Joel that if things worked out right we could always build a rabbit cage in the shady area outside the laundry room. Sort of thing we might rope Francis into as well.

Francis. Quick lift of eyebrows over sleepy eyes – laughing eyes but a little droopy, as if partially awakened to an entertaining situation. A roguish twinkle. Impossible to think of Francis without smiling. His was not a stunningly handsome face, like Connor's, but it was jovial – thickening a little now, yet appealing as ever. Cynnie had grown up closely enough with her cousin to bring him inexorably under her thumb. "Except the old Francis still refuses to bathe more than once a day," she'd remarked gloomily during an earlier visit. "You'd have thought Charlene would prevail on him." Not that this grim failing had put Cyn off from agreeing to a Tobago visit that Francis promised for whenever they could manage the second trip.

This Tobago lime had failed to materialize when Connor did not arrive, but Francis contented himself with chauffeuring Cyn and the children to the water park and nature reserve. So yes, Francis would help entertain them and might even insist on the rabbit and promise to clean the cage himself.

You wish, said a voice inside. Francis did not always deliver on promises about tedious chores. "Vie-ke-vie," I called him when complaining about his carefree ways to Joel.

"Never mind that," Joel replied. "However skittish he is on his own time, he's foot and foot with you in an emergency."

And one never knew what might come up with children. I thought of Cynnie's little sniffles that segued into barking coughs and fevers climbing, contemptuous of baby Panadol and sponging. But no. Why go there? Three hearty little people for Joel and me to enjoy.

Then the clatter of Tinsel in the next room, accompanied by the diatribe she maintained softly but audibly, drew a snort of laughter from me, for she would irritate us as much as she helped. Right now she was holding forth on the plumber, who had come in about a non-functional toilet and who had not noticed or fixed a dripping pipe in another bathroom. The drip had manifested itself days after his visit in any case, but Bartholomew, or, as Tinsel called him, Battalomeo, was clearly at fault. "Because when it leggo completely and flood the place, is me to ketch," she concluded. "Who else going mop that up?" She swayed side to side thoughtfully and grinned. "I go have to swim like a fish. Wait nah! It have fish on the chart, number 28. My mind tell me to pick 28. When I win lottery, I go thank Battalomeo."

Joel snatched up his car keys and headed for the door, mumbling, "Nostradamus in every doorway."

She was a book in herself, I reflected, not for the first time. Sorting through pillowcases and cushion covers, I again laid out in my head our adventures with Tinsel, shuffling confrontations and backchat. The idea of fictionalizing her had diverted me from time to time over the past couple years and kept my responses to her good-humoured. The usual trance came over me as I bent my mind around characterization. Unfixity mesmerized me, or was it perhaps the bottomlessness of personalities, level after level giving way to the unsuspected.

Or did the instability lurk in my own view? The habitual pacing having landed me back to the study, I jotted a few notes – confidently, for I don't actually believe myself madder than the rest of my acquaintances. Still, our lives had included significant upendings of reason. My thoughts travelled back to Joel's anguish over Cyn's departure. He had encouraged her to go, thrown himself into every stage of her relocation and, later, rejoiced over her marriage. But he could not take her absence. My Skype conversations with Cyn had connected us, however intangibly, but Joel missed her physically at every turn. He seemed overwhelmed by yearnings to squeeze Cyn's hand and follow her with his eyes.

At first, he'd viewed Connor with suspicion as his name popped up more and more in her news. We hadn't bargained on anything pinning her that side of the world. "Why he can't go sniff around someone else's daughter?" Joel argued. For a while he referred to Cyn's boyfriend as The Dingo. But I foresaw he'd never close his heart to a man Cynnie loved. In weeks Joel was as eager to meet Connor as I was.

Still, only days after the marriage fixed her in Australia, Joel fastened himself to the treadmill more and more often, for longer and longer, running faster and faster. He pounded on, obstinately deaf to my scolding and to the advice of every doctor I called on. He cranked up the regime and rendered himself clammy and corpse grey by the end of each session. What could I do but look on, agonized, at this compulsive race for oblivion – someone so fine, brave, strong, funny, and so much dearer to me than myself – rushing headlong over the cliff.

Thank God I was the one to get the heart attack. Mind you, he'd argue it was his regime that protected him. However that might be, I was self-aware enough to notice the occasional cramp. He'd have just jogged on. Mild as my attack was it checked him so he collected himself to watch over me. Then, over the years as other signals led to the bypass, we held each other up. Because now there was a new and palpable horror – that I might leave him, alone.

Cyn's phone call had gleefully upended such sombre pondering. One evening just a couple weeks later, Joel paused in a prolonged session of flicking through the TV channels to ask whether I knew the Ninja Turtles had made a comeback. He continued, "Twins too big for them, eh?" I supposed so. "Real turtles then? Set up a bowl beside the TV –?" He broke off and regarded me a bit sheepishly.

"It's OK," I said. "I'm in the same damn fool condition."

We exchanged watery smiles and huddled thankfully together over two glasses of Cabernet for a half hour before the flipping screen got through to me again, and I gently detached myself to head for the stairs. "I have those old postgrad files to weed before we can open out the extra bed in my study," I reminded him, and he nodded without shifting his eyes from the scramble of images. His dreamy smile deepened at one corner of his lips to an impish twist. But his intense gaze at the screen, like the truncated sentences, belied that sleepy vagueness. And now, taking in again his long, spare face, my mind skidded to a new anxiety. He had always been on the thin side. Lean, I'd said even forty years earlier when there was all the agility of youth. Nimble fingers on the typewriter, then the keyboard. Now the years, his father's decline, the scattering of siblings, Cynnie's relocation, my surgery – amidst decades of absorption in the news of local crises – had left him wiry, two fingers apt to stroke his stomach appeasingly.

His gaze shifted to me, those bright expressive eyes that could sometimes, unaccountably, go inscrutable. (Like that day or two of frantic secrecy in the '70s. We'd been married only a few years. *Don't ask me.*

Nothing he could talk about, he'd said, ever. And then months of tension, leaching slowly away. He'd never explained. Only, *You know you can trust me.* When I said I knew, he responded, *Well then. Just let it go.*)

Now he fastened on the only soap opera I'd ever seen him throw himself into – that bedlam the media funnelled in from the outside world. With shameless hilarity, Joel threw himself into the tortuous real-life dramas played out in powerful countries. He'd collapse them to one-liners or subordinate clauses – about which world leaders were chatty with each other although they had never spoken; where thousands of Muslims had cheered in close proximity to the crumbling World Trade Center in 9/11 so as to be overlooked by onlookers; what made financial disclosure that was required forbidden; how colleagues who had to be fired transformed into great guys while great guys who were indispensable transformed into traitors who had to be fired; why women qualified as fat pigs, slobs and disgusting animals by bleeding in all directions and, above all, how a world leader who invited an exquisite mix of revulsion and ridicule around the globe could still be termed by both followers and revilers as *the leader of the free world.*

Unreliable narration and plot twists in world affairs intrigued me too, but time seemed short enough to draw me back swiftly to my own storyline. At my desk I opened the diary, flexing its spine so it would flatten out and show up the purple and black of major and minor commitments and accompanying lists on yellow Post-its. *Unmaskings,* in purple, reminded me about slowing character revelation so I could mirror the long, circuitous process of coming to know anyone.

I'd thought of telling my story from the outside as if coming upon it little by little, but more naturally my tales rose from within. They surfaced into view, level after level. Even academically my most blinding discoveries have been gradual. Only after decades of fixation on the technicalities of storytelling did the obvious strike home, that the fiction I'd been interpreting was itself interpretation at ground zero. What this meant – basic, almost banal as it was – pierced me not just academically but viscerally, how every tale broke and realigned events according to its teller's interests.

I was ready to lay down scholarly criticism altogether. "As of now," I announced to Joel, "my mania for interpretation channels into spinning it myself." So. Healed of academia. Or had I succumbed further? I was still sorting the credible from the unbelievable, the known from the imagined. Only, the joke was that shielding sources rather than acknowledging them became a matter of honour.

When I came back to the specific place and time in which I sat – my study, mid-morning – I discovered my mouth and throat parched. Aha. Fallen behind with the day's half gallon of water. But now the ideas poured fast, my fingers flying over the keys, and when Joel set a tray beside me on the desk with a frosted jug and a glass packed with ice, I was speechless with gratitude. I tore my eyes from the screen to stare at him and shake my head in wonder. But he just grinned and wandered off to the bedroom, clutching the remote more purposefully than ever, no doubt possessed by such issues as whether a country that funds terrorists is an ideal base at which to locate ten thousand troops for fighting terrorism, and whether a nation's dream could best be achieved by deporting dreamers.

Why was Joel – a retired newspaperman – hooked on absurdity in foreign headlines? That was a no-brainer: he was avoiding our own news, despite persistent efforts of his associates to drag him back.

Now and then I heard him on the phone with a younger colleague. This fellow, Walters, had dropped in at our house a year or two ago and broken down. "I catching hell with this crime coverage," he'd said. "Property tax and so – OK. But the crime, Oh Gawd." The worst was that woman caught in crossfire just outside her gate. The bandit had had an automatic weapon, and there was her brother sponging blood off the wall, scrubbing and sobbing. His son – the woman's six-year-old nephew – did see the whole thing. "This little child keep saying over an' over how he auntie mash up and ting coming outta she."

Yes, they shot the gunman down. The young reporter had pictures of a youth sprawled on the asphalt with his legs apart, the area marked off by yellow police tape that someone had broken on one side so as to see the body good. The bright ribbon fluttered cheerfully to the side of the corpse. Suddenly I wondered whether this was the right place for Cynnie and Con to come back to, to bring up children.

"They should come back, shouldn't they?" I asked Joel. "Even with the crime and thing." Then I said, "You look baffled."

"Am." I glanced at him insistently, so he added. "You're baffling."

"Sorry."

"No need. Little bafflement not necessarily amiss." He tipped his head towards CNN's coverage of the latest school shooting. "Where you have in mind for them?"

"I don't know," I said. "It's got to be wrong for me to feel reassured when I watch foreign news and see brutality isn't confined to our corner of the world." I gestured at the TV before he switched channels again. Even in the most powerful of nations where the connection between gun crimes and the availability of guns was denied fervently enough to perpetuate mass shootings, strange reinterpretations of violence seemed underway.

Joel's clicking took him from one political somersault to the next. "Dream inverted to nightmare," he said, picking up my line of thought. "Any particular genre to suggest?"

"Gothic," I returned promptly. "Some monster lain comatose for years, doped by sugared assurances of freedom and equality. Now it's caught the soft hiss of hatred, muted, then louder, felt the kiss, and stirred." I reached up to draw my fingers through his hair. "Only it's for real. *You*'d write that one better than I could."

Everyday brain teasers on-screen amalgamated disgust with humour, and I almost followed Joel to view the latest international fiasco. But my usual compulsions overrode the lure, and I locked off the world outside to seize again on my narrative while I had time.

Time gurgled downstream, evaporating with an inaudible fizz. For there is nothing gentle about the onslaught of old age. However subtle its approach, it comes on and on with silent but unrelenting ferocity. You head into its driving force with what steady courage you can muster, but only because the alternative is . . . what it is. Except, once you gaze directly at it, at age, you may detect some different courage it confers, other competencies it calls forth. So now I think perhaps I would not turn back even if I could. We grow on, room opening up for surprise after surprise. Look – our Cynnie coming home. And the children.

Their arrival date had seemed distant when she called but rushed on us in no time. Joel threw up his hands as I whisked from room to room. "*In every cabin, she flam'd amazement,*" he muttered, though he was similarly fired.

"They'll like the pool," he reflected, jingling the car keys nervously the afternoon we were locking up to leave for the airport. "But Cyn's barely making a turnaround, and we don't know what position she and

Connor might take. I'm a strong swimmer but . . . you know." Jangle of keys thrown up with the left, caught awkwardly with the right, thrown up with the left, dropped.

"They'll be fine." I rubbed his back after he dived to retrieve the bunch. "We've got this."

3

KINDRED GAMES

ARRIVALS.

THE FOUR OF THEM CROWDED FORWARD. "Oh dear God the relief," Cynnie said, grabbing hold of her father while the children jostled each other to see us, curious as we were. Micah and Melody seemed warm and confident, Mattie shyer but easily won over. There was that in Melody that hooked me, though. I caught myself staring, trying to pin it down.

Her face more oval than those of the boys, she swung her chin first in the direction she meant to take (and God help you if you got in its way, I thought). The hair, though. Neither Cyn's dark mop nor Connor's glossy black waves, but a tussle of fine, unruly curls that turned a fiery halo of fluff if the light took it, clustering around her head like a brightening cloud at daybreak. The boys had their father's face but for a tilted nose with no bridge to speak of and faintly flared nostrils above appealingly curved lips. They had his eyes too, wide-set under the flyaway brows and thick hair, but more wiry curls that would go shaggy if left to themselves.

Soon all the house vibrated with bustle and chatter, the boys inclined to romp and Melody at ease yet more self-contained. What shocked us was Cyn — worn thin, she seemed, and surprisingly relieved at having got *this far* with the plan.

"Rough flight?" I asked. "Relax, child. Why you so fixated on getting back at once?"

"No, not a day to spare. Connor returns from his course less than two weeks from now and I've everything to do before then."

Odd, Joel and I agreed later. We'd seen how willing and capable Con proved on household matters – and not just in gadget repair or barbequing. The man ironed, folded clean laundry and cooked a wicked pelau. Still, if he was hypertensive it would be like her to spare him.

"Think he's less eager to come back?" Joel wondered aloud to me.

"Not likely." I caught sight of the usual young people jogging past our gate and remembered Con and Cynnie taking an evening run on that first visit. And there it was again – that surge of relief I'd felt. No. Jubilation – that Cynnie would have what *we* had, that rare thing most of the world thought was make-believe.

Watching the two of them, I hadn't even realized Joel had come up behind me till he squeezed my shoulders and said, "Yup."

So later that evening when Connor said how nervous he'd been about meeting us, he looked mildly hurt when I laughed.

"It's just – we were on tenterhooks too," I explained.

"OK." His smile dawned. "Because I want you to know it's official. You're my parents."

"Blood." I raised a glass, and he touched his to it, echoing solemnly, "Blood."

Anyway, Australia was no more his country than Cyn's, and Joel reminded me how Connor had fallen in love with our lives. This was his dream, he'd once said – family home with front lawn and backyard. Children romping all over the place. Cyn had shuddered histrionically. "Two'd be my limit," she countered. "If any."

Now, I tried to picture their life in Sydney, but found I was making it up in some vast formless setting built of rumour and supposition, rather as Dickens might have assembled a handy version of the West Indies. For what did we know of the place?

Sinking onto the couch the minute we got in from the airport, Cynnie looked too tired for us to ply her with questions. "So wiped out, Mom." The tremor in her voice stilled me. "Fill you in when I get back and we settle down. Promise."

Meanwhile, the children responded to us readily, despite a passing dither about what to call us. Joel wasn't about to be called Joel, so I steered them away from calling me Aria. Joel had acclimatized to Connor addressing him by his name, but I knew it couldn't work from small children. So I hinted that friends they made in Trinidad would call their grandparents Mama and Papa and think it odd to use their actual names. Micah and

Melody appeared to find this quaint but adopted it graciously, and Mattie followed their lead.

Once she pulled out a few essentials – the children's nightwear, an inhalant and insect repellent, Cyn spent those few hours with us sleeping – well, responding to our talk but nodding off wherever she sat down and eventually climbing into bed with the children packed tight around her. In the morning she barely made it onto the couch again and stayed unmoving for hours.

Another glance at her startled me with the thought that she made less of an impression on the cushions than before. Always a small woman, she was thinner, paler, stiller but for an occasional twitch. From childhood she had seemed in constant motion – feet tapping, eyes snapping, hair electric, fighting spirit almost visible. That was the Cyn indelible in my mind. Now, this inertia.

It had kept me up most of the night. *Might she be ill and not telling me?* After that I'd flitted in and out of sleep till my phone alarm released me from the bed.

An odd downpour in dry season had the morning dim and sodden until noon when she hugged us hastily before setting off in a taxi. We had agreed the airport parting might be too much for Mattie, and I'd need Joel home to help with three children whose mother was flying out even if it were only for a couple weeks. As Cyn opened the door of the taxi, Melody broke away and ran through the downpour to clutch her mother, face upturned and washed with rain – not tears: my certainty of that jolted me. She took her mother's face in both hands, and I could feel on my palms the velvet of Cyn's cheeks at the child's age. Melody gazed fiercely into her mother's eyes, her body rigid with the tightness of that grip before Cyn tore herself away.

"Love you, Cyn," Melody shouted as she backed towards us. "Be safe." Then she ran back to the door, soaked. Like her, Micah remained surprisingly steady – they had each other, I suppose – but Mattie dissolved. He pushed me away firmly and howled when Joel bent to pick him up. Then Melody nudged Micah towards us, and as he put his arm around Mattie the wails subdued to sobs then hiccups. In a minute or two the little fellow tumbled into my arms and put his head on my shoulder. I read Joel's glance and realized he had seen it too, the wordless paths of understanding among the three.

In a couple hours the phone rang and it was Cyn. "Boarding shortly," she said, "and like a fool I've walked off with the children's passports and stuff in my bag. Nothing to be done. Don't book for Disney World before I get back."

Laughter, kisses on the mouthpiece, and she was off.

⁓⁓

Two days later, walking through Trincity Mall, Micah remarked that it was weird without Cyn, and Melody asked, "What did you expect?"

"Nothing." He spread his hands. "Just . . . we never went anywhere without her before. Even one night."

Mattie scowled. "I want Cynnie an Con," he said.

Micah suggested we WhatsApp once we got home.

"The time difference, dear," I reminded him, while Joel shot me a look and mouthed, "home." I responded with a complicit nudge.

"Cyn'll call us when she can," Melody said.

"A diversion," Joel decided when we got back to the house. "I get tickets; you pack."

A flurry of excitement, and by the following day we were in Tobago for an overnight trip, rolling around in the shallows of Store Bay.

"Weren't we supposed to present their ID for the flight?" I asked Joel, and he raised his shoulders.

"Forgot. When I remembered, no one asked. Didn't remind them."

The two of us ate curried crab and dumpling while the children had hamburgers under almond trees whose branches fluttered layer upon layer of flat leaves between us and the dry-season sun. Then we caught a taxi back to the hotel.

By morning we were spread out under the almond trees on that beach, helping Micah construct edifices of sand.

"Listen," Melody interrupted, pointing.

Marking out the swimming area ran a barricade of green-black rocks, tops baked ashen by the sun – only, no, coated with grey-white bird poop. A host of seabirds alighted and jostled, shrill honking, rapid and persistent as demented merrymakers at 11:58 on Old Year's night. Then from another corner of the rock wall sounded a dissident fluting, out of harmony with the honks and contentious interruptions in various octaves.

Something off key came back to me, and I nudged Joel. "Cynnie's
OK, right?"

"Couldn't you just ask her if she was ill or something?"

"She'd worry about my heart."

"Used to confide in me too. Of course, she might assume we knew
each other's thoughts," he added.

"Might," I agreed, a trifle drily.

Looking back, I thought it was that heart attack that had saved me
all those years ago. Had it been a decade already? A pounding gathered
momentum, knocked my breath away and cramped my right arm. The
green ink pen for editing slid from my fingers. In a daze I watched it roll
off the desk and land against the lines of the tiles.

My cardiologist declared me stabilized on a slew of meds – including
nitroglycerine of all things – and ordered rest. I'd have liked a few days
on this very beach, but the best I could do was download five novels
on my Kindle. Only Joel placed no faith in them keeping me quiet for
any time.

"And how much longer do you put the other sides of your life on
hold?" he'd demanded. The tilt of his head and penetrating sidelong
glance signalled his shift to analytic mode. "Like the novel you've been
muttering about since we met. You have the choice to retire next year
and you needn't hang on another five." He flipped his fingers casually.
"Our affairs are under control."

Which I knew already. Neither of us had worked for huge salaries,
but Joel had juggled bonds, stocks and other imponderables so we could
live out our days in comfort.

Joel's reminder had echoed on over the following weeks that barely
offered time for leisure reading, let alone sea-bathing. Then, two months
later the vision flashed on me as I plodded downstairs from a board
meeting in an admin building, laptop under my arm with the wad of
papers that had been laid on the table. I saw myself shoving aside thick
folders of minutes, even texts I'd stayed with only because of some syllabus
or student dissertation. Some brilliantly written books flashed scenes of
cruelty I'd found more and more unbearable. One I've struggled to blot
out is of a boy forcing a knife into a girl's mouth while promising to
slit the corners of her lips into a permanent grin. This wasn't supposed
to faze the modern reader – but. Retirement would free me from any

pretence of being open to the dark and gritty. I could give myself up to random and entirely selfish samplings of verse and prose.

And what if I myself had time to write? Time to write myself. The thing seduced me, one restraint after the next falling away till nothing held me back from surrender to the whispers from inside. "Go for it, Mom," Cynnie had cheered me on by Skype.

I'd had no idea what I was doing, what it meant to open up myself. No one had told me and I never guessed the enormity of committing one's soul to anything as fragile and enduring and inflammatory as paper. So then I found myself negotiating that slippery path between remembered and imagined circumstances. Some memories I walled off, even those that were now mine alone. My father, in the late '60s, dying in an ambulance that was stuck in traffic – who was left to be offended if I detailed that? Yet it struck me as an intrusion, even a betrayal. I'm not at home in this post-privacy world.

The warm water of Store Bay gurgling between my toes, I wondered vaguely how I'd ever get the sand out of Melody's hair, even as I relived my transition from one type of writing to the next. I had clung to the verge of real experience, writing *around* things, slicing, excising, and the missing parts throbbed on. Eyeing these gaps uneasily, I'd dug out a file of notes, the earliest pages crumbling at the edges, paper clips seized up with rust and a broken rubber band melted to glue a couple of the leaves together. "Years now I've been slinging this stuff in a box," I complained to Cyn, "And the worst of it is – somewhere in all that a shape's been taking form."

Furious about having kept the thing in limbo, I wrote obsessively – building in layer upon layer of flesh and bone, thought and sensation, only to rip it out and lay it in again.

Still, I worried about my narrator. Not blunt enough.

"You're never going to pack in the required obscenities," Cyn said. "So much for realism."

"Well, what about telling it through a reticent onlooker," I argued. "One with laserlike vision. Someone like my mother." I added, "Wish you'd known her."

"Get her in there and I shall," Cyn said.

"Not nearly contentious enough," I groaned when I was ready to send off the manuscript for the press to dispatch to its readers. I braced myself for some sort of jangling disagreement between them, in which the loudest was likeliest to win. But through it went. A year later, when *Candlefly Season* by Aria Roche launched successfully, I felt I had recaptured my mother's voice.

Restraint, she used to command, softly drowning out louder promptings to jump, jam, stamp, wine, don a mask and let it go. I've never had it in me to let it go. Bookish and boring, I apologized to Cyn one year when she invited me to play mas with her and I declined. So off she chipped with a flip of the hand that was exactly Joel's, and vanished into the Carnival fray.

Now she was back, or would be in a matter of weeks, and here was Mattie tumbling around us in the sand while Micah somehow concentrated on burying Melody even as he kept an eye on the birds. A silent pelican lingered a few bored moments and then flapped off to sail on his own business before plunging, rising with its beak jerking at each gulp, and gliding off. And still in the cacophony of revellers, the party flutes and staccato of cries like ribald laughter went on and on, the birds perched motionless or a-flutter to exchange places with a frantic battering of wings. All the while the pelicans pursued their affairs with contrasting dignity – a circle, a swoop and plunge, explosion of sea spray then heavy lift and beating away.

Micah was entranced. "We can't stay one more night?" he begged.

When we promised to return in a month or so with his parents, he was satisfied, although Mattie put in, "Con doesn' like birds."

"Who says?" Micah took him up on it at once. "Does so."

"Doesn't." Mattie scowled.

"You two stop chooking each other." Joel opened a bag of plantain chips and rattled it. Then he hustled us out to Crown Point Airport – an hour before check-in – where we read, exchanged riddles and bought pink and white coconut sugar cake that vanished before we boarded.

Back in Trinidad, Joel half-heartedly suggested a visit to the Pitch Lake for the following day, but the shimmering heat dissuaded us and we settled for a movie – pictures, the children called it – consuming foolish amounts of frozen yoghurt in the mall. "No sorbet," I complained, turning away with Melody, who had selected and polished off her cone, and we left the rest vacillating between candy and nut toppings while we dove into a bookstore. Driving home, we stopped for them to watch a doubles vendor in outsize blue plastic gloves dealing out the hot soft bara with its filling of curried channa. "Chickpeas," Joel explained, but the twins eyed it with revulsion. "I just want the outside part," Mattie said, and then wolfed it down.

Next morning we set out despite rain streaming over the windscreen, and squinted through the glass fogged over from hot humid air outside against the chill of air conditioning within. The twins amused themselves reading street signs. They pointed, shouted, dissolved in laughter all the way to the zoo, and I thought they might crash after this exuberance, disappointed in our small affair, but they were delighted. "Ace," Micah declared, as we sat on the damp bench facing the giraffes.

"I never went to a zoo before," Mattie announced. He was still bouncing about when we got home, and while he slid behind the glider for his paints, Micah told us he and Melody had gone so long ago they could hardly remember.

"But your zoos there must be grand," Joel objected. And that was the first time we glimpsed it: a screen drawn softly between us.

Micah muttered something about their not having been able to get out much over the past months, and a funny signal flashed between him and Melody, one I could not translate.

"What was the difficulty?" Joel asked.

Micah shrugged, and only Mattie piped up, "Lojistics." He glanced up from his finger painting, startled by our shout of laughter. His eyes engulfed us. "Well, tha's what Cyn says." He scrupulously cleaned his fingers of cobalt blue on the jersey that stretched over his belly and reached for a pot of yellow.

By the following morning Mattie had taken to watching the door – dreamily at first, his attention straying to the gold-flecked crotons just outside or off to a towering pommecythere tree. He frowned in concentration as if someone might step out anytime from behind a stand of spiny fan palms. His eyes followed the odd walker one could barely make out along the road beyond the fence, or the helper coming in through the pedestrian gate on her way to work. The way he held his head – it was a listening posture, interrupted by a start and swift turn if the electric gate grated open and a vehicle rumbled in over the loose gravel of the car park.

Then he dragged the poof to a new spot opposite the door and clambered onto it to keep watch. He could be quiet for a long while, only a finger tapping time with the click-click of the wall clock. But at last he would fly into a temper when no one arrived. More and more we caught sight of these flashes of anger about his mother having left him. "You don't just leave children and fly away on a plane." He would scowl mutinously.

Melody threw me a look of apology. "But the grands are cool," she reasoned with him. "Aren't they being nice to us till Cyn 'n Connor get here? 'S just four more days."

He nodded unwillingly, but insisted, "We should've stayed home and come together."

Micah pulled a sleek grey and white speckled feather from his pocket and held it up. "You want this or what?"

"Yeh!"

"Then quit whingeing."

"'K." And Mattie skipped off bearing his feather aloft – happy for the moment, I thought, but Joel's chuckle of satisfaction made me shrug on my workaday mantle of serenity. Alongside all that churned and gnawed at me inside, Joel dwelt unperturbed in his oddly guilt-free state. Whatever emergency he was holding down, he would pause on the brink only to decide on what seemed right and then throw himself into it.

The social turbulence that erupted in newsworthy bloodshed or the odd outrage (batter down, chop up or blow away) that laid waste families or rival gangs – it had all come under his professional scrutiny. Occasionally his shudder of aversion was visible, but nothing turned his eyes away. "Can't afford to miss what triggered it," he'd say, "story behind the story." Even now, as he avoided local news of crime or corruption, he could not altogether evade it when reporters who had come in under him called for advice.

"Some of them just won't let go," I complained.

"Like Walters," Joel reflected. "Probably the most sensitive investigative reporter I've known – which only makes him the most vulnerable." Certainly, Walters made it increasingly hard for Joel to elude the grimmer social realities from which he'd tried to retire. If only the guy would leave Joel alone.

"What about the two who open fire on the birthday party," Walters' voice crackled over the speaker Joel had automatically turned on.

"Spraying bullets all over the place so birthday-boy end up in operating theatre. Instead of recovering from a few drinks, the man critical. That was bullet right through. Kill the man child. Child from the first woman. She done walk off and leave him with it years now and he wife take care of the boy like her own son. Stone dead."

I cast an eye around frantically, but the children were out of earshot.

"The man have a daughter with this wife too. So, now he in hospital, the family that leave at home getting threat over the phone. No arrest. Everyone know who these men are and where they hang out, and they still out there. Calling the house every other day about what they going do next. The mother say she don't let the little girl answer the phone. And this whole thing is like is inside the office with us." Walters paused, and then reflected. "Like you had some knack of distancing yourself from it, don't mind how concerned. I don't know. I sorry you don't have time to come in occasionally and chat with us."

No way. That was exactly what we needed to seal out. It remained unreal to me and I wanted to keep it that way. Besides, there was no time for it. In whatever ways we had governed our lives, this interlude with the children derailed basic routines, and we let slide most of our pursuits, Joel content that he had only to pick them up later. For me, in my navel-gazing and self-recrimination, it was more of a wrench letting things go.

I had my mother's dearest friend to visit. Each time over the past two years I'd found her further receded into a peaceful blur. "So very," she'd said when last I dropped in. "We were all. When we. Yes. Delighted you could. Such a joy. We did. A real. Tell every, every. So happy." She paused and nodded, smiling. "When," she concluded. I was anxious to see her, to summon up for her what little I could while the deep past still whispered to her. But my own present swept me along inexorably.

"Where does the day go?" Joel complained one night. We'd fallen on the bed laughing over some turn of phrase Mattie had produced, but Joel said he was aching in places he hadn't known he had. "We concentrate on them non-stop, that's what," he said.

I confided with a little jolt of surprise that I was sleeping even more lightly, and right away I could put my finger exactly on when it had started. A couple nights after our return from Tobago, we had fallen asleep with Mattie between us as usual. He persistently found his way to our bed and that night he clambered in earlier than usual. When I got up for my two o'clock trip to the bathroom he was gone. We eventually found him seated on the toilet at the far end of the passage, sound asleep. He didn't wake when Joel lifted him back to our bed.

In the morning he laughed as loud as the rest. "I was sitting there trying and trying and I must have falled asleep," he said, "because nothing happened."

My mind went at once to bananas, because he did not like prunes, and I was surprised by Micah's crack of laughter. "Motion denied!" He pointed at Mattie, laughing.

Mattie gurgled too as if at a familiar joke, but Melody cut them off. "Cyn said not to be vulgar."

So we could hardly enquire further about what had startled me as an adult quip.

In any case, Mattie circled back. "What I told you, Mama? Like how I got there? Or crazy things?" He yawned and a little thread of saliva stretched and popped.

To my surprise Micah's face went rigid, but Melody put in, "No. You stayed asleep, right?"

She had thrown it out hurriedly, and I had a sense, not for the first time, that they censored each other's comments in a curious way. But then, not having known us long, they might be anxious about how they came across. As soon as their parents arrived and settled in, we would all relax.

Then a weather alert brought warning of a mild tropical storm. "Early for that," Joel reflected. "Guess the rains really are here. Seasons all messed up."

The children were enthralled. "Not a hurricane," I reminded them. "Only a little extra rain and wind." Still, we picked up anything that could be blown around outside or bashed by flying branches or light chairs. We brought in a few heavy clay pots of fern and a dendrobium with its shower of pale lilac.

I had made pasta that day with the usual unwholesome pepperoni, bacon crisps and extra cheese, and we brought out leftovers for supper. Joel stared meaningfully at my hand wavering away from the chicken breasts and whipped sweet potatoes, towards the pasta dish with its medallions of glorious cholesterol among trickles of melted gold.

"If you have that, so will I," he warned. "Then we'll both be too sick to enjoy the storm."

"Not me," I returned with satisfaction, knowing the alacrity of his acid reflux. "It takes a while longer to do me in."

"True," he said, bowing. "Will be a privilege and a pleasure to predecease you."

"Viper."

The children stayed up to watch the rain beat on the windows and the wind picking up.

"Can their plane fly through our storm?" Mattie studied the thrashing branches through the glass of the sliding door.

"This will pass long before your mom and dad board, Matts," Joel said. "Won't get much stronger than this."

The three of them went to bed more disappointed than relieved. The wind died down, tall slender palms outside barely bending, although by then other parts of the island were sodden and roofs of a few small homes had ripped off.

"'s not fair," Mattie objected next morning as the TV showed the damage. "How come they don' get to keep their roofs like us?" By the time Joel felt around for his reply Mattie had run off.

We lost electricity for an hour or two, but when Cyn got through on Skype to make sure we were OK, Mattie said, "'Course we are. We slept right through."

There was no sleeping through Joel's mobile. "You don't think you should cool down Walters a little?" I asked. "Perhaps tell him you retired to escape all that and you don't even watch TV6?"

"Hate to put him off." Joel squeezed the gate control absentmindedly, and I made a note to separate the different gadgets so that the gate wouldn't just open and stand yawning while we sat and wondered why the TV wasn't coming on. "Truth is, I don't think Walters is handling things. Not his competence, I mean – no question about that. It's how he's standing up to close encounters with people near to the . . . event."

"You should come in and give us your thoughts," Walters had urged, and I'd felt to slap him. Only his voice had pitched a bit higher than usual, and I realized Joel was right. Walters was freaking out. "You heard the same fellows came back and stabbed up the woman – the man wife who did trying to mind they little girl while he still in hospital – and they gone with the Toyota? No, man. The same-same fellows."

I was sorry for Walters, and for all who had to pore over sickening violence. But I had neither time nor stomach to brood with him.

~⁄⁄ᴵᵡ~

The next afternoon we made the mistake of telling the children their parents would board that evening. Joel added that, by then, it would actually be next morning in Sydney. Mattie looked up, wide-eyed, his body heaving with shallow breaths. He cast a glance at the door, ignoring the reminder that it would take them until day after tomorrow to arrive.

"I mean *our* day after tomorrow," Joel said, making it worse.

By evening, it was clear there'd be no getting Mattie or even the twins into bed that night. "They'll call from L.A.," I said. "I'm sure they will. And we'll wake you to talk to them, I promise."

But Mattie perched on his poof, arms twined around his legs, a knot of anticipation. The smell of cake from the oven filled the room, yet there he remained, on the watch. Although Micah and Melody knew better, they too wound up more and more as bedtime passed. Set up a camp in the living room then? Make some game out of it? I cast my mind around for anything to distract them. It had been a mild day, and all was quiet now but for a liquid throb from a flying frog or the shrill rasp of crickets. Three faces gazed at me in expectation.

That was when Francis dropped in like manna from heaven. "Is so?" he demanded critically. "But what sort of lime allyou running here? Oh Geed! This ent no fête. Come, come – music, lights, glasses, cards." He snapped his fingers and the three stumbled over each other to snatch up whatever he demanded. He hauled a few balloons out of a back pocket and bellowed, "Pump!"

Off I went to a leisurely bath while he played cards with them, and Joel stretched out on the couch to fortify himself for a restless night. When I got back to the living room, Francis had finished playing Snap and soldiered on through Chinese Checkers, and the children were shifting around on tenterhooks once more. Joel sat up just as Francis pulled off the light zipped jacket he often wore, and now the house was locked up for the night he was sitting in the tank top that exposed his tight curls of chest hair and the muscles he had knotted across his chest and biceps through rigorous exercise.

"Schwarzenegger," Joel acknowledged him briefly, then cocked his head. "Nah. You'd have to shave that and varnish. Connor will supervise."

Francis grinned but looked a bit harassed. "Hear nah. We need something else to pass the time." He threw me an urgent glance, and I sat down with them again.

"Melly," I asked, "anything special you'd all like to do tonight?"

"Don't call me Melly!" she screamed at me, and in the shocked silence the child froze, staring at me. "Sorry, Mama." She darted forward and locked her arms round my neck.

"What happened?" When I folded her in I could not see her face, and she was silent.

"Only Con gets to call her that," Micah said, his tone offhand, and as I released her she threw him a glance I could not read. A mix of accusation and gratitude?

"Not Con," Mattie objected.

But Joel put in, "Let's play The Game," unleashing a babble of questions and explanation.

The moment Micah caught on, he said, "Melody can be *It*."

She began by breaking the rule that it must be some family other than one's own, but no one cared once she was engaged. As Elder, Joel accepted her tight folded paper that identified the mystery member. Clearly her father, for she began by acting a tumble of rough play, and then a different response – someone jumping up and down before running to the door, arms out flung.

"That's your dad," I sang out, but Mattie swung round in surprise, and before I could ask why, the phone rang.

The hand phone not being in its cradle or anywhere to be seen, Joel pounded upstairs two steps at a time for the one by our bed. "Yes, Kevin," I heard him shout.

Joel came back down looking puzzled and said, unnecessarily, "That was Kevin. He asked me to come over right away."

"Weird," I said. "At this hour?"

"It's just across the way, and barely ten," Francis objected.

"Right." I shoved the house key into Joel's hand. "Kevin doesn't even answer the phone during the News. And it's late for him to call anyway. Maybe he's ill. Better hurry."

"Who's ill?" Mattie regarded me seriously with his wide dark eyes.

"A neighbour. Or perhaps he's OK."

"Let's go on with The Game," Micah urged.

"Can't," Melody objected. "Papa's the Elder."

Micah grabbed my mobile, his fingers tapping expertly. "I'll video for him. Go on."

We were screaming with laughter at Melody's presentation of Mattie's antics, no one more boisterously than Mattie himself, when I realized Joel had come back in, accompanied by Kevin. Not accompanied: Kevin had an arm round Joel's waist and seemed almost to be holding him up. Francis sprang up to go to them.

"Papa sick?" Mattie asked, his head cocked anxiously.

"No." Joel fumbled his hand over Mattie's hair with an expression that stopped my breath. He leaned, as if steadying himself against the wall, then grabbed my arm and drew me out of the room. He shut the door gently and gripped my shoulders.

"The plane . . ."

⌐ノı∖⌐

It had been Joel's voice after the bypass that drew me back into the world, suturing, sealing. In my dream I was cold and laid out straight, and I thought, *I must have died then. Not made it. Joel, Joel, so sorry.* My heart was breaking for him – I remember pleading wordlessly that he would make it through, and then his voice had come, "Went well. You're good." Other times – my father's sudden death, a colleague's malice, my mother's slow, slow disintegration, Cyn flying out – I could talk myself calm but not into wholeness. Only Joel's voice could accomplish that.

Now all he could get out was, "The plane . . . with . . . Cyn and Connor."

His whisper cleaved my brain, gaps between the words unable to cushion, helpless to shield or soothe any more than the hands on my cheeks. His face, voice, arms – all incapable of dulling the thud in my chest that reverberated with gathering intensity, blocking the sound from his lips and forcing him to repeat what was unbearable to utter. As he stared down, I picked up the swift dive of his hand into the pocket where he always carried a Nitroderm spray for me, but I waved it away, my eyes unwavering on his.

Vanished. All track of the flight lost. Breathe in slowly. Out. Open. Raise tongue. He puffed the Nitroderm in my mouth. *No. No clue.*

But when, where? I couldn't push through the blur, barely framed the sounds with numb lips, and he shook his head. It comes back to me now as being like one of those dreams where a weight pressed down my tongue so I could not cry out, only it was not a dream.

Slowly, breathe. He had no answers because there were none.

How? I stared at his lips, waiting for him to at least sum up.

Nothing, he told me again, wiping my eyes then his. How could he sum up when nothing was known, and nothing hung together? Then Joel's glance wavered from mine to the door beyond which the children had fallen silent, waiting on us.

For news.

The impact of their waiting – a separate, consequent blow – resounded in the silence. "We must," Joel whispered, inclining his head to the door, and I nodded but stood a few minutes more with my eyes shut, the prayer unworded, only the slim urge sent up. The thudding spaced out. Less wildly, more deliberately.

We wound our fingers together – awkwardly, all feeling drained from mine – and we turned unsteadily to go back to the children. To tell them . . . tell . . . what?

⤜⟩⟨⤛

A little at a time? I don't know which of us said it but it may have been me, because Joel nodded as he lifted Mattie to carry him outside.

"Let's take a walk, son," he said. "May have a wait still, you see."

Francis had already followed Kevin to the porch, and I could see their shapes through the doorway, one figure bent double and the other dragging over a chair. Micah and Melody had their backs to the doorway but froze as their eyes fastened on my face.

"Mama?"

"You feel bad," Melody added. And Micah got up saying he'd get Papa.

I shook my head and tried to moisten the lining of my mouth with my tongue, but that was dry too. I got out something about us trying to get news of the plane. It seemed to have gone . . . off-radar. Or something. A barrage of questions broke out, and I said, "The airline . . . said it was . . . *proving difficult to re-establish contact.*"

"Mr Cambridge said something to Francis about *news*," Micah said, going for the TV remote.

"No." I tried to snatch it, but too late.

"They gotta know something," he insisted. But TV6 News was over – there was some stupid interview – and he flicked it off again in disgust.

I seized the remote before he thought to try foreign channels.

"We have to wait till they can tell us more," I said, as Joel walked back in with Mattie flopped over his shoulder, asleep but jolted mildly by the occasional hiccup.

"He was crying." More a statement than a question from Micah. "Disappointed. Now he'll go on and on about it till they get here." But he reached up and rubbed Mattie's foot gently.

The twins got off to bed eventually, because we promised to wake them if we heard anything more. Then, back in the living room, Francis, Joel and I crouched close to the set, the volume turned low, while Kevin kept watch near the door. Every now and then Joel got up to try the hotline.

I can't remember the order in which we got to know – *know* is the wrong word. Perhaps, what little seemed know*able*? Apart from the few sympathetic but guarded statements through the hotline (when we eventually got through) the . . . the *circumstances* came in slivers from the television– intermittent and as if it had not happened to us but to other, unknown people far away, as if we were trying to get the details of someone else's calamity through whatever scraps we might pick up. Through the night we fastened on bits and pieces of conflicting announcements or speculation.

The aircraft had cruised safely for a time, and then, midway in the flight – and with no distress call, no radio for help – voice contact ceased. Soon after that, the signal disappeared from radar. "We cannot rule out terrorism in accounting for . . ." "Aircraft deployed to assist in a search over a radius of . . ."

Television announcers with faces set for professional delivery of bad news released the little they had, shock by shock. They told the world that aviation analysts insisted there was no indication of mechanical or technical failure. Nor a storm system anywhere near. ". . . With planes, boats, helicopters out scouring the ocean. But officials are now advising the public to prepare for the worst-case scenario . . ."

The world changing under our eyes, emptying out. The clichéd plea jabbering in my brain: *Let me wake up and it will all have been an obscene dream.* We did not wake because we did not sleep. We spent the whole night trying to learn more and, in the haze, to figure out what to say to the children.

But in the morning – it was still dark – Melody and Micah tumbled back into the living room, insistent, almost belligerent. "You didn't wake us and you promised. You said as soon as you heard –"

"Nothing," I whispered. "There's nothing new." I reached my arms out for them to come close on the couch.

We had all run out of words when Joel left us to get into Mattie's bed, so he could be there when the child woke up. The twins were halfheartedly eating boxed cereal or some other rubbish when Mattie finally came into the living room. By then the phone was ringing continuously, the children clustering around for each pick-up, so it was even harder to talk openly. Kevin had gone home in the wee hours, and Francis had left by midmorning, promising to return by afternoon. In a few hours, I knew, friends would begin to drop in.

It was getting impossible to police the TV, and we had no choice but to tell the children that the airline had declared the plane lost. Joel took Mattie away again, barely in time before Micah demanded, "What does that mean? You mean they're, like, *dead*?"

"What sort of *lost*?" Melody tugged my arm gently, then jerked it frantically against Micah's disjointed babble. (". . . And not winter there, so the water wouldn't be that cold . . .). "*Lost* means different things, Mama," Melody urged.

Outside, Mattie's voice rose plaintively. "Papa, did they find my parents' plane yet so they can come?"

I walked to the front door and saw Joel had him on the porch. Mattie flattened his palm and squeezed his fingers tight so he could swoop his hand down and run it along the table.

"*Vvvwwww.* See it's dark and cloudy and people couldn't see the plane even with instramens. And now it comes out the cloud. *Vvvwwww.*"

He ran back in as Melody asked, "Mama, do they mean . . . *misplaced* kind of lost?"

Three faces tilted towards Joel and me, Mattie fretful, the twins stunned.

There are things that happen to other people, never to you and rarely to anyone you know. You hear about them and wonder: how does anyone live through that?

"But they said *lost*, Mama. So doesn't that mean they can be —"

Joel took them into the kitchen for something to eat, and I got onto my phone.

". . . Traces of shredded fabric . . . ash . . ." and then, ". . . are calling it the most devastating air catastrophe to have . . ." But that last was not a continuation from the phrase before, so it must have been my mind flashing on and off, registering smatterings of intelligence. "A crisis centre at Los Angeles Airport and emergency lines set up for family and friends . . . besieged by calls." But Cyn and Connor were just flying home to us (I tried to grasp it), coming to join their children. Millions of parents do that all over the world. ". . . Nor rule out possible terrorist activity."

Familiar words, household words almost — but in conversation about news from far away. Staggering news, but news of other people. What had we or ours to do with it? None of it was our quarrel. How do you set out to go home and find yourself in the middle of someone else's war? Or not find yourself, or never be found? The news we tapped when we could brought nothing together. How to summarize what was cut short and scattered? The senselessness of it ripped the ground from beneath us. Yet somehow Joel and I mechanically deferred our own desolation so as to buffer the children's. I wondered, unable to word it, whether I seemed cold under the veil of calm I drew over the screaming and wailing that clamoured inside.

By dusk, Mattie was scowling. Another letdown. Another put-off. I'd hidden the remote, but as the ringing of doorbell and landline distracted us, the twins had unearthed it. They'd caught some news, besides picking up snippets from tablets or phones. By the time the house quieted there was Melody, distraught, her lips framing questions I could not hear; Micah's rich bronze had faded queerly to yellow-grey. He heaved as if to vomit. "But what's it *mean*?" He caught his breath and whispered to Joel, "Like, couldn't it be pieces of some other . . . Like, a mistake?"

Mattie burst out, "They *said* they would come. I hate them. I hate them!"

Melody screamed, "Stop it." Yet she turned and hugged him. "'s not their fault."

"I still hate them."

"Shh!" she said. "There's no one to hate."

Something in that unfastened Micah's last forlorn hope, and he plunged wildly for the door. Francis darted after him, and it could have been a quarter or half an hour before they came back, Micah limping, his face contorted with pain. "It's broke. I know it's broke."

What? The question must have been on my face. I could get nothing out.

"My foot, my toe," he wailed. "Everything."

Whatever Joel asked, Micah kept shouting it was broken, so Francis hurried him out to the nearest medical centre for x-ray and splinting.

When they returned, Francis reported that the doctor had insisted on an answer, and Micah divulged that he had kicked the mango tree. At Joel's blank look, Francis continued, "Had to kick something, apparently?" It was almost a question – Francis as disoriented as the rest of us. "Seemed the best thing to do at the time." After a while he added, "Only thing."

We tried to make Micah sit still, but he limped straight over to Mattie and grabbed him close.

So it went on. Over the blur of the next days, Joel relayed what he could pick up from one or other of the international calls he managed to put through. We tried to hold each other up, a sort of living raft. Then, at last, it was put into words.

"As far as we know, there are no survivors."

Joel and I held each other, rocking forward and back, and all we could get out was, "What do we say to them?"

That was the evening when Francis made out, through a daze of TV babble, that the passenger list confirmed a Trinidadian had been aboard. Mattie was in the bath, but the twins heard him tell us.

"They're gone. Aren't they, Mama? They're never going to get here. That's what it is, right?" Was it Melody or Micah who whispered it?

So it was ripped from me. "I think that . . . may be true."

The next morning we told Mattie that the plane had been damaged and his parents were in danger of being hurt, so it seemed God had taken them to keep them safe. They mightn't be able to come to us after all.

He said no. They'd promised and they'd have to get here somehow.

Rain poured down. Sheets of water swirled over the windowpanes. The pommecythere tree dropped sodden leaves that plastered themselves on the cars that found their way to our complex, cluttered untidily among the palms and pasted themselves over the walkway. Kevin Cambridge stepped over and swept our doorstep as if sleepwalking through a nightmare. Visitors bundled dripping umbrellas behind the door, dropped cake, pone, roti, pelau, and sat with us for short stretches, wordless for the most part, before melting away. The rain pounded on beyond the ceaseless jangle of phones.

Above it all, Mattie's voice persisted. "Well, *when* then?"

4

EXTRACTION

I CAN GRAPPLE UP NO COHERENT account of the days that followed. Through the fog I made out words, kindness. I tried to move my lips appropriately. God knows what I said.

Joel's younger brother and sister, Patrick and Andrea, called from Canada and Scandinavia respectively. They'd left Trinidad a few years after Joel and I married, yet they seemed strangers to me. Now their anguished faces on WhatsApp drew them close.

From across the way Kevin dropped in with a bag of pastries for the children. "I guess all kids eat currents roll," he said, his voice hoarse and eyes red-rimmed. From next door Meera smuggled a macaroni pie onto the kitchen counter, subtly, as if the introduction of anything so trivial might give offence.

It was a fact that the sight and smell of food turned my stomach. One morning after being unable to face clearing up the kitchen the night before, I'd been almost overpowered by the odour of grease seeped into a Styrotex container. Suddenly, everything around me was tainted – an intimation of mould from under the sink, of rotting pommecythere beneath the tree beyond the window, of a damp dog padding past on the far side of the fence. On the sill outside, a couple lizard droppings, crisp white at their pointed ends, together with the sight of soaked leaves coming apart on the walkway beyond, became unbearable. With an immense effort, I disconnected so as to carry on. That way I registered not sensations, but being severed from them. The wrench was of nerves fraying and untwisting like overburdened rope. Yet a certainty gathered, that my coming undone would unravel the rest of them.

I know I steeled myself to go through the motions, recalibrating from mother to grandparent – except *now*, without Cyn's intervening authority, what was I but a mother again? When that discovery arrested me one morning, I stopped brushing my hair and stared in the mirror at the roots, which I'd lost time or will to touch up. Probably all white by now.

I snatched up the Nitroderm spray and wedged it between my breasts, because the slacks had no pockets, and I tried to recall whether I'd taken Brilinta the night before. I wrote a note on the diary to put some system in place. So Cyn had ruled, on that brief turnaround visit when we had seen her last.

Last.

She had propped her face sleepily on one hand, trying to take in my routine of sorting and swallowing pills. "Too complicated. List, then tick off day by day. Or no. Get the little plastic gizmo and set them out week by week." She turned an ear to the window. "Oh Pete. Just listen to that. I'd forgotten." Her ready smile broke out at the anthem of small creatures celebrating rain.

And now she was gone again from their audience.

⟶⟩⟨⟵

How did we get here – we who live on an island seven miles off the coast of South America, far from the stratagems of powerful nations. The twin island state – not two thousand square miles – riddled with mountain ranges and fertile alluvial valleys, with mangroves and waterfalls, with beaches hedged by coral reefs. Rich for a little country in the Caribbean, not just in physical beauty but in oil and natural gas deposits, even the larger, Trinidad, a tiny landmass luckily placed to escape most hurricanes or catastrophic earthquakes, prompting inane boasts that God is a Trini, among the many coexisting religions, among the more serious believers and non-believers, and the irreligious, party-minded, riotously colourful population complacent in their jewel-like surroundings, the flutter of over six hundred and fifty types of butterfly, and the surrounding hues in bold combination – palm green, ibis white, poui gold, Congo pepper red, melongene purple, tanager blue, kiskidee striped, monarch flared and bordered, waving among the songs of almost five hundred types of birds, and musicians and singers with voices forged by the confluence of uncounted cultures protesting, singing, lamenting, taunting, against the challenge and revelry of calypso and masquerade, of picong and pan.

Yes, we had seen trouble, a saga of violence through slavery, indentureship, uprising, coup, domestic battery, drug trade, human trafficking and the runaway murder toll. Reports on local connections to foreign terror had come our way, but we read of it with vague outrage, as the tragedy of strangers. We knew ourselves to be untouched and innocent, and felt certain to remain so (God being unarguably a Trini). Pristine.

Then, far away, a plane fell out the sky.

Francis helped us keep afloat. Somehow. Wiping his own eyes while picking up after visitors, fetching groceries and checking on payments for cable, Wi-Fi, landline, electricity and water. He moved us forward in baby steps one day to the next, from one life to another. He supported us through the service he helped organize. He inspected my medication, counting tablets to ensure I'd actually swallowed them. But I had started using the plastic case he bought. "I'm not going to die on Joel and leave him with three children to bring up by himself," I told him.

Joel swung round, gazed intently at an empty hook on the wall, then dashed out without explanation, returning home an hour and a half later to say a king-size bed would be delivered shortly. Suddenly I was again aware of what we were about. Over the years we had steadfastly resisted the idea of a king-size as totally unnecessary to two medium-size adults who slept tightly curled together. But I saw now what nightfall had become – in every mind a replay of *that* night – muted, but blatant on each face. I recognized this purchase as a turning point, perhaps only the first in a series of adjustments, modest or radical. Some would be permanent, others ephemeral – just to tide us over.

By nine that night, the five of us were huddled in the bed that filled up most of the room, snacking among the covers (a thing I had never let Cyn do), and talking about how to move forward.

Micah lay on his belly with his back to me and his feet wormed between the narrow wooden lathes of the bed head. Melody thoughtfully drew his feet out – for which I was thankful, as the slats were not mahogany or anything else likely to stand up to pressure. The bed was just a utility that should last our time. She planted her back gently against the lathes (whatever rubbish they were made of) and pulled Micah's feet onto her lap.

"Mama," she said. "If we can't have . . ." She paused then found voice again. "We don't want to go back."

Micah rolled over and sat up. "We're gonna stay with you, right?"

"I don't like planes," Mattie pronounced. "I'm gonna wait here for Cynnie to bring Con."

"Yes, yes," Joel and I chorused, and he added, "Here you stay." Then we turned them out to brush teeth, welcoming the interval in which to choose our words.

"Of course this is where you belong," Joel picked up the conversation again when they scrambled back up. "We need to make contact with your father's family, but your parents had listed us as your guardians if anything ever . . . This is your home now." He paused to steady his voice. "Having you means everything to us." My lips framed *everything* but not a sound emerged, and only Melody's eyes showed she had picked it up.

"And Cyn 'n' Con will stay here too. When their plane lands." Mattie turned over peaceably and went to sleep.

When all three had passed out, strewn here and there between us on the king-size, the two of us occupied ourselves with our own thoughts for a time. A glance at Joel's face confirmed that he was looking back to past and separate losses, perhaps including those he once had preferred not to word.

I knew his mother had died just before he entered his teens. He remembered best the unreal quality of the months that followed. His father visibly summoned strength to undertake her roles, moving through the house like a zombie by day, but night after night racked with sobs. Other ordeals had come later, more trying still, but regarding those Joel only shut his eyes and shook his head.

Now I saw suddenly that Joel's legs were thin below the covers. Lean by nature, he had shed flesh over the past fortnight. In the face of his devastation, I'd braced myself, staving off feeling yet reluctant to abandon him in it. Perhaps he saw I dared not begin a descent I could not reverse. All the time some unspoken agreement kept us searching out what lighter moments we could hold out to the children.

At exactly the same instant we exchanged glances, and Joel said, "What do you suggest now?"

I glanced at Mattie, snuggled in between Joel and Micah, the latter having again turned his head to the foot of the bed with his own feet resting on Melody's back, and Melody wedged tight between Micah and me.

"I'd say, turf out the tenants from the house down south and move back in," I replied. "Rent out this one."

He nodded. "Thought I'd give them notice tomorrow. Better see them personally."

"But isn't tomorrow that meeting with your group? On coastal erosion."

"Not going to happen."

In a while I continued, "I'll have to give Tinsel notice too."

"Always a silver lining."

I swung away, bringing up my knees as the words knifed me, but I covered the hurt at once by snatching a notebook from the table beside me. Turning back, I caught his own grimace and swift look to see if I'd recognized the insensitive quip for what it was – a survival tactic. So I served up Tinsel, while scribbling a reminder to myself.

"Maddening woman, but easy for you to dispense with," I grumbled. "How do I manage?"

"Ena." He'd obviously given it thought. "Visit her. Buy food on the way. Sort of outing for the children." He had not grasped that what I was wondering was how one contrived to give Tinsel notice. "Guarantee Ena'll come back," he concluded.

That was when I realized my breathing had been fast, because now it slowed and my heart resumed its normal gait. The thought of Ena making her way deliberately around my house, leaving a trail of order and quiet – balm.

⁓⁄⁞⁊⁓

Next morning when Joel and the children had gone to the supermarket, I told Tinsel we would move back south in a couple months, and closer to that time I'd help her find work with someone else. I was racking my brain to think who I could impose Tinsel on when I noticed she was laughing and shaking her head.

She would never think of leaving me so, she assured me – as how ting turn out. She alone could know how I must be feeling. She did dream the crash, she said, before it happen, and all dem poor people how dem burn up. Nah, she wasn't going to leave me so. She would just travel down south, put my three days together and spend the two nights with us before she came back up north. That way, she said, she could help out in the evenings and we would only have the two passage to pay, one south then the one back north. "And it go be a saving," she pronounced.

I explained there wouldn't be a room for her to sleep over and that I needed the three days spaced out. She assured me she would organize the work so the week's business would be done whether the days were together or not. As for room and ting, she wasn't fussy. She could sleep in the living room on the couch. Ent it had living room with couch? Right. I should know she wasn't going to take offence at that. Dat nah notting. Everything would wo'k out. You go see, she promised.

I felt my way upstairs and took to my bed for a half hour, resolutely avoiding the TV and reflecting that the king-size was going to fit much better in the bedroom of our house.

The house – I turned it over in my head, feeling its edges gingerly.

In those old days, from our porch that overlooked the sea, we had been able to make out San Fernando Hill before the light faded. The Gulf of Paria spread darkening but for paler streaks behind small boats making their way to land. Lights from other vessels anchored for the evening set off shattered gleams that trembled away and dissolved. The remains of the hill after years of quarrying stood stark against the fading sky. Afterwards, those bits that had been chomped out shadowed our awareness like a vague and disturbing memory, the sort of thing I would duck from as from a bat fluttering erratically over the porch.

Sometimes Joel worded it though. "How much of the view you think we'll have left a decade from now?" Even a couple decades ago we dreaded having it whittled away or blotted out by some tasteless edifice. Attendant questions I dared not word. How intact and comprehensible would our lives remain?

"I worry about our house now Mom's gone," our neighbour, Indira, fretted. Only her sister lived in the old place now, and once when her car failed, we undertook to drive her home. Along the way she spouted complaints about deterioration in her neighbourhood. "We coulda ever see this coming?" She flapped a hand at walls of nearby houses topped with double rows of coiling razor wire, each loop entwined with vines. Some flowered hypocritically along the brutal edges. "Watch!" She pointed dramatically. Toolum's Mini Mart had opened at the corner and a stall just beyond said, *Duck pluck and gut.*

Lamp posts with sagging wires tilted at different angles, matted thickly by vines as if a giant spider had spun drunkenly for a while before falling comatose midway, enmeshed in his own design. Only, no. The thickest were not vines at all but electrical cables looped, knotted, unravelling, caught up, hitched and tangling again, with foliage sprouting out between them in the most unlikely way. What she called a skid betrayed itself through gathering untidiness.

"Elitism," one of my bright young colleagues had sneered when another wondered anxiously about the future of the area in which she had recently invested. I'd invited a few friends from the department including the couple youngsters.

The reply came, milder than it might. "Well, I'm paying for it from the rent. Rougher the neighbourhood looks, harder it'll be to make my payments. And hear nah," she couldn't resist adding, "*my* contract ent tenure track. I might yet need that rent so as to eat bread."

I held my peace though I could have reassured her. The sneer had not been for her but for me, for my view of the sea and my comfortably appointed house. So, fine. I'd worked a fourteen-hour day all my adult life. My widowed mother had finished educating me on her salary as part-time music teacher knocking about country schools, and her father had raised her by digging trenches for pipelines. None of this compensated. Accustomed as I was to reverse snobbery, I held my tongue and offered coconut ice cream.

The girl Joel later christened Sneerer accepted grudgingly, adding that ice cream was a luxury she refused to buy.

"This looks like homemade though. *Love* homemade." Really, Sneeree had the gentlest of manners. "So we're not supporting some exorbitant brand. See?" Her voice slicked sweet and smooth as the ice cream.

"I do generally make my own," I confirmed, and Sneerer muttered something about wishing she had the time.

That house down south and those nearby had seemed unchanged only months ago when we dipped by, out of our way for we were en route to a wedding at St Paul's. But who could tell what changes might overtake it by the time we needed to sell? Long after my father died, leaving my mother resettled in Princes Town, she had sold for little or nothing the tiny house in an area behind God's back where I had romped in the rain with my first dog and learnt to make coconut ice cream. Ways of life were fragile as spiderweb. Where might the slide in the energy industry take us all, sweeping before it an economy we had taken for granted?

Indira and her husband Rodney had moved onto the Petrotrin camp before we relocated to St Augustine, and they had rented out their house on the road parallel to ours in Bay View. Now the refinery had shut down, they had been forced like other residents to move off camp, and they were back in their old home.

"That little rent was an income we could well do with now we have no medical scheme," Indira whispered to me when we met up in a mall. "But, girl, what to do?"

Moving back was our answer. The house. It would fit again.

"And I could do a extra day in the week for you if it suit you," Tinsel bawled from downstairs. "Eh? Ms Roach?"

Then the children poured back in, and Tinsel was mercifully forgotten.

―᠁᠁―

There were two pressing questions, Joel said. "One's financial."

He seemed stuck there unable to continue, although I knew that was the less urgent consideration. We were well set up for our own comfort and foreseeable emergencies, but we had lived on the premise that Cyn and her husband had good jobs, better paying than ours had been, and they would take care of their children. Us too if need be.

We had ensured there'd be no need of that, but it had been reassuring to feel factored in. I knew Connor shared Cyn's concern for us, however much I resisted it. One day I must have forgotten to wipe my shoes, and it could only have been some of that loose sand from the patch of grass we were trying to inveigle into covering the cesspit. In the kitchen my feet took off on the polished tiles and the floor slammed up cold and hard.

Connor reached me before Joel, holding me still. "Don't move yet," he said. "Mom, don't get up."

"I'm fine," I protested. "Pride a bit bruised, is all." I rubbed my right arm and leg (flesh too soft already without battering it further, I thought) and eased over to press a palm and knee to the tiles as hands reached forward to steady me.

"Hmm." Con's eyes swept me, troubled. "Why did you fall? You were dizzy?"

"Not at all." I realized I sounded gruff. (I hate a fuss.) "Thank you, my dear," I added.

Joel said. "You tear around so. Wouldn't hurt to walk normally." He'd gone pale, and I patted his cheek so he'd know I meant to try. The two of them got me up and were surveying me critically when Cynnie burst in.

"What was all that?" she demanded.

I took in front. "I'm perfectly all right. Slid, went down, am back up. End of story." So ungracious. "But it's good to be cherished." Then I couldn't help it – they looked so comical I burst out laughing.

Afterwards I heard Con tell her, "She's a grand lady. Tough and soft at the same time. Don't tell her I said so, though – she might think I'm trying to suck up."

"As if you need to." She chuckled. "You obviously fell for each other at sight. The question is – later. If they need care."

"They come live with us," he said. As if it were obvious.

So, no. We had ceased to need any special provision for Cyn. We'd cashed in life insurance once our only child was grown and independent. But now Joel was peering along a different road.

"What do we put in place for these three? No point selling off property. Rent might fund some emergency later or help with university." When he stalled again I knew it was because we had no idea what their parents might have put in place for them by the time . . . By that time.

There was the vortex, and there was that blast of obligations that pinned us close enough to the top for the anguish not to suck us into its depths forever. The aftermath of the blow afforded little time for reflection, what with children to feed, clothe, occupy and decipher. And educate. It dawned on us that there could be extra lessons besides doctors' and orthodontists' bills. There should be guitar and taekwondo.

How to occupy them right now, though, how to divert? Yes, there were boxes and boxes of children's books to unearth from the storeroom, puzzles and games to stave off the tablet that Mattie, especially, would clutch and stare into as if his whole soul were being sucked through the screen into some deep maw far beyond our view. We searched our memories for how we had invented games, saved stuff for craft – bottle corks, Popsicle sticks, fabric scraps and feathers.

The children's needs forced us through the slough in which it was most natural to sink, kept us focused on them. Joel mislaid Mattie's tablet till the charge ran down, announced he was having it fixed, then produced it again on the understanding that it could work only for short stints or was liable to break down again, permanently. "Now to fill that gap," he told me, and inside I plummeted again. Everything, everything, resounded with the crash.

Unaware of my reaction, he'd already turned to dig out photo albums with Cynnie on her bike, marshalling friends, hugging the dog or dangling from the mango tree. He mopped his face and shouted for the children, for now every picture became a story from which laughter could be exhumed. Joel climbed the ladder to fetch down the old globe from its corner atop a bookshelf, and I unearthed a flaking plastic bag with Ludo, Snakes and Ladders, and Tiddlywinks. There was a lot we need not buy. But the real expenditure loomed ahead, far enough into the future to frighten us – especially as our own futures shortened. University, Joel bantered, needed to be accounted for while we could still count.

Beyond it all, the TV dribbled news of the airline's investigations. Following the dredging up of the black box and the release of the odd text or video sent before takeoff, some vague reconstruction of events took shape. The inquiry had thrown up a breach of security that allowed a passenger to bypass a checkpoint. Another passenger's mobile, held up for a selfie, had caught and WhatsApp'd the image of a shadowy figure running along the aisle towards the front of the plane and flourishing an indistinct object. The investigation pointed to the cockpit as the probable site of the initial explosion.

Although some details suggested terrorism, others pinned responsibility on the airline and talk turned to compensation for families. "But could it be anything much? And how would one apply?" Joel pressed four fingers to his stomach and bent forward.

Still, we had to enquire. We learnt that such settlements varied all over the world. Then we stumbled to a halt before the enormity of the effort, and the sheer unlikelihood of any significant sum coming the way of three children in the Caribbean. Who to ask, and how? We opened our laptops to begin with a Google search, then closed them cravenly before the distance that yawned between us and whoever might respond, the uncertainty of any useful outcome, the agony rushing back. The indecency of the word, *compensation*.

"What if I went back to work?" I asked Joel. Outside, the insistent shrill of crickets rose to a crescendo, unless it was a scream in my head that I was trying to drown out with my most tranquil demeanour. "I retired early. Something might be possible." But even as I spoke I cross-examined myself: possible to secure a teaching appointment, or possible to resume routine duties and perform as I used to? An idea half formed that work might dull the pain, but contemplating class preparation, marking, student consultations – all through the miasma that hung on over us – made the thought unbearable.

Besides, we had our own proliferating limitations – mine the cardiac disorder, serious though invisible. Joel's health issues were more obvious but not life threatening. So far he had remained only near the border of diabetes, so it was the heartburn and arthritis that brought most discomfort, while a cataract had all but halted driving at night. That surgery was one of the things we had postponed to the following year, in favour of the Australian trip we had been planning before Cyn's call.

How could I lock myself into a timetable in the day, with children to transport back and forth to school – or in the evening with Joel stewing over what might have befallen me on the road home. Then, there was that quiet terror we never put into words, of whatever might fell one of us and leave the other, alone.

Besides – I examined myself as soapy dishes spun in my hand under warm water, and I reached for a dishcloth – *did* I want to go back to work? Nowadays, teaching seemed to involve entertaining students. I'd held attention successfully through the old ways and later built in PowerPoint, but now media had proliferated in mysterious ways. If I leapt in and floundered – I pictured the students exchanging glances of ridicule. Or fidgeting, those lower body movements that gave them away. Whatever attentive expression pasted on face after face, they might be politely bored out of their wits – which would be hard to bear because I'd been a good teacher. I knew I had. Then, nowadays, there were the uncouth ones who might yawn loudly and stretch.

"We'd need full-time help," Joel pointed out.

"Lots don't. They have to manage on their own. Some choose to."

"Those are parents. Parents are young people." He was scrabbling around at the back of a kitchen cupboard while he spoke, and I surveyed warily the carnage of plastic containers and ancient appliances.

"What you looking for?"

"Aha!" He wrested out a warped box bound with duct tape. "Ice cream contraption." He spared a reassuring glance. "I'll make it. Just tell me how. Right. So I think we need to be with them, not farm them out while we go off and try to earn." He untangled himself with a groan from the foray into the cupboard and straightened incompletely.

I could not look as him when I said, "You realize Mattie is still waiting."

"Head turns every time the gate creaks." After a pause Joel was able to continue. "If only we could track down Connor's family, these youngsters might get some sense of . . . continuity." He intercepted my question before it reached my lips. "Of course he had family. If he couldn't come five years ago because of family reasons, he had family. Must be someone. And Firaki's not a common name."

"Unless that was the given reason, not the real one."

"Cynnie never lied. Remember? She'd say, personal matters she couldn't discuss. Or something." After a minute he continued uneasily. "Children not telling us anything, are they? About home, I mean."

Melody and Micah operated according to mutual understanding, though they had their differences. "We're not from here" – Micah's voice reached me through the kitchen window a few weeks after the disaster – "and we don't have to do everything their way."

"Well, we're here now," Melody said, "where Cyn meant us to be."

"But it's not a proper visit." When Mattie backed Micah up, I went to the door where I could see them. "Cynnie shouldn' have made us stay without her and Con." He scowled. "They need to get here fast."

Melody did her best. "It's a good deal we three got here together, though. Right?" But Mattie swung away from her and grabbed onto Micah.

They were odd pairs rather than a threesome. Mattie consulted Micah with a glance yet resisted him with the same iron will that Micah exerted towards him. Melody drew them after her, Micah directly and Mattie through Micah. Micah and Melody, Micah and Mattie – hurled into an unknown space by the wreck of their parents – had oriented themselves into a constellation.

―᾿〉᾿〈―

Our neighbours from the San Fernando days, Rodney and Indira Fortune, had driven up to see us when they heard the news, and they dropped in again at the end of July.

"What do you guys plan to do about schools?" Indy enquired.

After the first outpouring of sympathy when the word got around, actual communication narrowed to a few close friends. We didn't mind telling Rod and Indy about our early morning trips down the highway to visit primary schools in south Trinidad, or west to the Ministry in Port-of-Spain. At last the twins were safely on the list for the school we wanted.

"The principal's been . . . incredibly kind." I seemed to run out of voice when any response to our loss had to be mentioned or even implied.

In the little pause that followed we sought out through the wrought iron scrollwork that enclosed the porch those few erratic pinpoints of green light zigzagging amid fine drizzle. About Mattie we were less sure.

"What about you two?" Joel asked. "You said the medical plan folded when Petrotrin closed down?"

Rodney looked away, but Indy responded baldly. "Our real problem is the dialysis." Rodney waved it off, and we didn't persist.

"How he'll handle that?" I asked Joel later. "I don't think they have much left after that Credit Union fiasco, and they both worked in the oil company. That's two medical plans gone."

"No idea." He regarded me gloomily. "No end of retirees set adrift. Think the public system can take up the slack?"

I know a rhetorical question when I hear one, so I gathered up the glasses and went my way.

Rain thundered down that night but held up next morning as we drove south for the children to see the house, plan their rooms and weigh in on where to put up the swings. The outing brought relief from the confines of the townhouse and from the barrage of condolences; but it underscored the finality of the children's relocation and the absoluteness of that *cleaving*. Automatically I split the word into its two opposing meanings even as I shrank from the sense of my very heart on the edge of the cleaver. The finality of this simultaneous severing and joining of lives struck home while I kept up the light chatter of plans for the move south.

The car in which we clustered glided, bubble-like, along a cataract of pain. We huddled there in this flimsy shield that could pop at any time. The highway unwound, the world outside the car windows bending out of shape while we fought to hold it in place. It staggered me – that I could be sitting here in one piece rather than disintegrating, molecules of blood and bone and brain rushing apart into nothingness.

Beyond that film of normalcy which contained us, the way south opened out as it always had, surprising the children with details Joel and I had stopped noticing. Cyn would have picked up on the silken gleam of broad grass blades bent dampened over a drain so the light rippled along them, then, the fountain of yellow tinted bamboo. A stand of scraggy banana trees flashed by, and Micah exclaimed at the lights of an unused stadium burning brightly in midmorning. Joel pointed out billboards whose signs the little storm weeks ago had cheerfully stripped and swept away, leaving their metal frames lurched forward drunkenly. And more bamboo, this lot smashed to lie radiating flat on a hillside between the almost luminous green that new grass takes on after heavy rain. Then other shrubs, tall sometimes but delicate, quivered untouched, softly insisting that the world was still here.

The rain-slick road parted for the wide, steep turn from the exit. Cars shuffled into lane and then squeezed to the inevitable bottlenecks nearing the mall. A tuft of grass shooting broomlike blooms had sprouted up on the roof of a Massy supermarket that had opened years ago at a nearby corner but now looked spanking new again after a recent coat of paint. The misplaced weed whipped back and forth in the wind as if it thought it was growing from a hillside.

Weeds, traffic – all the stuff one did not want, still here. I closed my eyes and gave myself up to the familiar motion of the car bringing us home, corner after corner towards Bay View. Later I would wonder how I had borne this approach to the house where Cynnie had grown up, but at the time I only registered that I was drawing near to the place where we had all been together.

Only, then, as we coasted up to our gate, I saw that new people had moved in opposite us and painted their house a dismal purple. Not lavender or orchid or some delicate, light shade but funereal purple. I surveyed it in grim silence for so long that Joel leaned across and with both hands physically turned my face towards his.

"I can make you grateful to the new owners," he said. I gaped at him and he tightened his hold on my chin to keep me focused. "They could have gone up another floor."

"And blotted out the sea," I finished, automatically.

"Look past it, over it. Beyond."

Right. Spiritual guidance for the day. And they had planted a holly hedge, so perhaps that would grow to obscure some of it, or even climb over the whole eyesore. Why were we just sitting here, then? Joel eyed my purse meaningfully so I would perhaps get the gate open, and I gathered my wits to dig out the remote.

Melody asked, "This one?" She was eyeing the house opposite with foreboding.

"Nope. Not The Purple Monstrosity." Joel turned up our drive, and she exhaled audibly.

The children scrambled out and began to race about on the uncut grass like puppies released from their cardboard box. Mattie tore around wildly, colliding with Micah. Joel nodded agreement with my unspoken thought. "Accidentally for spite," he pronounced.

Micah peeped in the windows, and I could tell he was wondering why the living room was so small.

"Bedroom. This house is upside down," I explained to him. "Living and dining upstairs." I saw he didn't like to ask, so I continued. "The original owner built it around the view from the upstairs porch. The sea."

"Can we swim in that sea?" Mattie pointed, bouncing up and down, up and down.

"No," Joel said reluctantly. "Lots of mud and mangrove roots before you can get to clean water. Pretty deep there." He turned away to figure out the keys, leaving me to explain *mangrove roots*. Then a hoarse bird call from a nearby house interrupted me, and all three raced off to peer diagonally across the road and return clamouring about a big bird with a huge beak in a small cage.

"Just over there." Melody pointed indignantly at the house next to the purple one. "A toucan."

"Well, first let's see what we find in this one," Joel said calmly and led the way in.

Home. Stark in its emptiness but crowded with memories, it closed around me in its parental sort of way, comforting, protective, steadying, ordered. Enfolding. How could concrete, wood, glass and steel wrap themselves around one's heart with the warmth absorbed from the lives tumbling through past years. Even the memories of its smells came back

– the scent of polished wood, rind on uncurling orange peel, rain riding in from the sea, thyme on baking meat, the warm valley between Joel's shoulder blades where my nose fitted for sleep. A baby's skin.

This bare shell of the place drew me back to our first viewing decades ago. Like many Trinidad houses it had begun on one level, elevated on pillars with an open space beneath for parking cars, drying clothes, tying some wretched dog. Its main appeal was a 120-degree view of the sea. Then, a subsequent owner had put in maid's quarters downstairs, so that plumbing on that level was already installed when we bought it. We had kept the upstairs intact but added an inside staircase, downstairs rooms with bathrooms, and a generous back porch.

Upstairs I took off my shoes and allowed the soft pile of the living room rug to caress my feet. *Consolement*, I decided. A respectable derivation for the circumstances, and every cell in my body cried out for it. But Joel's impatient nudge called me to attention. "Here for a purpose," I agreed and dug out of my bag the usual small hardcover black book.

Joel and I were working out what firm we should call on to clean the carpets when Melody said, "No carpets in Mattie's room, Papa." Mattie and Micah were to share a room and they had mentioned bunk beds when we encouraged them to tell us what they were accustomed to.

"Not even bedside rugs? Why ever not?" I asked.

"Asthma. If it gets bad so the spray we have from the chemist doesn't work, then he has to go to hospital," she said importantly.

Micah favoured us with a performance of rasping breaths giving way to strangulated gasps and concluding with a terrifying mime in which he clutched his throat and collapsed, writhing on the ground. Melody aimed a hearty kick which she stopped barely short of connecting with him.

"That would be a good show for The Game," she said and forced a laugh, turning at once to stare at the sea hard as if it had offended her, but I assumed it was to outsmart tears.

Then I saw there were no tears, just that fierce unyielding gaze back at the night it had happened.

Strains of Indian music of the high-pitched, nasal variety floated over from the purple house, and I winced. Even with my eyes averted there was no closing out that dirge of colour, and in the wailing music I missed whatever it was that Micah said, whatever it was that Mattie laughed at louder and almost more heartily than we could bear. But Joel and I moved on in our deliberations, exchanging glances of understanding that all carpeting throughout the house might need to be ripped up and tiles put down. I turned to the page with my running list and noted *inhalant*.

If you ask how we could plan, let alone smile, how we could engage with such trivia as swings or whiney-whiney music against the enormity of what had befallen us, I can only say that trivia offered a twig to reach for. The move itself was something to snatch at – distraction from the haze of loss that seemed to expand indefinitely, so far-reaching, so encompassing as to be hard to take in – of such proportions as to seem unreal. Joel and I – we kept nosing out the bits and pieces of normal life we divined through the haze, to nudge these in the direction of the children and towards each other.

"I'd been thinking," I said that evening, then stopped. But Joel looked at me insistently. "No use. I only thought it might have been just the thing to have a younger woman helping us. Jasmine was nearer Cyn's age and the children might have related so well to her. Playful . . ." I was losing control of my voice and I broke off, although the Jasmine thing had been ten or twelve years before. Because it was all of a piece. Inexplicable death.

That had been shocking news – this girl who had worked with us before Tinsel, savagely murdered. Jasmine had come to us after Ena left and stayed on into Francis's recovery from the accident, only her mother fell ill and she had to go in the middle of Cyn and Connor's visit. Horribly inconvenient, but what could she do? And Jasmine was a lovely girl. Then, a year or so later, her death had been sprawled over the newspaper with rambling speculations about motive and opportunity. But even before Joel retired, I had begun to avoid reading such ghastliness. It was only when the picture came out on the front page that I knew. Little Jasmine. It didn't help to think of it – especially now in the wake of . . .

Oh Lord God.

Once again, plunged down into the senselessness, into the unthinkable. Together or separately Joel and I kept sliding into the murk, and then clawing our way up only to plummet again. So then, what of the children? What was it doing to them, inside, where we could not see?

Ravi and Meera, from next door in our complex, must have sensed what we could not express between ourselves. From the beginning they had unobtrusively conveyed one dish after the other onto our kitchen counter: roti and curry, fry bake and shark, plantain pie and stewed pork, or it was sweet rice or cassava pone – anything they put their hands to that might, however fleetingly, foster some sensation other than pain.

On the first evening after our trip south with the children, Ravi and Meera dropped in as usual and unpacked two loaves of homemade bread still warm enough for one to break apart when I began slicing. We left the children to sit over it slapping on butter and cheese, while we drifted out onto the porch. Meera wondered in a carefully offhand voice whether we'd thought of counselling.

"The kids don't seem overwhelmed," she admitted. "But it may be they haven't quite realized . . ." As she went on, tucking in an added message (counselling for us, for Joel and me), her voice receded before my realization of how little I knew about even the children's physical health. I had barely been aware of Mattie's inhaler. What did I know of their minds?

Then the thought of the asthma sharpened. Hold on the dog then?

Kevin Cambridge had shown a wistful interest in the children from the beginning, and when he dropped by next evening, he brought up security measures for us to consider as we moved away from a gated community. I had thought vaguely of the three romping outside in our own yard and pictured them running hither and thither in the neighbourhood as our own child had . . . Our own child, barefoot in the grass with a puppy that would soon be twice her size. A dog long dead . . . You sidestepped the anguish lurking on your path and turned your mind along some other track only to find you had circled back, for it to whip out venomously.

Cyn was gone so swiftly and unequivocally it was as if I had made her up, invented the child I had longed for and did not deserve, and then invented her death to account for her absence. Bare feet on grass with a puppy. Then gone – through some hole in the sky.

What the children made of it I hardly dared speculate. Later, I thought. I would try to grasp that later. Meanwhile the three bore us up, even as they reminded us unrelentingly.

"No, no. You must have a serious dog," Kevin was maintaining when I came back to where I was. "If you don't see what you need in the Classifieds, I could help you bring one in." His job had something to do with the Port Authority or Customs. I'd never known exactly. "I could help you find the right thing," he insisted. "Get something for the boys to handle – probably too much for a little girl, but never mind that. The guys will deal with it."

Mechanically I set aside the mouldiness of his ideas because he was trying to help, but I could get any dog I wanted right here and intended to do so myself. "We're watching the allergies first," I explained. I looked forward to a dog; it was what I had missed most in moving north to the townhouse. But Kevin was the managing sort who could well turn up at our door holding out a leash with something huge and shedding at the other end.

"Is it true we're getting a dog?" Micah asked later that night. We were sitting on what porch the townhouse afforded, looking in towards the grassy patch that passed for a garden in our complex where fine sparks of green light wafted randomly under the sparse Poinciana.

"Perhaps no dog right away," I replied. "You know – I wondered about the asthma."

"We had a dog at home," Melody said. "He just couldn't come in the house."

The thought arrested me. "What arrangement . . .?" I couldn't word it.

"He sort of died. Cyn said we had to wait until we moved before talking about another," Micah responded.

"And now we've moved," Melody added helpfully, though I made no answer. I was still working on *sort of died*.

Mattie worded it. "What happened to Chase?" he demanded.

"Died," Melody said, with the automatic emphasis of one seeing herself doomed to endless repetition of the unpleasant.

"What means *died*?"

Micah shouted, "Shut up," and Mattie began to wail, a tired monotonous howl of inexpressible disappointment over an abandonment no one could explain to him.

"OK. Sorry." Micah reached for him but received a sound kick for his pains.

Joel came running and picked Mattie up, and the child pounded his fists on him and began to scream, then on and on – a directionless fury at finding himself discarded. He yelled till he ran out of breath and had to take a whiff from his inhalant. Eventually, still shaken by little croaking sobs, he lay across our laps, his eyes following the meandering pinpoints of light then closing at last.

It had been on a night like this down south when, shelling peas at my kitchen door, I had heard Cyn and Connor downstairs on the back porch.

"Candleflies," she said happily.

I glanced down where they sat with a couple glasses in a pool of light. Then a prized bottle of Blood Red Connor had brought slipped through her fingers and smashed.

"I'm so sorry, Con," she exclaimed.

"Don't worry." He grinned. "More will rise in its wake."

I called out to them and tossed out the paper roll I kept by the door. They seemed surprised I was there – at my own kitchen sink, for godsake – and I wondered again whether all my family thought me deaf when they demonstrated amazement at how much I knew about them.

Con's nimble fingers dodged the shattered glass to sop up the mess in between and came up dripping for more paper roll until he had cleaned up the macabre pool of crimson with its islands of broken bottle. He turned to wash his hands at the sink a few steps away.

"No splinters?" She intervened anxiously, grabbing his wrists before he could put them under the flow and peering at his fingers. They had obviously forgotten me again.

"Nope." He slid a forefinger down her forehead to the tip of her nose and then bent forward and licked the trail he had left. "Yum."

She shoved at him, scandalized. "How could you take such a risk?"

"With your face or my tongue?" He laughed. "I think I'll buy a bottle and wash you down with it completely, then . . ."

She shrieked and pushed him again, so he went down laughing and pulled her with him.

"Good job I wiped up all the glass," he murmured. "Well, most."

"What you mean?"

He hunched a shoulder to her, and I caught the glint of a sliver oozing red around the edges.

When she pulled it out and washed it, he said, "That's the difference between us, Firefly. See, I'd have licked it for you."

"Yeh. Right. Hey, Mom! Where you are?" She yelled for me to hunt down some of the vermillion stuff I'd always kept for cuts and told him to let that dry before he ruined another shirt.

Cyn was hasty though, sometimes unreasonable. The morning after this intimate exchange she was so cold to Connor I wondered what he could possibly have done in so short a space of time to alienate her. And he looked . . . numb.

"I told you that's not how I meant it," he insisted when she walked past him at the table and went out to the porch. He followed, reaching for her arm, and she flung his hand away. "At least listen."

At least listen, I echoed mentally as she shook him off. Here I was barely able to believe her good luck, and she was going on as if good men crop up on fruit stand at street corner.

"We want the same thing after all," he added. "I was just coming to it from a different angle." When she clanged the wrought iron gate behind her and jogged down the steps, he turned back, saw me and forced a smile. "I didn't get that right," he murmured.

But she would come about. He picked up his phone and went to fiddling with it automatically as if nothing had happened, and, sure enough, by evening all seemed fine.

Why this had come back to mind I couldn't think, sitting on the townhouse porch all those years later when the children had gone to sleep. Then, Joel came out with cocoa and rice crackers, and I sat inhaling the chocolate that infused the evening and curled round us before we took up the analysis where we had left it last. It was not the sort of talk to lead into dejection, because it revolved only around matters of immediate urgency. Once we started we pelted on through, so as to get off to sleep in time to wake up.

Yet the recollection of mild disagreement between Cyn and Con must have showed on me, for Joel leaned forward to study me in the dim light and ran his fingers down my cheek. So I shook off the doldrums and settled down to the topic.

It was about a school for Mattie, which Joel thought regimented. "Or can't he stay out a bit longer? Four years old. How can that blast his education?"

"But you don't think he needs something new and riveting to take over his mind?" I asked.

In the end we would opt for an organized school with an inviting range of activities. Meanwhile I excused myself from Bible Study and skipped book club so as to spend more time reading and building with Mattie.

"You're going to make lots of new friends at school," I promised.

"No thank you, Mama," he said politely, patting my hand. "'s OK. Cynnie 'n' Con'll take me to school when their plane lands."

5

THE CANNONBALL TREE

BEFORE MOVING BACK SOUTH WE HAD years of furniture and appliances to dispose of from this house we had been renting out fully furnished. We upgraded our second car, a stuttering pre-Y2K station wagon, to an SUV.

"And better lay in antiallergenic pillows and mattress covers," I said.

Joel agreed. "Matts roves from bed to bed." On further thought, he ran down a new, more powerful vacuum cleaner.

Nowhere in all this could I make out the narrowest aperture for preparing a keynote address. Wistfully, I regarded the invitation to the conference in September, but if I could even get my mind to engage with a topic, there'd be no time to catch up on the reading. And right here in Trinidad too, I thought. No need to leave Joel and the children. Yet, no. I'd decline, well aware that if I kept that up, everyone in the world of letters would accept I was dead. There wasn't even time before moving house to address the pigeons that had taken over the eaves of the old house and strutted everywhere, as a matter of course pooping copiously on the back steps.

Once we did move there was space for the children to spread themselves. Yet we continued huddling – in the backyard or in one bedroom or the other. A break in the rainy season and repairs to the next-door house raised up gusts of cement dust that sent us scurrying to lock windows so as to avoid setting Mattie off. "A/C draws air from that side," Joel pointed out. "Got a fan? Less expensive to run anyway, and it'll blow against dust, mosquitoes, whatever."

Mosquitoes were going to be the problem when the rains resumed, and the relentless march of ants up and down the walls was already maddening. "Can't very well spray insecticide," Joel said, his eyes following Mattie.

"Get more windows screened," I concluded, taking in the inconsistent width of sills in the old house and pondering how non-standard measurements might drive up costs. "We need to keep the grass down too."

I expected back the gardener we had had before, odd as he was. Ghany was a thin stooping man who arrived early, refused to eat a morsel till he had finished work and, until then, trimmed, dug and weed-whacked tirelessly in the flimsiest of shortpants. "Do you have his number?"

"The Mahatma? Somewhere, I suppose." Joel shrugged him off as if gardeners were easy to pick up.

Recognizing I was on my own, I made a note in the kitchen book to search my back diaries.

Over the past couple days we had unpacked enough for me to whip up a sponge cake while Joel and the children clustered round the kitchen table sticking out forefingers for raw batter. Later we piled into the car to run down to the road parallel to the sea where they could see the ibis assembling before nightfall, flapping through the mangroves to jostle for favourite spots on overhanging trees.

A few days later we shopped for school clothes. "We can find Nike in one of these stores, Mama." Micah pointed. "Right round the corner. It doesn't have to be Air Max. Really."

"You're too kind. Nice try." Then I spun to Melody. "What? Say what? Boots? Must be rubber boots for playing in mud. Watch. I've run down *Haunted Lady*. And sure, talk to me about Roald Dahl. Who? Addison Cooke? No problem once I read 'em first. But what *are* designer boots?"

"We're expecting snow," Joel put in helpfully, and they grinned. They were not whiners: they were like their mother. The thought shafted and lifted me at the same time.

From the mall we whisked them up San Fernando Hill to point out landmarks like the hospital and refinery, and show them the direction of their schools.

Other days, we would drive by the creek for the excitement of waves trying to slap up onto the road, or we turned in past the rusting oil tanks in Pointe-a-Pierre to the Wildfowl Trust with its dreamlike floats of broad leaves and lotus flowers, jolted here and there by bustling ducks. For the children all this was novel, while for us the prevailing normalcy was reassuring yet incongruent.

So step by step we stumbled forward – reinforced, offended and kept on course by the cliché that life goes on. We sought our way through a maze of paradox.

As outings tapered to weekend treats, the children contented themselves with romping in the backyard, diverted by the squawk of parrots erupting from the coconut tree, which – it came back to us – had to come down now there were three small heads beneath it. Years before, we had planned to have that tree cut, but two brilliant macaws took it up and were back and forth morning and evening, tails streaming, glistening blue. Now, the macaws long gone, the palm had shot up beyond the possibility of reaping its nuts.

So. *Get c'nut tree cut.* Another jotting of something long unattended to, now urgent. I was forever juggling notes of what to buy, what to get fixed, whom to call, encasing myself in the sort of scheduling I feared might harden me into one of these old women of rigid habits, trapped in some losing battle to keep up – especially with the children. There was no separating them.

Micah and Melody were forever consulting, or bickering about Mattie, and Mattie shadowed Micah relentlessly, while we had a sense that Micah would best read Mattie to us. In between sliding among the bookcases or going invisible on the floor in front the lower shelves, Melody elected to be near the others even if she was immersed in a book. She was as comfortable under the mango tree as on the sofa. I realized, without the heart to voice it to Joel, that the three were bound, most of all, by shipwreck.

We found them best content out amidst the thrumming, lavish greenery until the twilight brooded briefly before shutting down. This left me little time inside, and so the basic housekeeping that I barely tolerated had begun to overwhelm me. If I was to write at all I needed someone steady in the house.

Ena had picked up news of the crash vaguely but had realized only a week or so ago that the Trinidadian involved was *her CynCyn*. She had called to condole and found herself weeping over the phone and then apologizing because she had meant to comfort me. But Ena and I went far, far back. All we had ever differed on was her overprotectiveness towards Cyn, whom I knew could take care of herself and probably the rest of us as well. Ena viewed with suspicion everyone who paused in Cyn's vicinity. "She does be over-trusting, you see," Ena had insisted.

Now she heartbroken.

Whether Ena could come back to work with us was a question I could hardly pose over the phone, so we appointed a day for the visit.

—⁓—

Ena Partap had seen the type of confusion and callousness routinely shared out to poor women. When she left us to take care of her granddaughter – she never defined the crisis, and we did not pry – we took on a younger woman, hardly more than a girl, but only because Ena assured us she would not be back. Two months later she called to say that her problem was resolved after all but that she knew we had found someone, so she had taken a position as cleaner in a government office. No, no. She didn't want this new girl (what she name? Jasmine?) to lose the likkle work. After all, Ena said, she wasn't even sure her granddaughter's recovery was permanent.

"Recovery?" I asked.

But all Ena said was, "Penny good now."

We left it at that but stayed in touch, working out she would be entitled to a modest pension or other emolument from that office when she retired. Ena chuckled at the idea of retirement. People like her worked as long as anyone would have them. Her hope was to carry on until she dropped.

Then, in her sixties, Ena noticed a lump. Her immediate boss was a decent man and gave her leave, but she might need surgery and God knew what else. "Like I well going have to retire after all," she said.

Preparatory tests through the public hospital were free, but that appointment was in four months' time, so we got her to a private lab. Stage two, they said. "Could be a lot worse." Joel breathed a sigh of relief. "Even though she leaves the job, she gets something from them too."

Surgery was free and went off successfully. The chemo nightmare passed. She made it through, encouraged, bullied, coddled and pleaded with by Penny. Ena had raised the girl after the daughter absconded to the States, and Penny had grown up fiercely protective of her grandmother.

With what we gave Ena and what little she had put away over the years she stayed home to build her strength before the next battery of tests. She acquired her wig and travelled back and forth by route taxi to the appointments in Port-of-Spain. Then came a hitch: the clinic had to await Ministry of Health approval for the free follow-up treatment. Radiation needed to start by a certain date though, the clinic warned. After a tense fortnight, word came from the Ministry that the approval was coming through. But a day later Ena called me. "The lady in the medical centre tell me how they have to postpone again. She say, like my file misplace."

Meanwhile, Ena visited her former workplace in San Fernando for word of the sort-of-pension. A concerned voice urged her to stay in touch, come in regularly and keep checking by phone. "Like phone card and taxi fare does be free," Ena muttered.

Cyn had been messaging me every couple days, furious about Ena's predicament, but it was only at that point that the Water and Sewerage Authority began work downhill of Ena's house. A trench wormed its way along the western slope, scooping away rows of dasheen bush with its promise of hot, deep green bhagee, and another trench plowed along the southern side. For a while Ena assumed the trenches would meet. "I mean, I say they must. Ent?"

By then the rainy season had set in and water gushed from every direction, tumbled along the unfinished and incoherent trenches and overflowed, scouring the foundations of her house. The work stopped but the scouring went on. She appealed to the one workman left guarding the jobsite, and he watched her hard. "So why you doesn' fix the wo'k, if it don't suit you?" he said. Then, as if his contempt weren't patent enough, he cut his eye from her and steupsed.

She called her former workplace about the payment and learnt that her record was unusual. Looking back over her years with them, they found no note of leave for her in any form. "It didn' have no arrangement for leave with pay," she explained. "As how I never get sick I didn't take no time off."

They swooped down on that. Hadn't she been so ill recently that she had to leave the job? Cancer, she reminded them. Was the first time since she born that she had more than fresh cold or likkle arthritis. But payment for so many years of unbroken service was unusual, they insisted. "They mean is suspicious, Mrs Roche," she told me. "Like I must be cook up some way to look like I working, while I really spread out on beach."

They insisted her claim needed serious investigation. Meanwhile the Port-of-Spain clinic called to say that her medical file had turned up and to fix her next appointment. So she topped up her mobile and set off with Penny. Soon I messaged Cyn that at least Ena was through with radiation and building back up. "Mouth strong as ever," I added.

At night, though, Ena's house creaked on its wooden supports. She and Penny took turns staying awake. The house groaned more loudly and tilted. She appealed to the Water and Sewerage Authority, where an officer directed her to someone in Housing, so she found her way there to a clerk who produced nebulous words of comfort and advice. She went home to pack what she could and store a mattress and a bundle or two at a neighbour's house. More than that she didn't like to ask.

"No Mrs Roche. Thank you, but how I go leave Penny? How we go leave the house? Is we house – everything we have in it. Who to watch it but we self?"

Weeks passed in one enquiry after the next, phone costs mounting, and nights of alternating shifts, she and her granddaughter on watch between troubled dreams with an ear to the agonized moan of straining wood.

Then, one morning at 5:45, the house lurched – a convulsive jerk beneath their feet and a shudder of the walls. Ena and Penny dropped the mugs of hot Lipton and grabbed their purses, which they had kept continuously at arm's reach over the past month, and rushed for the door. They stood in the wet grass, fixated, as the house eased itself downhill, settled for a minute or two just short of the half-drums that overflowed with tomatoes, peppers and Spanish thyme, and then slid again to hitch, tilted as if a breath would bring it crunching down. The smell of rending soil and of shredded chives and bhandanya rose around them.

Above the silent wail of the torn garden grated the sliding stove, the fridge with magnets friends had brought from afar, the tearing wood of cupboards with clothes and linen, the dining table and cabinet, the crash of crockery. Somewhere in it shattered the bowl from which Ena's mother had liked to drink cow-heel soup – and, muted in all that, the crushed doilies a friend had embroidered. The armchair Ena sat in to follow her favourite show ("I does never miss Bold and Beautiful") slid forward to smash the TV and the small china cross that had stood on it.

Ena and Penny scrambled up to the main road. On the other side they ducked under the barbed wire fence to get to the neighbour's back porch. Clematis had overgrown the enclosing lattice, so their mattress and packages were dry. They squatted, backs propped against the board wall, and watched their house shuffle down a further two feet.

When the neighbour awoke and let them in, they got their phones charged and Ena placed more calls. Sundry government officials condoled and advised her to monitor the situation. The medical centre in Port-of-Spain reported that all tests showed her treatment to have been successful. Her former employers assured her they were looking into her claim and she should keep in touch.

"Any of the younger fellows want a human interest story?" Joel asked Walters. The interview came out in the papers with pictures of Ena and Penny pointing at the collapsing house. Then, after some ugliness about their going to the press, a government office contrived to provide a one-bedroom with sitting and bathroom, deep in from the main road where there was no public transport, water or electricity. But at least, Ena said, she was well enough to go back to work.

Then she realized she had told her employers there was nothing for her to live on until their payment came through. They had invited her back to work, at least for a while, but at the time she was waiting on radiation. If she went back to them now, she reasoned, how long could she work? Afterwards, would they pay the pension? Or if they found out she had gone to someone else – hnn! That would be, as she said, a nex' set of comess. Either way, they'd stop processing the claim, if only to rethink it.

Up to the night of Cyn's call announcing the move back home, Ena's claim had dragged on over four years regardless of her visits and our letters. Whatever help we sent, Joel said, the firm still owed her what it owed her.

But she had survived.

⇒∕⎸∖⇐

Now we sat on her tiny porch looking at the rugged countryside, broken only by the narrow, pitted road that had brought us there.

"I wish Penny was here to see you," she said, "but she gone out to make grocery. Is once a month we get a ride out to buy everything, but I so glad you come today – I was going to call. You never guess what happen: the claim approve. So I free to come back and work by you." She grinned as Joel exclaimed and I jumped up and hugged her. "They say I to collect a lump sum in a fortnight or so," she reported. "They go call me to come pick up the cheque."

It would be just three days a week, but Joel telephoned Mr Farley about repairs to the flat in the backyard where Ena could overnight when it suited her. Though she had never chosen to spend more than the occasional night there, the garden bench just outside in the shade of the cannonball tree had been one of her favourite places when Cynnie was small. Later, while Francis pushed Cyn on the swing, Ena would sit watching and shelling pigeon peas. It was two decades or so afterwards that we had taken on Jasmine when Ena left to nurse her granddaughter through some illness, as we surmised from the urgency of her departure.

I knew very well now that Ena would not stay for long nor move at her old pace. She was, after all, slightly older than I. Still, she'd come out in the next few days. By midweek, she'd said.

What I didn't reckon on was Tinsel, and I should have foreseen it in view of what had passed. The Monday after our move south, Tinsel had journeyed down the highway and threaded her way from one taxi stand to the next. She arrived when I had finally got into the shower and had to wait for me to cut the bathing short as best I could and get to the door. By then the house was tidy and lunch almost out the way. But she would be earlier next time, she said. All that was required was for me to meet her at the taxi stand in San Fernando and spare her that last leg of the journey. "Because the sun is very hot," she pointed out. "Don't mind people there inside, in the AC, they must realize how hot. Like it decide to come out stinging this morning."

But no problem: was just once a week, because when she went back up in two days' time it would be evening. Cool, thank God. The whiney music rose from across the road, and she swayed to it for a couple seconds, nodding approval. She plonked her bag in the living room behind the sofa, so none of us would even know she was there. OK, so the couch go jook out a likkle, but I wasn't to push it in because she must be able to reach she bag. She looked about for the mop. "Don't tell me they have the mop at the other end of dem step. They want me wear out my soul-case on the stair or what?" She threw me a mischievous look. "You know is joke I making, ent?"

I reached a snap decision about absolute secrecy regarding the flat at the back, and explained we needed our living room that very evening and would be using it well into the night. So I'd be dropping her at the taxi stand that afternoon.

She was quite put-out. Obviously she would have to leave early so as not to be on the road at night. She pointed out in a voice of gentle reproof that *she* had no car. So now it meant she had to hustle if she was to finish the *set* of work she could see watching her from every side. I could not find the strength to remind her she no longer worked for us.

By then the others had come in from the supermarket, and I was barely out of earshot before Joel set upon me demanding to know why I hadn't made things clear to the woman in the first place and, now, why I was pussyfooting around and promising to chauffeur her about. I regarded him with far more patience than I felt.

"You think I should have slung her back out onto the road in the hot sun?"

"Didn't say that," he mumbled. "Well, what is it you intend?"

"To pay her for today, including her fares, and drop her at the taxi stand."

"But she'll be back."

"Nope. I'll phone her tonight and remind her I left the sum I promised with Mr Cambridge, as arranged, that I'm finding days' work for her up north, and she's not to come south to us again. I have to get her out the house and have her on the phone before I go into that again."

That evening, however, before I could telephone, a tearful call came in from Tinsel. She wouldn't able come tomorrow because she well sick and on her way to hospital. She opined, in sepulchral tones, that it might be the sun that morning when she did come by me, walking up that hill to the gate and standing outside the door so long before I make time to let she in. I asked if there was anything she needed, and she said nah, she there in the taxi already. She would call again when she well enough to come back to work.

This was clearly not the time for me to lay out again our arrangements for paying her off. I dialled Kevin, who said she'd never called for the money we left with him. He'd phoned her, but she willfully misunderstood and said she had no extra days to spare him. "Not while I working for the Roach and dem," she said.

Meanwhile, we'd seen Ena and she had offered to start at once, since the pension matter was just about resolved.

She arrived the Wednesday after our visit and set about her affairs in that relaxed way that underplayed how much she was getting done. Washer, dryer and oven went about their business while she vacuumed the boys' room. On the way in she had discovered a bird floundering beside the driveway, its feathers mysteriously glued together. Fed and cleaned, it cheeped loudly in a box on the kitchen table under Micah's supervision, perhaps fortified by the aroma from the oven. By afternoon, nourished on the few sweetbread crumbs that remained, it was nowhere to be seen, having apparently found its wings workable.

The thought of crumbs made me glance round, puzzled. "Ena, what you did with the ants?"

She grinned at me. "You was using them, Mrs Roche?" She had a good chuckle and pointed to a bottle of clove oil.

"You brought that with you?" I asked.

"Nah. I take a look in you cabinet. I wipe it all along where they walk and they doesn't like that."

I noticed the muscles in my neck unknotting and my heartbeat resuming its preferred rhythm. The music across the road rose to a wail, and Ena steupsed and turned the vacuum to high.

At six o'clock the next evening I returned from the supermarket to find Francis playing Snakes and Ladders with the children and Ena hovering tiredly in the background.

"Why you didn't go ahead?" I asked her. "Francis was here. When he called and said he'd just driven in, I told him stay for dinner and assumed you'd leave at your usual time. That's why I didn't rush back."

"I don't like to leave them till I see you," she said. "Is no trouble."

"Miss Ena, let me drop you at the taxi stand," Francis offered.

"Nah. I good." She picked up her cash and made her way out.

I thought she could have thanked him for offering. But Francis shrugged. He wasn't too sorry she'd refused the lift, he said, because there was something he had to tell me about.

The fact was Charlene had left him. No. No idea what was wrong – was a complete shock. They had an ideal marriage, and he'd been living for the baby to arrive. He'd worried about Charlene travelling on her own, and she had argued it was to be a short trip – couple days in Canada nah, a little break with some girlfriends, she said. He was spearheading the investigation of a police officer and couldn't leave the country for a couple weeks. Afterwards, he promised, he'd get a few days to take her. She said, "Sure. No sweat." Next evening he come home and she gone.

"Just so?" I was startled.

"Just so. She leave a note to say she wouldn't be back. And the worst thing is how she sneak off as if . . ." He looked ghastly. "But you don't need to hear anything unpleasant now," he added. "I only wanted to forestall any stupid rumour reaching back to you."

Joel wasn't as surprised as I expected when he came in half an hour after Francis left and I told him about Charlene's defection. "Thought she was looking drawn," he said. "Couple weeks back when I asked how things were, she switched on this bright, brittle grin and insisted she was fine and I mustn't say anything to worry Francie. So, I wondered. Well. Poor boy."

"Or poor girl. Have you ever noticed," I asked Joel, "that Ena can't stand him?"

He stared in surprise. "What would make you say that?" But I couldn't put my finger on it. "You're imagining it." He waved it off irritably. "Some little thing you're blowing up."

Well, I left that right there and took to my laptop. It was on the dining table so I could be in the midst of the children. I'd set out neat stacks of games and puzzles which I often found occupied them – that way I could work near them undisturbed for an hour or so. Now they all crouched over a spinosaurus skeleton they were assembling on the floor.

They were peculiarly undemanding – Melody and Micah so insulated, whatever other children they encountered, that Joel prophesied they would be immune to peer pressure. Why need they try to belong when they had little interest in any group outside themselves? Even if they wrestled with each other at times, they joined forces against anyone else, except Mattie. In fact, Joel reminded me, they had barely bothered with the Jameson or Ali children who romped in the common space between the St Augustine townhouses.

Still, they weren't unfriendly. Ena they liked at once. Francis had become a playmate in no time. Tinsel – well.

It was the sort of thing Tinsel did. On her day south she had walked between them and the TV exactly when Bilbo Baggins was dodging the dragon's eye. She stopped in front the screen to throw an impish glance. "So how the M&Ms today? What happen to you, boy?" She observed Micah merrily. "I blocking you?"

Some days after my last contact with Tinsel, she called to say she was – well, not better but perhaps 70 per cent and so. What she wanted, she said, was to try get and see Michael Jackson doctor. Ent they did say he come back? Whenever, nah. Ent he there in office? But of course, if is Michael Jackson selec' he, then he mus be the best. She wasn't going to take on what chupidee people say in the news. Any time she could get the appointment she would go and make him check she out. Anyway, she would come out to work again the following week, please God.

When I explained once again the arrangement for collecting her package from Mr Cambridge, she said, "What? What it is you saying? You firing me?"

I took a deep breath. "You don't remember I told you about this move months ago? Last month I reminded you again."

"So when I come by you last time, you never say nothing. And I call you that evening self . . ."

"You were ill. Going hospital, remember? I had told you well before, and left the money with Mr Cambridge for you to collect, just as I said. You came the Monday despite all I had told you, and when we spoke afterwards you were ill so . . ."

"So you fire me. You mean after I work with allyou so long you fire me because I get sick? But people does really get on so? You really fire me for being sick?"

I struggled for a while, then put down the phone. Joel and I had worked out that Tinsel could clean the townhouse for the new tenants to move in and see whether they wanted her to continue with them; but I was tired. There was a level at which I had been under siege, deep beyond the reach of Tinsel's ravings to penetrate, or so I'd thought. But whatever protective layers I may have developed were raw and perforated, and I found I could not stand . . . certain voices – a shrill timbre of resentment, curiosity, excitement, even sympathy. An hour or so later I forced myself to send Tinsel a text confirming that Mr Cambridge was expecting her to collect the envelope.

Then I went to dig out the ancient Ludo board I'd found again when packing up the townhouse. We wanted the children in the best frame of mind for starting school, and our clustering around a game, photo albums of our travels, stacks of school gear, mangoes gathered from the backyard – these knitted us up.

That afternoon, as Micah, Melody and I crowded close over Ludo while Mattie napped on the sofa, Joel rubbed my back with his hand, his fingers seeming to plead; and I nodded, signalling another mental pledge to relax and feeling the tension ebb. I picked up the egg cup with the dice and rattled it with genuine enthusiasm. Ena placed a glass of water, packed with ice, at my elbow, picked up her cash and said, "Until," before letting herself out.

Joel retreated for an avid quarter of an hour to his newspaper, skirting the actual news, I knew, because he chuckled occasionally and at one point gestured at a couple ads in the Classifieds for my attention. One was for *a refined Indian lady* and another for *a black armful*, and I gasped. "Have you nothing better to do?" But of course he did. That was what he was trying to evade.

In the next couple days Kevin dropped in and reported that Tinsel had collected her envelope as cheerfully as ever and told him she still had one day free to work for him. Kevin had made himself comfortable with us now as a fixture on Thursday evenings, inclined to play the host if anyone else came in.

"What would he have been like if Cyn had married him?" I whispered to Joel, watching Kevin spread the day's newspapers around him. He found himself a coaster for the drink he knew would arrive at any time (he wasn't rushing anyone), and he had eased his feet out of his sandals and was flexing his toes in carefully mended socks.

When we asked him about Tinsel, he said we were well shot of that one; we'd have parted with her long-time if we'd asked his advice. "I've seen her sidling up, but I'm giving her a wide berth," he told us. At least she seemed to have filled two of the three days she had been working with us since the children arrived. "Not everyone sees what they're getting themselves into, poor devils." There was a sort of strutting benevolence about Kevin and a sense of being naturally endowed with the right to make whatever pungent remarks came to tongue.

"Not a bad fellow, though," Joel said after we waved him off from the front door.

"Well intentioned," I agreed. "Soft-hearted. After all, who can blame him for steering clear of Tinsel?"

By the end of the week, though, I unbent. Although Ena was willing to go up and clean the apartment, I fired off a text to Tinsel in case she wanted that job and offered to contact the incoming tenants. I never told Joel I was going to do any such thing, because I knew what he would say and that he would be right.

By next morning Tinsel called the house and Ena answered, so Tinsel engaged her in a chat. Ena knew Tinsel well enough to put the phone on speaker and say *mm-hmm* regularly while reaching under the kitchen table with the cocoyea broom she favoured above my store-bought one. Her mechanical responses to Tinsel's chatter worked well for a while. Tinsel talked continuously, even when she was alone. Once I'd pointed this out to her gently, and she said, "Well, is a company for me. If nobody talking to me – what? I go just stay dumb?"

After a while, talking to Ena, Tinsel became more specific. "So you there now," she said, a statement rather than a question. "Is just like I thought."

They had met occasionally, and Tinsel had preserved the connection through the odd call. Somehow she had gathered a bit of Ena's story. So first she went on to enquire solicitously about Ena's health and rejoice at her recovery. Then she asked about that pension matter that had been held up for so long. Her *oooh* of commiseration rose lingeringly up the scale and descended again as slowly into the depths. "How people could be *so*?"

She shared the experience of a friend who had waited years until some claim of hers was coming through, only to learn on the day she went to collect the cheque that the approval was withdrawn. Somebody tell the firm how this lady never really retire because she sick. She did really wo'king with different people all the time she was collecting salary from the firm while she on sick leave. Someone did see she coming and going to the nex employer and report she. "You know," Tinsel told Ena, "people does be watching you watching you all the time."

Ena cut the call, dropped the phone back on its stand and went to stand at the window, gazing through.

I grabbed up the phone and called Tinsel back. "Watch me," I told her. "You see if anything happen to Ena claim? I publishing the true story of Anastasia Penrose (alias Tinsel) in the Sunday papers. Is going be the story of a woman who make mischief at every opportunity and throw people house into comess. When I done, let me see who going to ever employ you again."

"But Ms Roach, what it is you saying?"

"I saying watch yourself. You see me here? I ready to send police to search you house for every last thing I lose over the past couple years. You better pray for Ena every day, because any inconvenience she suffer after this going land on your head whether you have anything to do with it or not." I slammed down the phone.

Ena stood watching me appalled but clearly impressed, and I gave a long, cleansing steups before stomping off and confessing to Joel that I had been soft in the brain.

He emitted an even more prolonged steups and said if I had lived while Jesus walked the earth I'd have tried to work out a reconciliation for Judas. But Joel was never one to kick you when you were down, so he left it at that, only muttering as he snatched up his car keys, "*What fools these mortals be.*"

He hustled Ena into the car and drove to the office of her former employers immediately, to enquire again about the cheque. As she told me later, they rebuked her gently for not coming for it before, when it had been in there for collection months now. It was two days short of stale date, they said. What happen? She didn' need the money or what?

Without letting her stop to say any of what came to mind, Joel got Ena back in the car and headed for the bank so she could get the payment into her account. So at least good sense had prevailed *somewhere*, Joel reported, scrupulously directing his gaze past me.

But I'd moved on already. Or rather, my head swarmed with questions about how to go forward.

⇀⫯↽

The vision of a return to teaching was seductive. I'd only retired so as to write – and spend months at a time in Australia. I'd wanted to pack in all my competing interests without my heart giving out.

One thing playing with the idea; but what real chance was there? With tightening financial stringency, the university's funds for part-time employment had shrivelled. Cautious department chairs scooped up grad students desperate for a couple tutorial hours, rather than blowing the allocation on a retired professor. Besides, the new chair was Aiden Bartlett, relocated from the Cave Hill Campus in Barbados and originally attracted to the sun from Northern Ireland. Aids – as Joel had inevitably named him – liked me no better than I liked him. He knew little about the Caribbean and cared less, but postured to foreign scholars as an expert. I'd schooled myself to protest that he meant well, but there was no arguing with an old friend, acting for the dean, when she remarked sadly that the man was utterly lacking in ballast. Were Bartlett even inclined to fight for me, he would carry little weight.

The graduate programme offered a stronger case for re-employing me but involved evening lectures for students employed by day. Our three would be in from school and at a loose end, and Ena would have left. Cynnie alone had occupied Joel and me fully when we were decades younger. There was no question of leaving him to oversee three of them singlehanded, evening after evening.

And yet. Images of bygone staff rose around as phantasmal presences – from my past, although I sensed myself still, somehow, in their ranks. Myself as I had been. And with them swept back the grandeur of the whole world of ideas and the delirium of discovery, the hunger for research that took hold with the force of addiction.

But then, too, the tedium of meetings returned to me, and the clenching of my stomach over submissions to the Bursary. "But you're good at administration," Joel exclaimed when I voiced this. "Why would you expect anything to go wrong?" I held back the observation that he was ready enough to imagine physical terrors lurking on main roads and highways, in my path or Cyn's. My bugbears were his painless routines of life. I'd managed a budget as well as anyone, but I loathed it. Not that I'd told anyone but him: there was no point feeding the gender stereotypes.

For more tricky financial management people like me sought Joel out for help. Such a quiet man, almost withdrawn, yet magnetic – and not only to *the fellows*. Women saw in him the sort of man they wished their father, husband or brother were like or the sort they wanted their son to be. Children gravitated to him.

Early for an appointment with the principal of the school we had chosen for Mattie, we lingered outside observing the playground, and

Joel asked a delicate slip of a girl hovering on the outskirts what game was underway. In no time she had taken hold of one finger and was chatting away, her face lifted to his. If he'd been sitting, I swear she might have clambered onto his knee. While I stood by racked by the thought of how trustful she was – for suppose Joel had been one of those dangerous men – she positively nestled against the arm she kept hold of by the forefinger, until the principal's secretary came out. This was a greying thickset woman, younger than I but in depressingly sensible shoes.

"You must be Professor and Mrs Roche," she said, detaching the child gently. "Ms Sibley's on an overseas call, but come on into the office. I'll see you comfortable before I run out to the bank." In no time she was chatting away with Joel about some shares that had disappointed her. "Could I call you to talk more about this?" she asked when the principal's buzzer sounded, and she took down his number. Usual story: the complete stranger's instinctive confidence in him.

Yet there were limits to Joel's trust in others. Some suspicious streak had prompted him always to lock his den on Wednesdays when Tinsel worked. He didn't believe in everyone.

—)(~—

In general, though, he believed in the future. The day after Cyn's marriage, Joel had spent slamming the garden fork into two sunny patches of ground in the backyard. "She'll be back. Sometime." On weekends in between his terrifying routine on the treadmill he'd gouged out a couple gaping holes and filled in soil filched from garden beds and flowerpots before tenderly setting young fruit trees for grandchildren who must visit Trinidad eventually. "Stands to reason," he said. Then he moulded and fertilized trees we'd had before. So now grandchildren had materialized and mangoes rained down from the old trees. The cherry, lone survivor of the newer ones and hardy despite prolonged neglect, blossomed luxuriantly, putting out fruit low enough for Mattie to pick and stand munching underneath.

As well that the children ate fruit. "What to cook," I groaned in response to Joel's lift of an eyebrow when I dropped my chin in both palms. "You know they've no concept of eating fish."

"Can fix that." And he did, shepherding them out with homemade rods to some jetty I knew nothing off, and they returned clamouring over a couple sprats we then cleaned and fried crisp.

Still, the three cast looks of repulsion at red beans, lentils, dhal – let alone callaloo. Worse, we discovered they barely tolerated rice. Mattie revealed their mother had warned them at Sydney Airport: if they wanted this trip to Trinidad, they must make up their minds to eat rice – unless they were setting out to be troublemakers. Mattie asked shyly whether eating potato would make him a troublemaker, and although Melody elbowed him violently, it was out already. "Potato," I said thankfully, having begun to suspect darkly that I was doomed to cook pasta every day.

"And buy red meat," Joel agreed. "We can do enough fish to cover us. Can't chinks on their food." He paused and thought some more. "We could cut alcohol except for wine. Forget bottled water unless supply goes suspect."

"And the dog?"

"A mutt, like when we were children. Needn't sign up for one set of vet fees – unless you're still hankering after an Afgan? All that fur, though."

"They don't shed, remember?"

But I'd lost him. He was surveying, eyes narrowed, searching. "Something gone?"

"Flower beds mown down. I kept the palms – and a few pots of bougainvillea. Those in the ground had to go, for why would anyone take on the thorns unless you fork out an exorbitant sum? But I'll miss the blooms."

"I'd have trimmed them for you if you'd told me."

"Right." I hurried on. (No point allowing myself to be sidetracked down that road. Again.) "Mr Farley's workman tided me over this time, but I want back my old gardener. Look, I had out that bush with the bell flowers, one-time."

"Mattie." He nodded.

An impulse to nail in every precaution and keep constant watch had taken possession of us as the children presented one trivial surprise after the next. That morning the neighbour's cherished white Persian had whisked by outside the window, holding aloft a tail dyed glowing pink and so accounting for the disappearance of food colouring from my kitchen cupboard. Outside, squeals of delight beyond my view from the study window confirmed that Micah was at the prankster age with Mattie eager to follow his lead and Melody to cover up or even instigate. Joel and I had nothing to prepare us for any of that, and I threw a hunted glance at the phone, wondering what I would say when old Mrs Mendez called.

The cat was a well-bred female, so groomed, sheltered and demur there could be no objection to the children petting her, at least no objection on our side, and Micah had quickly charmed Mrs Mendez into bestowing permission. But Mystique had a follower, a gaunt striped male of no known address that shadowed her when she left home and who, when she returned, draped himself longingly outside Mrs Mendez's door until the next appearance. Mrs Mendez was unfazed, Mystique having been spayed a year before, but I suspected that at the very least the besotted tomcat had fleas. The undesirable connection was so firmly established that the children had insisted I find a name for him, so he was now known as Philander. I made it an absolute rule that they were never to touch him, but Philander let no one near him anyway, nor betrayed the slightest respect for anyone but Mystique.

As Mystique darted back to her house with a flirtatious flourish of rose-pink tail, I searched my mind for some new adventure to divert Micah from mischief – and Mattie with him. Melody might not set out to play a prank, but could be depended on, if consulted, to produce an original idea – not for the sake of a trick but for the joy of the idea itself. I had recognized this in her almost on sight. Her mind was aflame.

"What are you *doing*?" Micah haunted her when she shifted her attention from him.

"Knock, knock," she snapped.

"Who's there?"

"Cantcha."

"Cantcha who?"

"Cantcha leave me alone – I'm reading."

Thankfully, when Mrs Mendez glanced up from her crossword at Mystique's arrival on the windowsill, she was diverted. "But how stylish," she remarked later, when I called to apologize. "And I'd never have thought of it. No, no. quite harmless. And such a sweet feminine shade."

6

MINCING WORDS

FRANCIS DROPPED IN OFTEN NOW. NO one to go home to – not that Charlene had necessarily been there when he did, he added. It had always been that restlessness about her. In truth, it turned him on to begin with, made her unpredictable so he couldn't take his eyes off her. Rendered home life a bit unsteady but – say what. He guessed we hadn't even noticed. They'd been cool because he understood her, or thought he did, and the baby was bound to settle her.

"Only – like how she always on the go – you could see her raising child? I mean, on her own." Then he paused and the inevitable thought flashed across his face before he worded it. "That is *if* she on she own. Ent?"

When Francis stepped off to the bathroom, Joel confided to me that he had always thought Charlene's head was full of sargassum seaweed. "Thought Francis hadn't noticed. Now turns out he had – and thrived on it."

When Francis got back and slumped down in his chair, we realized he was set on a straight course for the dismals. One could hardly blame him, and we reached around for some diversion. We turned the conversation to the children and he brightened up, so I felt him out regarding childish pranks. He saw no cause for alarm.

"Micah? No. Absolutely normal kid. Not a wild streak in him." And Mattie little more than a baby, no clue about all that had happened or the enormity of what it meant. Melody? "Nah! Too placid to be that shaken up inside. Not the type."

But Melody's face the night before we moved south when a plane flew overhead; and Melody's face when the news carried some passing reference to the crash. Then Mattie's insistence up to recently that his parents were still to arrive. No. I didn't buy Francis's characterization of Melody or Mattie. But he might be right about Micah, for what did I know? He'd have taken Micah around with him, but there was no separating the three, and all would have been a handful. Besides, I recalled talk of Francis being pretty unruly, growing up. (Well, the mother was helpless. Perhaps there was more I could have done?)

In any case Francis needed support regarding his own troubles, so we kept him close when we could. In a couple weeks he announced he was in touch (did he call it FaceTime?) with a friend he and Charlene had stayed with on trips to Toronto. Now, he understood, Charlene was tossing down tequila and smoking as normal – like she wasn't pregnant. How he could help worrying about the baby?

When I flourished the ice tray in his direction, he drew a hand over his glass protectively.

"Rum?" Joel offered.

"No, ta," Francis responded absently. Whisky and, OK, he supposed he could take a little coconut water in it. Unless Joel had the Kraken? Joel did not, so he brought out the last couple inches of Johnnie Walker we would have in the house for the foreseeable future. Not that I cared.

From all Francis said, Charlene wasn't prepared to sacrifice one sip or puff of her usual socializing for the sake of a healthy child. "Life come like one endless lime to her, yes."

As I turned into the kitchen for ackra that Ena had put by in the usual Styrofoam box, I heard Francis expand further, now he thought he had Joel's ear alone.

"And fête? Don't talk bout fête. Much less dance. If is wind on a bumsee you want in fête – well, look Charlene."

A despairing moan rose and fell outside as if Philander heard and empathized. I steupsed, then glanced over my shoulder, because that was a vulgar sound I didn't want the children picking up – at least, not from me. And then Francis's remarks – but I need not have worried. Francis would never have expressed himself in those terms if they'd been around.

Thinking I heard a car arriving, I stepped onto the kitchen landing and glanced out. A silver-grey Toyota Corona coasted to a stop immediately beyond our gate as if the driver meant to get out and ring our bell. Instead she got out, crossed the road and walked briskly back uphill past a couple houses, only to open a pedestrian gate under the street light and step through. A pompek yapped automatically but wagged and scampered off inside ahead of her. I stood rooted to the landing for a few minutes staring at the car. Not in my way but – an oddity.

Still there was the ackra to take inside. When I reached the living room and the smell of soft, fried saltfish balls diverted Francis, he continued his reminiscences in a more restrained vein. He said we'd have realized Charlene never was the serious homemaker, and that was all right. The meticulous type would probably not have grabbed him to begin with, so he'd been happy to take up the slack. The truth was, precious little would have been done in the house if he hadn't turned on the stove or taken up mop and bucket the minute he got in from work. "If I even start looking about to see if it have food, she would say, 'Don't ask me nothing. Ent you say you could take care of youself? You is a big man. Don't you can't done tell me that?'"

Yet another alternative story to the precious little Charlene had let drop, I reflected, and who knew which was closest to whatever had actually occurred. Then Francis's voice brought me back to his original anxiety: he would have sworn that at this stage Charlene would be thinking of the child. True she had abandoned *him* – he said it without rancor, as a realist – but this *was* his child.

Then he fell silent, the next thought widening his eyes before he worded it: Or perhaps not. What had she left him for? Or whom? How long had this absconsion been in the works? "How I know is my child?"

I protested feebly and Joel tried to reassure him, but in the end there was nothing for it but to listen and warn Francis not to jump to conclusions that would sink him in deeper misery.

Minutes later Joel raised a forefinger and cocked an ear towards the window. In the distance tassa drumming rolled insistent, celebratory, provocative, inflammatory, contemptuous of inhibition. A wedding? It made our silence louder, underscored our loss for words that might buoy Francis up.

"Anyway, I'm sorry to keep on and on." He forced a valiant smile. "Nothing you guys can do for me – and God knows you've done so much. I wish I could help *you*, but I can't pretend to know anything about grandparenting. Surely you have contemporaries you can sit with to knock around ideas?"

Which made sense. And we were uneasy rather than alarmed, concerned about being out of practice and missing some vital sign. Our own possible deficiencies worried us.

"The Arindells?" I threw out.

"There you go," Francis said, leaning forward to tuck a flyaway strand or two behind my ear.

The Arindells were a large tight family, and Cecile had stayed closest to me through secondary school. While she had no children of her own, a grappe of nieces and nephews had been in and out of her house as they grew up. Although her brother and sisters had decamped to Tampa, it seemed safe to assume that Cecile, who travelled every year, lived in frequent contact with those growing families.

"Bound to be as close to a practising grandparent as you can find," said Francis.

He embarked on fond recollections of romping with Cecile's nephew and nieces, and now disclosed that it was Cecile's niece (he used to have a crush on Shelley – did we know that?) who had introduced him to Charlene. He should have stuck to Shelley, he reflected. Instead, she had married this boring guy – now *there* was a loyal devoted wife. But enough of that. Yes. Aunt Cecile. You know she was really the one who brought up Shelley and Arnold and the rest, right? Aha. Definitely talk to Aunt Ceiley.

But the next day my call to Cecile brought an unexpected revelation. "Oh-ho. We not really in contact, *oui*," Cecile said. "Years now I ent hear nothing from one of them, except Shelley. The rest didn't even call when Lance passed. They knew. They *knew* my husband died, and not a card, not a word self. After he had their children running tame in his house weekends, sometimes half the school vacation. You remember because Francis was there too – and Charlene, because she and Shelley was thick. Still thick too. For Shelley-self pick up Charlene at the airport when she run Canada not too long now. Charlene call Shelley when she was boarding the plane and she wear Shelley clothes till she could buy what she need. Oh yes, Shelley and them call when Lance went. But the parents? Not one word."

It turned out that Cecile's ongoing enquiries regarding the children she had helped to raise gave their parents offence. One sister had told her baldly to let go, and the other threw out that God would have given her a child if she had really been cut out to be the ideal mother. Her brother merely went silent.

"Visit what?" Cecile emitted a mirthless laugh. When she travelled it was to see the world. Cosmos Tours was her family now, she said.

Afterwards, when we went over this revelation with Francis, I left out any reference to Charlene. For one thing, I was still trying to process her setting forth without her extensive wardrobe, let alone a few changes of clothes. So I focused on Cecile's predicament instead.

"How does that happen?" I asked.

Joel and Francis were mildly shocked, but inclined to move on. I couldn't leave it like that. I'd been in school with Cecile and one sister, and in and out their home. They were – well, *seemed* – so close-knit when we were growing up. It was the parents holding it together, I surmised, and when the old people died, the connections withered.

Like each of my parents I'd been an only child. "Nary a cousin," I told Francis. "To my mind, Cecile and them were a clan."

Joel had siblings, and although I'd rarely interacted with them I knew they remained connected. Patrick lived in Calgary or some such place, while Andrea – single as ever and a US citizen – was still flying all over the globe. In the past weeks Joel had spoken to them by phone and maybe exchanged the odd e-mail. Perhaps Patrick and Andrea kept in touch through newer stuff I couldn't even put a name to, but Joel stuck to his ancient devices. As for me, short on family, I had close friends no minor disagreement could shake off. Cecile's alienation from her siblings rocked my understanding of how the world held together.

Francis even reminded us how the Arindells had seemed to be all about *home*, about each other – not about *things* at all, he said. Not like how Charlene made a god of furniture so you couldn't even be comfortable in the house. He'd expected Aunt Ceiley and them to stick together. He gazed into space while searching his mind. "Like Aunty Jackie and her sisters," he concluded. "Tight."

Just so, I thought. Running my mind along these lines made me long to look up Jackie. Inseparable from primary school, we had stayed close even when university took us along different paths. Her children lived abroad, married late and divorced early. The daughter in Michigan had two children, but there were no grands here, not even nieces and nephews, for Jackie's sisters had never married. Joel said he could see why Tonia mightn't have, but Gabriel was a beautiful girl. Mind you, they gave everything up to nurse their parents, and then poor Tonia lingering through that rare muscular disorder.

With a jolt I registered that we hadn't visited recently, shut in as they were. Gabriel had worked up to a year or two ago, but Jackie had stayed home as chief nurse. What could it have been like inside that house day in day out? They had phoned, of course, after hearing . . .

Jackie had realized the children might be with me and listening in. She tiptoed through the conversation. Her delicacy had always been phenomenal. Then she reminded me that she knew how much I'd suppress. "You probably can't be convinced to talk, but allow yourself to feel. Don't postpone it too long. Promise."

"I might just pop by them in the morning," I said. "They've probably forgotten how to go out."

While I got ready next morning, shouts and squeals rose to my window. Joel was running races with the children and losing – essential for Mattie not to come in last. As I got downstairs and picked up my keys, along with the regular car bag with its clutter of extra shoes and spectacles, medication and other spare parts, Ena interrupted to say a lady named Mrs Hamilton had driven up outside and was asking to see me. Not a name I could place, but when she came in she seemed vaguely familiar and said she recalled me attending a service at her house after Jasmine died.

And yes, I remembered now.

Showing her to the living room I looked more closely and saw her as I had those years ago. Striking face above black linen with white buttons and a stunning collar. Jasmine had worked for us until leaving abruptly when her mother took ill. That was during Cyn's first visit from Sydney, and by the time Jasmine was ready to return to us, we had moved north. So she picked up the job with the Hamiltons.

Then the grisly case spread itself all over the front page, and I turned it over as soon as I saw the bold black headline. But half an hour later when Joel was deep in the paper, I heard a faint groan. He looked at me and folded it up quickly.

"You don't mean it's someone we know," I said. And he came over and put his arms around me. Snatching the paper, I stared at a faint but unmistakable picture of Jasmine. I caught a sound I must have made, more like a little croak, and he said, "Beastly." He gave me an extra squeeze before releasing me so I could go busy myself as he knew I must.

That night I'd demanded, "Why would anyone hurt Jasmine?"

Joel raised a shoulder. "One of the Deadlies. Wrath, Lust, what have you. Generally is, I guess. Poor little soul."

"What sort of monster?"

"If they ever find out, someone will say no. Couldn't have. Not an angel, but no. Would never have gone so far." After a while he added, "It's hard to take in. Sort of thing only too familiar in the news. but impossible near home."

At the funeral was this couple we had never seen before, sitting in the front row with Jasmine's family. I asked the woman beside me in the row of chairs behind the family, and she said was them people the dead girl did wo'king for.

But all that was years and years ago. My perplexity must have been patent.

"What I wanted to ask was whether you knew of any boyfriend," said Mrs Hamilton now, watching me closely. Jasmine had been seeing some man but then broke it off – only his calls kept on coming. Mrs Hamilton had noticed that the girl's cell phone kept ringing – and she was not a girl like that. Quiet, hardworking child. Not a talker, never discourteous, but sometimes you couldn't get more than a monosyllable out of her. She had just got this new phone – a gift, she said. It looked expensive too. Mrs Hamilton spoke to her about the continual calls, and Jasmine said her mother wasn't well so she had to keep the phone on. No arguing with that.

I was able to confirm I knew about a sickly mother and that was why Jasmine had left us. I smiled when I remarked that whenever we had a helper we really liked, they seemed to develop an ailing relative.

Mrs Hamilton was not to be deflected. I felt immediately ashamed of being flippant, but she paid no attention to that, only leaned forward earnestly. "Whenever the phone rang and this girl glanced at it, she would swipe off without answering. Eventually she admitted there was this fellow she was trying to dodge." Jasmine said she'd really liked him at first, for quite a while in fact. Then he got a little weird. Clingy. "Like he felt he could share her with he pardner."

Some response was clearly expected of me. "They never found the culprit, did they?" Not a conversation I felt up to, but I saw no immediate way out.

She shook her head.

"Has something new come out?" I asked, at a loss regarding her visit. "I mean it's been ten years, Twelve. Anything recent?"

No. And that was the point, Mrs Hamilton said. She had come across pictures of Jasmine with her children, and it brought the thing back to her. The police had got nowhere with the case, and how was she to just accept what had happened to this lovely young woman? While she was working for them too. Right there in their land. Did we know that was where they found it . . . her? After a moment to collect herself, Mrs Hamilton added that Jasmine had mentioned being happy with us. A young girl like that – Mrs Hamilton was sure I'd have been alert to anything untoward.

"So long ago. I don't remember much she said about her family, or anyone else." I assured Mrs Hamilton no one had visited and I hadn't noticed calls. "Back then, they'd have been on our landline." Besides, I didn't know anyone who would do something so vicious.

This was true enough. I lived among people I could trust with my life, people I had trusted with my child's life. I saw my visitor out, still wondering why she had come after all that time. What could I add to a case that cold? How could I, at this stage, point even indirectly to a killer? And how would I even be acquainted with one?

Yet it was also true I sometimes found myself rethinking people I knew well. Even my closest friends surprised me from time to time with some new quirk, some departure from the expected. Look at Cecile's family. Had I ever really known them? Had she?

Then, how did one account for people whom one liked and trusted but who did not like or trust each other? Two colleagues I had treasured for decades despised each other, people whose judgement I respected. I loved them both. And what of friends I'd grown up with taken off along trajectories I could not have foreseen, their children unknown to me although our parents, even grandparents walked to work or church together. Vast unknowns yawned in the lives of those who remained part of who I was. Well. Who I thought they were had remained part of who I was.

So, yes, longstanding acquaintances and even friends might surprise or disappoint. But not horrify, I thought, watching Mrs Hamilton's Benz glide down the road. None I could imagine myself wanting to cast off or escape.

Indeed, now there were even cases of people endeared to me *only* by time – people I had never actually liked much, let alone approved of. How, for example, had Larry Moore come by so much money with few if any qualifications and no visible job? I had always thought it suspicious. Now, though, his hair silver and his fingers trembling with the first intimation of Parkinson's, his eyes still sparkled and his quick repartee and good humour remained unimpaired. And I recognized a surge of affection I cannot account for except for the occasional overlap of our lives over fifty years, and accumulation of small, not unpleasant exchanges. Such short, scattered infusions of goodwill had amassed to the euphoria of finding someone (anyone) from my youth still around. I mean, still living here in Trinidad. Actually, I mean still above ground.

But Jackie and Gabriel Bradley meant more to me than Larry. I'd known them fifty years (nearer sixty, for God's sake), and Jackie was Cyn's godmother. Still, when I totted it up, a year had passed since we'd met.

Joel and I arranged to drop the children at school for that first day of term and then spend a couple hours with Jackie and Gabriel.

―⁄|∖―

We went to St Teresa's first, though Mattie's school was nearer, for Micah and Melody would get out the car without a fuss. After all, they were going not only to the same school but the same class.

As Joel set off with them, Mattie stared at the crush of children, parents, teachers, his alarm building visibly. Then Micah doubled back and signalled to me to wind down the glass. I braced myself for a jibe that might break down Mattie's last reserves, but Micah said, "Hey, you – make sure you're in one piece when I finish here and get to your kindie. No bawling and rubbish. If you're covered in snot, I'm not taking you back."

"You're coming for me? After school?" Mattie's eyes lit up.

"What did you think, Ratbag? I'd leave a little pest like you loose?" Micah stuck out his tongue encouragingly and Mattie followed suit.

I suppressed my sentiments on polite behaviour, and Micah ran off.

Mattie proffered a plump hand and squeezed mine comfortably. "You coming for me too?" When I nodded and kissed his hand, he breathed a small sigh of relief.

So although he was sniffing and biting his lower lip when we relinquished him to his class teacher, Mattie was not the screaming mess we had half expected. Mind you, he had gone with us twice before to see the school – Aglow, it was called – and since we had driven directly from home, he knew we were close. The week before, he'd pointed out landmarks along the way. So perhaps that reassured him.

It wasn't everyone we felt to visit. So many kept bringing us up to date on whatever their younger relatives had conveyed from continuing media coverage of the crash – most of it unhelpful. But Jackie and Gabriel had neither Facebook nor Twitter, so Joel and I set off from Aglow in reasonable spirits and reached their house half an hour after that. At least we reached their gate.

Once there, what I thought of was Sleeping Beauty behind her wall of impenetrable green bristling with thorns. Even the gate was overgrown, yet beyond, a fresh oil spot glistened on the driveway. At the far end stood the ancient car that had been their father's.

"Old man died – what? Decade gone?" Joel pondered it further. "Couldn't have driven eight years before that." We studied the wall of green doubtfully, and he continued, "You phoned, right?"

I called out, while Joel turned back to the car to honk the horn.

"Ah!" Jackie's voice emanated from inside the house. "You found us? Coming out then."

After a while, we heard doors creaking inside, barking and commands, and at last bolts scraping back on the wrought iron at the front door.

Gabrielle appeared and laughed at us from the other side of the overgrown gate to the driveway. "I bet Jackie you'd never work out how to get in." Eyes snapping with fun, she watched for our reactions while reaching into the tangle of green. She pulled a bolt invisible from our side and swung the gate in carefully. Each stem alongside it was trimmed, so when she swung the gate closed it became again an indistinguishable part of the hedge.

Joel flung back his head and laughed.

"But why?" I asked.

"Because I could." Gabrielle shrugged and broke out into the old faraway, almost dreamy grin. That was when a good-size dog of indeterminate breed and ferocious aspect rounded the corner of the house, paused and stared at us in shock, then lunged forward.

Gabriel seized his collar. "None of that," she said calmly. And between them they escorted us inside.

"Don't mind the house." She tossed the words over her shoulder gaily while hustling us in and closing out the dog. Then she opened the door again, just a crack, and said, "Sorry, boy," before shutting it definitively.

Furious barking and deep bass growls came from further inside, perhaps the bedroom that had been Tonia's, and nearer at hand from behind the door to the kitchen. They had always been dog people, but so had I, which meant it didn't faze me – although the barking seemed to come from more directions than usual.

"Break-ins all along the road, every house but this one," Gabrielle boasted.

Jackie slid out of the kitchen, pushed in the door and gave the handle an extra testing tug. "Whew!"

Hugs all round and seats taken before the usual questions.

"So, children gone to school?" Jackie held her head then raked her fingers frantically through her hair. "You're parenting all over again then?"

We summarized where we stood and enquired for Jackie's two, one firmly settled in Edmonton and the other in Michigan. "They're not too amused about us having been unable to visit for years, but we couldn't leave Tonia, and she's been gone just eighteen months. Seems like days. We haven't got our lives back yet. The two children have actually applied separately to bring us over, and we've got through with Canada. Not that we've made up our minds. We've hardly gone anywhere for ages except for the odd foray to the supermarket or pharmacy. And no one comes here."

In the procession of illnesses they had overseen, while the crime rate soared and they barricaded themselves inside, Gabrielle and Jackie had become harder to visit and lost touch with one friend after the next. "Except for those who really count," Jackie added.

Gabrielle leaned forward, clearly wanting to shift topic to something that really mattered. "And your grands? Adjusting, you think?"

"To all appearances, astonishingly well," Joel replied.

I could see him searching for a way to go forward but finding nothing to hold onto – and not for want of interest or compassion from Gabrielle or Jackie. It came to me that we and our friends replicated each other in innumerable ways, so they were hardly equipped to fill our gaps. What with the younger set drifting off to other pastures, our contemporaries hadn't managed the lives of small children for decades.

A generation ago, our daily balancing acts of earning a living, while meeting the demands of body, mind and spirit, went forward against that urgent, mystifying, compulsive challenge of contriving futures far out of sight. Most of our lot – however they had interpreted child-rearing – now lived retired, some on shrivelling means, hanging on to news from adult children who had settled abroad and were juggling their own households in another world.

Mostly, our friends were as we had been, a heartbeat before.

So we left Jackie and Gabrielle refreshed but no wiser about how to go forward. It came to us that we should have crystallized what questions to ask.

Indeed, we seemed to be feeling our way among proliferating mysteries. Even as we turned into our gateway with the children, we caught a soft gleam of silver and the Toyota Corona slowed into position just beyond the gate. The smartly dressed driver settled in her preferred parking lot alongside our hedge, from which to cross the road and walk several yards uphill.

"She lives there or not?" I demanded, caught by a slightly enigmatic expression on Joel's face.

"Who? Ms Parker?" He paused for the children to chase on ahead. "Not officially. Gentleman of the house married to other party elsewhere. Arrangement mustn't get back to wife, so no extraneous cars to be parked at his own gate." At my questioning look he went on. "Good newsman never reveals his sources." Then he relented. "Rod's heard stuff."

On and off during the day I spun facetious scenarios of accosting Ms Parker about her designs on the gentleman of my house. About whether she realized he had a live-on wife. Only, that night, the laughter was driven out of my head by a shrill cry from a house up the road. Then two voices raised, one shouting, the other bawling. "Oh God, No! Stop. Nah, man. Oh God, don't!"

Could it be Parker? I turned off the bedroom light and ran to stare through a window, but that house was dark and the road quiet again except for dogs barking furiously, one a hysterical treble yelp. Joel came out of the shower having heard nothing, and when I told him, he asked if I was sure.

"Only of what I heard. Not where it came from."

And now, nothing more than the usual sounds of vehicles up and down, humming car engines, occasional horns and thudding base. A group of belated walkers chatted breathlessly, announced by excited barking along the way. I hadn't checked my mail for the day. Mattie needed his story first or he'd get tired and cranky. Joel muttered about having forgotten the garbage. We could only hurry on with the evening.

And never enough evenings in the week. On the second Saturday of September, I skipped book club for the third time. Soon enough, I realized I had dropped it. We tried orienting the week around fewer demands, but I gave up even my Bible group – only for a while, I insisted mentally.

Overseeing the townhouses we had rented to students became an unbearable irritant, what with carelessly handled fixtures to replace, or irate neighbours phoning about music that throbbed deep into the night. Joel began to talk about getting the students out if he could negotiate with the university to resume our original arrangement and rent it for incoming staff or visitors. But then, he said some of the students were such nice young people – and in the midst of their programmes too.

Mentioning this headache by chance to Isaac, my sole remaining graduate student, I said we probably needed an agent.

"If it comes to that, perhaps what you need is me." He tugged his beard thoughtfully. "My parents are driving me mad with the quarrelling – is like living in a war zone – and right now I only longing for a place out of earshot. Jus' now." He uplifted a finger, signalling a breakthrough. "What if you rent one unit to *me* at a reduced rate and I oversee the rest for you?"

"But I want the thesis finished. And not a day later because of you managing my property."

"I'll be nearer the library and my tutorials, and in quiet surroundings. Oh yes, I have work to do – so there won't be any loud music in the night, not on my watch." As I wavered, he added, "Is not to say you're my examiner or anything, now they changed the rules."

After a quick check with an admin office to ensure it was an acceptable arrangement, we agreed to go ahead. "Matter fix," Isaac concluded.

Isaac had been a particularly brilliant undergrad in both the Shakespeare courses, one compulsory at level 2 and the other a final-year option. So I'd been glad to accept him as a tutor when he registered for the doctorate.

I'd have taken him immediately after graduation, but off he had gone to seek his fortune at an excellent European university his parents could more than afford. He returned disillusioned by uncaring supervision of his MPhil.

Two years earlier, he had rejoiced over his assignment to a world-class scholar, but soon enough he discovered Professor Cavendish was interested almost exclusively in his own publications, and papers he could present all over the world. He wanted completed doctorates to chalk up on the vitae too, but doctoral candidates who were worth their salt could manage more or less on their own. The more humble MA and MPhil candidates would just have to demonstrate once and for all whether they could come up to scratch (again, on their own) so as to be considered for acceptance to a doctoral programme.

Isaac completed his MPhil with distinction but came home in the hope of closer supervision for the PhD. I could have told him that any international institution harboured its share of self-seeking staff and we could produce a couple of our own. But then I heard who was to supervise him here, and I held my peace. In good hands, I murmured. The best.

"Not all my friends lucked out like me," he confided. "I wish I could bring one to talk to you. But lemme try this: suppose it was me wanting to escape my adviser. What recourse I'd have?"

Having an idea of his friends, I suspected which supervisor prompted the question, but I steered clear. "Any student can come for a chat. But tell your friend the regulations have guidelines for requesting a change of supervision."

"She's fond of him. I don't mean in any *way*, you know. But she doesn't want to make trouble or whatever."

"Some students request a change of topic – not enough to call for radical overhaul of the project, just a departure that shifts the expertise needed for oversight."

"Aha."

I inherited Isaac as a student when his own supervisor, a young colleague I had valued deeply, died suddenly, needlessly, smashed into on the highway by some sot who was never held accountable. The circumstances made it impossible for me to refuse accepting a doctoral student even after retirement, especially one whom I knew to be both hardworking and gifted. So I found myself, torn by anger at this needless loss and sympathy for a visibly shaken student, reading the first chapters of his thesis: "*Haply for I am black*: Cultural Reconstructions of Ethnicity in the Vale of Years, with special reference to *Rupert Gray*". So we had grown close – as often happened with my graduate students.

─╱╿╲─

Even as the demands of our townhouses sorted out, Joel and I found our day-to-day routines expanded along forgotten paths. There were the children's teachers to work with or work around. Mrs Khan, the twins' "Miss", was a tough but kindly woman; Mr McCarthy, who presided over the form above, prided himself on being a terror. He made it his business to strike fear into every child who would face him the following year. As vice principal, he contrived to descend abruptly on the class below his when Mrs Khan left the room, and to convince them of torments that awaited them if they brought their dunciness forward to his class. Micah merely ridiculed him in nightly presentations after supper, but Melody was visibly boiling up to deliver him a piece of her mind. That was for Joel to head off. Not me. It would be all I could do not to lay into the obnoxious McCarthy myself.

Mattie's preschool harboured Dorothy Sobers, a.k.a. Auntie Dorie, a soft timorous soul who said "uuuu" about most things, while Auntie Nicky spread herself over her work and Dorie's. Principal Sibley was Auntie Jan, apart from others who had nothing to do with Mattie. He was the first to say everyone was nice and there was cool stuff to do. But he did not want to be there. When his parents came they would find the right school, but for now he preferred do play at home, with Mama and Papa.

The first time Mattie ran away from school, they had brought him back before I found out. I felt I'd have died if they had got me on the phone the first time they rang. By the time the call came through on the landline, they could tell us he was all right, and we tore over to collect him. Principal Sibley said to come in and discuss it next morning when we dropped him off. Meanwhile, we should chat with him as calmly as we could. The clothes? Oh, he'd been soaking wet when they found him, but they always had spares on hand.

Wet? Mattie?

Well, rain had been pouring too.

Once home, bathed and dried out, he perched happily on Joel's lap, and I nestled his hand in mine.

"Why, sweetheart?" I asked.

"Didn't want to be there." Quietly said. Confidingly.

The rest of the discussion added nothing. Of course we warned him it must never happen again.

What *it* was, we did not find out until next morning's meeting with Jan Sibley.

"Do you know where we caught up with him?" she said.

I remember shaking my head dumbly and seeing Joel's hands stray involuntarily over his ears.

"He had slid under the back fence and walked through the next-door warehouse yard, then across a field with cows (and a bull), then under that fence to the highway. Which he crossed." After a pause in which she studied me narrowly for my reaction, the principal resumed. "You will wonder what we were doing all that time. We scattered in all directions – there is never an excuse, but we hadn't experienced anything like this before. I don't mind telling you there was widespread panic while we tried getting you on the phone. A few teachers joined up their classes so others could get out on the road without leaving the rest of the children unsupervised. So all work stopped –"

"Where was Mattie, then?"

Jan Sibley turned a quelling eye and continued in her own way. "Nicky followed the fence around the premises till she found the gap under the wire at the back and the mud beneath churned up. Probably just minutes after he slipped out. There was no space for her to follow, so she returned for clippers and then got back to cut open the wire mesh. I went after her but stopped to ask around in the warehouse while she ran on across to the next fence. She climbed that one and edged her way round the cows (she is terrified of cows as it turns out – some childhood experience), and on the other side she was cutting through the hedge when she glimpsed this little boy heading into the traffic on the highway.

"She was afraid to shout and panic him. By the time she got through to the road, the traffic had stopped and he was on the other side, so they let her pass too, but a couple drivers cursed her in the foulest way for *allowing* a small child onto the highway – and that was when Nicky called to him. He turned at once and asked her to take him home. Very politely. You know he's an unusually well-spoken and respectful child. She explained it was far to walk and dangerous in the traffic, and she held his hand while phoning me to come for them." There was another long pause before she asked, "What has *he* said?"

When we left the principal's office (Joel with the name and phone number of a counsellor in his breast pocket), we sat quietly in the car for a long time. Some bird flying overhead pooped on the windscreen, browny beige green, splat on the glass. I opened the glove compartment for paper roll, but Joel ignored it. He drew out the card that said *Dr F. Harvey Marcelle, Child Psychologist* and studied it so intently, I wondered if he could hear me.

"Is this how it's going to be?" I don't know what I looked like, staring at him. "You're good to take it this way."

He shook his head. "Never been so afraid in my life," he said. "But we'll make it through this, because . . ."

". . . Because we must," I concluded.

That had always been our mantra and we clung to it.

7

PREDATORY EYES

—⁀⁄⁀—

CONSTANT RAIN HAD BEATEN DOWN LEAVES all over the yard, and the grass sprouted high. I waited for Joel to finish the lunatic routine on the treadmill — oh yes, he had begun it again — before I asked him to call the gardener and find out where he was. Mahatma, as Joel irreverently called him, had promised seven in the morning on Saturday and now it was eight. Everyone knew that whatever time he arrived, he slowed down after lunch and appeared dressed for payment and departure by 2:45.

Joel said, "The thing is, he's so unprepossessing."

I couldn't believe my ears. "We won't mow the lawn because the gardener we had for three years when we lived here before is *unprepossessing*?" Since moving back, I had tried one temporary gardener after the next, so I was chuckling as I fumbled through an old kitchen book that might have phone numbers. But Joel laid a hand on mine, squeezing my fingers hard.

"Sort of told him we wouldn't need him after all," he said.

I gaped at him.

"That my grandson and I would handle it together," he concluded lamely.

I walked away and contemplated the overgrown yard, but I wasn't seeing any of it. I was wondering whether Joel was losing touch. And what that would mean.

When I turned my face to him, he rushed over, saying, "We'll get someone else. I'll ask those people who trim the stupid holly hedge across the way." He peered at me. "But how you could look so tragic? Not to say this is any emergency."

I tried to collect myself. "Apart from high, drenched grass and the dengue or Zika factor, and from disappointing a poor man who has worked well for us in the past, and from this daft idea sprung up from nowhere, I guess you could say there's no emergency."

As I took in the troubled expression in his eyes, though, my faith in his good sense welled back. I squeezed his hand and led him to the sofa. Then I leaned close and peered into his eyes, to see into his brain. "What's changed?"

"Was trying to spare you one extra twinge. Remember when Ghany had worked with us for a year or so and a comment came back to us that he had been 'inside'? Actually done time?"

"Yes. I'd forgotten. But by then he had been so reliable, so respectful and . . . and handy . . ."

"Right. Then when I asked him straight out, he said it was some trumped-up ganja charge, and we dropped it." I nodded. "Well," he continued, "what with the children now, I made some extra enquiries, someone who could check court records – a connection through Francis. The old Ghany's conviction was for something quite different."

"So tell me."

"Child molestation."

"Father God!"

"I was thinking we could just have those guys who do so many yards in the area," he added, "husband and wife team. Maybe get their number from the toucan people."

I nodded wordlessly, hugging his nearest arm and shaking my head as if that might somehow clear our way.

"Should have told you," he went on, "but I figured – one thing less to jar on you. Your point about dengue, though, is well taken. I did spray Mattie down before he went outside." He craned his neck to glance through the window at Mattie, rolling over and over in the wet grass with his imaginary friend. "Matts, come in for a dry top," he called.

By then Mattie was already wheezing. "Too damp at this hour, son," I said. "You can't wallow in the wet like that."

Melody had come into the kitchen with some intractable math problem for Joel, and she shook her head. "I don't think the wet troubles him, Mama. It's the grass. Cyn used to take him for a drive whenever the mowers came." She settled down still in pyjamas to get the homework out of the way, presumably so she could read without interruption for the rest of the weekend.

By the time I had run the bath and got Mattie in, Joel was on the net. "Grass pollen?" he called to Melody.

She got up to look over his shoulder and nodded. "Or it could be the repellent. Sometimes he gets a rash too, from the grass." She thought a bit. "Or the repellent."

"What's *arash*?" Mattie called from the warm bath clouded with menthol fumes. In response to a shout of explanation from Melody, he bellowed, "I don't have no arash!" Loud enough to reassure us about his lung capacity.

But after a day of his wheezing and snuffling, we inclined to make it a quiet evening. At any rate, I discouraged the more boisterous larks in which Joel and the three of them delighted. Then Mattie demanded to play the game. When Joel asked which, Mattie said, "The same one. *The Game.*"

Joel and I exchanged startled glances, and Melody said, "Let's not" – my thought exactly as that last session came back to me. But when Mattie asked why not, I found no words. Then, while we were temporizing, Micah too asked why not. It wasn't to say anything like *that* could ever happen again, he pointed out. So we gave in.

"I'm *It*," Micah said. And the truth was we were laughing over his antics in no time.

He'd defined his game family as Joel and me, along with our neighbours from St Augustine – Kevin Cambridge as well as Ravi and Meera. At first, as we realized what he was doing, we reminded him it should be one actual family, but he said he didn't know any other families in Trinidad yet, and this was a nice little group. Somehow he captured Kevin exactly, the arrogant gestures, the wagging forefinger. Kevin can be such a stinker, I'd often told Joel. I would say I didn't know why I liked him. But I recognized it was because he was genuinely a kind man beneath the posturing. And it wasn't as if he'd ever had a chance with Cyn.

One of the sore places Kevin had recently trampled was the issue of guardianship. He had dropped in the evening before, after a mysterious appointment in the south, before going back up the highway. How did we know we were entitled to the children? he demanded. He cross-examined Melody about her father's family and elicited a faltering response. I would almost have called it evasive. She planted her palms on the table nine inches apart and exactly parallel, braced her arms as if nothing would ever move her, and tipped her chin towards an open window, assuming her most wooden expression. There was no one left, she insisted.

Joel made a hasty signal to Kevin, who had the grace to shift topics. But Melody was quiet for the rest of the evening.

"As if it isn't bad enough generally fielding the odd reference to Australia, to fatal accidents, to air travel . . . He's kind of a loose cannon," I complained to Joel when we were alone. "Why have people got to *dig*?"

"Genuine concern in Kevin's case," Joel said.

"Knows everything," I grumbled.

"That too."

Later, when I asked Melody whether she had been very upset by Mr Cambridge, she turned sulky. "What's he trying to make you give us away for? 'S not his business."

True enough. But I told her, "I think he just wants to help."

"How's it help to keep passing us on?"

"Pass who on? What?" Joel snatched her and swept her along as if to toss her to Micah. "A ball? Old shoes? A secret?" He waved her about a bit more. By this time she was squealing and giggling. "Pass on? Pass over? Pass out!"

So that passed, especially as Francis rang the doorbell two minutes later. One look at his face made Joel plant a drink in his hand and plonk him in front of the TV.

"We won't be long," Joel assured him.

Francis nodded silently. He seemed to be in some sort of daze, and I was glad Joel had relented and laid in another bottle of Johnnie Walker. It didn't take long to put the children to bed, and we got our wine, switched off the box and settled down with him.

Francis spared a disapproving glance at Joel and asked, "Then why you walking crookedy so?"

"I'm fine," Joel said.

"He thought he could twirl an eight-year-old girl like a baton, without his vertebrae demurring," I explained. "What about you now?"

He should have expected it, Francis said. Charlene was a young woman – why wouldn't she remarry? After all, since that first bald message from Toronto she had given him no cause to expect her back.

Especially, I thought, since he may have given no indication of being lonely. Joel and I had registered signs that he'd been taking comfort in one girlfriend after the next. Mind you, he'd played around quite wildly before his marriage too. Then he was at the altar – on a whim, it seemed. "Too early," Joel had said. "Too young and callow, the two of them."

Now, Francis wondered aloud about whether she had liked this other man long-time, for why else would she have left a perfectly loving husband in the first place. But I had already come to wonder whether it was the other way around and that she had left him because he was a womanizer.

It was no point closing our eyes to it just because we loved him, I told Joel later when we were alone. Francis had a roving eye, and I had seen it rove. Which was not to say that I thought for a minute he could ever hurt anyone, I added hastily.

"Why would you even say that?" Joel paused before settling in his usual chair on the porch. He looked startled and a little offended.

"God knows." I shrugged it off. For who was I to judge? And what guidance had I ever offered Francis?

By now Melody slept in her own room and Micah on the top bunk in his. Mattie stayed with us till he fell asleep and then Joel carried him to his bottom bunk, but he woke up during the night and padded back more or less in his sleep to our room, worming his way in between us. That was hours away, though, and we could unwind before heading in to bed.

"What could that family matter have been, to keep Con from coming on the second visit?" Joel reverted to what he thought relevant. "Or rather, who?"

"No parents left, I think. Remember him saying he wanted a place of his own? Something substantial his parents could never have imagined *had they lived*."

"Suppose there might be an uncle or something," Joel said.

"I did ask Melody about her dad's family – whether there was an aunt or uncle – and she hesitated. Then Mattie said something like 'Barry.' She looked at him very oddly, and I didn't like to ask anything more in case it set him off. When Melody took him outside, I asked Micah who Barry was, and he said, 'Just Mattie's stupid imaginary friend.' But I felt there was more to it."

"Could try to find out whether there's a Barry Firaki in Sydney. Or a Barrington. Pretty sure we heard Connor's parents were dead, so you're probably right. Barry could be an uncle." Joel thought a bit. "You know," he continued "Francis is good on the Net and all that stuff. He'd help us

. . ." Joel's voice trailed off as he watched, bemused, while the usual Toyota drew up just beyond our gate and the driver got out in the rain, crossed and scurried up the road, holding a sagging newspaper over her head.

"You claim to have solved that one definitively?" I asked, and he grinned.

"Yup."

"So there's more? Aren't you going to tell me?"

"Same thing. Parker kind of lives with fellow up the hill. Doesn't want wife to know, so Parker leaves car near our gate."

"Well, you'd said *that*, but wife doesn't notice when Parker gets inside and goes to bed with them?" I asked. "She must have returned from her travels by now."

"Nah. Not travelling – just lives elsewhere. Maybe Venezuela. He's working here, or in some racket, and sends back money to her and the children. Doesn't want any report getting back though. Anyway, forget them. We've more pressing stuff to figure out."

In a few minutes we had decided to get Francis talking with Micah so as to find out what he could about Barry.

—)⟨—

The two spent quite an afternoon together the following Saturday, for it was a clear, dry day – telling silly jokes, raking leaves, talking over the fence to someone in the next yard and shooting at the basketball hoop. Later, Francis said he had an idea there might be some legal firm Barry had worked with, and he would find out what he could. That was promising, because it came back to me that Cyn had once mentioned something about Connor having had a lawyer in the family.

But we were never able to track anyone named Barry Firaki.

Afterwards, I found myself with two problems. One was that on Sunday morning Micah referred to the helper next door as a *sweet piece of skin*, defending himself righteously with the claim that "Francis *said*". The other was that Mattie was grossly offended at having been left out of the big-boys' lime and would have nothing to do with Micah the following day.

So I devoted the morning to his entertainment. I pushed Mattie on the swing until I had to ask him to come down and play something else.

"Better stop for a rest," I said.

"I'm not tired," he assured me, kicking his sturdy little legs vigorously but not with enough coordination to pump him back and forth.

"I am," I admitted. "I get tired faster than you." I led him to the front, and we strolled a little way up the road. Along the edge I caught a sparkle of broken glass shattered so fine it seemed part of the sand and gravel between the asphalt and the grass. I glanced at Mattie to make sure he had on his sandals and noticed his feet seemed to be manoeuvring around some other pair I could not see. But he paused to look up at me.

"Why?" Mattie urged. I turned to him, confused, and he insisted, "Why you get tired, Mama?"

So hard to explain. "I'm older than you guys, and sometimes I have to rest." The heat I had never noticed years ago was searing holes in my skin, and I led him back in through the gate. Before I could continue, he was scampering up the drive and onto the grass, skipping and holding out his hand to help an invisible someone jump over a pipe.

"Are you playing with your friend?" I called.

"Yes, we're playing run-away."

"Catch?"

"No."

"No, Mama," I reminded him. "Hide and seek?"

"No, Mama. Run-away."

Icy prickles on my scalp. I hurried after him and leaned close. "What's your friend's name, darling?"

"Barry." But he wouldn't tell me anything more. He seemed not to hear me, and I decided not to make a big thing of it. I tried asking Micah about Barry later, but he said not to bother about Mattie because he had 'roos loose in the top paddock.

When I talked it over with Joel later, all we could come up with was to listen intently while continuing enquiries about the Sydney family. We sat on, on the porch, as another of the white vans that regularly drew up at the house with the toucan sounded its horn for someone inside to open the gate. The toucan joined in with its habitual croaks and snores.

"Some business with deliveries coming and going at all hours," Joel remarked. "Has to be above board or they wouldn't make so much noise."

"You'd think they'd give the driver a remote," I said, "out of consideration for the rest of us."

Joel shook his head. "Too many vans, too many drivers, too many remotes."

"Then the driver should get out and press the buzzer."

"They don't need a buzzer," Joel said. "They have the toucan." Which was unanswerable.

Ravi and Meera drove south that evening with containers of hot roti, chicken and curried mango in a well-padded cardboard box, and Micah said, "See? Told you they were family," which delighted them no end. But beyond the normalcy assembling on the surface of our lives, something was building up and pressing its way out into my consciousness. Everywhere I turned was something disturbingly nebulous about family borders, disintegrating relationships, or elusive family members like those my son-in-law may have had.

⌁

The following afternoon when no one else was home, I cornered Ena and asked her point-blank what she had against Francis.

At first she hemmed and hawed. "Mrs Roche, how you could say that? Look how long I know he. From he this high and Cyn-Cyn not even in school."

"Exactly. And you were so good to him through one scrape after the next. But then, later, you seemed to cool towards him, and recently you don't feel able to leave the children with him before I get home. Whatever it is I'm grateful, because I realize you care about them. But I need to know, Ena."

"But suppose I wrong now," she whispered. "He so pleasant. And he play with them like he a child heself."

"But what if you're right? OK – I might think you are wrong – whatever it is. But suppose you *are* right about whatever concerns you and you don't tell me? I mean, you know me too long to believe I could be angry about whatever you think. You can't trust me, Ena?"

Ena shifted uneasily, studying me. "Is not what I think." Her face grew determined then, and her voice slightly belligerent. "Is what I see and hear. This boy, Francis, used to come how far to my house and talk with my granddaughter after he see her once come here to meet me. But when I tell Penny that he not too long married and she and he have

– 116 –

nowhere going, she send he away." After a pause she continued. "And not for nothing he would *go*. And she young, don't know how to manage a big man like he. She might be have seventeen years, and he well up in he twenties. He call, he call. He wait for she coming from work – she did just get a little job. He follow she to church. After a while it get to be disgusting, like he a pest."

It hit me without warning, not only this new side of Francis but the position Ena had been in while I fretted over my routines in that gentle blindness natural to those who do not live in a state of crisis.

She glanced at my face and stopped. "I know I shouldn' say nothing."

"No. You right to tell me."

"Well, he tell she he going to leave he wife and he taking she, Penny. And he and she going an live Tobago. Ms Roche, you ever hear ting like that? When she tell him she mama going have to talk to police if he call her or come by them again, he get blue vex and say if she make that happen, then he and she going somewhere together for good where nobody couldn't bring them back from."

I just . . . my mouth couldn't frame a word. I dropped down, limp, on a seat at the kitchen table, and she drew a chair too. After a time I said, "Ena. You couldn't tell me before?"

"How I go do that? I tell you I had emergency, and you ask if Penny sick, so I say had to stay home and mind she."

"I remember. That was about Francis?"

Ena gazed back, her eyes troubled. "Mrs Roche, don't take this thing on, you know. It done with long time. After a while, ent he stop? He had to stop some time. How long a man go nurse tabanca? Like he find something else to interest him."

The thought of him laughing and playing with Cyn came back, and Ena must have read it on my face for she blurted, "But he did always treat Cynnie good. Like she was he blood sister. And I feel he well love you and Mr Roche." Her voice became uncertain, apologetic. "Cyn-Cyn was younger, but he grow with her. I can't feel good bout leaving he to watch dem children, especially Melody –" She broke off suddenly as if she had been about to continue and thought better of it.

I hesitated, my affection for Francis surging up. Then my certainty of Ena's integrity bore me forward.

"I have to know everything, Ena, I really do," I pleaded.

"You see, he used to boast about how he and he pardner and dem does always get any woman they like. One day, not long after I think he cool down, he call back out of the blues. He say she better think it over, because it have some men don't eat nice. He tell she how real man don' let he woman just walk away."

An odd sensation gave me pause, some slight numbness in my lips. I felt the squeeze in my chest but had to ask, "Did he ever name any other woman?"

"No. I feel he have someone in mind, but I not even sure he was talking bout heself or if he thinking bout some wickedness one of he pardner do. You know, it have a type of man is just duttiness. But I never see or hear he do anything – well, to say, violent."

I thanked her and went upstairs, took a whiff of my nitroglycerine spray. The cramp had passed and no one ever knew I'd had it. Which was just as well, because Ena would have blamed herself. I saw with absolute clarity that Francis was never going to be alone with any of the children again till I knew who he was. Then I sat at my desk and put on the laptop so as to worry this little shred of narrative, trying not to tense up again while writing but to tease it out. For my own sanity I needed to write Ena's Francis into bearable shape. Or write him into some other shape. If, someday, Francis recognized himself in one of my evil characters, his feelings wouldn't matter, but there was Ena to consider. If he didn't recognize himself, then good. Off the hook. Nothing to be hurt about.

It mattered to me whom I hurt. Deeply. And I didn't care to dispel my restraint under some other word. No. Let me brave the contempt for manners, respect, concern (near synonyms, in my estimation). I took note of the fashionable disdain that boiled down scruples through faulty diction: courtesy misread as suck-up, reservation as timidity, self-control as repression, discipline as inhibition or regimentation, consideration as grovelling. So much of what held me together also held me back, but how to relinquish my restraints without falling apart? That left me with little to put on the page that evening, and I got up knowing neither Ena nor Francis better than before.

The next Monday Joel dropped the children at school, leaving me to dip into the supermarket early, because Ena had called to say the man who normally passed for her was down with flu and she couldn't find another drive that day. I wanted fries I could just sling in the oven.

Joel suggested I ask Ena, when she came back, what she thought of her granddaughter, Penny, filling in for her on occasion.

"Mmm," I said.

"Why not?"

"I didn't say not."

"Said 'Mmm', which is effectively 'not'."

I thought fast. "No drive for Ena means no drive for Penny. Anyway, I want to believe Penny's working somewhere. I'll make something quick." I hurried off to cut the talk.

Massy Stores was close by, so it was hardly midmorning when I got back to the house and found Mattie sitting on the front step. The door was still locked and his pants were wet. He was very pale.

"You feel bad? Why you came home early?" I asked. "Who brought you? And left you all by yourself? Mattie, why aren't you in school?"

"I didn' want to be there, Mama."

"How did you get here?"

"I walked, Mama."

"What?" I spoke louder, more sharply than I should, and he recoiled. I knew it was the worst way to have responded, but it had been wrenched from me.

Mattie clapped his hands over his ears and shut his eyes tight. "'S not my fault, Mama. I had to, had to. I have to do what I'm told – I'm just small."

By now he was wailing, and I gathered him in my arms and tried to calm him down.

All the while the road map took shape in my brain: heavy morning traffic, taxis blaring, trucks reversing blind to anything of his height, Rottweilers and pit bulls in shortcuts through backyards. I rocked him back and forth, surreptitiously flashing from my cheeks unaccustomed tears. Then I tried again.

"Who told you to walk home, baby? Who told you such a thing?" He opened his eyes, and they were dark and scared. He took my face in both his hands and looked right into my eyes, his mouth dropped open as if in shock. "Who told you to?" I whispered.

"Barry."

Every number for Aglow beeped busy. I called Joel frantically to drop whatever he had been picking up at the fruit stand and get home. When we eventually got through to the school, they were still searching for him.

"There was no contacting you." The principal was furious. "Don't you answer your phone?"

No point explaining that I couldn't hear the mobile in my purse and the pants I wore had no pockets. I pushed my hand into my purse to check the mobile and saw nine missed calls. I shoved the unwieldy thing into my bra, knowing it would have to hitch there for the foreseeable future.

"We've been out our minds hunting for him this forty-five minutes," she went on.

"Wait, wait. I've been trying to call you since I came home. I don't know when he got here, and it would have taken a while. When did you miss him? How could he be gone for any time and not be missed?"

The implied criticism opened the floodgates. Her teachers were the most caring and reliable in the country, the principal shouted into the phone. The child lied to his class teacher – *lied*, she reiterated. The boy told his Miss that someone had said the principal wanted to see him, and when Miss asked who said so, he said *Parrie*, so his teacher thought the principal had really sent Perry, the messenger, and she let Mattie leave the playground and walk back inside to the office. Only, he walked past the principal's door and straight through the building, and it was only when Nicky wondered why Jan was keeping him so long that she came to see what was wrong and they began to search. "But, Madame, *why* you won't answer your phone?"

That night, the review Joel and I embarked on in bed was mostly about Barry. "The mishearing – *Perry* for *Barry* wasn't that strange," Joel reflected. "But they should have followed up earlier."

I was almost too furious to talk, but not with the school or anything I could rationally direct my anger towards. My thoughts knotted around Barry. How could the imaginary friend of a four-year-old be this disruptive? I could have conceived of it being troublesome – but dangerous? What had we overlooked?

"Counsellor," Joel said, agreeing with my inevitable next thought. How else to root out this suddenly troubling influence?

When we arrived at the principal's office next morning it was to face another tirade, this time because we hadn't yet taken him to the counsellor she had suggested.

"Dr Marcelle is highly respected," she insisted.

It struck me suddenly what a sour face she had. Good features but sharp. Pinched around the mouth.

"When we spoke to Mattie after that first incident, he seemed settled," Joel explained. "We really thought he'd be all right. Will certainly take him now."

Jan Sibley held her head in both hands, and I realized she looked hard and miserable because she had been petrified with fear. I was instantly at one with another woman who was trying desperately to hold it down.

"Please, let's work together on this," I begged her. "I can hardly begin to tell you what we're dealing with. What the children have been through, we can't even imagine."

She went very still, and when she raised her face to me it had softened. "Of course." Then firmly, "But this can't happen again."

Easily said. Apart from road hogs amid bumper-to-bumper traffic, the escalating crime in the country and rumours about a resurgence of kidnappings sharpened to dread the thought of Mattie alone on the road. Jan Sibley directed one of the junior aides to keep track of Mattie, but the child proved he could disappear under her eyes. Kevin, who turned out to be the principal's cousin, called us to say he had heard and to commiserate. He put the problem down to the disappearance of the belt from schools.

"He's a nice little fellow," Kevin said, "not a wicked child at all. I mean, is not to say he harden. If he knew he was in for a good licking once he went under the fence, he would stay put." He realized after all we had been through we would want to treat the children as if they were made of glass. But it wouldn't be best for them in the end. It had all kinda people out there, he reminded us.

Some things just go straight through, out the other ear. Joel muttered something about Kevin being a dinosaur, but I didn't stop to engage with it.

We helped the school secure their back fence, and Mattie zeroed in on a hole near the front gate by the guard hut. Auntie Dorie said was like something get into the child, and why we never take him to a pastor who had the hand for that sort of thing. Nothing weird, she hastened to add. Just a power to heal.

We got Mattie a Ninja Turtle watch with a monitor, which he wore proudly to school then removed and strapped to the wrist of some other child he'd taken a liking for.

Meanwhile, Dr Marcelle, to whom we had taken Mattie promptly after this second incident, put it to us that the child had not dealt with the loss of his parents, and Joel's one nod with the barest lift of a shoulder marked the obviousness of the statement but probably struck Marcelle as dismissive.

The doctor turned sternly to me, and I said, "That's why we're here."

Marcelle questioned the account we must have given the child and massaged his temples when we revealed that we'd told Mattie about his parents going to be with God. "You see, that's what I feared," he said. "All you've achieved is to leave them, the parents, up in the air when they're at the bottom of the sea – whatever's left of them. A set of sugary superstition won't help the child to keep his grip on reality."

That one lodged in me, but I tightened my lips.

"We can only guide the child according to our own beliefs – and his mother's," Joel responded with admirable restraint while gripping the handle of his chair so his knuckles bulged pale. "No idea what his father thought about such things. What concerns us now is this imaginary friend urging him to run off."

"Well, but haven't you set him on a path peopled with imaginary presences?" The counsellor had modulated his voice to gentle, conveying limitless patience now he had betrayed his initial irritation.

"We have had to deal with advice ranging from a bush bath to a beating," I told him. "I don't think a sense of the absolute extinction of his parents will be any more helpful. Nor do I think it will work. He still expects them to arrive at any moment."

"Then I encourage you to re-examine your approach to his bereavement," Dr Marcelle pronounced firmly. "I can hardly help the child, once a week, to let go of this Barry and rely on the real world, if you are steadfastly undermining me with Jesus and Casper and the tooth fairy."

Another concern he voiced was about the children having to call us Mama and Papa. "You encourage confidence and intimacy if you leave them free to use your names. I certainly told Mattie to call me Harvey. He said he couldn't because you wouldn't like it. Because he was *just small*."

I considered him thoughtfully. I'd always urged younger colleagues to call me Aria and genuinely wanted that, but I was of a generation that expected a say in the matter. The leap of a young stranger to automatic familiarity was still a surprise.

"A self-confident adult doesn't need to cling to this vertical orientation," Marcelle concluded crisply.

Despite all this, if he hadn't taken off his glasses and pointed the arm at me things might have gone differently.

"Oddly, you didn't correct me when I addressed you as *Doctor*," I returned. "Look – don't worry to fix *us*. We'll all just try to work together on Mattie, OK?"

Joel touched his fingertips to his forehead in a gesture I knew well.

"I know," I said afterwards, in the car, screwing on the cover of the water bottle I had begun to sip from and then digging off the damaged Blue Waters label with my thumbnail before I could drink any more. "But we have friends of all faiths and of none, and the whole of us manage to treat each other with respect. Who the hell does Marcelle think he is?"

"Guy whose business it is to help us out of this hole. You're the one always making excuses for people. Perhaps you could've approached him more . . . subtly?"

"Nope. That wouldn't have worked: his business is to see through people, so he'd have spotted what I thought of him right off." Joel breathed hard and I glared at him. I crumpled the label and shoved it into the small bag I kept in my purse for what Cynnie had called "surprise trash". Then I boiled down a bit. "Subtlety is vastly overrated anyway," I threw out.

The next day, we asked Principal Sibley whether she had another counsellor to suggest, and we had to explain why. She protested that this was hardly a matter that required a doctor of any specific faith, and we agreed.

Joel said, "We just want the child talking to someone who'll focus on getting him into a frame of mind in which he won't run away from school, in the first instance, and then begin getting him beyond the loss of his parents."

"Did you tell Dr Marcelle that?" Ms Sibley asked.

"Yes," I replied, ignoring a warning eye from Joel. "He takes the position that our faith is our way of running away, and we're putting it into the child with a whole lot of authoritarian claptrap. He disapproves of us being *Mama* and *Papa*. Listen, Ms Sibley. My view is that our religious belief is not his business. Your school has morning worship for those whose parents want it, and the children call their teachers *Auntie*."

The principal looked thoughtful for a while. "I can seek advice on an alternative counsellor. I'm coming around, though, to the feeling that Mattie may not be quite ready for school and perhaps we shouldn't push him."

"But, say we keep him home now, mightn't he fill the day with Barry?" Joel's tone was his most persuasive. "Better if we work together with you on this. You have so much to offer him."

"Well." Jan softened visibly. "He's a dear little fellow, and unusually bright."

So that was something.

But on the way home Walters called about the case he was currently investigating. He sounded too traumatized to put off. Joel got Walters on speaker so as to continue driving and mouthed "sorry" at me. I tried watching the raindrops on the windshield wavering along parallel paths, each darting bead leaving a bit of a tail, like a translucent tadpole. But Walters' voice bludgeoned its way into my consciousness.

". . . Wrench open the back door and spring in holding a knife to the driver neck, and the driver – mother of two children, one in the car – she holds herself together. She drive with the knife at her throat and the three-year-old in the car seat behind her screaming, until the man order her to stop the car. This beast unbuckle the seat and roll it and the child out onto the roadside."

It turned out someone had found the car seat and child later in a pile of raked-up grass, flattened plastic bottles and soggy paper bags, but meanwhile the man yelled at the mother to keep driving. So she did. Then the traffic slowed and the car coasted near the entrance of the police station, where she swerved in, knife or no knife, and ran the car up to the station steps where two officers were talking. And this guy in the back opens the car door with one hand and slits her throat with the other before he springs out. Right there on the police premises. And he runs off leaving her collapsed over the wheel with her life pulsing away.

By then, someone had retrieved the three-year-old from the roadside, though what they found to say to him when he screeched for his mother, or what he would become later, who could say. All this happened two days before, but we could hear it replaying in front of Walters as he spoke.

"Man," Joel said, in the even tone that I had come to depend on, "you see when you get back to you house on evenings? You have to put that down outside. You see that kinda thing? You have to write up your report, but you don't carry it round. You have to put it down outside your door."

I didn't hear the rest, because I was berating myself for my hard-heartedness in resenting Walters' intrusions.

Joel and I didn't get to talk about Mattie again until hours later, when we reached home after school pickup.

"It's going to be much worse if they put Mattie out the school," I whispered to Joel while we were getting the snack together, and I was too busy slicing up homemade pizza to realize Micah was in earshot.

That evening Micah backed Mattie against the wall and threatened to cuff him down. "Tomorrow, Ratbag – tomorrow Mama's going to pick us up first, then we're coming to your stupid little school and you better be there, or when I get home I'll cut your tail." Micah was picking up Trini talk fast.

I told him we appreciated his support but that he had to tone down the ferocity. Only, he said if someone didn't frighten Mattie out of running away, the little beast wouldn't stop. If Mattie wasn't afraid of teachers or bulls or traffic, he would go on and get himself killed. Micah said his mother had told them there were things people needed to be frightened of so as to stay alive.

This sent a chill, but I packaged that for later. "Do you want him frightened of you?" I asked.

"Yeh. Enough to keep him alive. But it's not me he needs to be afraid of."

"What?" The expression in Micah's eyes arrested me. "Who you thinking of?"

He wouldn't answer, and Joel signalled me not to press him, but Mattie had edged after us into the kitchen and put in sulkily, "He means Barry."

Joel glanced at Micah in surprise. "His imaginary friend?"

"Yeh, right." Micah rolled his eyes.

Then Melody tugged at him, and the twins ran off together and sat out at the bottom of the steps from the kitchen whispering for a while. Micah was arguing, Melody disagreeing.

"Cyn said *no*," she insisted. And he nodded but looked mutinous.

Not for the first time, Micah spoke angrily about his mother. "It's all her fault anyway," he told Melody. "If she never made us move, none of this would have happened. They wouldn't . . . wouldn't be crashed somewhere." He sprang up in a fury, pushing her away, and blundered off to the seat under the cannonball tree.

"She couldn't help it," she screamed after him. "She said it was the only thing to do."

When I went to comfort her, she held my hand and squeezed my fingers, but she wouldn't explain. I disciplined myself so as not to follow her around, but I stayed close. I couldn't afford to miss anything she might say. I couldn't take my eyes off her.

That was when Jackie phoned and offered help. "Let me babysit sometimes so you guys can just go out and see a movie or have dinner somewhere," she said. "What about this evening? You told us yourself they're wonderful children. I'm sure they won't be any trouble."

I was deeply moved. Jackie had always come through for me, from school days. But I could not take her up on it. Melody wasn't going to talk to her. She wasn't likely to talk to me, but I couldn't be out of range if she tried.

If only they could feel connected with someone or something they had known before, Joel and I would say to each other in a hundred different ways.

"Did you have a best friend at home? Was it Cindy-Ann?" I had been brushing Melody's hair while she told me about the girls in her class, and suddenly I felt what it was to be her age again and forgot myself so far as to ask, "Would you like to send a postcard?"

"What's a postcard?"

"Right. What about trying to locate your friend on Skype? Or, how did you guys plan to stay in touch?'

Melody shook her head. "I don't."

"Why?"

"She said mean stuff." At my questioning glance, she went on hurriedly. "I don't want to talk about her. I'm just going to be friends with Dernelle, in my class."

I wondered how much she might tell Dernelle that she wouldn't tell me and hoped to God Dernelle would hit on a helpful response.

"It's OK, Mama," Melody insisted. "I like it here with you and Papa." Her tone was frank, but when her face swung to the mirror it was unreadable.

At night the questions, images and suppositions tumbled through my head, the flood too hectic for me to let go and drift off to sleep. Scenarios flashed through my head unbidden, intolerable. Mattie ducking out from under the school fence as a car swerved around the bend, braked. Barely a breath of relief before a door opened and a muscular arm shot out, scooping him up, and then the car screeched away again. Mattie wandering in through a gate on some imagined shortcut. Nice doggie. A pit bull charging forward so violently its lead snapped. Mattie startled by a group of strangers headed his way, sliding down a sodden bank to hide until they passed but losing his footing and skidding towards a drain. Suddenly the rushing water tumbled the child away, reddening and thickening into a torrent of blood.

I sat up, my cry choked by terror, then fled from the bed, closing the room door behind me as quietly as I could. I turned on every light along the way to my study.

Write. Inscribe the pain. Trap it on paper to see what it's made of. I found myself writing – not about losing my child but about writing about it. On I typed, trying to orient myself to the unavoidable yet unapproachable, but skirting it cravenly until it was time to turn out the lights and start breakfast. With a shock I realized I hadn't saved it, and when I prepared to, I arrived inevitably at the file name, *Untimely Ripped*.

The next day the children seemed back to normal, and Joel and I agreed to continue somehow with Dr Marcelle. What alternative did we have?

—⟩⟨—

When three weeks had passed without Mattie running away from school again, we ordered barbecued wings and hunted out the most recent version of *Jungle Book* we could find on YouTube.

"Movie time," Joel announced.

"Let's watch it tomorrow," Mattie protested. "Want to play The Game instead."

I was willing to go along with him in case he was afraid of the snake, for we had watched the trailer. Eventually the others agreed, provided that afterwards they would sit up and see the movie, for it was Friday anyway. And they were right about him being too small to profile the mystery person through the reactions of others. He just acted Cyn out and, instead of miming, brought forth a few of her defining phrases – a good act really for a four-year-old. Only, when Micah and then Melody shouted that that was their mother, he objected, growing more and more frantic. That wasn't his mother he bawled, that wasn't his mother.

The twins were obviously shocked and dropped it.

While quieting Mattie down, Joel fell asleep with him on his bunk, so after Micah and Melody had watched their movie and gone to bed leaving me wide awake, there was little I could do but go back to my desk.

This time, I didn't pick up a pen or open the laptop. I sat rethinking the past twelve years, scouring my mind for anything Cyn had passed on about Sydney, or anyone she had got to know there. I drew up Connor – his sweetness and devotion to her, camaraderie with Francis, playful but respectful affection towards Joel and me – yet I could think of nothing he or Cyn had said about family over there. His parents had left Trinidad shortly after he was born, but were long gone, surely. Nor had we picked up any mention of a sibling who might have relocated to Sydney so as to be near a caring and successful brother. Still. An uncle?

Outside, from the house beside the purple one, the toucan croaked pitifully from jail while a white van honked for entry until the gate screeched open rustily along its track. Philander yowled his proclamation of passion at Mrs Mendez's locked door, and the neighbourhood dogs took up their protest against an unfamiliar pedestrian wandering past their premises in the dead of night.

Inside I sifted for that level of routine events – persistent, troubling, perhaps mysterious – anything Cyn might have passed on in regaling us with the children's sayings, or her challenges at work, or even repairs to their house. I came up with so little that I realized, for the first time, she must have hidden something under all the wealth of updates and photos of the children. I couldn't help wondering what it was in me that had blocked her openness, but then I caught myself. This was not about me, but about retrieving her story.

I sat on for what must have been hours, probing my memory for a hint of whatever might lie suppressed. The deep narrative.

8

ON REFLECTIONS AND ECHOES

IN THE OLD DAYS I WAS OBSESSED with structure and left genre to take care of itself. In planning my first novel, a couple years before retiring, I'd wavered between two distinct storylines as ordinary-seeming lives seethed or splintered beneath the surface.

The better type of student often helps one to tidy out the inside of one's head. So when I got going on the first novel, I had talked it out with Isaac, the graduate tutor I later inherited as a doctoral student, when he drove south to discuss coursework scripts with me and tell me about the research he had in mind for the PhD. On the one hand, I told him, I felt as if I should write the sort of slow reflective piece readers might well expect from an older literary scholar. On the other, I was besieged by lurid situations that people I knew of were living out, circumstances one might hail as melodrama in a novel but that were unravelling around us all the time in real life.

Isaac became so excited he flung off his cap, scooped back his locks and twisted them to a knot out of the way so he could throw his whole body into the argument. I must not on any account listen to pseudo-affirmative chupidness from people who probably couldn't string two events together themselves. He pounded his fist on my desk, then caught himself and said, "I sorry, Prof. But that is the kind of thing that does really grind me. Tell me something: What you listening to them kinda people for? Write it as you see it and let them live with that."

Even so, I explained, there was really no choosing between the two types of story, because people who conducted decorous and organized lives were so often, in private, riven by unthinkable tragedy, or torn between impossible choices. This was partly why, for *Candlefly Season*, I ended up constructing two stories that began quite separately and eventually drew parallel, finally intercepting and permeating each other.

But before I got there, after chatting with Isaac and packing him off with a bag of mangoes, I sat on, looking back.

How little time I'd had to write amid the undergraduate courses, graduate supervision, meetings of committees on funding for research, programme revision, disciplinary matters, examination and assessment. More challenging than structuring two types of story in one novel had been the managing of my own life with all its disparate strands. Let alone deciphering those who partook of my life and helped define me as a character. Apart from conflicting currents in the writing process, other forces churned, pressuring and sculpting me.

As my academic and creative selves had locked in a battle for dominance, I'd felt myself propelled through time, limbs grown leaden, my stomach clenching until a band tightened round my chest, my breath catching. I wrote it off as stress.

And so it most probably was, Dr Staple had concurred genially as he wrote up directions for my tests.

"Angiogram? Impossible." I was shocked. Incredible now – how I had blocked the connection between these sensations and the mild attack two years before.

"Not according to the results of the ECG or Echo," Ben Staple had returned calmly. He explained that I might need a stent, but my results showed 90-per cent blockage here . . . there . . .

The days flew before the bypass and crawled afterwards. My impatience with it might have brought me down if not for Joel at my elbow and Cynnie as steady on Skype and then on WhatsApp.

That surgery tucked neatly into the mid-year vacation of '09, and for a while I was strictly guarded, even from sketching ideas for the novel I had in mind. By the time I took it up again in September, teaching had resumed. Along with Joel's prodding, it made me think – about all I wanted to do before I died and, if possible, instead of dying prematurely. What about the fiction around which I would have to contort days and nights so as to poke it into crevices in my schedule?

I had a choice, now Joel reminded me. My contract enabled me to retire at sixty, for I had joined the university before the retirement age bumped up to sixty-five.

Retirement turned out to be a wrench of sorts. Mine evoked protest from some staff and no doubt a gusty sigh of relief from others. Lovely sendoff, gratifying remarks by colleagues. I was deeply moved even in the disorientation amid colliding sensations of gratitude, relief, regret, nostalgia – of casting away, reaching for, severing from, shrugging off and shouldering. There was the confusion of seeing myself anew through the eyes of others, while on the point of metamorphosis into an unknown entity. In the midst of this upheaval in self-awareness, I let go of it – the place, its procedures, the *idea* of it. I unclasped my hold on it and its hold on me tenderly, suffused with the bittersweetness of release.

At first, I held on to research students and the odd course per semester – or they held onto me, perhaps the same thing. But as books that had queued up in me for years jostled each other restlessly, I let go of the teaching and of those graduate students still fumbling for topic and approach. It was a couple years afterwards I accepted that single new doctoral candidate, Isaac. Not wise, when I had at last succeeded in disentangling myself from the workplace, but his mind was of a quality impossible to resist. And then the topic – to die for. Still I took him only because his supervisor was senselessly, tragically struck down.

Even before that, when Isaac had returned from the United Kingdom for doctoral work with Carol Nanan and teaching assistance for me, I was unknown to most undergraduates. By the time I undertook Isaac's supervision, newer staff nodded to me on the corridor in vague recognition. I didn't care, because *Candlefly Season* was out along with academic articles and book chapters that had lingered in the pipeline. More than that, I was assembling impressions for a second novel.

Then Isaac faltered. In his writing and teaching the joy seemed snuffed out. I prised it out of him that he was under attack from another student, and something out of tune in his last graduate seminar came back to me. He had fielded snide comments from a singularly know-it-all young woman who dismissed his analysis of Shakespearean references in Caribbean fiction as irrelevant to the region's needs and issues.

"But apart from the usual clichés she trotted out," I argued when he paused, "there must be something else going on. I mean – the venom. Who is she?"

"Well, it's a sad story," he responded after a long pause, and I groaned inwardly, for he seemed hesitant about bringing it forward. Then he appeared to steel himself. "OK. A couple years back I ran the tutorials for Dr Nanan's final-year Shakespeare course, and Shereen was in it, not attending regularly nor showing signs of having read anything. The coursework essay comes in, too good for her track record. So I check it out. Straight from the Net. I told her I'd have to attach the copy of the original to the essay when I turned the scripts over to Dr Nanan. Of course Shereen protested angrily, then set up a big bawling – not loud, you know, but frantic. When she saw she wasn't getting anywhere she made me . . . an offer."

"Wow."

"But I passed all the info on as I'd said."

"So how's she in the graduate programme now?"

"Well, Prof, Doc was soft-hearted, you know. She gave her an F for the assignment but didn't make an official report. That final year course was optional, so Shereen dropped it – medical reasons, she said – and took another in its stead. She made an A in that (*how* I don't want to guess) and graduated with honours. Then she got accepted to a Master's in the States and came out with distinction. Earlier this year when she applied for the PhD here, Doc was . . . gone. Only I knew the history, and that done drop from my mind long time. But you think it easy? Out of the blues I meet up with Shereen in the corridor, on the way to class in Research Methods."

"OK. Disgusting. But why let it affect *you* so much?"

"I see you haven't heard. I assumed you must have and was wondering what you and everyone else was thinking of me."

"Well?"

"This woman has been putting it around that I propositioned *her* and when she turn me down I set up a smear campaign about her having stolen work from the Net. Watch: a student in my tutorial look to ask me about it." He paused, took a breath. "Prof, you see me? I just feel to put this whole thing down and done, yes. Thesis, university, every last thing."

I thought fast. "I was Second Examiner," I said.

"Say what?"

"I was Second Examiner for the course, and Dr Nanan told me all about it."

"Nah!" The relief on his face was all I'd have needed if I had doubted him – which I never had.

"Tell the woman I still have the essay and the printout from the Net."

"You do?"

"Certainly not. Just tell her. Perhaps mention that I'm willing to circulate it."

He grinned, and went his way rejoicing.

Not that Dr Nanan had told me a word about it. She and Isaac would have marked that coursework together, and as Second Examiner, I would only have received scripts for the final exam, which the wretched girl hadn't sat. I don't normally lie, but I felt good about that one.

Nevertheless, I began to stay away from the department more, not because I felt any less connected but because that sort of thing turned my stomach. Versions of Isaac's story pop up at universities across the globe, but even this indirect encounter, where I belonged but could do nothing concrete about it, made me feel oddly unreal. And I found myself disinclined towards ghosting the corridors when I knew myself to be more vibrantly alive than ever. My life was elsewhere.

So was Joel's, and still is, elsewhere from his old world. Yet echoes of that world broke through fitfully via Walters. Walters had been sent to do a follow-up with *that same family* – what was left of them – and he met with the grandfather. This old man holding up his hands, palms together, begging the people who kill his daughter and grandchild to come back for him because it have nothing leave for him to live for. At first glance, Walters said, he had thought the old man was smiling at him, but it was some sort of muscle spasm or something. Like his mouth was fixed in a shriek he couldn't get out.

"You might as well be reading all the newspapers," I complained to Joel, "or doing the rounds with Walters. I don't know how long you can keep it up – listening to him, I mean."

"Don't know if the boy himself can keep it up." He sighed. "*Somebody* better keep an ear on him."

And who else to keep this ear? And how could Joel possibly fit in Walters and the like on top of all the rest?

More and more I became aware of a sensation foreign to me, something that had seeped in like some corrosive chemical with an unpleasant smell. Anyone to whom it posed no threat would overlook it, in the same way no one but Mattie might pick up a faint whiff of smoke or insecticide. But this was not an odour or vibration, or anything else detectable to the senses, but something that jarred mentally, unfamiliar and worrying. It rose inside as a sort of collective fume – of Joel's gathering apprehension about Barrie, of Walters' agitation, of Ena's unease about Francis – that sort of thing, condensing to a film of general distrust, a widening taint.

Now, suddenly, as if something in this murkiness set it off, the question flashed: What would we have done if we had found ourselves with the three children while we were still working full time? A wave of gratitude reinforced my thankfulness for the children themselves, and I mentally pledged more time to researching Mattie. If we could trace no one who had known him in Sydney, at least we could consult others besides ourselves who saw him every day in Trinidad. Joel and I must get as close to his teachers as we could.

"Brace yourself," Joel warned. "We have to consult Dorie Sobstory."

~⁄⁄∖~

Outside Mattie's classroom at Aglow, Dorie Sobers opened her eyes very wide. They were light brown eyes, clear and liquid but strangely empty. "If you hear all what he says. Just like he talking to somebody he could see." She clasped her lips tightly. "I wouldn' like to say. Sometimes it isn't nice, I tell you."

Joel squeezed my arm in warning without taking his eyes off Dorie, and I held my tongue. "You see," he said, "we can help him better if you do tell us."

Dorie closed the eyes tight and shook her head. "You don't understand," she said virtuously, "when I tell you it doesn't be nice, I mean it doesn't be *nice*."

Mattie dragged his bookbag out of the classroom along the red clay tiles and onto the asphalt, peeping up sideways to see whether he would get a rise out of Auntie Dorie.

"Papa," I said, "remind me to buy extra garbage bags to replace that Spiderman book bag when it bursts, OK?"

"Sure thing," Joel agreed, sliding paper and a pen from his breast pocket and muttering, "Just jot that down."

Mattie hoisted the bag and dusted it reverently as Nicky came up.

"That's better," she said bracingly, while Dorie scampered away in relief. We asked Nicky what lay behind Dorie's warnings.

Nicky was the class teacher, and an altogether different customer to Dorie. "No idea," she said. "But it's mildly worrying. There's bound to be a kernel of truth in there somewhere."

"But *you've* noticed nothing," I prompted.

"Well, but it's Dorie who sits with them through lunch, and watches the playground," Nicky said. Her white cotton shirt gleamed against sleek grey slacks. Complex swirls of meticulous cane-row plaits and chunky earrings set off her striking profile. "You can get an imaginary friend in class, but the playground offers more scope."

Still, we felt better. Nicky's manner was direct, her eyes alert. We had seen her call to order a boy yards away from her in a blur of other small bodies, for being *about to* yank Savitri's long glossy braid. "I know you'll call if you notice anything unusual," I said as we parted.

Nicky called that night. She told us to look out for an envelope she would put in Mattie's bag next day. This was just between her and us, she emphasized, because the principal was still a bit rattled by Mattie's earlier exploits.

The following day when we brought him home, we restrained ourselves till he spread himself out on the tiles with his dinosaurs. He was cooing to a particularly hideous ornithopod when we opened the envelope and smoothed out on the table the sheet we found inside. It was like any of his paintings that we regularly admired without having the least idea of what they portrayed. A Post-it with Nicky's name and number clung to it. When we called, she took us through, Joel making swift notes in his left-handed ketch-a-crab writing.

The small smudge of blue-green colour near the bottom was Mattie, and the big pink and brown swirl was his friend. Long orange lines fountained from the top of the swirl; his friend had long hair. *Long long*, Mattie had said. Most of the rest of the page was marked by bold, wildly scratched purple lines.

"Trees? Clouds?" I guessed. "Rain?"

"Knives." Nicky must have been waiting for a reaction, for a few seconds passed before her voice came again, more gently. "Are you still there?"

I'd taken a deep breath and shaken my arms hard to stave off the shiver. "Yes," I replied. "Now these knives . . ."

"They belong to the friend."

"Are you telling me that this little baby is living in fear of some made-up character in his head?"

"Not at all. His friend will protect him. That is what the knives are for."

"Protect him from what? Whom?"

"That has not yet emerged."

That night, hugging Mattie in bed, I went over and over Nicky's explanation, digging at it compulsively. He mightn't know what Barry was protecting him from. It didn't seem to be in the picture. I was still holding him when the room began to shake violently. I heard the lathes in the bedhead rattling. Then I saw that the roof and walls were gone, and the sky filled with streaks of light-like meteors flashing down, and they were not meteors at all but blades, razor sharp, gleaming down all around to stab the earth, shivering on impact, until they formed a fence of quivering steel around our bed, under the open sky.

Something soft on my cheek and it was Mattie's, the velvet plumpness he had not yet lost. He was rubbing my face with his, then pausing to crank open my eyelids with his forefinger and thumb. He wanted to ask me something 'portant, he said.

Now it will come, I thought, and steeled myself. "What, darling?"

He asked, "What's your best favourite dinosaur?"

A normal four-year-old, engaging, yet, in part, unknowable. While the three were eating breakfast and Joel and I packed their kits in the kitchen, Joel told me he remembered his own imaginary friend, who had stayed with him when he went to school. In fact, now he thought about it, the friend had moved up with him to the next class, but Joel had never spoken of him in case the others teased him.

"What did people at home say about your friend?"

"Nobody cared."

I'd have cared, I thought. Then – I wouldn't have shown it though, would I?

Now we knew to listen out for it, we sometimes caught Barry's name. From the tones of voice we picked up in a largely inaudible exchange among the children, we concluded that Mattie trusted his friend but Micah seemed not to.

"My money's on Micah," Joel said.

How many children had them, I wondered, visualizing the shadows of countless imaginary friends flitting playfully among the tumble of flesh-and-blood boys. If Micah's reaction was anything to go by, the difference was that Mattie's friend seemed, at best, violent – at worst, psychotic.

"And suppose," Joel whispered to me later that morning when we had dropped them off, lacing his fingers through mine and crunching them so urgently I winced, "suppose he's *not* imaginary?"

"Right." We'd arrived at that in the same instant, so I crushed his hand to my heart and clutched it there while I plunged on. "Remember that day Mattie said he didn't like the counsellor because he kept saying people weren't real when they were? And we assumed Dr Marcelle had been having a go at Jesus?" He nodded, and I continued recklessly. "I don't think so again. The thing is, I went to Marcelle's office and asked him not to interfere in issues of religion that were not his concern. He said he hadn't uttered a word on the subject to Mattie, and he was obviously offended that we thought he might act so unethically."

Joel stared at me. "Really said that to the man?"

"I probably owe him an apology."

"You think?"

He inhaled deeply, caught up the air in his mouth, the lean cheeks puffed out like a hamster, then blew it out slowly, endlessly, as if he were trying to empty every air pocket in his body. He started up the car and drove in silence for a while until he spun the wheel to turn up our drive, and there was no time for more.

We set off in our different directions, about what had to be done before pickup time. For one thing there was Walters to check on. Joel hadn't been able to get him back and kept saying he hoped some bandit hadn't shot the poor chap. He said it as if being facetious, but often enough to confirm that he was seriously concerned.

By evening, though, Walters was on speaker, his voice cranked up another octave. "Yes, I called the counsellor's office like you said, and I had the appointment, but yesterday was craziness and I had to postpone till next week. We had got this tip about the guy who's been missing for two weeks. All over the papers: you'd have seen it. So when we followed up we found the car, well, the shell really, with him . . . with this thing. You know. Burnt to death. Beyond, beyond."

I wanted to make him stop. This place Walters spoke from was not my country. Besides, it was not a description Joel needed to hear at this time. I turned the vacuum on, but Joel flagged a hand at me and I stopped it. He had switched the phone from speaker but gripped it so his hand shook.

Joel's face was grey, but he went on. "Yes, boy. So how they knew it was Bradley?" Voice steady but not as powerful as usual. "When did the DNA results come out then?"

All I could do was get out of earshot myself.

⁓⁓⁓

Later in the afternoon, Melody approached me hesitantly.

"Mama, can I ask you something?"

"Of course."

"Suppose I can't tell you why I ask you the thing." She studied me closely. "Will you make me explain?"

I was at a loss. "I can't make you say anything . . ." I faltered. "I can only hope you will tell me whatever you can." My arms ached to hold her, but I kept off. "Please trust me, Melody," I whispered. She was still very quiet, and I reached my fingers for hers gently. "Is it something that can help us with Mattie?"

"I don't know," she said, and I waited. "Mama, what does *passed down* mean?" While I considered, trying not to frame my answer as a question, she swept on, "Does it have to do with things that go wrong with people in a family?"

"Ah. Yes it can." Terror flashed unmistakably across her face, so I added hurriedly, "I think most things that are hereditary (as they call it) are simply *possible*, though. They don't *have* to happen." I watched her, praying for more.

"There was this show on TV about a test for something that was *passed down*. I don't know what it was. If they test you for something and find it, can they cure it?" She sat rigid in the chair, eyes fixed on mine.

"I suppose it depends on what *it* is." I smiled encouragingly. "Nowadays there are cures for most things." I soldiered on bravely. "Shall we find out?"

"What if it's a sickness in one's mind?"

"You mean an illness one *thinks* one has?"

"No. Something wrong with your mind. Like if your mind is sick."

"There are doctors and treatments." I crushed the rush of questions in my head as she reached for the handle of the door. "It's like being sick in any other part of your body. You find a doctor."

"Or a hospital if it's very bad?" She had turned back and dropped in the chair again, her arms flopping loosely at her side. Her eyes wandered from my face, and she began playing absently with the hem of her skirt, but she still seemed fixed on whatever was working through her head.

"Yes, but I'm sure there'd be lots of treatments to try first." I waited, on tenterhooks.

Then she stood and ran off.

How I controlled myself I do not know. I wandered out to the porch and sat studying the yard with its limp croton leaves, thinking I should turn the hose on them and knowing I wouldn't. The seasons were all inside out now, drizzling dry seasons and sun-baked rainy ones, but the years still sped from frantic partying for Christmas and Old Year's through Carnival fêtes and back to Christmas, different sectors of the community pausing for breath at Easter, Bocas Lit Fest, Eid, Carifesta, Divali. There were still templates for imposing order. Somewhere.

If I could get some chance to think I'd see my way.

My eyes followed a line of bachac, red-brown soldiers the length of my thumbnail, marching along a wrought-iron bar bearing neat slices of pink and green from a potted plant they were demolishing before my eyes. If I could trace them back to the nest, a pot of boiling water might do until we got the bait. Then I turned my glance up at a couple circling corbeaux without coming up with any theory of what they were about. The air smelled clean except for a slight smokiness from the direction of Embacadere, some twelve minutes away. I rocked on the porch for an hour, processing the likelihood that Barry was real, a close relative, possibly deranged. Even violent. Each tightening of the screw focused me more, so I could set aside sensation and force my mind forward. How to get Melody talking again?

I sauntered into the dining room, where she and Micah had their heads together over homework, and set down a tray bearing lemonade and crackers with cheese spread spotted with tiny chips of pimento pepper.

Back in the kitchen I went about my business like a zombie, slicing green apples to turn in vinegar, garlic and other seasonings without even thinking to pinch a sliver for my own mouth. In half an hour I floated back with a cloth to wipe up crumbs. Then, at a loss for another excuse, I found myself back on the porch, rocking and staring into the blue – there was no doing anything. I watched the mowers next door and counted the boats at sea. I took note of a sandy mound that marked termites in the wooden porch set. I listened to the blasted pigeons in the eaves.

If Melody was fretting about a mental illness *passed down*, it must be someone very close. A grandfather? We had understood that Con's parents were dead, but, if not, could Mattie's grandfather be institutionalized? But would they call him Barry? They might. They would have called us Joel and Aria if we had not steered them along the traditional lines eschewed by Dr Marcelle. A kiskidee alighted on a thick stalk of orchids, with little hops so frivolous I could have slapped it in my present state of mind. It eyed me roguishly, almost derisively. No wonder: if a grandfather (senile or raving), how would that account for Mattie thinking of him as a playmate? Barry was younger.

I needed to get into the car for a visit I had promised myself to make. Joel had agreed to occupy the children while I looked in on an old acquaintance living just beyond San Fernando, still in her own home but in poor shape. I had known Edith Jessop from I was born – a neighbour, with no children of her own, who had showered me with kindness before leaving Princes Town for her new house in Valsayn. She had ended up moving back south into a townhouse.

A fine athlete in her day, Edith was immobilized now, stricken by some circulatory disorder that remained a mystery to me. The pain made talking about it unbearable as well as useless. On my last visit – I had counted on it being the last – she thanked me for coming. What a trial, she commiserated with me breathlessly, to see someone in such a condition, unable to offer me a cup of tea (though I should take anything I liked) or even exchange a comfortable word or two. She was perfectly lucid, only unable to engage connectedly with anything but the racking vascular pain.

"So glad to see you. Hnnnnnh. Darling girl. You didn't shouldn't have to. Nnnnhn. But good to . . . rest my eyes on you again."

She was in too much agony for me to stay for any length of time, too tortured to hold still for a kiss. I heard myself say, "I have loved you all my life."

A smile squeezed between the spasms. "And I you. I you." She was glad I had come. "Aaaahnnnn."

I prayed then that it would be the last visit. That she would be let go. But still she lived, and I was determined to go again.

Only, just as I was picking up the keys, Melody came out and showed me her homework, her eyes searching my face. She twisted her hem around her finger, looked at me and away, and then drifted off again. There'd be no visiting of the sick this afternoon. Melody and I circled each other for the rest of the evening.

That night when I went to tuck her in, all Pears Soap and peppermint toothpaste, the Wonder Woman sheets scattered with books, she said, "Mama, suppose we all went for a checkup. Like how you went to your card . . . cardio . . ."

"My cardiologist. Last week. Right. Just to make sure all was well."

"And it was?"

"Oh yes. Dr Staple was pleased. And that's good to know, eh?"

"Yes." She ran a tentative finger along my cheek. "What if we all went for a checkup?"

"Sure. Papa, me and you guys? Not a problem. What sort of doctor would you suggest?"

"One for the mind."

I hugged her and said we'd make an appointment, because it felt so good to get a clean bill of health. I was still explaining what that phrase meant when I saw she was asleep and I could rest my forehead on the bed beside her and just listen to her breathe.

Joel agreed that appointment must take precedence over all else.

What about turning over the whole matter of tracing Con's relative to Francis? "Leave that with him?" he suggested. "He chats easily with the children. Younger than us and all that. May elicit more about their Sydney life than we can."

I said I wished we could do that ourselves, but gave no particular reason. I didn't feel up to passing on any of Ena's account yet, and for the time being I decided not to leave the children alone with Francis till I was sure she was mistaken. Or, at least, until Joel and I had talked it out. Then, when I acknowledged that *at least*, I realized how much of me believed Ena. And *talked it out*? It?

It pulsated beneath the tight surface. Some things we can only make out by writing them into sight and hearing. Listening for their faint echo is nearly addictive, the pull irresistible. Wording *it* tightens to a visceral need, the compulsion to *find out* something on which life or sanity hinges. But. Mattie first.

Dr Angelo Mohammed was a relaxed man of around forty-five with an uncanny resemblance to Con – which was why we chose him over the other psychologist, a plump, comfortable-looking woman with a youthful face and lively eyes. I had thought a woman might draw out Melody, but when I saw Dr Mohammed I agreed with Joel that the resemblance to their father might encourage the children's confidence. Neither of us had spared Dr F Harvey Marcelle a thought.

Nevertheless Micah clammed up from the outset. Mattie sniffed the air cautiously, and I wondered whether the mixed aroma of aftershave and leather upholstery meant anything to him. Then, when the doctor posed a question or two, Melody, who had paused in the doorway before edging in warily, grew very still and her face went blank.

"This is the thing," Joel put in hurriedly. "That is, if you guys don't mind my starting with my own problems?"

Micah and I chorused encouragement, and Joel skimmed over the tragedy itself to say how the children had made basic operations like eating and sleeping possible and made waking up worthwhile. In the midst of unutterable loss, they were a godsend. But he said he kept worrying that we weren't doing all we should for them.

"It's been so long since we brought up a child," I agreed. "These three have saved us, for how else could we ever have found our way through . . . this whole . . . Only there's so much we don't know about their lives in Sydney – how they spent their time, what friends they had, what family on that side. Places they loved. We've never been to Sydney, though we'd planned to go."

"Did you guys have lots of friends there?" Angelo Mohammed glanced around at their faces pleasantly, and Micah forced a nod without making eye contact. "What about here? Did you make friends on this side yet?"

There ensued a stilted discussion of friends in Trinidad and Australia. Mattie maintained a stern silence. Melody leaned close to me and asked whether the doctor wasn't going to test us.

"He'll decide what he needs to do, darling," I whispered.

"But, Mama . . ." Then she looked away, placing her palms flat on her thighs. Her mouth settled into a straight line, and she looked towards the door, her chin jutting ominously.

"I don't like doctors," Mattie burst out rebelliously. I caught Dr Mohammed's eye, and asked Mattie why.

"Because they locked up my friend."

"That's very sad," Dr Mohammed said. "I'm glad I'm not a doctor like that. Tell me about your friend."

"They locked up Barry, and I'm going to . . . to burst down the door and let out Barry and Barry will kill all the bad people."

"Why did they lock up Barry?" The doctor's tone was shocked and sympathetic at once.

At the perimeter of my field of vision I caught a frantic exchange of glances between Micah and Melody.

"Because they're bad. Barry will kill them. Barry has knifes."

"Where?"

"What where?"

"Where would Barry keep knives?"

Mattie caught himself and slowed down. "Barry just has them, OK?" He regarded the doctor narrowly, cautious about giving out information.

"Really? Even now Barry is locked up?"

"No. When I let Barry out, Barry will get more knifes."

"Barry is Mattie's imaginary friend," Melody broke in.

"What's 'maginary?" Mattie asked suspiciously.

"Not real," Dr Mohammed answered.

"No," Mattie shouted. "Barry *is* real. Cynnie 'n' Con aren't real anymore. But Barry wasn' on the plane."

"It's OK, Matts," Joel said. "Don't be cross with us."

But Dr Mohammed intervened. "The thing is, Papa, that it's OK to be angry when bad things happen. We have to be careful what we do when we're angry, but it's no point pretending we aren't angry. Are you angry, Mattie?"

"Yes. Very angry." The child was smouldering. "I am very very angry."

"What about if you tell me why you're angry."

"The plane didn' bring my parents, that's why, and they said they would come an they never, and Barry's all locked up and I can't *find* people. It's very very bad, that's why."

Angelo Mohammed looked around at Micah and Melody. "Who's Barry?" he asked conversationally.

Micah might have answered, but Melody cut in. "My mother said not to talk about it to anyone, especially anyone outside the family. My mother said . . . *said* . . ." She was shaking.

"All right." The doctor had a tissue in his hand before I could ferret one from my purse, and he passed it to her. But she waved it off it imperiously: she looked agitated, cornered, but she was not about to cry. She was trembling with rage. "I'm sorry, Melody. And I won't ask you to tell me stuff your mom trusted you to keep private. It's not like you know me well yet. But perhaps your mom would want you to talk to her mom – about the sort of things you used to talk about when you lived in Sydney."

It was there in Melody's tightly compressed mouth and hunted but determined eyes that challenged us with her steady gaze. Barry was fact. Not childish fantasy, nor, thank God, the delusion of a fevered brain. But perhaps worse? Flesh and blood one can't dispel.

In the deathly still room, Melody regarded the doctor frigidly, but after a pause he continued.

"Do you think your mom would really want you to have no one to talk to about stuff?" Melody shook her head, barely, and glanced towards me. "All I want you to do, Melody, is to think about talking to your mama just like you would talk to your mom. Because I believe that's what your mom would like." She turned her eyes back to the doctor and considered him with the same cold fury. "I don't know your mom, it's true," he conceded, "but I think most mothers would want that."

Then he swung back to Mattie. "Hey, big guy. You're a loyal friend. You know that? I wish you were my friend. Are you friends with your brother here? Yeh? Is he cool or what? Micah? Mattie can depend on you, right?" He gave high-fives all round. "You guys come and see me again, OK? Together or separately – just as you like. I enjoyed chatting with you. You're great kids." He looked at Joel and me and nodded. "Great kids."

9

BLOODLINE

‿⁊⸜⸍⸝‾

BUT, MAMA, HOW COME HE DIDN'T TEST US? No I'm just – I promised Cyn. Still, I guess she'd want me to.

OK, Mama. So it's true Barrie's real. She's our aunt, and she's the same age as Con because he said they used to celebrate birthdays together and thing when they were real close. Only, then, they stopped getting on at all. They were *always* quarrelling. 'S why we had to move. Cyn wanted to come live near you guys, but mostly she said she was moving away from *that situation*. And Cyn was OK – I mean she wasn't a wuss or anything.

And it's not like we never loved Barrie. She was kinda exciting, into fun stuff, new games. Cool shoes – she bought us brands. She chatted about what we could do together, where we'd travel, who she wished she could meet, what we'd like to do when we got big. She'd swing from one thing to the next and she was happy being with us – not just everyday happy but like over the top. Only, now and then we'd find her real down – once she told us she felt like all her best friends had died, only how'd that make sense when we were there, she said, and she loved us most in the world. "So grab any stuff you need to make yourselves happy," she says. "I got my eye on you. But next time you come, I'm gonna be way more fun." And she was too.

I sort of remember a time we were small, and Micah and me would go to Barrie's big house where she and Con used to live. Her mother left her the house, but Con and Cynnie had our own house where we lived, and long ago – Micah and me must have been in kindie – we'd pester them to take us to Barrie at the old house. Mom would drop us off now and then. Then Barrie'd make a bushland in the yard and she was the phantom cat and we were her cubs. She said, "You guys are all the cubs I'll ever have, 'cause I sure won't be bothered with a husband." I don't remember anything more from so long. Like L.A.? I don't know if I remember L.A. or only remember what they said.

Barrie was a lawyer. That was in Sydney, right? But like she didn't always go to office. Con said Barrie was super smart and she'd be the best in the country if she'd been able to *hold it together*. "Brainy like her mother," he said. But it didn't sound like a compliment.

Last year Micah asked Con, "So how's she live? How's Barrie make a rooboy when she doesn't work? 'Cause she always seems to be taking sickies." And Con told him drop it. Then Cyn said big people had problems we wouldn't understand.

But before that, like when we started at that school, Barrie didn't look like she had problems; she made jokes and romped with us, Micah and me. When she put on black tights and pounced and rolled, we couldn't stop laughing. Only, sometimes – you know when you laugh until it hurts? Like when someone tickles you and you're mad but you can't stop laughing?

She was mostly happy, with us. Then something happened – I don't know what – and she got real ill, and Cyn ended up taking care of her till she was well enough to go home to the old house. That was the first time, I think. I kind of get the different times mixed up.

Barrie's house wasn't old like falling down, you know. It was just that it had been there so long her grandparents had lived in it. It was real big and had this garden, besides all the crops and stuff farther out. She said her mom died years after her dad had gone off and left them. Afterwards, only Barrie and Con lived there before he moved out. He never wanted to leave but he said Barrie . . . he said she *had her claws into the place*.

When Barrie got ill, she'd have been all alone, because Con had warned her to keep away – and I heard him tell Cyn, "The woman's dangerous." But when Cyn found out Barrie'd been real ill (that was the second time, right?), she got Barrie from the hospital and took care of her, although it was hard with Mattie so little. Then Barrie wanted Mattie with her all the time. Like *all* the time. She wanted all of us, but she said Mattie was hers. She said Connor and Cyndra had a child each and this one was for her, at last.

Cyn didn't like that – said it was weird – but Con told her, "Look, you're the one who brought this on, letting her get close to the children. From now on, leave her to me. I'm the one who knows her through and through. OK?" He said Barrie insisted this big huge place she lived in was all hers, so why didn't she stay there and leave his children alone? Cyn said we should make allowances for Barrie in view of everything. No. I don't know what. Like I said, Barrie was ill, but then she got better and she shouted, "Who, *me*? Stay another night in your house? No way." Only she kept on about having to see Mattie.

Cyn said the Barrie situation was *bizarre*, although I'm not sure what that situation was – but Con said we were all to stay away from Barrie because she was *messed up*.

And, Mama, there was something about people phoning other people and telling them stuff. My friend Cindy-Ann said her mother knew things about my mother because someone had called and warned her. Cyn heard later that someone had told her patients about mal-, mal-something. "Someone spreading poison," she said. "And no doubt about who that would be." But that part came much later. Con said we needed to keep to ourselves, not talk to Barrie or share a helper with her or anyone else.

Yes, the cleaner who had worked with Barrie and Con when they lived in the old house, she worked for us too for a while, but then Con made her stop. "Too awkward," was all he would say when I asked him why. And he said our place was a lot smaller and we should be able to manage. He didn't want anyone working for Barrie to get near his children.

Con was – I don't know – he said he was *frustrated*. He had *pressure*. He lost weight and Cyn said it was side effects of whatever he was taking. Cyn got to worrying about him all the time, plus about how everything cost so much and how we'd have to cut down on all kinds of stuff and watch the money because of *obligations*. I don't know what.

One day I heard Cyn on her phone "Wait a minute. What? Slow down. Barrie, what've you done? Listen – have you hurt yourself? Barrie, answer me. Where are you?" And I couldn't tell what Barrie had done to herself. Was that the first or the second time? I'm not sure, but it was a time Cyn brought her home. And she looked real bad, pale and skinny, and her cheeks gone in. Under her eyes was a sort of purply-grey. Con said he didn't like it, Barrie being home with us, and if she was so sick she belonged in hospital. But Cyn said since *she* was a doctor it was OK to have Barrie at our house, so Barrie stayed in my room while she was sick, and I moved in with Micah. She had a nurse and a tall thingo with a bag hanging and tubes taking medicine into her arm through a needle.

Under her eyes though – that was . . . anyone would notice because Barrie always used to dress and make up real nice. She wore this perfume she called *FF*, and when I asked what that meant she said it was fragrance made by a man called Ford. And now she smelled like the alcohol they wipe you with before your shots and her hair was like strings. She had this long curly red hair and it was like strings on a mop, I used to brush it for her then stop, then a little again then stop, because of the knots. Cyn said what Barrie's hair needed was cutting, but she wasn't bringing that up.

Then one day Con said he needed to get more out of this nurse about Barrie's real condition, and while they were talking, Nurse got real mad and shouted and slammed the door.

After the nurse left, Barrie stayed a day or so more, but then *she* started shouting at Con. "You're the one," she said. "You did this to me."

He told her stop the madness 'cause he'd let her stay with us even though that was crazy. He said, "You're only alive because we've taken care of you."

Then Barrie said, "Right." And she yanked the needle out her arm and shouted at him, "Try and take care of me now." And she grabbed up her stuff and pushed it in a pillowcase and knotted the end. All the time she cursed, all sorts of words I can't, well, not supposed to . . . you know.

Then she shouted, "I'll be back for my baby," and slammed the door behind her. And she takes off with the blood running down her arm.

It was January and almost midday, so Cyn went chasing out after her to drive her home. Con wanted to stop Cyn, but she said, "You don't see she'll walk and walk in the hot sun and drop down on the road?"

After that, I don't know. It was a long time. I kept wondering what happened to Barrie because we didn't see her again for weeks or, or months. Con said we mustn't touch the phone if it rang, so I guess she could have talked to him without us hearing. Mama, you know what he said too? That we were never to be alone outside.

Cyn said she saw Barrie sometimes driving or walking somewhere and that she was always dressed in like high platforms and matching Gucci handbags. She told Con, "Outfits that scream Ellery," and Barrie mightn't even be working regularly, so how could she always look like she came straight from the hairdresser, and wear brands? "Even if the firm's still OK, where's money like that coming from?" Cyn asked. "You mean you never noticed?" And Con told her no, he didn't care enough about that stuff to notice. But he looked real hung-up.

A couple days later, I heard them talking about like Barrie sold some of the land near the old house. And Con said it was the last straw, because of some claim he had, although Cyn said – how could there be doubt, because who was it left to? Cyn said, "I thought I heard it was to Barrie and any daughters she might have, because of how the old lady'd got to hate men." And Con said things didn't work like that. There was property in both their names, and Barrie couldn't just start taking it over. He had his children to think about.

"So how'd she pull it off?" Cynnie wanted to know, and Con said he and Barrie could always write like each other and had kept copies of each other's documents for safety, like driving permits and stuff, and maybe she signed his name or got something done in the firm. Anyway, he said if she'd sold this land and got away with it, maybe next thing would be the house.

All that time, Cynnie went to work and came home and cooked and cleaned and looked at our homework, because Con worked real late and sometimes he had to travel. When we got home, Cynnie would look at the house a bit before opening the door and say, "Still standing. Let's see what's inside." She used to make like jokes that weren't really jokes. Only, if Con was there, he'd come out grinning at us with his arms spread out like he was going to fly or something, and we would all just walk into them. But it took a while before she breathed right. Once he said, "Relax, girl. You'll freak out the kids," and then she put her arms round all of us and said, "Oh no. I'm good."

Then one day Barrie phoned to speak with Mattie. He didn't know how things were and he had it on speaker, so her voice kinda filled up the room. Cyn runs in and picks it up. A little after she turned off speaker, she said, "Yes, Barrie, I was thinking that myself." Then she listened a few minutes and said, "But why not?" And after that she hardly said anything, but when she put the phone down there was a puddle on the floor and she had wet herself. I mean . . . a grownup, and not sick or anything.

She saw me looking at her and she said get some old newspaper for her and don't tell anyone and don't worry because nothing Barrie could say to her would ever hurt her again. She said whatever we did we mustn't worry Con, because he wasn't well and I must leave it to her to talk to him about Barrie so they'd work out together what to do.

One day the three of us were in this taxi with Cyn, and Mattie was asleep on her lap, and that was when she told us we were on the way to the airport – we were leaving and it was a secret. "Con and I planned it out," she said. "You know he had to go off on this course, and by the time I get you guys to Trinidad, he'll be home to help me pack up our stuff. You'll be having so much fun you won't even notice while I nip back and get him." So then she and Con would come join us in Trinidad, but Barrie wasn't to know about anything. And no one was to know about Barrie. Cyn told Micah and me that even when we got here we mustn't talk about Barrie and Con, because their problems were too complicated for us to understand and it was a sad thing and . . . and private. She didn't want people talking about anyone in our family.

Cyn told us all sorts of stuff on the plane when we were coming. She was like . . . I don't know. Not just happy. Like she'd got loose from . . . some cage, or something. When she got here she sort of folded up, tired I guess. But on the plane she'd said she had just about given up everything to meet her . . . her *obligations*. But now she'd come to Trinidad and get her life back. *Get her life back* was what she said.

Only . . .

10

THE OCEAN WHISPERS BACK

MELODY'S VOICE TRAILED AWAY, AND A minute or so passed before I realized she was done. When I looked at her questioningly, she said, "That's all, Mama."

All.

I'd been perched on the edge of the armchair but got up to sit by her on the bed. Then I leaned and fell back, and she threw herself down beside me. We stayed like that a while, thinking our own different thoughts. Or perhaps they were the same.

No, for I thought of all Cyn had tried to do for Barrie and pondered Cynnie struggling to protect her husband by swearing the children to silence about his twin. From there I got hung up on how, strewn between the goodhearted banter of the Trinidadian in the street lurked another strange, demented culture with its hard cackle at pain and jeering at integrity. Cyn had been right in trying to protect Con from that, even though it meant hiding from us these upheavals with his sister. How could Cyn have foreseen we would need to know?

"Is it all right for me to tell Papa?" I asked, and Melody nodded.

So the moment I got Joel to myself I poured it all out.

"Melody unchained," Joel concluded. "So, now we know." He exhaled slowly, cheeks puffed till he'd emptied it all out. "Have a private chat with the psychologist, you think?"

"You mean to clear up Mattie's obsession with Barrie?"

"You'd call it an obsession?" Joel objected. "He's mostly a regular happy child. Warm. Curiously gentle, in fact. Interested in everything going on."

"Mmm." I felt something else, a difference in Mattie. Something new I could not put words to.

"More confident with us, doing OK at school," Joel insisted. "Even stopped running away. Just looks like a mini Micah to me . . ."

That he certainly was. I'd thrown my mind back to Micah on his first visit, when I heard him call out. I caught Joel's sleeve and drew him to the window. Micah had strolled out towards the mango tree and paused under our window a few feet away from where Mattie was intent on drilling the tree trunk with a short stick. They chatted away at full volume as usual.

"You like it here, ent?" Micah asked. He was becoming more Trini by the day.

"Yup."

"So why you keep on and on about Barrie?"

Matty looked up at him sideways, warily. "What you mean, keep on?"

"I mean, you're good with the grands, right?"

"Yup."

"So forget the aunt."

"What aunt?"

"Barrie."

"Barrie's not my aunt."

"How come?"

"Barrie's my mom. She says I'm hers for always. She's alive. Not gone in some plane. And she's coming for me."

"What you talking about?"

"She called. She says she's coming for *me*."

⇜⇝

So now there was this new development in the fixation, or whatever it was.

The difference I had observed in Mattie crystallized in my mind. He had become purposeful. He may have stopped talking and playing with Barrie as an imaginary friend, but he had not let go. Now it was planted in his head – she was coming for him.

Dreaming, Joel insisted. But I wasn't sure. Mattie was positive. And there was a new big-boy confidence about him.

The following day we picked up the message. A woman's voice on the phone said, "Hello? . . . This is Mattie's mother. I'm just letting you know I'll be collecting him shortly. Be assured I have the necessary paperwork. Please call me back at this number."

I dropped down on the chair by the phone, and Joel drew up one from the dining table. He eased the receiver out from my fingers, which had gone stiff, his eyes fixed on my face.

"No calling back. She didn't leave the number," I said, my mind spinning through possible moves. Then I added, "Perhaps she doesn't really want us to call back."

"And no chance of tracing it," he agreed. We'd never put caller ID on the landline.

I propped my elbow on the table and rested my chin on the back of my hand to regard him but also to keep it steady. After a while he shook his head, said, "Figure it out later," and got up to see where the children were. But his fingers strayed to his stomach, and I knew he needed time to settle before talking it out.

I stayed pinned there. The convincing ring of the impossible chimed now with actuality. Her voice – abrupt, determined, words somehow a little blurred – resounded in my head, flipping my sense of what was real or illusory inside out. Flesh and blood, I registered, with a sickening lurch in the pit of my belly. Suddenly Melody's revelations, establishing that Barrie was far from imaginary, seemed long ago. At that time, only weeks before, we had seen her as a hazard, but now, *now* she had materialized into an impending menace.

Joel was trailing after the children, reluctant to let them from sight. I hung back, desperate to figure out what Barrie might do.

I began feeling my way around what I knew of her – in my usual style, as if she were a potential character for a book. Except I must invent nothing, only decipher.

The same age as Con – shared birthday – so, a twin. I hitched there, my mind spinning over what it must have been like for Cyn, negotiating around this intimate part of her husband's life. Tentative at first. Then, perhaps uneasy? After my first attack, Cynnie had grown a bit hyper about causing me anxiety. And she'd never mentioned Barrie to us. Not once. So had Barrie's resentment grown up over the years, as Melody's story seemed to imply? Or had it been there from the beginning, a potential hotspot. It would be like Cyn to postpone mentioning her, to shield me.

Barrie's possessiveness must have glowered under whatever film of acceptance Cyn put forward. With more and more to draw away Con's attention from herself, his sister's obsession with him must have eaten away at her till it ignited, flared. Perhaps it cooled periodically, but always some new landmark in his marriage might heat it to flashpoint. And now – Cyn and Connor taken out of the picture – I grew excruciatingly aware of Barrie not just as some deranged aunt left stranded in her obsession with her brother's children. For her to want Cyn's child, to pursue him across the world for herself, I saw her as a fury. Only, what fuelled such chthonic wrath?

Stupidness. I told myself I had to be blowing it up. In the mirror I looked myself sternly in the eye and said, *Get a grip*. But when I asked Joel, he only said, "Mad. We protect them by any means possible."

As if we did not have enough to think about, Walters had begun to call Joel almost daily, unburdening himself as if to a therapist. I had glimpsed him only once, but as a result I could visualize behind the voice on the phone this short, caving figure with a sweet somewhat wistful smile beneath a ragged moustache. But there was no smile in his voice now. "They'd gagged her, but it was stuffed too tight and throttled her. So she didn't even know what they did to him."

Had Walters seen the doctor? I wondered. He had promised Joel. But his urgent narrative drowned out my thoughts. "By the time the neighbours . . . yes, quite a crowd, because – although the bullet in he chest and thing – he was alive until . . . no they set him alight and he ran down the road blazing till he fell down and . . ."

I suddenly saw my life as hypernormal, so sheltered as to be utterly at variance to the day-to-day observations of Walters, even though I too was living with the unthinkable. But I was trying to avoid nightmares, sleeping and waking.

Unexpectedly my attention was deflected from Mattie. Over the past four weeks I'd been avoiding the television news, because it no longer added real information about the tragedy that had taken place three months before – only hype, which was unbearable. But it was just like Kevin to bring up every new reference in the media. It seemed the international news had begun touching less and less on the circumstances surrounding the crash in favour of human-interest stories about passengers or the relatives or dependents they left behind.

It seemed a teenager's mother had posted on Facebook a video her boy had sent her during the flight from which he never returned. I cringed then left the room every time it played on TV. Over and over. There followed other messages, texts, images, reports of furtive calls that opened up enquiries about the airline's responsibility. The electronic stuff went viral, speculation rife about whether an official had let the plane take off under suspicious circumstances. Because I refused to watch through any of the footage, I couldn't form an opinion. But after that, more and more, updates on the accident began to focus on arrangements for damages.

Melody's account to me made it seem unlikely that any funds to assist in the children's upbringing could emerge from her parents' affairs – if we ever got at their papers. So Joel argued, "Means we must apply for damages." We owed it to the children to follow up whatever the airline might grant, despite the queasiness that accompanied the concept of compensation. Eventually, we had sent a query.

The day after hearing Barrie's voice in the message promising to collect Mattie, a response came from the airline company.

As you may be aware, compensation on behalf of the children surviving Connor Firaki has already been requested by their most immediate relative, Barrie Firaki, with substantial documentation. As this application is already under consideration, we advise that you contact Ms Firaki for any further information.

"Realer than ever now." Joel threw up both hands then dropped onto sofa and stared blankly at the wall. From that point what encroached on every other consideration – certainly on attention to Walters or Francis – were scattered details of Barrie. Or, more exactly, questions about Barrie refracted and broke apart and collided again bewilderingly. Had Melody said something about Barrie being a lawyer, or even (I could not quite recall) the head of a legal firm? "Could she take Mattie from us?" I asked Joel. "Or all three? Or, you know, twist things through some technicality . . . or, what if she has some *right*?"

"You mean, suppose there are papers somewhere about guardianship? Stuff we know nothing about?"

"I mean, what proof have we of any rights at all? Perhaps Barrie – as their father's sister – *would* be the obvious guardian," I said. What documentation had we? Even the most basic papers like the children's passports had vanished with Cyn "A court might say we're old, with fewer years ahead than their aunt. Unequipped." I could hear the arguments:

the oldest boy given to senseless pranks; the girl withdrawn or secretive; the youngest and most disturbed in denial, regularly running away from school up to recently, which meant he had repeatedly been in mortal danger. All of them on record as having required counselling.

It played out in my head as I left Joel's den and turned upstairs, back to my study. What if we retained guardianship? Their future with us passed before me with its inevitable gruelling losses – the illness and death of parents (which we had now become) brought forward by decades. Before that, they would still be needing support rather than having to give it – having to hold a trembling hand, guide a wheelchair, interview a caregiver. I grieved for them that they should have to bear such things too soon.

By the time they had to make decisions about education, careers, marriages and investments, our thoughts might be outdated or vague. I recalled the joint account my mother opened with me when I first went on campus, the site visit with Joel's father when we were considering this house. I remembered the ticket we bought for Cynnie's flight to Australia. For Micah, Melody and Mattie, *we* would not be on hand, or we would (at best) be in our late eighties or early nineties, a responsibility rather than a support. And it wrung my heart.

But then it hardened my resolve to preserve myself, body and mind. The gym had long slipped off my weekly routine. "I'm setting the phone for half an hour earlier in the mornings," I warned Joel that night, "to accommodate a stint on the treadmill myself. Perhaps forty-five minutes to include arm lifts or whatever." I actually made it an hour, to plan the day better.

So much waiting to be done, the column of reminders lengthening, bending out of sight. Rust worked up through the white gloss paint on wrought iron along the porch and gnawed down to the base of the iron pins that protected us from falling off.

"We're not keeping up," I declared to Joel next morning when I plonked down my diary.

"A court mightn't view us positively." He picked up from where we had left off the day before. "Ageing couple in circumstances not straitened but fixed. Pensions, rent, some investments. The aunt might seem equipped to give them everything, a qualified lawyer."

"But what means *does* she have?" I wondered. "We don't know if she's still employed, or competent to practise."

"If so — hmm. Twin sister of their lost father, living in the same country as the children's original home, more likely to know the parents' wishes." Right. The grandparents' lifetime of achievements might count for nothing. Ruthlessly, in my mind, I set the image of the young professional alongside that of a couple old people who had met two of the three children once before in their lives and met their father only once.

Even our uninformed and incoherent reflections forced the conclusion that shimmered into view and blocked out all else. "We can't prove any right to the children," I whispered.

It swirled there. The dizziness turned me back to our room to check my pressure:180/90. Who had time for that?

Then I took hold of myself. What there was no time for was a stroke or heart attack. I *must* sacrifice my early morning session on the laptop — my most productive time — for one on the treadmill. But even this would not be enough. Holding back on matters I would normally discuss with Joel had ramped up the tension.

How was I to pile more on him than the mysteries surrounding the children, all the time with Walters in his ear ("When we arrived the police were there, but the couple were already dead. Multiple . . . No, you don't understand: lemme explain . . ."). Disquieting questions about Francis chewed around the edges of my mind.

Yet if I made myself ill, that would only pressure Joel more. And what if I died leaving him uninformed, inadequately equipped to deal with potential crises I could at least vaguely foresee at this point? I was not protecting him, I realized: I was dodging.

To better evade awareness of my evasions, I turned my thoughts to hidden factors that might lurk in our obligations to the children, crucial issues we may have forgotten or overlooked, and a sudden recognition jolted me. The lawyer. We had not contacted Cranshawe regarding the business of guardianship even though it was everywhere in our thoughts.

I hurried to Joel's den and blurted it out. "Cranshawe!"

He kindly refrained from pointing out how much further along we'd be if I'd agreed to rope in Francis, and, much as I needed to explain my reluctance, I could only focus on the core issue — whether Barrie could take away the children.

I suddenly loathed her. It was this almost conscious surrender to an unfamiliar and corrosive sensation. But it was as if — why waste time?

Conserve energy and give way to the only rational response. Yes, rational: she had made my daughter's life hell – that much was obvious. Barrie had pushed Cyn into uprooting herself and the children so as to take them out of reach. And now – Mattie. What had begun as an irritant and developed into a nuisance and then a worrying influence on an impressionable child closed in now.

It was Micah who answered the next call from Barrie, and, in case we still had room for doubt, the child dropped the phone on the floor and ran yelling to us, "Papa, stop her. Stop her. Mama, make her stop. She says Mattie's hers and she's taking him away." I hurried to him.

"Hello?" Her voice, on speaker, seemed to come up from under my feet. "Micah, it's me, Barrie. Please put on one of your grandparents. They didn't call me back. I need them to know I'll be there Thursday." Then came an angry mutter: "Why the hell won't someone take my call?"

By the time I grabbed at the phone it had clicked off. We stood staring at it. "You kids don't have her number?" I asked Micah, and he shook his head.

"We weren't allowed to call her." There was a guilty pause, then he added, "I tried once from Con's phone, but she'd blocked him, and when I Googled – nothing. It wasn't listed."

When Joel got in and I told him, his terse response was, "Lawyer."

So now Thursday thundered in my head. And with it, a sense of Barrie consuming our lives more and more, as if every drop of attention diverted from her brought on calamity. But I forced my mind back to the issue. Custody. Cyn had told us once it was in her will, wherever that was.

"You kept saying you would go over the matter with Cranshawe," I reminded Joel, feeling mean about seeming to blame him. "I know how busy you've been," I added lamely. But it was more than that. Even more than that private service we had gone through in a trance, the will we needed was that official line that ruled Cyn off. Gone.

Joel buried his face in his hands. I could do nothing but wrap my arms around him and throttle my own sobs. Then we gathered ourselves again. For what loomed now was worse than the crash.

"Thursday," Joel repeated.

Today was Sunday.

I set off upstairs to Melody's room. "Darling," I began cautiously, as I smoothed and straightened her pillows without being aware of what my hands were about. "I promised not to coerce you into telling me anything, but the problem is – I need to know all I can to keep Mattie safe."

"But now I told you everything, Mama."

I believed her absolutely. "I know. It's just – we have to get your parents' papers – anything they might have left about your care if . . . if . . . Would you have any idea where they kept important documents?" My heart fell when she shook her head apologetically.

"Not home. Cyn said she didn't want anyone *digging up in her things.* She said there was a safe-something-box."

Relief slid over me at the probability that their papers had not fallen into Barrie's possession. I kissed Melody and made for the door, instantly preoccupied with how one might locate and access Cyn's safety deposit box.

"I *knew* her," I said, under my breath. "She wrote it down. She wrote everything down. There's an envelope with something, somewhere."

A little strangled sound from Melody turned me around. "Mama, I'm sorry. I only just remembered." She headed for a drawer where she had a few old books and puzzles she had outgrown, but her mother had brought them along knowing they had been favourites the child wouldn't want to leave behind. "Before she left here for the airport Cyn told me put this up and never open it – only give you if anything . . . and I couldn't give her back." When I stared at her, she continued falteringly. "She told me forget I had it and I . . . I guess I did. Till now. True, Mama."

A small white envelope was addressed, "Mom from Cyn." Inside was a single sheet of paper with a password for something stored on a cloud (whatever that meant): *MLimbs3!* Below that:

Promise me that if one day you wake up and hear I'm dead, you will write my story. Promise.

Then the ground gave way and the walls keeled. I tried to call out, but my mouth quivered out of control. *God, no, not at a time like this.* Grabbing the back of a chair, I felt tingling in my right arm. I snatched out the spray from my bra with my left hand and puffed, then turned my face to Melody, and mouthed, "Papa."

What ate up time was determining why I fell, and all that time the possibilities gnawed at me. Not a stroke, I reasoned. Everything worked fine on both sides of my body. But if it was a mild heart attack, they would all force me to slow down. I couldn't afford to slow down.

After a lot of poking around, an EKG and Echo, Staple ruled out the need for another angiogram. I'd hit my head on the floor, though not hard enough to cause more than a bruise, so Joel raised the question of concussion. No further dizziness, though, no nausea. I could go home. Just rest a bit, Staple said. By this time we had lost the rest of Sunday, all of Monday and most of Tuesday.

Tuesday night was coming on before I could talk to Joel about Cyn's note, which I had barely had time and strength to slip into his hand when he gathered me up from the thin mat beside Melody's bed. By now I had arranged my face so that the turmoil behind it was sealed off. At most, I looked grave.

"Micah might know about this cloud business," Joel said. "Bound to. All these young people know that type of stuff. Except, well, Melody's entirely into books." Then we glanced at each other furtively. Not knowing what was there, was it wise to let Micah in on it?

Next morning I joined Micah at the table to find out, as he crammed his cereal, whether he could give me directions before he left for school. How would I access this *cloud* thing? He regarded me blankly. "What's that?"

It was almost ten when Joel called to say that the lawyer was confident he could block any arbitrary attempt to remove the children from our care. By then I'd swallowed my pride, called campus to consult someone in IT and taken copious notes of his directions. Then exhaustion descended on me. Certain I could access the file in no time, I still stayed pinned to the couch. I owed it to them to lie quiet with the kitchen door open so Ena could hear me. I woke in the afternoon to the faint grating of the gate, the clack of the padlock on the grillwork and chatter of the children arriving home with Joel, tumbling in and clunking down bookbags at the top of the stairs.

I knew they'd rush in to see how I was, so I got to the mirror and scraped the comb through my hair. As an afterthought I brushed a little mascara around the hairline.

"Back to normal!" I announced.

During homework time, Joel sifted the files I got open and printed the essentials. A letter – heartbreakingly brief and hurried – ended with safety deposit box information and summarized its contents. The document list included at least one will, presumably Cyn's, property transactions, bonds, and correspondence regarding employment in the Caribbean. The file contained some electronic copies, Cyn's password to her Yahoo account, a note of addresses and another on the children's medical information, warning against exposing Mattie to mould, smoke, insecticide, chlorides, lilies, strong perfumes, or honey. Honey had been underlined twice, and I went cold at the recollection of how – purely by chance – I had decided against buying that oats and honey cereal the week before.

Then my attention caught on a single letter: *B*. One file was entitled *BMatters*. But we could not open that.

Nothing suggested that Cyn or Connor had left significant property; nothing explained Barrie's fixation on Mattie.

The next day was Thursday with no time to seek help regarding the *B* file. The technician I consulted by phone said it might be *encrypted*. Or *corrupted*? Was that what he said? I asked Joel.

"Whatever. Written that off for now." He shrugged.

Unless Barrie had been bluffing, we were out of time. We'd kept the children home from school lest she contrive to collect any of them there – who knew what she could do? – and we waited with Cranshawe. I stole glances at the tall, exquisitely clad lawyer reading some brief at the glass table on my front porch. How much would we have to pay?

As the day was frittered away, I got to wondering how we were managing to hold a policeman idling on our porch, with so much to claim him elsewhere throughout the country. It seemed only yesterday that there had been the hoo-ha about a container, the two doors at the back chained and clamped with a shiny padlock at least four inches in diameter. It stood a few minutes from the dock in the noonday sun while hands slippery with sweat hammered on the inside, skidding on the inner surface of the door. Two women were dead and three little girls critical before the police broke in, with Walters and his photographer close at hand. So they missed another truck incident developing at the same time a few streets away. But Walters knew all about that too.

This other truck had its low tray covered in yellow tarpaulin neatly roped down and printed *Landscape and Garden*. A few sacks showed, presumably of soil, manure or ornamental stones. On one side, however, a sole policeman watched with fascination a corner where the yellow tarp had come untied and flapped back to expose part of one sack with a small but widening crimson patch. Joel took Walters' second call patiently as we sat on the porch, watching the gate.

Barrie did not come. But anything could delay an appointment at the end of a journey from Australia to the Caribbean, so we stayed on tenterhooks through Friday. Our lawyer verified that no one named Barrie Firaki, or any other Firaki had deplaned at Piarco.

I can't pretend I was relieved: that would be too frivolous a word for having a blow deferred to later. In truth, I felt let down: I had braced for impact only to find it would come some other time. Maybe the following day she would waltz in and demand the children. For all of our unspecified future, it could be the following day. Or the one after that. It took hours to fall asleep that night, and in no time I was awake again.

Perhaps it will be tomorrow. The thought drummed in my head, mocking the silence till I dropped off once more. It woke me next morning too – *Or today* – and would come back as I opened my eyes for countless mornings after. In fact, after that Thursday I became aware that every time we registered a period of ease and relaxed slightly, cautiously, towards normalcy, Barrie loomed again.

⌒⑂⌒

We had written back to the airline immediately after getting their first response, and that second correspondence regarding damages elicited another and surprisingly prompt email message that arrived the day after Barrie's non-appearance. It again referred directly to Ms Firaki regarding provision for the children. Presumably, then, she had been or was to be granted damages for their support. We could only surmise, bitterly.

We contemplated her going after the miserable money, which could never make up for what the children had lost but could at least have been invested for their future. The idea of her enriching herself through the deaths of their parents filled me with revulsion. Recalling Melody's account, I tried visualizing Barrie through younger eyes but could only draw her up a wicked fairy of fantasy, slender and beautiful in a flowing robe of blood red background with pastel, pinkish-green vines spilling from it like pale intestines.

"It's been, what, a week now?" Joel said on Friday, fingers sifting what he had brought up from the mailbox. "Since . . . The Day Barry Didn't Come, I mean."

"A week since the day after – which was a nightmare too," I told Joel sinking onto a porch chair.

"Frenzied Friday," he agreed without looking up.

"She's wholly evil." I said, and, getting no answer, added, "Vile."

"Mmm," he responded absently.

I was startled. We had got to the porch late. Having missed sunset, we'd got rid of everything that needed to be done and come out after nine. And here he sat, his shiraz untouched, riffling through the day's mail, seemingly oblivious to my reaction. Then I saw that although his fingers fiddled with the small pile of envelopes before us, his eyes were fixed on one. Without a word he shoved it across the table to me.

The bill inside was headed *Specialist Health Services, Private Choice Reproductive Clinic*, a medical centre we had never heard of. It came to us as near kin named by a patient they had failed to contact, although the SHS had treated Cyndra Firaki over the years. Attempts had also failed to contact her husband, joint owner of material in their possession and named as immediate next of kin on her file.

And now, the reproductive clinic was requesting payment for rental space that accommodated two frozen embryos left after successful implantations in Cyndra Firaki.

How little we know about those we know best. Joel and I stared at each other open-mouthed for several seconds.

"A 2010 procedure," he said, and I replied, "Nine years." Then, "The twins."

We pulled ourselves together somehow and noted the phone number, before starting to calculate the time difference between San Fernando and Los Angeles. Business offices would be closed by now. We'd have to wait for tomorrow.

꧁⸱⫍⸱꧂

When we telephoned the next day after lunch, the woman at the other end evinced no interest in us beyond our willingness to pay, or our ability to convince the responsible party or parties to sign off for disposal. Then Joel explained about Cyndra having been on Flight 198 that had mysteriously vanished, and there was a swift intake of breath and a stumbling but genuine-sounding exclamation, "Oh God, no. Oh, I'm so sorry, sir. Please hold."

Another voice, apparently a doctor's, came on, concerned, even distressed. The problem was how to help without compromising patient privacy, he explained. They would keep the embryos for now but would need evidence of our identity and reasonable proof that the patient and her husband were deceased before they could release further information.

At least we were sure now that Cyn and Connor had used the clinic to conceive Micah and Melody. Multiple births were more common with IVF, even if twins had not been in Connor's family. The problem was that the clinic's privacy limitations blocked any hint of activity in the last five years. So, no clue about Mattie. Good God.

The following morning my mind was still worrying every possible implication of that as I got the twins out and negotiated the traffic. At about eight-thirty, when I got back from the school run, I glanced at the sky before going inside. Far above, fine wings sailed, tilting, borne along by invisible currents. It occurred to me that we knew as little about my child as about that bird, and she seemed to have been as much at the mercy of forces in a domain beyond my experience.

When I went inside, Joel was just starting on the treadmill, and shortly after he got going, one of the long-stemmed crystal glasses in the cabinet on the dining room side of the wall tipped and shattered. I wiped my eyes and gathered it up. No point telling myself how unimportant it was, for it had been one of a set and its place was now forever empty. Besides, this had never happened before, so he was pounding harder, and who knew whether he would hurt himself. I mopped, burnt the tip of a needle and picked the splinter from my left thumb. Then I got on with the day.

A call that evening derailed for a while any further enquiries we could make regarding the clinic. It came from a student in one of our St Augustine townhouses, to let us know about uncollected mail that was piling up. Isaac would have told us more promptly, but he had warned us he'd be digging around in the British Library online and the Folger for most of the month, to the exclusion of all else. "Thesis *still?*" Joel had asked. "Thought he submitted long time." And I'd explained it was a post-doc project Isaac meant to follow up once his dissertation was examined. Briefly at least, he'd taken his eye off our apartment.

Angie, the tenant who called, said the stack included notices from Trinidad and Tobago Port Authority and seemed to refer to something from Sydney.

"Perhaps we should have asked Angie to pass them on to Kevin Cambridge to open for us," I said, then added, "that is, if we want Kevin in the matter at all."

Joel said, "How confidential could it be? Well."

We began to speculate wildly, and that went on for the rest of the day. Perhaps a family member of Connor's sending forward something for the children?

"Barrie, you think?" I whispered. "I mean, I suppose she does love them."

"Don't know that," he said.

"Don't know why she didn't come or why she meant to or whether she meant to. Don't know much of anything," I replied grumpily.

We turned in for what would be a restless night. Joel thrashed about, knees and elbows boring me at intervals, as I battered on in my mind for a possible explanation.

⁓⁾⁾⟨⟨⟨⁓

Next morning Joel set off for St Augustine by six, leaving the school run to me. I regarded his errand with foreboding. I dreaded unpacking whatever unaccompanied luggage might have dawdled in from Sydney. Neither Micah nor Melody recollected their mother mentioning clothes, books or other items to be shipped, but the children had been with us during the final stages of their parents packing up, so how could they know anything about that?

"Bound to be books," Joel had concluded, and I wondered silently what we would do with a pile of medical tomes. Perhaps the university library? Publications over a decade old, though.

Then I caught sight of Mattie's face, alight with hope – as if news of any arrival from the other side of the world brought his parents' landing closer. Something inside me plummeted, and I hurried the children to the car so as to get back to my laptop and lace my thoughts together along entirely different lines.

Midmorning, I heard Joel mounting the stairs with a peculiar drag to his tread. My door stood ajar, and he pushed into the study with the gait of a zombie, speechlessly holding forth a notification that a container of household furniture and other personal property of Cyndra Firaki awaited clearance, subject to payment of various tariffs and overdues for storage. Failure to contact the office within six days of the date of this last notice could result in the disposal of unclaimed goods.

I sat him at my desk and coaxed tea from the Keurig while he got on the phone. After the inevitable disconnections while being passed along from one clerk to the next, he came off, an hour later, with instructions for clearing the cargo. Kevin Cambridge had dropped whatever he was doing when Joel phoned him for advice and had tracked down a reliable broker.

The next day Joel set out. "Valid forms of ID for agent's office," he confirmed, "and, yes, money for paying fees."

"More and more offices require cash now," I'd reminded him, "and no one tells you when you're making the appointment."

"Nope. Only at point of payment," he agreed. "Usually with fake grin of apology."

At last Joel had a bill of lading and instructions for clearing the cargo. Once the container was unstuffed, a Customs officer would tell him the fees to be paid.

"More money?" I asked.

Joel pushed a list towards me. I stared at it, unseeing at first and just wishing it could all disappear. But they came at me: *bunk beds, bicycles* and *dining table* leapt out from the paper.

There ensued our exhaustive discussion of how we could bring it all to our already fully furnished house. It popped into my head that if only the notices hadn't reached us before the deadline, it could all have gone away. We could have escaped unlocking and handling Cyn's treasures, picking over what to keep and working out how to get rid of the rest.

But how could we refuse to accept what our child had saved to bring with her, had packed up for her children? Connor and Cyn had sensibly shipped what they most wanted to keep, so as to avoid purchasing everything over again at greater cost. They had allowed for a generous storage period while finding a suitable house, and they had named Joel as recipient, confident that he knew the ropes in his own country or would be able to identify an agent to help them through.

And then the children. They had a right to their parents' stuff – and their own, as Joel reminded me. For the children, we had to get that much safely landed. But we needed time to prepare.

In vain Joel pleaded for a fortnight to make the necessary arrangements for delivery. He was advised stonily to have the haulier make an appointment at once and assured that appointments were given for the following day.

"And it had already cost so much," he explained that evening.

"What cost . . .?"

"Storage. Several notices, remember? All the time it stayed waiting to be cleared the cost mounted up."

"More money."

The shipment seemed enormous to Joel when he viewed it at Customs. "May need another house for the stuff," he reported when he got home. "Which was, after all, the plan. They were to have a house to fill with their stuff. Well, it's coming down the Hochoy Highway on Saturday and we'd better be ready."

"What's coming down the highway?" Melody asked.

So then there was all that to find words for.

That evening, while I cleared pebbles that had collected in the track of the gate, I mentally rearranged the house, scouring it for every cranny in which to squeeze items ranging in size from framed pictures to a fridge and queen-size bed. I must have been hidden from view by the front hedge. Just beyond it, the woman Joel called Parker was struggling to get the key into the car lock and wrench open the door, but the man with her slammed it and tugged her away from it.

"Leave me," she cried.

"Shut up," he snapped, glancing about. "People will hear."

"Good, I want them hear me." She was sobbing. "Make them hear how you does treat me. How you could hit me so? How you could do it?" She broke away, and he must have caught sight of me, because he swung away and went striding back across the road, then up swiftly to his house. Keeping her face turned from me, she started the car and screeched off.

The space in front our hedge was clear for two nights, and I thought, *Good for you, Parker.* But on Friday evening the Toyota coasted up again.

Saturday morning was a clear day, thank God. Francis arrived early in shortpants and tank top, carrying a cooler with ice and soft drinks. Ena had got the pigeon peas simmering for pelau. The children grew more and more restive.

"Do you remember any of Connor's jokes?" Micah asked the others.

"Lots," Mattie answered.

"Like which ones?"

Mattie thought a little. "I can't tell them. Only Connor can tell them."

We heard the rumble far down the road before we saw it, and it growled louder as the container lumbered up to our gate.

"It's humongous," Melody breathed.

A stark rectangle like a warehouse interposed itself between our house and the Purple Monstrosity opposite. Then it eased forward and began to swing its front wheels away, avoiding Parker's car. A man sprang out of the front and began yelling instructions. The truck backed in, narrowly missing the gateposts and then the two plain slim pillars that defined the downstairs porch and helped to support the upstairs one. The truck and container halted with a shudder that vibrated through us. They filled the roomy front yard and blocked out the nearby trees, the sea beyond and even the San Fernando Hill.

Micah stared wide-mouthed, and Melody breathed, "'S almost as big as our house. Does it have *everything* in it?"

"Cool," Micah said when the back wall of the container lowered to form a ramp. Mattie sidled up close to him, intent on the men easing down a crate.

The men broke out the kitchen things first, storing most in the helper's quarters at the back, since Ena insisted on going home every evening anyway. The workmen grumbled about having to lug the heavy stuff all the way around the actual house, until Joel grew tired of them. "At least they not going upstairs to the kitchen," he snapped, his eye unwavering from the clipboard in his hand.

The biggest of them hoisted the brace he wore around his ample waist and steupsed. Then they unloaded the fridge.

"Good news is we're putting that on a patio down here." Joel grinned and signalled them to follow him. "Just round this corner."

"That's the fridge from my house," Mattie shouted suddenly. "'s got my SpongeBob stickers on it."

Then the workmen started on living and dining room furniture, while the children followed their every move. Mattie's eyes widened at the rocker and the recliner that somehow fit in among our living room chairs upstairs, but several miscellaneous chairs got abandoned in the garage for the time being. The men shoved the porch set onto our downstairs porch until there was no space left to walk, so Joel and Francis shifted our own wrought-iron chairs and table into the yard to allow the workmen room to pass with the beds.

These had to fit in our bedroom. We had had Mr Farley's men take down our bed and push the king-size mattress into the living room, leaned up behind the sofa. When the container had disgorged its contents, we could lay the mattress flat in the middle where we would sleep for now. With the rest of our bedroom furniture rammed against the walls, our room would serve for storage while we figured things out. No. As Joel pointed out, no dressing tables, chests of drawers or cabinets, thank God. Must have gone among the things Melody said her mother meant to sell off when she got back to Sydney after dropping the children with us.

Finally it got down to the children's stuff. Mattie watched them uncrate the small desk with the kangaroo and wallaby painted on it, the duckbilled platypus and the dingo. And he edged over.

"Where are they?" he demanded. "I want to see my parents *now*."

He surged forwards and I caught him.

"Wait, darling. Let's talk a minute."

"No." Not rude, just decisive. "I've waited an' waited. An' I want them *now*." He grabbed Micah's hand and tugged. His voice trembled with passion. "Those are our things from our house and how come *they* haven't come out yet? Make them come out."

Micah grabbed his arm. "Cyn and Connor aren't in the container, small man. It's just things they shipped over before . . . before they got on the plane."

Mattie pulled away and slumped onto one of our porch chairs. Then he shifted from the wrought iron to a padded dining room chair with curved wooden arms. He climbed slowly onto it as if in a dream and ran his fingers tenderly over the polished wood and touched his cheek to the padding at the back. Drawing up his knees and wrapping his arms around the cushioned back, he squeezed his eyes shut.

I was on my way to him when Joel clutched his lower back and sank groaning onto the iron loveseat from our porch set. At the same moment the most belligerent of the workmen bellowed, "So whe' dis have to go?" And in glancing between Joel and a delicate little desk in the man's arms, I took my eye off Mattie.

When I looked back, he was gone.

So everything came to a halt. The workmen were instantly on our side. A child had disappeared, and this had nothing to do with overwork in the hot sun or underpay every day of the year. This was a child.

"Watch in the house, Mammie," the big one bawled at me. "You," he hailed the others, "you, run down the street. And you, Redboy, go up the next way." He softened his voice for Micah and Melody. "Watch me. You two stay with you papa. Like he mash up he back."

On my way to the door Ena met me, out of breath. She had been watching from the upstairs porch. "He ent inside here, unless he hiding in some cupboard." But we both knew nothing would have prompted Mattie to go inside, let alone into a cupboard, while this unpacking continued. Meanwhile, the trundling and scraping of heavy furniture and equipment halted, as did the shouting, while the men turned in different directions to search, and in the hush that fell we made out the muffled, weirdly echoing cry.

"Where? Where're you, Cyn? Connooooor! Come *now.*" Mattie's voice from deep inside the container. And as he got farther in among the stuff that remained, the words became indistinct, muffled to a pulsing of two or three syllables at a time and the occasional emphatic *nowww* tolling out among them.

"We have to reach him," Francis said frantically. "Things have moved around in there. What if something topples . . .?"

Micah shot off from the downstairs porch.

"Stay with Melody," Joel told Francis before taking off too.

We got up the ramp – I shouted for Ena, and when I reached the top, she was on the upper porch yelling to the workmen – and we would all have blundered in if not for Micah stopping us with one palm raised and the other hand pressing a finger to his lips.

He turned his face to the narrow passage between the crates. "Hey,

Ratbag, stand where you are, lemme give you a hand." And before we could forestall him, he had dived in between the high wooden frames and wadding.

Joel held me back. "On no account do we want them messing around trying to avoid us and overturning anything or, or stumbling against . . . I don't know – nails . . . whatever." We froze, listening. Then after a while we heard them more distinctly.

". . . *My* desk. My own desk with the wallaby. And Cyn's chair. They're not crashed. They're good, look." The two boys appeared at the entrance of the container and stood squinting against the sudden glare, gazing down at the motley collection of all we had already unwrapped. Mattie didn't even look at us as he pointed. "See Cyn's chair isn' crashed. Why *they* won't come out?"

Micah placed both hands on Mattie's shoulders. "You see," he said carefully. "Cyn 'n' Connor weren't in the container." Mattie recoiled, regarding him warily. "They put the container on a ship because the stuff in it was heavy," Micah went on, "and *they* got on the plane." He swiped at his own eyes angrily and grabbed hold of Mattie's hand again, then led him down the ramp, while I pulled Joel's arm through mine and we followed without a word.

Mattie paused partway down the ramp. He turned once and regarded us with his eyes huge and dark and hungry as if they could swallow us up. "They should've got in the container instead," he whispered.

Francis was crying when he reached up and lifted him down and gave Joel a hand. The workmen clustered away in the shade of the truck, the bossman listening attentively to Ena but with his eyes fixed on Mattie.

Then Mattie went back to the dining chair and sat up in it very straight, laying his arms along the curved mahogany arms. He watched, stony faced, as the rest of the stuff was unloaded. When one of the workmen brought down a package that was clearly a large painting or print, Joel looked away and laboured up the stairs to stretch out on the sofa. I stayed downstairs, sitting as near to Mattie as I dared, and refused Francis's offer to unwrap the picture, from its size and shape almost certainly the old van Gogh print that had gone across the world with Cyn and returned alone. Ena distributed bottles of cold water and had Francis organize an icepack for Joel.

After that, none of us cared where anything went. The workmen got the lot of it under shelter where rain wouldn't blow in and soak cushions or watermark wood. When they were ready to go, one came over to Mattie and stroked his head with a large callused finger, infinitely gentle.

"Small man, you want to go in the container and watch how it look now we take out allyou furnitures?" He gazed down on the child with his eyes full to overflowing.

Mattie shook his head.

"Big brother going to walk with you if you want," the man persisted.

"There's nothing to see," Mattie explained, his voice barely audible. "'S empty. And it didn' have what I wanted." Then he collected himself quickly and whispered, "But thank you for bringing it all the same, Uncle."

When the container eventually trundled away, he made his way inside and up the staircase to clamber onto Joel's lap. Joel held him on his chest. I knew Joel's back was breaking, but what else was there to be done?

⇀⁊⃒↼

Mattie insisted his desk with the wallaby slide in alongside the dining table Micah had claimed and lodged in the middle of Joel's den. Which was fine, Joel insisted, only a seven-piece set and he'd been meaning to push his own desk against the wall for years now.

There was another desk, though. Melody must have this, I resolved when I made them carry it upstairs, whether she parked it beside the boys' stuff (as they slowly elbowed Joel out) or kept it here by mine. She would want it here, I sensed, in the hush of my study.

But this desk.

Of all we had unpacked, it arrested and undid me. Solid but compact and poised on delicately tapered legs, riddled with nooks and crannies, it had to be Cyn's. She was the sort who would have suffered a plastic folding table for years until she saw the desk she wanted. This one was silky mahogany with slim, exquisitely turned legs rather than the pedestal type, and shallow drawers that enabled that light, open look she favoured. And it was lower than usual: a writing table for a woman little more than five feet tall, who didn't like the sensation of being boxed in even around the feet.

Particularly around her feet. I saw her untucking her bed linen every time I tidied it away, because, she insisted, going to sleep was nuisance

— 172 —

enough without half of her being tied down and her toes clamped. And all this unnecessary cloth – we didn't need half the stuff we had, she added. Yet now, here was this desk for someone who cared for the elegancies of life and could access at least some of them. It was furniture for passing down the generations, only she had had it so briefly. My mind meandered between the privileges of life, the right to it, and the fragility of any hold on it whatever. I had to shut down these reflections by wandering off from the two desks, out into the hurly-burly of a living room rearranged around the king-size mattress and a tumble of small bodies.

—⁄⁁⟍—

Following on what Joel came to call the Day of the Container, we made a quick survey of what we must keep versus the rest and weeded out less prized possessions. Over the next week we arranged for a truck to take stuff to the townhouses and then to Ena's new and still bare house.

One morning Joel set out, driving ahead of the truck and leaving me to get the children off to school. When I returned home, I picked from a haphazard cluster of odd pieces from the shipment the only chair likely to fit comfortably at that desk. It took several minutes to ease it up the steps. It was on wheels and without armrests, the back low enough to reach Cyn's shoulder blades. Once it was in place, I lowered myself gently onto the maroon padding – cautiously, almost as if it might dematerialize beneath me – and drew it close under the desk, which squeezed my thighs, for I am taller than she is.

Was.

I reached for a tissue from the box that would be in the right top drawer. But that was locked. I tried the other drawers, and they were locked too.

Cyn never locked things. *Why should I?* She'd have shrugged the idea off.

Quickly as it had arisen, my vague sense that the desk might not, after all, be hers dissolved before the solidity of this dainty yet durable arrangement of aged wood that stood before me. Somehow commanded me.

Through the dark rich mahogany, lighter tones broke through in elusive whorls of old gold or bronze like refracted gleams from the deep. Its fine polish, its smoothness drew my fingers to stroke downwards yearningly

— 173 —

along the sleek finish of one slight yet rounded leg. And somehow its poise, its elegant balance of fragility and indestructibility projected Cyn's presence and then overwhelmingly her absence, so that I flung my arms around it and clutched the sides where the grooves cornered in such a way that my thumbs fitted as if that small detail in its moderate carving had been constructed for my thumbs alone.

A wail tore through me. I cried with no one to hear me or be troubled or disturbed or further depressed by my dissolving uninhibitedly over an antique I had never seen before. The overpowering drought I had contrived and sustained inside broke in wrenching sobs that shuddered on at last beyond my control or my interest in controlling. My face jammed on the writing table and my breasts pressed painfully along its edge with my arms squeezing the planed sides, I gave in to all that welled up – the years of her separation from us for study and the finality of such geographical distance at our age, and that night, that appalling night of catastrophe that had never really let up over the succeeding months, and the growing insubstantiality of our hold on the children, the yawning emptiness that might lie in wait. And I thought it would never stop, the paroxysm of grief reverberating through me, so I can't say whether it was five minutes or twenty before it slowed to periodical heaving and shudders, and I raised the loose-fitting cotton top I was wearing to draw it across the desk and wipe away the moisture I had spread everywhere over the lustrous wooden surface.

I glanced again at the drawer that should have the tissues, locked, with no key taped to the underside of the desk as she would have done *if* she had locked it at all.

Cyn all over – rigorous about what she valued most, casual about what she regarded as peripheral. She had taken some care with her documents, I reflected, casting my mind back to the *cloud* and to the enigmatic *B* file. I studied the drawers along the front and hypothesized that they might be locked to prevent them sliding out and breaking. But then I remembered the wadding, bound tightly before the men ripped it off and prepared to lift the desk inside.

To avoid going downstairs and consulting the list on the fridge door, I turned back to my own desk and got onto my laptop, then searched through the numbers stored in the House file so as to call Mr Farley and ask whether he could pick or break a lock or two without damaging a bit of particularly fine furniture. I braced myself for a wait of a couple days, but he promised to come before I left to get the children home from school. He drove in and had the drawers open barely in time for me to leave for St Theresa's.

Then, at Aglow, I paused for a brief chat with Nicki, who was pleased about Mattie's progress. Even the principal, Jan Sibley, had remarked on how he'd settled over the last few weeks. As the weather turned cooler with dry days in between, the children played outside often, yet no one had heard any more of Barrie.

After straining my eyes for the parking lot where my car waited under a scraggy casuarina, I looked back to the bench nearby where I'd left Micah and Melody. They had taken their first opportunity to explore Aglow and had now settled under a Graham mango tree, studying those that hung well beyond reach. As I approached, the air was heady with the smell of the fruit. Nowadays I could eat only half of one at a time, but that was all right because that half had a stolen sweetness, more luscious than the two I would earlier have accommodated. Well, they were all out of reach anyway.

It was nearly four o'clock before the children, back home, had eaten their hot sada, slit and wedged with slices of yellow cheese that melted in the enfolding roti. Then they had settled over their books and homework. They were outside by the time Joel got back with his account of our Court Augustine townhouses – how the sofa-bed from Sydney had just slid under the living room window in one of them, and what the plumber had uncovered under the kitchen sink in the other. And what did I think? The new office that had opened up across the road to the townhouse had inflicted on the neighbourhood a glaring orange and green sign announcing Uterine Services.

Before I could tell him about the desk, the noise of slapping and grumbling made us check on the children – "The mozzies are out," Micah reported, "in a rage" – and call them in for the mild insect repellent cream that Mattie seemed to tolerate. By then it had occurred to me I should just check Cyn's desk drawers myself before getting up Joel's hopes –

The phone rang. Jackie was calling with the news that she and Gabrielle were relocating in a few months, selling the house and moving to be near one of the children, the son in Edmonton. Or at least Jackie would go ahead while Gabrielle worked out passages for the three dogs, one or more of the most ancient having died since our visit. Jackie was to fly out in the new year and might manage to visit the daughter in Michigan by next summer. The earth jolted beneath me yet again, gently yet definitively, another slab of bedrock loosened.

"Quiet tonight." Joel observed me, worry lines tightening around his eyes. "Feel OK?"

"Mm-hmm." It was possible to nibble a corn chip with hummus and sip a glass of wine but feel bereft, so harrowed by the years as to pick up that subtle hollowing-out that was continuously underway. Merely surviving could impoverish one.

He hadn't taken his eyes off me and touched my glass with his again as if our lives depended on that faint click, as indeed they did. After the children kissed us and trailed off to bed, we sat on there until even the night noises died away.

So it was ten-thirty, the children all asleep and Joel snoring lightly, before I wandered back to my study to go through Cyn's desk. Miscellaneous bills and receipts of recent date stuffed one side drawer. A few notes and cards, but mostly selected letters from Joel over the years filled the other. Fourteen years? I suppose they had tapered off as he succumbed to email. There was little from me, because I had lived on Skype and more recently made wobbly progress on WhatsApp.

I didn't read his letters to her. Once I knew what the bundle contained, I simply rested my fingers on it and her face lit up in my mind. Such a strong face, eyes steady and intent, mouth determined but quivering at the corners, ready for laughter.

Keep going, Mom. I swear I heard her say it.

I had left the narrow middle door for last, because it was over eight inches high and probably another eight deep from front to back. Inside lay a shallow stack of papers. I ran my fingers over them – then froze.

The documents I thumbed through related to Barrie and Connor, some in the form of printed email messages, others handwritten notes made about phone conversations or face-to-face encounters. A few turned out to be official documents like a hospital receipt and an invoice from a vet. Everything was numbered and dated, with the odd note in Cyn's hand and a few phrases underlined with heavy black marker. It began to look as if I might patch together what Cyn could tell me through her wad of notes.

They began on 12/03/05. She wrote, "The woman actually contacted me to warn me off. 'You have no ****ing idea what's in store,' she told me." I leafed on through the notes, connecting them up to see if I could salvage an account in Cyn's voice. In quoting Barrie, she used a lot of asterisks or thick black marker, which proved the notes were for me. ("Like how you're from the ark, Mom," she used to say.)

I shuffled through little oddments – disconnected comments and scattered records of conversation to put together whatever Cyn could tell me that might somehow help me write her back into being. I found myself teasing out whatever facts seemed to be suggested by a few sentences here and there, especially where I could link them with the occasional document.

I paused and studied one that came to hand. A copy of Barrie's birth certificate.

June? Not the same month as Connor's birthday. This was late June, and his was early July. *Not* twins then. Hold on: Barrie Intyre. Not Firaki. And the same year, but weeks apart. What? Not siblings at all?

This cramp in what I'd reasoned out wrenched me from the notes I had been jotting, and I turned from the laptop to scrabble through the pile beside it for another document. Two folded together. Divorce Certificate (decree nisi). Then, decree absolute. For a full minute I stared at the names uncomprehendingly.

PART II

As if, when after Phœbus is descended,
And leaves a light much as the past day's dawning,
And, every toil and labour wholly ended,
Each living creature draweth to his resting,
We should begin by such a parting light
To write the story of all ages past,
And end the same before the approaching night.

—SIR WALTER RALEIGH, CYNTHIA, XX, LL. 118–124

11

BREAKING NEWS

―⁘―

CYNNIE (DRAFT)

WE'D SET THE DATE, CON AND ME. Then, the message – my first exposure to Barrie, dated April 2005.

Clueless little bugger, aren't you, she wrote. *No inkling who you're ****ing with. Well, this will be one fight too goddamn bloody for you to survive.*

And from there on she rained down toxic email. Like spider season.

I saw through the venom one-time. From the outset Con had told me about the previous marriage and this ex who dumped him callously but figured no one else must lay a hand on him. Con called Barrie "deeply troubled". Though he admitted he hadn't seen it in the earlies.

But then, what if the woman thought my relationship with Con had begun before they parted? When that hit me, I began wondering whether she might even imagine I'd entrapped him, lured him away to start with. It would have been one way of her dodging responsibility for ill-using a husband that was any woman's dream.

For weeks I fought to block her out my mind, but the idea that someone, even Barrie, might think me a home-breaker nagged on. In the end I fired off this brisk corrective: I had never nor would ever involve myself with someone else's husband. I'd met Con when the divorce was already final, though he was still shattered. Now Con and I were married, we could all go forward along our separate paths in a civilized manner. End of story.

Next week a messenger from Barrie's office arrives at my clinic with copies of their divorce certificates, dates highlighted in yellow, the first (nisi) only weeks earlier than the date on our marriage certificate, the second only days. Photos in the package too, but dated long before either certificate and nothing to do with me, so I shoved them back into the envelope.

Barrie's covering note read, *Guess you deserve each other.*

It was like I fell off a cliff, down down into this . . . midden. Paralysed with guilt – like any decent woman, I suppose, finding out she'd strayed, however unknowingly, into someone else's marriage. When I tried to inhale there seemed to be no air, only this caustic mess I'd plunged into. I could taste it – shame – in the acid flooding my throat.

I had to write Barrie back. *I didn't know*, I told her. *Understood from beginning it was all over.*

But then, obviously, I started cross-questioning myself. Understood? What had Con actually said? By now I couldn't remember word for word, and it came to me I must have jumped to the conclusion. Wishful thinking, I suppose. That evening I showed Con the messages.

"But still, you gave me to understand," I whispered. "You did lead me to think . . ."

"I know. And it's been ripping me up inside. I can't believe I misled you – whatever it was I said came out before I could think, and then I was in this box: what to say to you to put it right? Mind you . . ." He paused. "This is exactly what she does, twists things so people end up distrusting each other. But. Enough of that. I've no interest in making her look worse, and the truth is I was so dead wrong. I let you believe . . ." He was silent a minute before continuing. "Look. I was afraid. You're . . . like Sunday-School-proper. Right? And I thought you'd look at me . . . the way you're looking at me now." He closed his eyes and turned his face away. "I was wrong, Cyn, so wrong, but I thought I'd lose you."

He groped for my hand, but tentatively, as if sure I'd draw away. "My love, I'm not a saint, and I won't pretend I was honest with you about my status at the time, but don't hold it against me. I knew that marriage was through, and I wanted you so . . . I thought I'd explode." Then he tugged me to him and buried his face in my hair, his anguish as well as the feel and smell of him driving Barrie out my head.

Yet I did draw back. "How could you have led me to believe you were free?" I could barely summon my voice against conflicting shock waves – outrage and blind enthrallment.

"Shhh!" he said. "I was afraid, I tell you. And it's all behind us now. Forgive me."

For what could be done at that point? And stacked up against it — this good, good man, not to mention gifted, sparkling. Irresistible. So, yes. That had been this awful lapse we could do nothing about now, and there was no holding out against the passion that had driven him in the first place, let alone against the remorse afterwards. After all, that divorce was through now, and we were married already. Barrie was going to have to deal with that. Caught up and swept along, I wiped her from my thoughts. There was only room in them for Con.

From our first encounter, there was this . . . *this*. I can't word it, can't define it. He set off in me — I don't *know* — like a chemical reaction or an electrical charge, magnetic force, power surge — whatever cliché. Everything else in me locked down before this overwhelming all-enveloping rush.

"Only I have to know nothing like that can ever happen another time," I managed to get out.

"How can it? Look. I can only swear I'll never mislead you again," he replied, catching up my fingers to his lips and kissing them one by one. Reverently.

I know a vow when I feel one.

And he meant that, for then he went on to tell me other stuff he need never have revealed. "I will never hide anything from you ever again," he swore.

There had been . . . someone. When life with Barrie got unbearable, yes, he had got involved in a brief — call it a fling then. They went out a couple times, but he stopped it before it developed, because he was determined to save his marriage. Then, although Barrie hadn't shown any such restraint, she pounced on that to use against him.

Aah. The photos, I recalled, not that I had noticed anything especially compromising about them.

"Exactly," Con said. "Nothing I did called up the hell she put me through. But then, nothing I've done makes me deserve you. I guess people rarely get what they deserve." Then there was only his whisper, breathing my deepest thoughts. "What we have now feels too good to be real," he said. "Like some dream." Not original thoughts, no, just the commonplaces we innovated warm and glowing as if we were forging them for the first time, time and time again. So we put the unpleasantness away and gave ourselves up to our own life, deliriously happy.

For a while.

Then, Barrie again. *Did he ****ing tell you he can't father a child?* Her message came about a fortnight later, and I was disgusted with her.

Certainly, I responded. *We don't lie to each other.*

Except about marital status, Barrie concluded. *GFY.* Which kind of put the lid on the conversation, such as it was.

Later I found out that he messaged Barrie. She forwarded it to me without comment. He'd said: *You wrecked my life before. Once is enough. Keep away from my wife or I'll wipe you out our lives myself. For good.*

"This was crazy." I showed him what she'd forwarded. "How you could say that?"

"You know that was to make her leave you alone," he said.

"Obviously. But what possessed you to threaten her? And – my God – in writing? And she's a lawyer?"

He was ironing a shirt with his usual level of meticulousness I could never flog myself to achieve, and he barely looked up. "Just delete whatever she sends you without reading it, love," he returned.

I tried to tell him he was playing into Barrie's hands, but he insisted the problem was my communicating with that harpy.

When I stared at him, he said OK and rested down the iron. So he'd made his own mistakes, he admitted. "But you have to understand Barrie's not only a very sick woman but an evil one." That stopped me. "In truth," he continued. "Beyond anything you can imagine. It's not something I say easily, but she makes mischief compulsively. She's like an engine, a contrivance for churning out misery." He left the board to come sit beside me and ran his forefinger along my cheek. "I need to ensure she makes no trouble for you, and the easiest way is by frightening her off. Listen. I have records of her visits to counsellors, as well as a referral to a psychiatrist and the copy of his prescription."

Right. As head of a mental health organization, he would know the ropes. He could prevent her from doing further damage, he said, but I had to accept it was better for all concerned if we just steered clear. On no account was I to entertain any further contact with Barrie.

I'm not clued on the obedience thing, but I saw his point. I blocked every connection with her.

Or so I thought.

But months after our trip home to Trinidad – a tweet. Then tweet delete. But it had flown in and I'd seen it already, a snide remark about clueless little wives and a photo I'd glimpsed before.

I dismissed it to begin with, yet that old picture brought fluttering back a vague unease I'd managed to smother. It had to do with timeframe. Those photographs connected with Barrie's case for divorce had seemed harmless, but irrelevant too – not only long before I met Con but a couple years in advance of their divorce. If they proved anything, why hadn't Barrie acted earlier? Con had said that flirtation ended almost before it began, while Barrie was too busy with her own affair to care. So then, what eventually got her going? And what would prompt anyone to dredge up a set of pointless photos now?

Something intangible unsettled me so much I picked up the phone. With a sense that I was about to rake up muck that would do nothing for me, I called her.

I've got to say the timbre of Barrie's voice disarmed me when I heard it first. It reminded me of Con's, and for a second I wondered if she had practised copying him – a voice deep and soft like it could wrap itself around you and keep you safe. It was a direct, convincing voice too – refined, unlike her messaging style, a voice that wouldn't set off a tremor of doubt. The thing was, I had called so as to work out an uncertainty of my own.

I made a hash of it. How could I word what I hadn't been able to think out? I managed a confused question to her about how the photos could mean anything, dated so long before she filed, and her tone hardened.

She whipped back. "You think those photos captured his only betrayals?" The sneer grew almost palpable, as the velvet in her voice coarsened to steel wool. "The man's a slagger. After a while his womanizing is in your face. Wait for it. He's a machine: the charm's a mechanism for consuming women like you, bright but naïve. You say he was open about his probable infertility, but did he tell you how he found out? No, don't go yet: this part's too good: some woman asked him to contribute sperm at this clinic where she wanted to conceive. A hunk like Connor should be a sure thing, right?" I tried to hang up but couldn't, frozen by her implication that there might be some child of Con's out there. "He found the request gratifying – except it then emerged his count was low.

"Never underestimate macho neuroses," Barrie continued. "I was there when one of his friends baited him. Heckled, I think you'd say? Anyway, a couple years into our marriage we met up this Trinidadian in Italy, and the *pardner* – so Connor had greeted him – demanded why there were no kids yet, and taunted him that bad seed was better than no seed. I guess any pardner of Connor would know about bad seed."

My hand slammed the call off without pausing to consult my brain, because what was there to think about? Nothing foul she would stop short of saying about him.

Delusional, was what he'd said – and I'd thought he was overdoing it. But he'd understated. I guessed he was shielding from view the diseased thinking of this woman who'd been his wife. I kind of honoured him for that.

See, I knew very well how desperately Con wanted a child. He'd told me, weeks before on that first trip home to Trinidad, his arms locked around me and his face hidden against my neck. At first Barrie had refused to consider having a baby, but he understood it was part of her being so messed up, only it turned out she was manipulative as well.

He admitted a bit sheepishly that, to begin with, he'd thought there'd be nothing to persuading her. She'd give in because there was no resisting this natural, compelling drive in any woman's make-up. Yes, yes – so he tripped up on the stereotypes, but also, *also* she tapped in on and *used* his own natural yearning for a family, his own mindset about gender. She began bargaining for this trip to Italy: she promised when they got back, she'd go along with him to the clinic.

So he and Barrie actually began the IVF process, and there he was, committed to this thing, when – abruptly – she cried off. No lead-up, no explanation. Embryos ready, and she deserted him and them – would hear nothing further about it. And now, *now* it was too late for him. He paused. "Except, well, in a way the child's actually there. Waiting."

Something cold crawled across the skin at the back of my neck. True. Like clammy little fingers. Spread then regrouped and skittered down my spine. I went dead still in his arms, then felt myself shrinking away.

"Don't. Don't flinch from me. Cyn, oh God, don't you turn away too. You know I'd never ask you to do anything you were uncomfortable with."

In a while we got back to where we'd been, and the trip passed well. Understatement. To be home in Trinidad, with Con? Ecstasy.

But he did return to the subject once we got back to Sydney after the '06 visit – little by little, as if were being torn from him. "I can't expect it of you, and it's OK. I just want you to know how the idea could even occur to me. I'd never been part of a tight family like yours, and here I was on the brink of having *a child*. I don't expect I can ever have any other." He cupped my hands in his, staring at them anxiously – like they were something precious and irreplaceable that could slip through his fingers any time. "That's all I'm saying."

Con tried to leave it like that, he did. But whatever he was doing or talking about, the pain and yearning in him was heavy in the air. A week or so afterwards, he couldn't help wondering whether – considering what we were to each other – I couldn't at least give it some thought. Was it that outlandish, the idea I might accept and bear that one child that could be his? The embryos in storage were his. Entirely. One of the terms of the divorce had been that Barrie signed them over to him absolutely. No, it was nothing she'd resisted, because – he knew I wouldn't believe it; he'd hardly got his mind around it either – she'd never wanted children anyway. She claimed she had chosen to remain child free, as she called it. What the hell was that? Child free?

He sat on the living room floor with his knees drawn up as if he were pinned in a mesh he could not claw out of. I walked past and looked through the window, but he didn't get up, didn't move. So I turned back and sat on the tiles beside him.

I gathered my resources to talk calmly, so he wouldn't pick up how much the idea had put me off. He wasn't, as I'd thought, accepting of his infertility: he was obsessed. But wasn't that a condition of a sort? I had to spare him my immediate reaction, the rawness of it.

"Listen," I told him softly. "So now, I'm done freaking out. OK? All I want to know is why you didn't just suggest the obvious. We do our own thing. Go to a clinic of our choice and begin from scratch."

"Cyn," he whispered. "You don't get it. The procedure is prohibitively expensive. So, just write off this huge investment and start over with it a couple years later when the price has probably gone up as much as my chances have gone down?" I couldn't hide my reaction to that, and he stopped, gritting his teeth, clenching and unclenching his fingers. "Oh God, no. No. Wrong answer. I'm sorry, Cynnie, I'm so sorry." He slapped his hands over his face for a few seconds. When he dropped them, his eyes were full of understanding, his voice unsteady with regret. "I can't believe I said that as if it was something to put a price on. Cyn – *darling*, of course I'd prefer it your way. It's just . . . time lost is gone."

I suppose I went on studying him as if he were a stranger, for he unravelled his limbs, got up and trudged away to sink into a nearby chair.

"Come," he said. "*Come.*"

When I went over, he drew me to him, clasping his hands on my neck and running his fingers along my throat to turn my face up to his. "Of course it's not just the money. Listen. I know you want your own child. Naturally. But I see this as . . . this *would* be yours, Cyn, from your body. It's the only way it really can be both yours and mine. Don't forget, my count has dropped farther by now, and while we spend precious time on an off-chance – remember, your clock is ticking too. But. No, I'm not going to push you into something you obviously find repellent."

He stood, pulling me up too, pressed his lips to my forehead and backed away, palms up. "OK? So I won't mention it again."

In the end, I did. The following night I pleaded with him to visit another clinic I'd identified. "One year," I insisted. "Let's at least give us one year."

"Another count?" His arm, crooked and upraised, elbow out, staved it off. "And with another set of people? I'm not rebuking you, I'm not. I know you can't imagine what this sort of thing does to a man, but it's more than that. What? All that's gone before just keeps on parallel to the new venture? Or what do we do with the embryos we have? Terminate? I mean *kill* them? Or just keep their little souls there in limbo indefinitely? Wait. No. You need to stop worrying about this altogether. You had no part in getting it going. I'm not about to drag you into it."

And he never mentioned it again, only headed off every effort I made to reintroduce the subject.

I felt like a beast.

I came to a point, worn down by this gentle reticence, I suppose, when I began to think it might be something I could contemplate. But if Barrie, the biological mother, objected, was I about to thrust myself into the middle of what had been the most intimate and agonizing issue of Con's former marriage? On the other hand, I was reluctant to open up the wound between Con and Barrie by pushing him into contact with her. This was barely a year into our marriage and since their divorce. Besides, any response from her would tempt him to raise the whole matter of ownership, and that was not what it was about. My decision had nothing to do with property. It rested on whether Barrie saw herself as the sole and incontestable mother of those embryos regardless of whether she'd ever wanted a child or not.

I had to speak with Barrie in person.

⁓⁓

I glanced around the coffee room she had suggested for the meeting, taking in its spotless linen, gleaming china and fresh flowers, then back at the woman I'd come to see.

Barrie was a good eight inches taller than me, more slender, more poised and a lot more chic. Grey slacks with a turquoise blouse of Italian silk. Grey shoes with pointed toes, but of leather so soft they must be cherishing her feet. Perhaps because it was Saturday she looked more like a model than a lawyer – except for her eyes. They were still but keen, collecting everything, giving nothing away.

She was not what I expected. She spoke gently and reasonably – I wondered whether she had taken something to cool her down. But she was clear on the fact that she had no comfort to offer and certainly no moral release or whatever I was asking her for. She'd never wanted children, and had married Connor happily when he said he didn't want and couldn't have them.

Then her tone sharpened with resentment. He'd inveigled her. Later, when she found the marriage falling apart, she refused to go further with the IVF. But it was more than that. She paused, but I refused to ask, so she went on anyway. The point was, he'd turned out to be – her words – *a horrible man*. So no, she said. It was not all right with her for me to bring into the world any child that Connor had contrived and meant to live with and to shape – because he was unfit.

You know when you can't believe your ears? "*Unfit?* For what?" I demanded.

"Where does one start?" She contemplated me absently, apparently calm again, and when she went on, her voice was cool, collected. "Unfit to exercise authority over anyone. Unfit to be on the same planet as a child. Unfit to ★★★★ing live."

I managed to pick up my keys and stroll out with my best unconcerned look pasted to my face. She didn't seem to notice I was going. But her reaction – the violence of it radiating from under that front of serenity and reason – had shaken me right through. I simply hadn't grasped how twisted and vengeful the woman was, even though Con had tried to explain. Nor had I fully realized how far I had bought into the idea of bearing the child. Now I went cold at the thought that I'd actually considered it. What if I hadn't checked Barrie's reaction? What if I'd gone ahead with Con while living in the same city as Barrie?

But one week later I was thinking – what if we could move somewhere else?

If we could only go home. Just like that it flooded over me – this yearning to get back where I belonged.

"Con, why don't we?" I ran my fingers through his hair, tugging his head so he would look around at me. "This isn't your home either. It's true we'd make less money in Trinidad, but we could afford a family of our own. Can't we just move home, or even somewhere, anywhere else, far away from Barrie."

He said, "You only have to ignore her." Then he froze, studying me. "You've been in touch with her again, haven't you? She's poisoning you – you can't see it? What it is I have to do to keep you away?"

I was sick of being told who I could or couldn't talk to, and I snapped, "Move away with me."

"Stupidness."

It blew up into our first real quarrel, and afterwards he must have called Barrie himself, for the next day she phoned me.

"Change of heart," she announced crisply. "Better you than who knows who. Go ahead with the goddamn embryo. And you know what? He'll be after you for another in no time, so tell them to pop in two while they're about it."

12

TWIN STATES

—

CYN'S VOICE, WHICH I'D BEEN SO painstakingly restoring in order of the dates on notes or messages, blew apart in my head, discharging a barrage of splintered thoughts. Micah and Melody? I clenched compulsively, crushing between my fingers the paper with her more recent jottings.

There I stuck for a while, cowering from what must come next, the icy dread of reading on creeping along my skin and prickling my scalp.

In a while I pushed away from the desk and got up, steadying myself against a bookshelf. I made my feet carry me to the window. The light in the backyard illuminated the mango tree. It rendered ethereal Mrs Mendez's white Persian picking her way elegantly from next door along a low branch that crossed the fence, before sitting to commence an elaborate toilet. I glanced around automatically, and there was Philander on the grass beneath, his head raised, eyes soulfully intent on Mystique's ablutions.

The ache in my fingers distracted me, and when I managed to focus on my hands they were cramped from gripping Cyn's notes. My mind ached more at the thought of analyzing further, let alone inscribing. The bin beside my desk beckoned. If I stopped here I need never know. I tossed the wad of papers away.

But then *I would never know*, so I snatched them up again. I smoothed them out, folded then smoothed them again while trying to take it in, trying to keep it out, even while knowing I'd go through the papers again and again searching for an alternative conclusion. But then I blundered on through the little wad of papers only to encounter a printed message from Barrie to Cyn, way out of order chronologically, and it was one prolonged rant:

O God make him stop this. I never believed he'd ****ing do it but now I know I'll keep away why would I want to be in contact? You got it wrong, ****ing wrong. He distraught? You don't know what it is to be alone locked in this goddamn sewer and if even out the room nowhere to go, day after day empty. Was glad you had your own babies, honest I was. So much better that way. As for embryos, get it in his bloody skull – IDC.

Thank God, my mind soared. Hers. Her own. Cynnie's.

I never interfered with you or even saw you before you asked to meet about the embryos. Never meant you harm or tried to hurt you, and you let this [blotched] to another woman? I tried [blotched] to your scream for help was what it was even if you don't realize. Get me out will stay the hell clear of you both. It's all I want. I never thought he'd turn on me like this, blank out my life, lie to colleagues clients neighbours in street, they look at me like Im filth. You cant believe I hurt Chase on purpose. ****! The children's dog?

There was more, but right there – stapled to that part of the page – was another, an undated note in a different font:

There was that day while we were on holiday, driving along a steep road overlooking the sea, and the dog in the way paused and looked up just before we hit him, and I heard myself wailing, "Stop. Stop the car. We have to do something."

"There's nothing we can do." Con turned his eyes to me, away from the rear-view. "Nothing to be done." He stopped a few minutes on, where the road was straight for a while, and put his arms around me, calm flowing from him and folding me in. "Poor thing. I didn't see it." When I raised my face to him, his eyes were dark and his mouth twisted before brushing my forehead. "At least it was fast."

We drove on in silence for a while after, and I turned on the radio. It may have been forty-five minutes or an hour later I asked, "But how you could be sure it's dead?"

And he said, sort of absently, "Sure what's dead?"

Then there was nothing else on that sheet and no sign of where it fitted, so I turned back to the email message it was clipped to, the appeal from Barrie to Cyn. I left out the strings of expletives in transcribing. It was no point just blacking up most of the page:

*Poor Chase got in the way when I was trying to back out your gate it's true I should never have been there but I only came to try and make you see. Then that madman screaming about locking me up he ****ed me off and I must have stamped down on the pedal. Hurt a dog on purpose? He knows very well I could never and I swear they could've saved Chase at the clinic if I'd taken him but of course I had to be vilified even at the cost of putting him down. And now even Micah and Melly behave like strangers, what with all the lies poured out about me.*

Then the writing began to break up again, jerky and uneven as if the writer were growing more and more agitated, frantic.

*Imagine this set of thugs swarming into your house, your house that was your mother's home, which they got into because some **** gave them keys so they could lay their filthy hands on and think, think when you try to fight them off and of course you ****ing fight you'd be mad not to they ram this bloody big needle in you drug you drag you off everything swimming blurring you feel yourself fall crashing down and you wake you're in this mausoleum no phone books tablet computer you have to beg crawl suck up to get a chance at email once week. Cant watch news they say lest upset you – UPSET? Like corrupt politicians or assaults in Kings Cross or whatever can upset when you been hauled away caged up after what I grew up with caged up in this ****hole urine on the floor rat crap under the tables nastiness the walls? Upset? For godsake make Connor get me out I'll do anything just get me the hell out they're trying to shut me down now for godsake tell Connor to think what we were to each*

Behind that page was another paper, empty except that across the middle of it, in Cyn's handwriting, ran a scrawled, undated note:

Can't go on with this. God knows the extent of her derangement. Yesterday's phone call proved Con right the whole time, and we were negligent not to have acted before. When they came for her, found knives behind night table beside her bed. And kitchen chopper, they said. My God – who knows what her genetic profile is like.
We just have to get out. Con must must listen.

No way of telling where this last note fitted in chronologically in the rest of the account. Nor could I work out whether there was one hideous flare-up that took Barrie to hospital or recurrent upheaval. Moreover, no further call or message had come in recently from Barrie to the children, not since the one Micah had answered.

But Mattie then. What happened after Cyn underwent her own procedure and had her twins? Secretly (while I took note of how I was hiding more and more from Joel – or protecting him, as I preferred to think) I tormented myself, speculating about whether and how Mattie might be Barrie's.

When I looked up, I met Mattie's glance from a picture on my wall. It so disarmed me that I suddenly caught sight of Barrie, as she might have been at that age, and, then, as she might well be now – a disturbed but devoted mother, deprived of her child, alone in some uncaring hospital from which she might be discharged to learn of the husband she had loved and lost, gone, en route to the other side of the world, his three children disappeared. All one had cared about vanished. Enough to send anyone over the edge.

Then I steupsed in irritation at myself. As if Barrie weren't over the edge already. Con's face lit up in my mind. My own home, with a backyard for children to play, he'd said, his eyes closed as he turned it over on his tongue like brandy. What would Barrie have cared when these three vanished? Child free indeed.

I knew it was well past midnight, perhaps after one or even two, and that I must catch a few hours sleep. But the night, which so efficiently magnifies even trivia, had blown up my mesh of terrors about Mattie to monstrous proportions. *Sleep?*

I was a compulsive three a.m. worrier in any case: how much time I could squeeze aside for the next book, what to cook the following day, when and how Joel and I might die and how the other might hang onto life and why, how I was going to get by without a dog, or manage one at this stage, and whether I really should have snapped at that imbecilic cashier two months ago as I did or just let her impertinence pass. Now all this was erased. No, no, lurking there but blocked – by something infinitely larger and darker: an impending loss so absolute as to defy comprehension. I strained to peer into the murk.

Had Barrie ever had any right to Mattie? If so, could Cynnie and Con have been awarded custody over the course of a breakdown that took Barrie out of circulation? And that confinement – a mental hospital? The thought jabbed at me: Or a prison? What might she have done?

I made my way downstairs to the living room and crawled onto the mattress beside Joel, setting my back firmly against his. I lay there raking my brain with it. Against a cacophony of crickets, frogs, owls and the blasted stray cat, *It* abstracted itself to what seemed a jumble of broken bottle and barbed wire inside me tearing soft tissue. I must have whimpered, because Joel rolled over and held me. Then *It* morphed into a child I enfolded, rocking, somehow absorbing into my body. Only the forceps, then the scalpel probed deep inside, pinched, sliced, gashed – until Joel said *shhh* again, and the gouging slowed, became almost tender. Stilled.

It seemed no time at all before Joel was calling, "I'm taking them."

"Who? Where?" I struggled to locate myself. I seemed to be sprawled on the floor of the living room.

"Children to school. Just wanted to see you were OK."

Right. Because I never sleep late. "You'll be home later when Farley comes to put our bed back up?" he called. "Then he'll transport the last of the other stuff to the townhouse."

"Hugs," I bawled, and the three ran in, crouching to get hold of me then tumbling over and around me on the mattress. "Off to Papa now." I was laughing but trying to catch my breath.

"Later, 'Gator," Mattie threw over his shoulder as he raced off.

~·)|(~·

I talked out the contents of Cyn's desk with Joel later that morning while the children were at school.

As I expected, he was stunned by the revelation that Barrie was Con's ex-wife but showed himself wary about the slightest sympathy for the woman. "She may have suffered," he agreed grudgingly. He did not quite say, *as she should.* "But let's not underrate how dangerous she is. I certainly won't believe Mattie's hers."

"Which brings to mind the clinic – to contact again," I said. "That's about the only source we can look to for answers."

He seemed otherwise preoccupied, and it turned out he was pondering the application for compensation. "And how to refer to That Woman? We can't give the impression of . . . vying with her in any way, much less invite a suggestion of possible cooperation. Nothing must get back that can encourage her." He stuck there, obsessing over Barrie. "She's just waiting for a chink to open up."

I couldn't even write. I settled down in front of the bookcases, one after the other, tugging and patting to bring the spines flush with the front edge of each shelf. Then it caught my eye. Another sandy-looking heap. I jotted an extra note to myself: *termite man.*

By evening, when Joel had come around to the idea of calling Los Angeles the following day, Kevin dropped in to bring our mail and to regale us with news of Tinsel. It turned out that she had inveigled our tenants at Court Augustine to employ her for both Saturday and Sunday each weekend, but she regularly stayed home one or other of the two days.

"But once I don't work, I doesn't expect no money," she argued. "I is not a tief. But ent everybody need at least one day off for the week? I can't understand why people does be too dotish to know that." The couple who employed her stipulated it must be one particular day they should expect her. Let it be the Saturday then. So they could plan their weekend. To which she had replied inscrutably, "Well, I go do me best. My bes' is all I could do."

It was November already, but with no showers lingering or impending. Four months gone, and my glance at the sky had been unconscious. It was that deep blue – not dry-season blue with its veil of dust or fleck of floating ash but an infinitely deep unhindered blue broken only occasionally by floating clouds, white at their tops but underlain by the pale grey that could darken so swiftly and dump rain after all. Still, it had stayed clear long enough for Kevin to get in.

We were beginning to suspect Kevin had no actual business down south but only missed the occasional natter and glass of wine. So he made his way along the Hochoy to San Fernando on whatever pretext came into his head. But we didn't mind. We knew that during and even after his impossible assay on Cynnie, he had remained attached to us. After he left and the children had gone to bed, we pondered the political gymnastics in the United States that came out as *breaking news* – a tautology, Joel pointed out triumphantly. It helped us not to obsess over what our next call to Los Angeles might uncover. Later, while Joel slept, I would rattle around the house adding to my lists.

Meanwhile I cotched on the sofa, turning them over in my head. Inside and outside, so much waited to be done – piled up, mostly invisibly, around me. The hose near the front of the house, less in use now the garden was reduced, coiled brown and mottled with mildew like a decaying snake. Rust that worked its way up through the white gloss paint on the wrought iron along the porch now also gnawed its way down into the cracking terrazzo at its base. Unchecked, it would eventually render the wrought iron work unsafe. I never leaned against any barricade on a height, but who knew what children might do. A glance upward reminded me of lightbulbs to change and, no, neither Joel nor I were braving the ladder unless it was to fetch Mattie stranded on top a cupboard, like yesterday. Nor would I be sending Ena. Francis?

I groaned.

And there was one TV gone dead, and the electric gate turned unresponsive to any remote and fixed on manual until Mr Farley could manage to locate a new gate man, the old one having migrated after his wife's attempted kidnapping. And the blasted pigeons defiling the back steps. More and more pigeons: more and more poop. Next thing – the garden snake hose was fixed to the front tap that had seized up rather than the one nearer the back of the house, so it was no longer an easy matter to haul a hose up the step and point it at the poop from splatter-safe distance. Now it was bucket and broom – a broom that must now not only be washed vigorously but must ever hereafter be designated pigeon-poop broom and labelled so it could never return to the kitchen.

"Hope Kevin made it back north before the rain," Joel muttered, his fingers groping absently for the remote I had surreptitiously slid under the sofa cushion before sitting.

Outside, yes, a breath, a whisper, a trembling of leaves and excited chirping before the soft *shhh* of light rain gathering to a shower. *Whoosh.* Then, stronger, a rush intensifying and deepening in tone, gusting by the windows then rapping at them, pounding the ground and roof, stilling the trees and drenching bushes, a downpour drowning out the other outside sounds as if that was the sum of it, relentless rain on all that might have gone on outdoors and everything now battered to submission.

A crack of thunder echoed, then a long drawn-out pounding that died away as water flooded down the windowpanes and everything beyond them disappeared. "Hope the phone holds out," Joel said.

To our relief we got through to the clinic next day, after our lunchtime to be sure they were open. Then, learning permission had been granted,

I used my card to settle the unpaid bills and arranged a further two months rental of space for the remaining two embryos. They offered a fragile trace of Cyn and Connor, one we couldn't as yet spare the strength to terminate. Besides, they justified ongoing communication with the clinic. If we temporized, perhaps we stood a chance of learning more.

Even as we spoke, I heard the notification chime on my laptop. The clinic had instantly emailed confirmation of payment. The receipt for storage of two embryos referred to some record of an original total – seven eggs (no date recorded), only five successfully fertilized and one of these had not thawed well. Two accounted for Micah and Melody, and that left the two in storage. The math terrified us.

Pointless asking the clinic for the information we urgently needed; it would only make them suspicious. We did ask about dates regarding the original embryos themselves, but even about this the finance officer apologized for the clinic's inability to share private information. They were sympathetic, however. They assured us that they had given the same answer to Mrs Barrie Firaki regarding her enquiries, even though she had registered her willingness to pay rental in the future. "And commandeer them from there on," Joel concluded after we rang off. "No telling what more she has in mind. You see what we're dealing with."

But that was exactly what I could not make out. By now we had tracked most of Cyn's documents without uncovering anything about Mattie, and it was becoming difficult to think in any focused way about anything else.

Later in the afternoon I took my laptop to the porch and, after an hour or so, paused to gaze at the horizon. To one side a huge tree blocked the view inexcusably except that it was a Poui and would in a few months exonerate itself by breaking out in pale pink or yellow (but I seemed to remember pink) for the couple days a year that justified its survival. Nearer, close to the garden pipe that had seized up, lay wire baskets I had rested temporarily on the ground while gathering the will to dump them, now I could no longer keep up with the watering. The remains of the plants had been shrivelling to a mass of gnarled grey-brown roots, but now the staghorns had flung out bright fronds, rejoicing because it had poured so frequently for weeks that they had every reason to suppose the rains would never stop. Beyond them, Boston ferns sprang out from their black mat that thickened almost beneath my eyes, spreading away to choke out a fine ground cover of grey pink leaves and drive their hold deeper into the damp earth.

Closer still, edging the porch, orchids thrust out spears studded with shining hard dark little buds in the moist air that tumbled across. The same wind raised the palms waving in celebration, and beyond, the coconut trees swaying set off a raucous party of parrots. Then, kiskidee, kiskidee, followed by assorted chirps, cheeky whistles, yearning flutes. A rusty hinge. The *flip, flip, flip-ip-ip-ip-ip* of startled pigeons winging away left the electric wires that sagged between pole and house bouncing in the breeze.

The normalcy of the physical world was almost unnerving alongside the tangled paths of our mental wanderings.

There was Mattie, now that someone had mentioned Christmas, suddenly adamant again that Barrie was his mother, not only because she had said so but *because* – a word howled with an exhausted, plaintive insistence that convinced Joel the child was laying claim to her mainly because she was alive.

"They're gone, Buddy," Micah said, wearily but with more patience than he could usually muster. Ena had set up a box of hot sada roti with tomato chokha, along with a dish of tiny fish fried so dry and crunchy as to seem skeletal, so Joel had called Francis and he was to spend the evening. This meant Micah looked forward to monopolizing him. But meanwhile, Micah rumpled Mattie's hair.

"Cynnie 'n' Con are gone, and we were all coming to Trinidad to *get away* from the whole Barrie thing. Me and Melody and the grands are what you got. It's cool we got you. Don't you, like, want *us*?" Mattie threw himself on Micah and clung to him wordlessly, and Micah continued, "Because, if your Barrie's kid, you're not *my* brother, Ratbag."

"I am. I am," Mattie wailed. "I'm your brother."

"Sure you are. Just thought you got tied up there for a while."

I could hear Joel breathe easier, and I resumed shuffling the cards. When Francis came in, we set up the children with the new Ludo board (a jungle version that made sense to Mattie) and settled in another corner to review progress with the Sydney furniture. Just as well they hadn't packed everything off to Trinidad, we agreed. We'd moved out the bed we originally provided for Melody. It had been Cynnie's, but Melody knew nothing of that, so we steeled ourselves to part with it, sending it off to one of the townhouses. In its stead, we set up her parents' bed – with which we felt no connection. I was planning to replace my rocker with Connor's recliner in the living room.

Francis looked doubtful. Mightn't that strengthen Mattie's expectation that his father would arrive to sit in it? And Joel said, "Quite right."

"Besides," Francis continued, "why you giving up your rocker for at this stage of your life?" I restrained myself, knowing he meant well. "It seems Connor left a good bit of his stuff behind, whatever arrangement he had in mind for it," he added. "Put their father's chair in the boys' room where they will see it as something of his passed on to them. It'll have plenty room for it there when you get shot of the extra bunk beds."

We went on to contemplate the fridge with the SpongeBob stickers. I flatly refused to part with my larger and newer fridge, so we decided SpongeBob would remain where he was downstairs on the back porch. Especially with Christmas coming up, I added. This reminded Joel that Tinsel had called in case we needed extra help for Christmas. She wouldn' even charge us her new rate. As is you, she had said.

The phone rang in the midst of Joel's harangue about Tinsel, and he hurried to answer it. But then he called that it was for me. I picked up an inflection of surprise when he realized it was Andrea, his half-sister. Both Patrick and Andrea had called several times since July, but Andrea, so many years younger and brought up in a different household to Joel, had shared far less of his life; so, their conversations tended to run dry. Or she had remained incurably stiff and awkward with him – I could not tell which.

I found myself without any such problem. Andrea and I chattered easily. She was thinking, she said, of how challenging it must be to find oneself a "new" mother in one's late sixties, and she wanted to be of practical help. Could she buy and send clothes, shoes, books – anything at all? Or, what about setting up an account for online reading or study material they might need at school. It was a short step from there to an exchange of views on novels we had enjoyed on Kindle or Nook. Andrea couldn't believe I had only just caught up with *The Handmaid's Tale*, and she reeled out her other favourites. Lovely, lovely woman.

It turned out she was writing fiction too. We hadn't known we were in the same business. Well, of course she'd heard I was an academic so I would have had scholarly publications – but the novel, she said, she was getting it that very night. And of course hers was not out yet, so how could I have known? It was due to appear in the new year.

Why hadn't I known Andrea all this time, I would demand of Joel afterwards, as he waved to Francis from the front door. At that point, though, while I had her on the phone, I merely insisted that she visit. "Come and get to know us better, the children especially. We're into building wholesome family connections for them. What about a stint in Tobago?"

"You never know where I'll turn up. I might suddenly call you from there to join me," she said with a chuckle that was deep, throaty, a little familiar.

After I put down the phone, I realized it had reminded me a bit of Mattie. But his was this long, infectious gurgle I knew well. Then it struck me – no, his was Cynnie's laugh.

13

NOT REMOTELY

"I ALWAYS FELT I WAS MISSING something, not knowing your folks more closely," I told Joel. "Well, your father, yes, I got close to him." Closer than any of them realized. That was unexpected.

In the early 1970s when first we met, Joel's father proved a reserved, undemonstrative man. Kind enough, I soon realized, genuinely glad to see me on every visit; but always, somehow, constrained. Constrained even with Joel, whom he was almost pitifully pleased to see however unable he was to word it. In those days old age was a foreign country. Even my parents never penetrated its borders, so my mind grappled awkwardly with the anxieties that besieged my father-in-law. Still, I knew Papa Roche best towards the end when he was becoming confused and saying things he should not. And my interest in Andrea grew exponentially.

So I was delighted when she called again on December 18 to find out whether my invitation to visit still stood. Joel took the call, shouting enthusiastic confirmation into the phone. "Just as well," I heard her yell back. "I'm on my way to Heathrow." As I could follow their conversation from the next room, I made a mental note that whatever else they might lack in common, they shared genes that compelled them to bellow over the phone.

When he came into the kitchen big with the news, I was able to recite it all calmly. "I doubt whether either of you needed the telephone for communication at all," I concluded, and the twins collapsed in merriment.

Mattie zoned in on the essentials. "Will she bring presents?"

It was an unexpectedly bearable close to such a year as we threw ourselves into preparation that would never have occurred to Joel and me if we had been on our own. Andrea diverted Francis from his growing fixation on the baby Charlene was to have shortly. Charlene neither answered messages nor took calls from him, and he was hurt and uptight. But Andrea helped Francis distract the children with a whirl of activity while I drew them along more quietly in my search for inexpensive outdoor lights and for the exactly right-size ham. They shrugged when I cooed over a lush pot of poinsettias and abandoned me to hang over Ena as she steeped and strained sorrel or filled pastelles to wrap and steam in leaves she had brought washed and cut for the purpose. They hung ornaments while Joel upheld a palm for silence so as to cock an ear for some quatro and shac-shac interpretation of "O Holy Night".

We drove up San Fernando Hill for the view and stumbled on a parang group that set them swaying and clapping. And everywhere – on Indy's porch, under a tree in Jackie's backyard against the disharmonious chorale of dogs penned in the house, or in the kitchen where they clustered around Ena – the children breathed in the aroma of the season. Yes, Cynnie had told them about ginger beer, curried wild meat, punch a crème, and now here were the tastes and smells – new but chiming with familiar words from their mother's tongue. So the season kept them afloat rather than sinking them deep into their parents' absence. In the process they buoyed us up.

"Listen," Joel said. It was Mattie singing softly along to music in the distance, his feet cupped in Andrea's hands. *Do you hear what I hear?* Joel caught his breath. A delightful treble, unlooked for from a child whose mother could barely hold a tune. So the carol service we coaxed them to attend turned out to be a success, because Matts impressed the twins and enchanted Andrea by warbling those songs he knew, whether or not the congregation was invited to join in.

For Joel, Andrea's visit was a revelation. His father had remarried three years after the death of the first wife, while Joel was at university. So this half-sister was roughly eighteen years younger, and they'd spent little time in each other's company. Blue nail polish and extra ear studs a half centimetre or so above the main ones – Joel was staggered. But after some moments' reflection he shrugged and said, "I suppose."

Her outspokenness acted on him like a tonic. When he ruminated aloud on how old we would be when the children were leaving secondary school, she said, "You going to let that prey on you? Watch – if either of you checks out, I'll pitch in. I'll help whichever of you to see the kids through. How's that?"

"But she can't actually mean that?" I asked him later. It was an unbelievable commitment to make. "I mean, who would do that? Promise out years of her life?"

"She absolutely means it. From what I know of her life – that's who she is," he said. "Suspect she'll let us name her as guardian in the event of us both dying or being rendered unfit."

"Why?"

"Why what?"

"What would make her do that for us?"

It was not a completely honest question, and perhaps something showed in my face, for he regarded me quizzically. "Sort of person I seem to find myself hooked up with, I suppose." Then he drifted off to hear Micah's case for fireworks on Old Year's night, before opening up the Médoc Andrea had brought along.

While we were sipping it, she raised the question: Hadn't we ever considered leaving?

"Leaving where?" I honestly had no idea what she meant.

"Trinidad," she said. "You guys really never thought of it?"

"Move?" I asked, genuinely surprised. "You mean – leave the Caribbean?" I turned it over in my head awkwardly. "What for?"

"And where to?" Joel added with a chuckle.

"Don't know where you'd fancy. England for the similarity in educational background maybe; Canada for outlook or lifestyle. But the States perhaps? For the convenience."

"Why would I tote my arthritis to England or Canada?" Joel said. "And now I've crossed the line from pre-diabetic to diabetic – well, pneumonia's even less appealing to me than hitherto. Would have to be Florida or something."

"You needn't get pneumonia. We have shots out there," she responded.

"Here too. Had ours. But yes, I know health care abroad is . . ."

". . . Worth moving for – apart from everything else," she finished.

"But why?" I tucked a bookmark into *The Reluctant Fundamentalist*, although I'd read it a few times and it no longer mattered where I restarted, and I took off my glasses, folded them and set them parallel to the book.

"Opportunities." Andrea tilted her head towards the living room where the children were spread out around Monopoly, Francis whispering in Mattie's ear. "So many problems here," she added.

"Problems everywhere," Joel returned. "Thing is, we're quiet coves. So much in these big places we don't even need." A squeal from inside made him grin. "And at least schoolrooms here don't have to be fitted with panic buttons." After a while he added, "But I admit we have our worries."

"The energy sector sliding, for one," she said, "and the economy with it. What's the future? Perhaps worth thinking about is all." Andrea held out her glass for a top-up and gestured at the book I had put down. "Did you read his recent one? With the portals?"

"And refugees," I answered. "I'm thankful not to be one."

"Anyway," she said, "count me in as far as the kids are concerned." As Joel had foretold, she added that we could name her as guardian if we liked.

Francis turned out to be a bit hurt when he heard. "You should know I would take care of them if anything happened to you guys," he told Joel.

Guys, my foot. But I held my peace while Joel appeased him by pointing out that Andrea was not only well-equipped financially but had dual citizenship – besides being a woman. "Mothering Melody might be a challenge for you. But we know you're there," Joel said, "and that's one huge comfort."

I got away as quickly as I could, leaving them clapping each other's backs.

So there was no hard feeling between Andrea and Francis. In fact, he talked openly to her about Charlene. "No clue where she is now. None." Indeed, Francis and Andrea got along just as Francis had with Cyn, which was comforting and painful at the same time. There wafted over me something akin to memory but more delicate, more elusive – a sensation of what it had been to feel our world secure on its axis, an inkling of normalcy all the more poignant for having been absent so long.

The holidays fled by, and Andrea was off again as "Jingle Bells" gave way to pounding soca music, Christmas Day having barely passed before Carnival edged up with mounting tempo. Yet for us there came a lull in the turbulence that had buffeted us from that night of the tragedy and through the ordeal of Mattie's distress and the circling threat of Barrie's claim to him. A settled order of things asserted itself, so it began to feel natural to plan on resuming whatever might remain of our old lives once we refitted to accommodate the children's. The twins had had their ninth birthday, and Mattie's fifth would be in a couple months.

"Time and past time to get back to Sunday service," Joel reflected. "Maybe take them off to the zoo afterwards."

I nodded. "Enroll them in the library. Then treat them to lunch at Fridays."

Now and then we did (as Andrea had suggested) give fleeting thought to moving away from our tiny corner of the world to a metropolis where we would be more sheltered by the sheer size and organization of such a society – from crime, from the elements, from culturally engrained heedlessness, from inadequate supplies of what we thought we needed, from the sort of foolish government that overtook us periodically. On the porch we would look up from some worrying newspaper headline and out from our small comfort zone of emerald foliage and cerulean sea and sky, cradled by salt breeze, and we would gaze at the horizon and then each other while we reflected: What it really have here?

Besides beauty. Besides each other (and anyway we would be moving together if we moved at all). Besides a way of thought we had grown in.

When we considered all we could have abroad, we did ask ourselves whether Andrea was right, and whether we really were mad to stay. But somehow the answer that fluttered back fitfully was always the same and, oddly, seemed to adopt Francis's voice: Keep your tail home. For the further afield we sent our thoughts the more unreadable the world appeared, the more uncertain the grip of the most developed nations on themselves. Look, China. Huge, civilized from antiquity, technologically advanced beyond our imagination. And over the past weeks (months really) accounts had come in of hundreds suffering from some new flu no one understood.

"Why do we need to get flu shots?" Micah protested.

"Shots?" Mattie asked, his brow furrowed. I drew him close. "A little medicine in your arm so you won't have to cough and cough." Micah stuck his thumb between his next two fingers and jabbed it at him.

"Behave," I snapped. "Matts, what about if we stop and buy Smarties, eh?"

He leaned in, and I could feel healing spread from the sheer sweetness of him.

"What?" Joel's voice. "Thousands?" Reports about China came blurred by vague math and distrust about some town with a name that slid right out one's head, presumably some remote little disorganized place. Joel shook his head. "No. That thing looks bad," he said.

But we were engrossed in getting the children back out to school, and Joel was at last arranging to sort out the cataract. China always had some virus, I argued, and he said, "Yup. It usually gets away too." Still, that was the other side of the world.

"Hoo-ha about some whistleblower," Joel added, his eyes fixed on the set, caught by the issue of how news might escape or be contained. From well before Christmas there had been talk, but we'd paid no mind. Now, as rumour concretized, I asked if he knew anything about this place where it was all happening, and he said, "Nope."

So I Googled it, and held my head at the realization of my abysmal ignorance. Wuhan, the epicentre, eleven million strong, London-sized with soaring buildings, multilane highways and sweeping bridges, high tech, rich cultured, deep historied – ravaged. Wuhan at the confluence of rivers, railways, expressways, grinding to a halt, its streets emptying.

Now cog by cog world news shifted gear but also genre, to sci-fi or fantasy, but not in some galaxy far far away. "What about us?" I peered past the TV and through the front door at the horizon, suspiciously. Commerce, tourism – I tried to engage with what catastrophe in China might mean for us, but it was too vast, too tentacled. Whatever had been spawned must already be on its way through Asia and beyond.

While the great nations discussed, denied, expostulated, our own small country discreetly closed its border to travellers from China, and this *thing* no one understood except that there was neither prevention nor cure. But so what if we were the first in our hemisphere to lock out China? Who out there knew we existed?

"*China*?" Francis was scandalized. "Source of 70 per cent of the world's smart phones?"

I caught a blur of fingers as Joel dismissed phones, wheelchairs, plastics, tea and whatever else that life might hang upon from China. He glued himself to local as well as international news. "I notice I don't have to duck into another room to catch a report now," I said, as he and Francis pitched from screen to screen – television, tablet, computer, phone, so we were sucked out of ourselves through glass into one baffling scene after the next.

"No Carnival." But then Joel heaved a sigh.

"As if!" I jeered.

"Nah, nah!" Francis objected. "People going say, *We ting.*"

"Tourists going to flood into the country and wind on our own set of party animals then fly out and leave us with their blasted flu. Mind you," I added, "they'll get it too."

"They'd have to have it in the first place for them to bring it in," Joel reminded me. "But then off they go, home to their well-equipped health centres with every conceivable comfort and treatment," he continued. "Where's that leave us?"

Consequences: even trivial decisions fraught with outcomes inevitable or random, often out of all proportion to one's actions. On screen the ad said, *Life comes at you fast.* Take in front, we say here. But most don't bother with precautions. "Nah, nah, nah. Don't take it on." I could hear in advance the usual cheery dismissal.

Abroad too. Always some new seasonal flu, world leaders reminded the public, usually more distressing than Corona. Cases were mild mostly, of course, more serious to adults over sixty with other conditions. But then everything was more serious to the elderly.

Hold on, though, I reflected as the little droplets of information trickled together. Back-back a little: that was *us*.

"Nah. Ent you guys done take your flu shot?" Francis said. "And you not tied to no office hours. You just steer clear of crowds, or whoever don't seem too wholesome."

Not flu, I reminded Francis. Nothing we'd had shots for. "There *are* no shots."

A clatter of footsteps, squeals and a sharp scream. I was hardly out my seat when Micah burst out onto the porch.

"Mama, it was not my fault, I was only throwing up the ball, I kinda missed the hoop and the ball wacked the coconut tree. I know something jumped down into the mango tree, and I was going to see what when this humongous green lizard raced down the trunk and across the yard, so I followed it."

"Chased it," Mattie corrected him.

"*Followed.* Only he ran inside, I mean fast you couldn't see his feet move, and well, he was right by the step —"

"So he ran away from you upstairs," Mattie interrupted.

Melody summed up calmly. "And now there's this big iguana in your study."

I stood frozen a good two minutes. Then I said, "When this is sorted out, you'd all better be sitting quiet, quiet over your homework."

"I did my homework already," Micah said virtuously.

"Find more to do," I shouted at him before Joel managed to tug me inside.

"Before it makes itself too at home," he suggested over his shoulder, crooking a finger at Francis to summon him along.

"You see me?" Francis muttered. "I ent no lizard person."

After a delicate and lengthy eviction process, we made sure all the outside doors were locked. "All this talk about people infringing on animal habitats," Joel remarked. "This one was moving in on us."

"It was Micah who bothered him," Mattie objected. "'sides. He was probably living here before we came."

"Right," I agreed.

Micah nudged Melody, who said, "So we can have TV now?"

I took a brief glance before surrendering the remote. From the other side of the world yet intimately in our living room, exhausted faces caught and held our gaze: doctors and nurses in masks and ponderous suits, bewildered patients overflowing hospitals, scientists shaking their heads. No known antiviral therapy. As graphs for positive cases tilted steeply uphill, what rendered the numbing numbers real were almond-shaped eyes shadowed by tragedy and exhaustion, their natural shape widened by shock. Faces haunted and haunting.

[Must highlight these notes for a rethink, lest later some sensitivity reader warns me of racist description. Mind you, my eyes too are narrow, gently slanted, pointed at the corners. Those on the screen could be my eyes, but for their tears – which make it harder to disengage.]

In the hurly-burly of trying to keep up with momentous but faraway emergencies, we lost hold on our own routines. Payments for cable and wireless slipped off our shortlist, and the Friday before Carnival, Joel shouted, "What's wrong with the remote?' Then he checked his records. "Cut off," he groaned, hurling the gadget at the sofa as the outside world blanked, leaving us to local channels that piped in the noise and colour of the street, the tent, the pan yard and determined revellers, local and foreign.

"Small ting." I had much more to think about – like Mattie coughing. Our open lifestyle let so much float in. As the dry season wind picked up, we turned fans against the windows to blow against dust before it filmed surfaces and set him off. We wiped the furniture down with oil and vinegar to avoid high-smelling cleansers and polishes. I smeared Vaseline inside Mattie's nostrils, closed his windows at night and ran the humidifier along with the air conditioner – infuriating because I knew fresh air was best, but dust rode in on it.

Joel stuffed his own ears with wedges of tissue paper to block the thud of a nearby fête, but there was no stopping the Carnival. Once we would have been on the street with them. More recently, at least we'd have tuned in to follow Rudder or hear Exodus. We'd strain for that glimpse of costume flaring and swirling its mesh of light that bobbed and shimmered round the body. Now this other, competing suspense tugged at us from far beyond our shores, but spreading, and the local channels were, well, local.

All we could divine seemed sun seared, base hammered, mind blown, seduced or bullied into festivity, sated with rhythm, cracked up over lyrics, intoxicated by damp bare skin winding, gleaming, rippling along the notes of stick-on-steel, strung out on the glitter, the thud, the sheen, the gyration and the slick gliding-sliding past of bodies possessed by kaiso. Heedless of constraint. Contemptuous of it.

"Then what?" I demanded of Joel. "Like is only the two of us fools taking it on?"

"Taking what on?" Francis had arrived, and Micah was fumbling eagerly with the padlock on the grille gate. "Step back, boy. I go hit it one lash." When he got in he repeated, "Taking what on? Who going to win Road March?" Much he cared about some nebulous thing laying waste the far side of the world.

I was uncomfortable. Far away as it was, it unnerved me that something so deadly could be undetectable. My unease deadened me to the rhythm and colour throbbing around us. As for Joel? "Our boy's in anything but Carnival mode," I reported to Andrea. At the end of January his first cataract surgery had come off at last, but then arthritis had nailed him to the house for days. "The eyes are out of sync, you know, so reading's uncomfortable. And now, just for the couple days, no wireless."

"He didn't want to step across to Miami and do it by laser?"

I counted to five mentally. "Not really. Nor to do it by laser here – as I suggested."

Reconnection immediately after Ash Wednesday brought back the international situation, turning us from our original plan for swift attention to the other eye. "Don't want anyone in my face," he muttered, his tone morose as the downturn of mouth and slump of shoulders.

No use pointing out he'd have healed more promptly from the laser option. Oh no. He had to stick obstinately to the old, less pricey way. Still, I reminded myself this was a minor challenge set against past crises. What hadn't I nursed the lot of them through? Cyn's whooping cough, Francis's fractures, Mom's cancer, and then there was Joel's father slipping through disorientation into dementia.

I had never known either wife – not Joel's mother nor her successor. I'd assumed his father's swift remarriage in the mid or late '50s must have hurt Joel or at least disturbed him. But he said after that first bewildered effort to grasp it, he came to terms. Inevitable, he explained. Looking back, he figured his father didn't know how not to be married. By then, Joel was mostly out the house – boarding in San Fernando near to school. He had little opportunity to know his stepmother or the children for a long time. Then she too died.

Before that death drew him close to his father again, Joel had shown little connection with Patrick and Andrea. From the outset, I'd been aware of an engaging young sister and the slightly truculent brother who was unusually protective of her, but Joel went to the house mainly to see his father, whose eyes followed him ceaselessly. "Says I look like Mom," Joel explained it away. I wondered if Patrick resented it, but Joel seemed not remotely curious about that. Even Patrick's wedding – a shotgun affair that welded two nineteen-year-olds together barely in time for the birth – elicited little comment from Joel. "Harden from small," was all he said. "Doesn't listen to a soul. But I wish him well."

"Should you make an effort to know your brother a bit better?" I'd asked.

Let it happen at its own pace, Joel had responded. He wasn't pushing.

Now, in the same way, the cataract, arthritis, diabetes – whatever presented itself – exacted whatever response his doctors prescribed. Neither shortcuts nor supplements seduced Joel. "You see this instant gratification thing?" He upraised a forefinger severely. "Gobble down fast food? Buy a car because a young fool in some thousand-dollar shades on TV can make it whizz along a winding cliff-hanger road? Dump and replace drapery for Christmas, pay down on furniture, appliances, Carnival costumes, take a loan to jump and wave, jump and wine, drink a rum? Nah!"

"Lord!" I patted his face. "Sour."

"Well, I can't even read *Wind in the Willows* for Mattie," he complained. "Fat lot of use I am."

As the period of healing dragged, he could only hang onto his phone for news of the outside world, harrowing as it was. Nearer at hand, Walters clung there at the other end, desperate as ever for an ear.

Not as rough a Carnival as he'd expected, Walters declared. Did Joel remember, a couple years back, that boldface attack at the fête? Joel signalled me to send the children out of earshot.

"Yes, man."

Three men in camouflage storming in and jostling one couple out from the rest before they start firing. Then the three walked backwards away through the space that opened up behind them. Outside, a woman waited at the wheel of an SUV, revving the engine till they clambered in and roared off. Later, police found the van abandoned, burnt. One resident in the vicinity recalled smoke. It had been black then lightened. Hours later grey blue smoke still rose, thinning, dissipating. No one thought to call and report it, so most attention stayed riveted on the fête brought to a standstill around the dead.

"Usual gang execution," Walters concluded. "Each one. Bullet to the head." Walters was again feeling the heat of crime reporting and phoned almost daily to offload the latest atrocity on Joel or to dredge up one from the past. Mostly, Joel kept the phone on speaker to leave his hands free, but I was too occupied to keep up with Walters' troubles. In running to seal up the place against flying ash from wildfires and the usual dry season dust, I failed to notice what Joel described later as a more than usually frantic tone to his voice. Even in the evenings I'd be juggling my writing and the children's homework against washing and cooking that had outmanoeuvred Ena in the day because of water lockoffs.

"Put in another water tank, you think?" Joel interrupted the international news in his most deadpan voice.

"What's a water tank got to do with all those sick people? Micah objected.

Extra washing ahead, I concluded. But what of areas where no water came through the line for months, or homes with no space to fit a tank if one could even pay for it? And how would the country's infrastructure support life if . . . if this thing . . .

On the television, masks and visors eliminated contrast between faces on either side the screen, shrouded hair texture, elided epicanthic folds, blurred lips and skin colour, so any of us could see ourselves reflected endlessly. This chaos could be reduplicated anywhere. On local channels the prime minister announced his single goal: save lives at any cost.

Afterwards?

Joel tapped the remote and cut off the questions from the media so we could eat supper in peace.

"And when the refinery done shut down," Francis groaned.

"That was bankrupting us anyway," Joel said. "Besides, gotta stay alive for there to be an afterwards."

⇀⁄↿⇀

Our outings tapered off. Up to about a year ago, Joel and I would set off for the occasional late show or function in Port-of-Spain. We'd stop over at the Kapok before breakfast and take a leisurely drive back south. But now, fork out for an extra room if we even found a show that children could attend? "Besides," Joel said, "bundle up in a line or pack ourselves into an audience?"

It was only one more small freedom curtailed. Bandits having broken in on an elderly couple three doors away and tied them up, I'd given up watering my ferns and potted plants at dusk, cool and inviting as it was with the shadows and wafting breeze. What if those shadows materialized into some intruder who forced me inside, more helpless than ever because of three small children at his mercy as well? So the ferns withered.

Yet these were day-to-day irritants, jostled by myriad other prowling apprehensions. Seventy soon, and Joel six years older. New terrain in which death was no longer if but when, illness no longer whether but how. One thing to face it in company, but one by one, anyone likely to be of comfort fell away. A bad dream, rumour, threat to be staved off, yet a certainty closing in – on the elderly and especially those with underlying conditions. Us.

Random new pains in my fingertips forced my attention to my hands, suddenly (as it seemed) closely lined, their veins standing out. The hand gripping the pen seemed less lined *because* it was gripping the pen. The other, relaxed on the left page of the book, seemed more stricken: not the one I'd grown with. Around each knuckle of the stranger's hand sprung suddenly from my own arm, the creases proliferated along the fingers. The nails, clean and trim though they were, showed uneven under the desk lamp.

Blast. I'd have to forego nail polish or stick to clear varnish. Yes, yes, a manicurist could smooth and polish the ridges, but that would eat up time. Time. Too vanishing for varnish. And a beautician, face bent towards me, pausing to sneeze? Peach Frizzle. Plum Glow. Mmm. I spared nail polish a sigh before a line whipped back, *A-tishoo! A-tishoo! We all fall down.*

The children's rhyme, dwindled from a grim medieval memento, swept aside the muddling trivia, and a door in my head creaked open on what I knew of past centuries. I refocused on the five of us, staring down the future. What if need came to lock ourselves in? It would be hard on the children, hard on us to get them through it. Then I realized they would get us through it.

Ena, though. How would she manage? When I sought her out, she replied she could stay quietly in her isolated house as she had up to recently, and now at least she had some funds. For what if she had found herself safely through radiation but without a dollar coming in while her house slid down the hillside? Even now she was at risk. I reminded her that if this thing hit us there could be no travelling back and forth in the crowded taxi.

Penny would go out to buy food, Ena said. "She visiting she brother, but soon as she come home she will make grocery and ting." Penny would be careful. But I thought: Penny could bring it home to you. How to word that?

As for me, bereft of Ena, I'd preserve a few time slots for writing only if I could avoid the kitchen, perhaps buy food now and then. The easier to acquire the more damaging, though, and worse with each new enhancement – batter coated, deep fried, crust cheese-stuffed, cream topped, sugar dusted, butter drizzled, flour dredged, simmered in coconut milk, extra marbled extra flakey extra spicy extra crunchy extra Nexium.

Lap it up, urged American ads. Ignore billowing flames and dragons swooping through the gut and swallow the touted antacid. Flames quenched and dragons brought to heel. Deny the symptoms and gulp down whatever would fade the sign off what was toxic, mute the whisper, dull that jab of warning. Here, too, heedless consumption surrounded me. Doubles for breakfast, paratha and curry goat for lunch. Common fowl curry stew (skin on), deep-fry okra, souse, gulab jamoon, crispy fried pork, pepper roti – all to a chorus of television inducements to partake in beefsteak or ice cream of metropolitan proportions (any single serving adequate to the average family I knew). "See? That's the size burger I want," Micah shouted to the others. "Watch!"

"The chips," Melody objected. "We get two orders, and you have both burgers, and I have two bags of chips."

"Mama, we're ordering burgers?" Mattie executed a somersault while giving a thumbs-up and ended up howling.

"Hmm. Outside food?" From unknown hands. Breathed on by *others*?

So much to consider, evade, search out from chaff, deflecting us from other, persistent emergencies. Barrie? Far away and unlikely to trouble us. Cases of Corona had cropped up in Asia and Europe, so what fool would set out across the world now?

China having shut down city after city, world leaders and commentators shook their heads over ruthless tactics. But even with China locked down and locked out, it was too late: contagion was sweeping the world softly, invisibly but all the more deadly for that – through Asia, Europe and America. Closing on us.

⁓⁝⁝⁓

I stared from the porch above the children and those bubbles that managed to waft up despite overenergetic shaking of the wands. The gulf seemed choppy, though I could not make out waves so far away. Waves. Pestilences had come in the past, wave upon wave, each crest more tumultuous. Yet now, all the time, from oceans around the earth, cruise ships disgorged their revellers, some frightened but healthy, others infected, infectious, infecting. And more boarded eagerly.

Suddenly the prospect of being isolated on a small and powerless island seemed less unnerving, almost reassuring. Only, with our economy already compromised, whatever drifted in could overwhelm our health system. Even regular dry season dust was hard enough to keep out.

"Knock knock."

Joel and I grinned as Micah called to Melody outside the living room door.

"Who's there?" she said patiently.

"Barry."

Joel flinched and glanced at me.

"Barrie who?" Melody asked, suddenly alert.

"Oh, barry anyone you like. My doze is too blocked to cub to the weddig."

They bickered and shoved at each other as we moved out of earshot, Joel kneading his stomach absently.

"Weeks since we heard anything from That Woman," he muttered, his other hand feeling for the remote before slapping it sharply on his knee to wake it up.

"Months," I corrected, totting it up with my face turned towards the screen while making a mental note to buy batteries before we got cut off from the news.

Wash hands, wash hands, wash hands. As Ministry of Health videos demonstrated the twenty-second lathering, the children crowded into the living room to watch, Melody explaining how people who were symptom-free could pass the virus on. Micah cast a covert glance at Joel and me and added, "'specially if older people have chest problems or diabetes. Well, other stuff. . ." His voice trailed off uncertainly, and Melody concluded, "Not bread, dairy and stuff Mama couldn't eat, though. That's nothing to do with Corona."

They stared at the TV cartoon on social distancing. "What about school?" Micah asked hopefully.

"Once we stay two metres apart," Melody said.

"What's *twometres*?" Mattie piped up.

"Like − you gotta have six feet," Melody replied.

Mattie's eyes widened. "Like a insect?"

And Melody held her brow while Micah and Joel shouted with laughter. For we could still laugh.

Yet it was sidling up. Unwillingly I registered it grappling onto my thoughts: what if this thing reached us here? And wasn't it inevitable?

"Oh, don't say that," Francis objected when he dropped in later.

He was coming to us more often now he had reduced the liming after work and on weekends. He'd adopted his most soothing voice. Say it, of course, I insisted. Word it as it is, as it may be. He shook his head and went on to talk of everything except what lay ahead or, at least, barely offshore.

"Charlene must have had the baby by now. How she can't realize I would want to know whether they alive or dead?" Then he suppressed that too, to talk of nothings. "We going get through OK, man."

But small and helpless here, I argued on wordlessly inside, compared to the great nations, naked. I scoured my mind and came upon Andrea's advice only weeks ago. I felt hunted, all of a sudden privy to that urge to run for cover elsewhere — somewhere larger, richer, bristling with technology. We'd scoop up what we needed along the way. But where to? Moving abroad took years of planning, applications, interviews — too late to think of. A waste of energy looking back to probe choices ossified by time.

We must gather wit and strength to dig in right here for as long as it took.

14

PESTE

OVER THE NEXT DAYS, THE LOGISTICS of hunkering down took me over. For if it were a hurricane in the Caribbean, wouldn't we stock our houses and batten down? Well, apart from those holding storm fêtes, and laughing: "Storm? Leh she come." Perhaps only I would batten down.

But this was not a hurricane; it was immeasurably worse.

I had been there. Writers of past centuries had taken me to far places unknown to almost everyone around me. Among these narratives wove guided journeys through hell. Figurative or actual, spiritual or physical, they opened on vistas of graphic suffering. Some landscapes of death loomed vivid in their grisly detail, and now, just as it swept through my head from Boccaccio, Chaucer, di Tura, Clyn, Shakespeare, Nashe, Defoe, Woolf, Camus, Porter, I could see it swiping our way – that scythe that felled old men young girls chubby infants labourers kings scholars sinners saints, all sickening, suffering, dying by scores, by hundreds, thousands. Millions. I pushed back the images of buboes, pustules, bleeding and suffocation, stuffed away unthinkable details behind the glowing fact that each wave had passed at last and a new changed world dawned. Only, all I suppressed waited in the dark for me to drop my guard.

I tightened my grip on the facts that there would soon be medication, vaccination and all too much information, but people were people, by turns dismissive or hysterical. I closed my eyes and watched the procession pass.

Is it only the stuff I've read surging clear in my mind, I began to wonder, or am I indeed clairvoyant, as they say? Or is that what clairvoyance is – flashbacks that cast up foreshadowings? Besides, to see beyond the nightmare may be to glimpse its recurrence. Gradually the rising number of cases crests then ebbs, and we breathe relief. But always that second wave backs up before it crashes down on the complacent, a tsunami that not even the most powerful would resist. And us? Here? Wouldn't we be utterly submerged?

In the shadowy parade of images from the macabre, a cowled form raises a bony finger and whispers one word: *Prepare.*

I can do that. It is one of the things I do best. I begin by supposing, throwing my mind along a narrative that bolts into the future. I can start anywhere in this narrative, because there is no plot as yet, only a setting and characters. Suppose. Suppose a kink in some supply chain through other stricken countries prevents some necessity from reaching us? Something like Mattie's Ventolyn. Or what about Janumet, Brillinta, Nitroderm? Or food. Rice? Wheat? Our country does not feed itself.

The children: potatoes, pasta, chicken, fruit juice — I jotted down what might keep them happy while spinning my mind over the rest of it. If they got it, they might never know they had, but Joel and I —

And who would care for them if we were picked off? Andrea might be quarantined on the other side of the Atlantic. Francis? Hmm.

Every possibility triggered developments of its own until the borders between story and life faded. As usual Joel and I arrived, together, at the same conclusion without even consulting each other: the minute news came of our first case, we would take the children out of school.

But getting serious too obviously would provoke disapproval or, more likely, ridicule (which would irritate the hell out of me), so we'd make each step privately. I arrived at my own formula: overkill or die. As usual exaggeration crystallized a discernible point of departure, and I set up a new list.

⁓⁄⁊⁖⁓

At the same time, we could not afford to shift attention from other fronts. I did expend some thought on Barrie. In the current circumstances, our fears about her began to seem blown up, her very existence illusory. Perversely worrying as this was, it brought relief that the children had settled into routines that pushed her further to the realm of the insubstantial. Mattie found it a huge adventure to rake up the leaves that whirled down everywhere, and Micah was glad to supervise him. The inconvenience of lockoffs had prompted Melody to take on the job of policing water tanks, rapping on the heavy plastic and listening with stern attention. I turned my mind to shopping, for essential medication and food, including chicken for Ena to clean, bag and freeze.

So Barrie's next phone call shocked me, because I'd set her aside, but especially because it was to my mobile. When it rang I fumbled for it in my purse.

"Mrs Roche? My name is Barrie." Instantly my finger jerked to shut down the call – automatically, as if the finger bore no connection with me. I couldn't believe I'd done that. I stared at the phone as her voice resounded briefly in my head, not harsh or belligerent, as I'd have expected, not even the crisp, businesslike voice on the phone message we'd had about Mattie, but soft, almost sad. A throb of longing. Where from?

I looked back at my phone log for the number. No area code, only a seven-digit number beginning with 660. Barrie was phoning from Tobago –

Cold, suddenly, causing me to glance at the sky. I'd experienced hail once, and it was like that, the sky shattering and raining down on me in shards so sudden and unrelenting it took a while to gather my wits even to dive for shelter. This time when I did regroup, I barely stopped myself from hurrying off to tell Joel about the call. His acid reflux had surged back more ferociously than ever, and what if it wasn't the usual heartburn but some ulcer gearing up to rupture? But I wouldn't have told him anyway before calling her back, because he would have been dead against it, and I had to get back to her, to find out what she was about.

Only, when I called, the number rang and rang. I Googled it with *Tobago hotel*, identified the hotel and found an alternative number. Then the charge on my cell ran out, and I shifted to our landline. In my study it was one of those old, old phones with the dials. What's that still doing here, Cynnie had asked, and Joel had defended me: "It works. Like your mother and me."

Cynnie gone, and Mattie now, Barrie had come for him. But what could she be about? Could she mean to take him, board a plane and fly, connections through one infection-ridden airport after the next to God knew where, in the middle of this gathering storm – worldwide – of suffering and death. My hand shook as my forefinger sought the little hole to turn the dial again. She wouldn't, an intelligent woman. Only, even now, with plague-laden ships locked out from ports and floating aimlessly, there were new passengers boarding other vessels for cruises. Still, wide-eyed and sightless. So many people in denial. A mad woman might take him out there into that, she might take him.

My thoughts spun wildly with me pinioned in the eye of the cyclone. Fly to Tobago, then, and try talking to her face to face? Lie to Joel and go, so as to dissuade her? Board a *plane*? When I came back, I wouldn't be able to enter the house, couldn't expose them. But Cynnie was gone, and what to do to keep Mattie?

It bloomed in my mind like a flame: *I am bound upon a wheel of fire* — a line that had lived in my head for over fifty years without a matching sensation. Until now.

I reached into my glass, my fingers trembling as I fished out a bit of ice and got it on my tongue. Then I dialled again and left a message about Mattie's state of mind, about his asthma, begging, *begging* her not to call the landline where he or anyone else might answer but to talk to me instead, only me, and as soon as she could. I promised I would take her call. It was after I sent the message that I wondered whether acknowledging Mattie's anxiety had provided evidence against us as custodians. But it was done.

I can't recall what I expected her to say. All I remember was how the thought of hearing her again clutched my chest, tightening it as if to lock her out, lest the whisper of her might sweep into the house and tear away everything inside. I got to the fridge for more ice and had crunched and swallowed every bit of it before my cell phone, still on its charger, rang again.

What I had not expected was what anyone should have foreseen. She sounded grief-stricken. Her voice, bravely controlled but for the occasional tremor, undermined my resistance. "The last thing I want is to unsettle Mattie." She sounded horrified. "Or to hurt or . . . or endanger any of . . . Please, I implore you — let me stay in touch so you can tell me when I can talk to him."

Implore. Did people say that still in natural speech? How much in that tone of sincerity was an act? I could only strain to catch each fleeting syllable and shade. So I lent my ear, while every inflection in her voice — restraint, compliance, humility, remorse, supplication — undercut the mental fortification I had rammed in place over the months. Through the minute apertures in my reserve welled something like empathy, dilute and grudging but undeniable. In my head, though, Joel's voice said, *You're letting her manipulate you.*

So I asked, "Why are you in Tobago?"

A pause yawned. "That was a mistake." Her voice came low, laboured, but now my response was colder. Crisp.

"*Mistake.*"

She worded my thoughts. "One doesn't find oneself from Sydney to Tobago by mistake. I know. Especially now." I waited in a cold fury. "No, I meant to come," she said. "But I was too precipitate. I felt if I didn't see the children quickly I might . . ."

"Might what?"

"Well. What other interest in life could I find? There was nothing left. I was . . . brought so low." There was a rasp to the voice, as if the effort to draw breath was too much for her. "I had never wanted a child. I never knew before how loving them would change me."

In my head I told Joel that Barrie killing herself would not make things better. In my head he seemed unconvinced; so I tuned him out for the time being. What I said to Barrie was, "Don't do anything hasty that you can't reverse. But you have to wait. You won't do the children good by forcing a meeting now. Besides, you're just off a plane: you're not coming near them."

She latched fast onto *wait* and *now*. "When do you foresee . . .?"

"What are you doing in Tobago?" I burst out. "What are you doing here all of a sudden when you threatened to come before and didn't show and didn't call? How in God's name could you even think of boarding an aircraft? You imagined you would cart away one of the children – or all – on a plane, in the middle of this . . . this . . .?"

"I know," she cried. "It must seem – look, my mind has been too much in uproar to . . . and then, you never returned my call. I guess I thought if I got stuck here then at least I would be near them. Through whatever happened. But by the time I nailed the flight, then actually travelled – even since boarding and my connection got delayed – it all changed, the situation worldwide. God, no, I won't expose them. Since calling you and hearing your message I brought forward the return. I'm leaving for the airport almost at once, because I've had to grab the one seat left. Who knows what's going to happen with flights. Only, you've gotta let me keep contact with you. So I can, like, hear about them. Otherwise

I've no reason . . ." I caught a sound of muffled crying before she cut off.

This number she called from was for a mobile, not the Tobago hotel. She could indeed be on the way to Crown Point Airport and routed back to Sydney, or she could be all set to stay in Tobago indefinitely.

Or Trinidad.

While I was fighting the urge to call her back, that struggle was taken out of my hands by another incoming call. It was Mrs Hamilton phoning to say she had remembered once when Jasmine was talking on the phone and telling the man not to call again, she had called a name that began with F.

Frederick?

No. Not Frederick, nah.

Fazal?

No. Sounded more like Frankie but not a nickname.

"I have an emergency, Mrs Hamilton. I need to go. I'm so sorry."

The draft from the door I ran to when I dropped the phone swept in chill with the blustering March wind. But March so cold? No, the wind had not set me shivering. This was exposure – to calamity creeping closer on every front; it was the peeling away of protective layers of certainty. And it was the blocking of my most secure outlet. More and more I found myself disoriented by all I was keeping from Joel.

Yet even if I approached him to raise beastly questions about Francis, how to blurt it out that Barrie was in Tobago, with Joel's stomach reacting violently to every fluctuation of stress? Even while we were hearing nothing from Barrie, the pain of Mattie's possible abduction had been steadily eating its way through Joel as if, he said, with uncharacteristic detail and drama, whatever was shafting his stomach would lance straight through and issue from his back in an eruption of blood and mangled flesh on sharp steel.

An ulcer then? I kept wondering. He refused to go to the doctor even when Francis badgered him. Who wanted to be in a doctor's waiting room now? The best I could do was mash potato and steam red snapper for him alongside whatever I cooked for the children. Thank God I'd laid in Pantecta, or whatever generic version. My mind forked, and one branch of it meandered along a trail of questions regarding the efficacy of less pricy alternatives to brand name drugs (for what did I know?) while the rest of my thoughts struck off on the separate path of pondering whether anything I did for Joel could be of use if I went on to torment him with an update on Barrie.

What to believe? What was real about parts of my life that had once been clear and substantial? I longed for Joel's certainty, yearned to wrap myself in my old belief in people we had known for decades. Instead, this Mrs Hamilton – about whom I knew nothing – was nudging me towards the inconceivable. Even so, it was not questions about Francis that possessed me, for there was no time to work out Francis, and relatively little urgency. Even as the pace of the epidemic picked up and bore it nearer, here was Barrie at our doorstep. Oh yes, she said she'd leave. But had she? She seemed to hover, howling or sighing round, here, there, a demon, a lost child – a shattered soul.

Was she really gone? Wherever she was, real and imagined, she taunted me with many voices – pleading, accusing, logically debating, threatening, hysterical, lulling, keening – a cacophony of tones, moods, intensities that she controlled with masterly accuracy or lost hold on so they swept in, gale force, with the power to tear Mattie from our arms.

Outside, while great nations stumbled around in the dark, our own government came out with clear warnings against unnecessary travel. Perhaps, I thought, our borders might close. If Barrie really had flown back to Sydney, she should be at a standstill for a while. Enforced social distance, Joel would have added incorrigibly, and I missed the freedom of our exchanges, of him in and out my brain, of uncensored chat.

For now, I had to assume Barrie gone so I could focus on moving forward here. How might we be forced to live?

Apart, the government advised.

With a sense of being exonerated in advance, I set out quietly to buy masks. By the time I had a couple boxes. the verdict came on TV: useless. Droplets from a sneeze would penetrate masks. Besides, not knowing how to manage one, you were more likely to infect yourself. Anyway, health workers would need them.

"Why?" Melody demanded. "What do they need 'em for if they're no use?"

"Well, I got ours already," I said in my so-there voice. "Haven't hogged them, just laid in a couple boxes. In case."

I'd purchased gloves too, but as I was tumbling these into my car trunk along with hand sanitizer, Clorox wipes and Lysol spray, a tall broad man of about my vintage — but too strapping, surely, to be harbouring any underlying condition — grinned derisively and shook his head. I'd slammed my trunk, crawled home and laid my purchases aside furtively. The bathroom downstairs accommodated my stocks in a cupboard I had never fully utilized. I squashed them back against the wall and assessed the remaining space unrepentantly.

As news bombarded us of mounting cases and deaths in the world outside, supermarket and pharmacy shelves gaped bare of masks and sanitizer. Yet perhaps it would not happen here. (Here where God is a Trini. "Corona? Nah. I ent getting dat. I can't get that. Like you forget I is man?") But there it was popping up all over the United States and the United Kingdom, while we had tourists in and out, travelling locals in and out.

Madness. Why were all these fools flying up and down? Behind the cool film of powder I patted over my most untroubled expression before picking up the car keys again, anger began to well up. For God's sake lock them in; lock them out; lock them up.

But then, if our borders closed in truth, how would we live? Even if essential supplies continued as the government promised, what if we found ourselves reluctant to leave the house? What needs might force us out? I picked up a pen and regarded the children sprawled in Saturday morning idleness.

"Are you drawing us?" Mattie asked, running over to look at my paper.

"After a fashion." I tucked the pen through a hole in his pyjamas and tickled him before I began writing.

My list split into multiple columns for different stores. I strolled along the aisles with the paper folded to whichever column pertained, and caught sight of one or two other cautious souls collecting basic items, quietly, against the gentle ridicule or forthright scolding on the media.

"Mama, could you buy a cage, just a small one I need?" Mattie met me at the door as I struggled in with the shopping bags. He held his palms up, parallel, about eight inches apart. "Small like this."

"Ah. And what's it for?"

He regarded me warily. "My caterpillar. I got this big stripy guy. Black and white and yellow. He's got red too. If there's space in the cage, we can have another — to keep him company. There's lots. The tree with the white flowers is covered with them."

Melody held out the phone. She said Ena had sent it for me.

I plonked everything down to pick up Jackie's call. She and Gabrielle had cancelled their airline tickets. "Postponing the move till we can face an airport." She paused. "Listen. We're talking about stocking up a bit." Then she added humbly, "You think we being paranoid?"

The next call was from Indy, admitting that the two of them were ducking out of hotel reservations in Florida, despite the condescending smiles of relatives and sturdy encouragement to have faith. A cousin had offered to take Indy to the malls herself – no need for any taxi, if she was really that frightened.

"What's it like out?" Joel asked as I hung up. He was trying not to look worried, so I didn't mention the more excitable shoppers loitering in aisles to exchange snippets of news.

"Bleach and disinfectant running low on the shelves," was all I said.

The Ministry of Health's announcement of our first case landed as a visceral blow. It was here.

Schools would close at once: no need for action on our part.

"Yippee!" Micah shouted.

What to do with them all day? I cast my mind over material I had put away for projects in the Easter vacation, and I totted up extra weeks. Well, months. (At least.) That prompted parallel notes to those I now kept for stocktaking: how to keep them sane at home. Bubble wand and paints for Mattie, check. Sodium bicarb for chem experiments, Cynnie's old microscope, et cetera, check. Books, books, books.

Coldly and methodically, Joel and I shifted into crisis mode. When we drove out at all now, we went separately to avoid taking the children into public spaces where they might finger who knew what. (Surfaces, the experts warned. Not aerosol: droplets.) Lines outside supermarkets snaked longer. Dawdlers turned out in full force, shopping in a confused way, listless, or clustering to put heads together anxiously right over the fruit. Joel or I ducked in and out, avoiding everyone we could and dropping our shoes outside the door when we got home.

"No, we've stopped visiting," we told Indy apologetically when she called, "except by phone."

We sifted messages to delete morbid speculation, inspirational reflections of the more insipid kind, end of world prophecy, jeering denial of the virus as a hoax, fake notifications about house-to-house delivery if one would only send one's bank account number and other personal information. The less we went out, the more we found ourselves clinging to those phones. "Like young people," Joel said with a wry grin.

"Can we have phones?" Micah put in urgently. "Since we hardly go out."

Curiously, many of our friends were calling no more frequently than before closing themselves in. And to our surprise, Jackie and Gabrielle seemed distraught at the idea of a long stay at home.

"When they ever go out anyway?" Joel demanded. "Doubt Gabrielle's left the house more than five times over the past year."

"But I guess she knew she could," I replied. "Thing is, they shy away from WhatsApp, which cuts them off more. Now your boy, Kevin, lives on WhatsApp. Forwards everything."

"Everything." Joel rolled his eyes. "And I get stuff from people I don't even know. Open, send. Open, forward. Open, post – people hypnotized by media alerts." But also galvanized into action, from what Francis said – at least the younger set, impelled out of their houses for the last lime or swim or even prayers before lockdown. To hear him tell it, beaches, bars, riversides, churches, every imaginable gathering place buzzed with activity.

"Nah! Exaggerated," Joel said. "Has to be."

"And how'd Francis know?" I demanded. "Unless he goes too?" My mind writhed.

"Probably his job to know," Joel said.

One government update after the next repeated and reinforced what we knew, what any fool could see, what fool after fool ignored: warnings against congregating and travelling, demonstrations on how to scrub off the virus with its crown of suction pads.

"Will get worse," Joel said.

As Mattie took his pinky out his nose and examined the finger closely, my mind wandered to the purchase of a home nebulizer. Who knew what else? One day everything from humidifiers to oxygen tanks could run short. If we locked down and the economy slid, foreign currency would shrivel.

Party-goers jeered and vacationers were still boarding cruise ships gaily when I was making my last run to PriceSmart. One or two shoppers in line for a cashier stared blankly ahead as if they had nothing to do with the freezers they were paying for. I was giving thanks for SpongeBob's extra freezer space when the circumstances that had brought it to me slammed down again. Then I plowed my way out once more from beneath the weight of recollection. I noticed two women in the line behind me counting cupcakes. "You think is enough for the prayers, though?" one asked. The other replied, "You forget is how much food it going to have. Partly only the children really going to eat cake."

Quite apart from uncaring fêters and drinking buddies, a hard core of the unthinking godly insisted on physically congregating for worship. Even as most worshippers from different faiths went online, a couple pastors had dug in their heels. "God will protect you," one proclaimed. "You think you could catch the virus in the house of the Most High? Nevaaah." He called on the faithful to come forth in their numbers.

"Why the hell they don' lock he up?" Francis took it up with Joel straight after the report. "He ent telling them pray from home because he have offering to collec'. That is what."

Offering, I jotted down. *Get account number for online.* A patch of dust under the tangle of wires in the corner prompted me to scratch a reminder to buy vinegar. We kept Mattie away while Ena mopped, but once we were on our own, we'd have to avoid pungent cleaners.

Ena List. I scrabbled in my purse for my notes on preparations for freezing as I turned along the chicken lane in Massy next morning. "You see if they lock down it could be weeks," I heard a woman say behind me. The mask conferred a vague sense of invisibility, and I made no effort to pretend I was minding my own business. I took in her companion's fuchsia tights.

"Everything have to put away now for now," declared the first woman, flashing a brilliant smile that reminded me how much I missed lipstick already. "I feel when I reach back here from New York with them children, the whole of the shelves in this place going bare. And you see that? I ent able with that."

On the aisle with the small box-drinks of Milo that were nowhere else to be found, a large man in multi-pocketed shortpants descended on the woman wheeling past me: "Gyul, where you going with so mucha toilet paper? Is you lungs the virus want, not you belly."

"Oh gooosh!" She flung her arms round him, kissed loudly and pressed cheeks. "What you doing here? Is when you reach? What you really come for?"

"Wedding, gyul. Me cousin getting tie up. But like you buying out the people whole supplies. Is just for a few weeks, man."

"I know, I know. But if it get sell out what I go do? Serious ting."

Weeks. I steered away to give them a wide berth, wondering if I was mad to envision a year or more, to think we would be lucky to escape outbreak after outbreak like those that had ripped through earlier centuries I had inhabited intellectually for decades. In desperation to stop the peste, Defoe's contemporaries slaughtered cats far and wide, and today, so far, there seemed little sign of more useful responses from the great cities I knew well. The thought of clueless tourists drifting in our direction set my scalp crawling, and growing talk about closing borders seemed to offer the only hope available.

In our house we closed ours. By now I'd laid away list after list. The children had helped me pack away soap, detergent, toilet paper, disinfectant, paper roll; dry, canned and frozen foods. Panadol, cough medicine, lozenges and inhalants; blood pressure, heart, and diabetic medication. There was drive-through for whatever else cropped up. Those who were habitually unready for whatever befell, scolded about panic buying. "Is people buying what they don't need and wouldn' use," they complained into any mike the media presented in garnering public opinion. "People want to hoard one set of unnecessary ting and make it scarce for who really need it."

"That is they," I said. Panic? I felt calm descend. I hoped not to need the lozenges, but we'd use everything else. "Little extras to prevent us having to leave the house more than necessary," I explained to Micah. "No need to done the peanuts in one week."

So we settled in to peer out at the world. "I'll have time now, at any rate," I told Joel, and put my feet up in front of the TV.

Only, in the spectacle of negligence, heroism and wrenching heartbreak, life reshaped faster than eye or mind could follow.

"You can't see me," Mattie sang out from a dusty nook under the sofa, and I called, "Come out of there or you'll be sneezing." But he was angling for a game.

"I can see you and you can't see me," he said.

"Nobody wants to see you," Micah snapped.

I was fixated on the news from outside that brought in scenes which peeled away our understandings of reality and erased lines between consciousness and nightmare.

Micah flattened himself on the floor to look Mattie in the eye. "Out!" he said, and Mattie crawled forth sulkily.

"You spoiled the game," he protested, nose stuffy already.

Rubbing on a smear of Vicks, I kept my eye on the TV, where the half-forgotten past and improbable future converged – not in witty speculations on what might come or dim woodcuts by some ancient moralizer but in blindingly sharp relief. At the touch of a button, channel after channel threw up mounting numbers of the dying, beleaguered healers, distraught mourners, and the clueless leaders who let go of them all to scrabble around keeping their grasp on power.

I must have been holding my breath, and when Mattie sneezed, I exhaled slowly, gathering him close as it dawned that survival lay in looking away from those in charge of the world and even past those in charge of our own country. Nothing for it but to take charge of our own house – this island within the island – and govern ourselves, each of us, with an iron will. The vastness of the problem made a mockery of borders, yet they were all we had.

"OK – so this makes no sense," I said to Joel, "but everything, island-wide and world-wide, depends on basic little choices we make ourselves."

"Plenty beyond individual control, though," he objected. "Access to water, money, physical space."

Right. I surveyed the cupboards I'd tidied out – even my clothes closet, to accommodate what I then gathered under shelves of neatly packed clothes. I know, I know: usual extremism.

"Aren't you kinda overdoing it, Mama?" Micah asked, the corners of his mouth twitching.

"I guess," I said. From different angles I peered at myself and realized, how ludicrous. "But I'll do what I want with my own cupboard."

"Not fair," Mattie complained, when Melody said I had more storage than millions of people had space to live in.

"I guess," I repeated. "All the more reason not to waste a square inch."

Everyone else we knew accepted that – all hell having broken out in Europe and America – it was a matter of time before the virus crushed our own fragile little systems.

"Perhaps we're tougher than that," Joel said one evening in the living room as the children set up a prehistoric world around our feet. Francis looked doubtful.

"If Covid goes rampant here, we can and must lock ourselves in," I told them. "Like people did in earlier ages." Francis mumbled some question about whether I knew the mental stamina that would take, and I reminded him that poets had gone into seclusion and composed verse that would amaze the world for centuries.

"Not as if a plague enforces idleness," Joel agreed.

And yet. "Bored," Kevin was moaning in no time.

How? Boredom was not a concept I got my mind around easily. "Well, he's alone, you know," Joel said afterwards. So. Lonely. I could grasp lonely.

But what was there to *do*? Indy sighed. When it would end? Heartless to point out that it had hardly begun, so I held my peace.

"You know," I told Joel, "I might be losing it by now as well if it weren't for the children." Then I whispered. "But can you imagine if they were little horrors?"

Micah piped up, "You mean we aren't?" He radiated delight in having caught me out.

I wondered whether he could lip read.

"You're a delight and comfort," I mouthed at him, and he grinned.

"You'd just write your books all day, that's all," Melody said. "'s what I'd do too if I were you."

And you are, I thought. You are me.

⸙

What to do was a persistent question, though. Members of the media repeated it to government ministers, reflecting pockets of impatience with the shutdown of schools, beaches, bars, churches and restaurants. The answer was always the same: Only the virus had a schedule. The prime minister referred us to Isaiah: *Shut your doors behind thee; hide yourselves for a little while until the fury has passed by.*

"Get out from under the bed, you little pest," Micah hollered so irritably that we rushed in to find Mattie crawling forth, wailing. "Why you keep going under things?"

"I'm just hiding," Matts said, breathlessly.

"What from?"

"Covid," he bawled, running to me.

'You're warm,' I protested, running my hands over his skin. "And what's wrong with your mouth now?"

"Dry," he moaned. "'S 'cause I can't close it – it always happens when my nose blocks."

While I poured him some water, Joel put a pot on the stove, and Melody whispered something to him.

"Right," he said.

When the water came to a boil, he sprinkled in menthol crystals. We got him breathing in steam till he nodded off and we put him to bed.

"What did Melody say?" I asked.

Joel sat on the edge of the bed studying Mattie. "Says once the sinuses get going, the asthma generally kicks in too."

I heard what he didn't say next, so I worded it. "How will we know *what* he has?"

But the next morning, to our relief, Mattie was fine. "Don't need the doctor," Joel concluded.

Micah looked scandalized. "You weren't taking him out, right?" Before we could respond, he added, "No one goes out: nothing comes in."

Only then, by courier, Andrea's novel came in, a brightly covered volume in yellow and green. Her note said she had postponed the launch until whenever the crisis might pass, but there were reviews already. She'd sent our copy with a clipping: *Longlisted for Major Prize.*

Precisely what I needed. I misted the transparent packaging with Lysol and allowed the volume a day's rest. Then I turned the children over to Joel so as to get into it.

"Won't keep you out of circulation long." He flicked his eyes over it with a grin. "Mere two hundred and fifty pages. You'll inhale it."

Except. While claiming to be set in 2015 Trinidad, the novel projected a '90s lifestyle. Yet a schoolboy named Garth opened fire on his principal and then ran along the corridor to mow down his classmates. I had to stop and grapple with that. When I resumed, his father, the class teacher, wrestled the gun away and turned it on himself, leaving the child's mother,

Alver, a highly paid executive who had surrounded herself with every luxury, more than ever desperate ("like anyone else", so the narrator said) to leave the island. Alver was going to New York even if she had to accept work as a maid.

Seriously? I pondered Caribbean classism. I moved on again, and then something in the woman's voice jarred, and I slowed once more to look more closely at the dialogue. Alver sounded like my mother's contemporaries rather than mine, let alone Cyn's. Besides, glimpses of social background seemed patched on, as if mined from secondhand memory or some online summary rather than coming alive through the characters.

Still, the author's use of language in the narrative was breathtaking. And I loved the voices of Alver's neighbours in the Bronx. Andrea was an able writer, I realized, picking up the plot again to race on.

Following the carnage at school, there flowed a truly insightful account of Garth in juvenile detention. No one could have got into the boy's head better. But alongside that ran this less persuasive tale of Alver's escape from the island to eke out a living as cleaner in some major airport. The airport was never named, but the usual brilliant prose evoked the J.F.K. International. And the mother and son stumbled upon each other in the last chapter on the point of the young man's deportation. Unknown to Alver, Garth too had been an illegal immigrant for years while he made a bloody living in the drug trade. The book closed with Alver watching her son led away for his return to the void.

The back cover write-up described the novel as a gritty evocation of the author's native land. The blurb was perfectly accurate about amazing technique. Andrea penetrated her characters' thoughts. But what triggered them and where they led – even how they were voiced most of the time – struck me as alien.

Now *this* mess settled in a sinkhole that had opened up somewhere behind my forehead, for I had thought I knew Andrea to the extent of considering us like-minded, and this book came out of – of where? And was popular. My quick check on the award site showed it had moved up into the shortlist. People were reading more than ever and further afield now their movements were curtailed.

Why was I annoyed? Because we had enough crime of our own without imposing some alien brand? Mmn. More to it than that. Andrea's estranged gaze hailed as an insider's revelation? I knew it was that, at least in part. Only, right here, *inside*, wasn't I estranged too? Apart from the havoc outside our shores, I glimpsed nearer at hand – in a parallel universe beyond my touch and sight – the beginnings of a cascading catastrophe. But what was I to do about faceless, gnawing want – what *could* I do? Helplessness mixed in with other nameless and unfamiliar sensations.

I stoppered them to take hold of what I might be able to manage, what I knew that I knew about. The reset transported me beyond the unlikely local circumstances Anthea had contrived in her fiction, to what was actually going on in parts of the world I'd got acquainted with through the odd visit or voracious reading. From Italy then Spain flashed video footage of pestilential homes for the aged, emptying streets and screaming ambulances. Then silent ambulances backed up outside overflowing hospitals with nurses worn out and mask-scarred, traumatized doctors admitting they must choose between patients for ventilators. Processions of coffins passed in the streets of European cities we had grown up regarding as bastions of civilization, wisdom and ordered existence.

I retreated to the bedroom, only to be set upon by the usual contrapuntal strains of US channels. This Chinese flu was just another flu, the president belted out. Focus on saving the economy and we'd be through by Easter. His cohort chorus swelled: A mild disease. Get out to work once you can walk. Medical voices advised: "Stay home and save yourselves and others." Fox scoffing rounded off the polyphony.

Pointing the remote merely shifted screen from one discordance to the next. Test and test again. No, test only the symptomatic. No, most of the tests were rubbish anyway. No, random testing was essential. No, tests only distorted the statistics, driving up the impression that the virus was out of control. No, tests provided the only reliable information. No, so many tests were faulty. No, there just weren't enough test kits to go around. No, the tests were part of the whole hoax.

"Reality seems more unlikely than Andrea's novel – or any other I've read," I told Joel. And this was just the beginning, I thought.

One day in late March, I turned off CNN's coverage of Covid to head outside in search of the children, but turned back when the phone rang. Jackie said her son had called and told her about his ex-wife's parents in Washington, where they resided in a seniors' complex now rife with the disease. Jackie's former daughter-in-law had remarried and settled in

Spain, so she couldn't travel, not that she would have been admitted to visit her parents in any case. The old people (what am I saying – they'd be our age, just people) – the *couple* – were confined to their rooms, terrified and bored. Jackie had made the mistake of telling her son that at least the two of them were together, and her son explained that was the main problem: they loathed each other. Nothing he could do but call sometimes, and they didn't like him either.

So at once my mother's friend popped into my head, the one I had been too busy to visit weeks ago. Probably months. She was in a home, which was rare enough here, but then she had no family. Did she remember where she was, or even who she was? If not, perhaps that was a mercy. And what of my beloved old neighbour with the vascular disorder, in her own house with her live-on caregiver? She knew very well all that went on, poor soul, but was in no shape to receive a phone call. I was staring helplessly at the phone when it jangled again, and cold sweat broke out all over me. Not only was I less composed than I pretended then; I wasn't even as calm as I'd supposed.

"Going out for printer cartridges," Francis announced. "What you need? Paper and ting?"

I'd laid in stationery weeks ago, so I thanked him anyway and rang off.

Unwisely, I paused halfway across the living room in a haze of disorientation before the set. In Europe, deaths tolled in hundreds, in thousands. In my head, darkening pages of old volumes turned again – one century, four centuries, seven centuries on, the great plague of our time. Closing in.

The next day was Mattie's birthday, and although we had ice cream and a cake with five candles, the children's enthusiasm in the games I had arranged was flagging by evening. Then Francis dropped in with sushi for us and beef pies for the children. From his far corner near the wrought-iron gate of the porch he produced a pump and balloons from his bag and blew them up, and Mattie exulted in Francis *bringing a party*. The concept of partying was already exotic, what with assemblies of over twenty-five formally outlawed, however the unruly persisted with their fêtes or religious gatherings.

"So lock them all up," Joel snapped.

But Francis shook his head. Impossible. At work, he said, it was hard enough figuring out how to reduce overcrowding in the prisons. What space it have for one set of hardened limers? Nah. "You know," he added gently. "Best I visit you guys on WhatsApp from now on."

Joel and I had already talked of bringing this up and were glad he beat us to it. "I'll shop for you, though," Francis added. "Just send your list." When he didn't kiss me on the way out, I realized with a jolt that he hadn't as he arrived. I felt relieved, then confused and guilty about why I felt relieved. And then, just guilty – but suddenly not about Francis; guilty because I could afford lists.

They were the shield I set up around my flesh-and-blood family, while all around, barricaded out of sight, darted children – without space to play, books or wireless, without adults who had time or spirit to talk or listen to them, without water from a tap, regular food, or cough medicine. I could not see them but they were real and unfriended. Jobless parents, perhaps, or older siblings strayed or abused. Even if a mother packed them off to school, they got there exhausted after a disturbed night, bellies empty of a sip of hot tea, unable to do more than stare uncomprehendingly or angrily at the harassed teacher. What did they know of the virus and how to stave it off? I had no list for them. Whose list were they on?

Joel fixed a knowing eye on me. "Berating yourself over something," he said. "As if going forward won't be challenging enough, what with our set of jokers here living from day to day without a thought in their heads. This is a whole new asquanky dispensation. Think we have enough people here going to hold a straight line so this thing doesn't wipe us out?"

The best-equipped nations of the world were in chaos, I agreed. At the top right of the TV, set for international news on the pandemic, red boxes of statistics lengthened even as the two cases here had given way to five, seven, nine.

I'd seen Ena off that evening, and she said she'd come fortnightly to collect her envelope. "But such a long way, Ena. And packed tight in the taxi?"

I handed her a flat sum for the month and promised to work out future arrangements by phone.

Lock after lock snapping in place. Keep in, the government urged. Stay in your home. The known cases were imported, so there would be state quarantine for all arrivals, including citizens. Only, then our borders closed to non-nationals. Keep out.

"Still the nine cases," Joel said. "Not bad."

What? No, the government said. No cruise ship would be allowed to dock. Nationals? Sorry. Oh, very well.

"Airlifting them," Joel announced. "Nationals to be flown in and quarantined. Still nine, though." Definitely a lull. Hope.

Then the Ministry of Health explained it at a media conference. Sixty-eight nationals from a cruise ship had quarantined at Balandra, and forty tested positive. The authorities had transferred the forty, mainly elderly, to Couva hospital and held the other twenty-eight at Balandra for re-testing. They were a mixed lot – some compliant, some complaining. Some hammered their smart phones to arrange legal representation.

Meanwhile, a forlorn group in Margarita moaned about abandonment. If Venezuela had closed its borders, what was he to do, demanded a harried Minister of National Security.

On Joel's phone there was Francis, ready to explode. "What the arse they was doing on cruise ship anyway?" Joel threw up his hands, unable to get a word in. "If people can't read ent they at least sit in front the TV? They don't see what going on? Watch me," Francis concluded. "I better get back to work yes, before I say someting."

"Can't Francis come any more?" Micah pleaded that evening, and we hadn't the heart to say more than *perhaps soon*. But we knew normalcy was receding faster than ever.

No assembly of more than ten now, the prime minister ruled. "Please. We are trying to save lives." Ours, I recognized, reassured but unnerved at once. I shifted my thoughts hurriedly to settle on something that had nothing to do with the virus. But – like what? Job loss? Family disruption? Academic procedures? Isaac's dissertation was limping through the examination process, because his External Examiner in the United Kingdom had died of Covid and had to be replaced. I wondered what the new man would make of Isaac's arguments; I thought them groundbreaking. What was there that had nothing to do with the virus?

When Francis cut through again on the phone, I assured him we could manage curbside shopping for ourselves. Then I lent an ear to his latest account of the Charlene predicament. He'd heard she'd had the baby, but he still had no idea where they were. Shelley had left Toronto and travelled to Florida with her ex-husband to see her mother-in-law, who was dying of the virus – not that the home had admitted either of them.

The home had made it clear in advance, but Shelley said of course they must let her in when they saw she'd come all that way.

Francis said Charlene had no one else but Shelley to stay with. She'd wanted to go with Shelley but couldn't, for what if she didn't get back into Canada? "The borders and ting nah. So now no one really know where Charlene. Or the baby, of course." In the end everything came back to the pandemic and its ramifying dislocations.

Then, a death. Here.

A sweep of my hand closed that window with the Ministry of Health update. The children were huddled over homework, so I took cover in my mail, alerted by an optimistic chirp from the computer.

Amid a flurry of messages – a request for a job reference, an invitation to submit an article, notifications from academia.edu – was an email from Barrie (dear God – I had forgotten Barrie). She had forwarded in a brief chain a message that Cyn had written later than any of the notes wedged in her desk. It was dated last year and said, "You were absolutely right all along. But I never knew, Barrie. Can you ever forgive me?"

Another broadside. Was there then something, anything, Barrie could have been right about or had she eventually sucked Cyn in? And Barrie's characteristically *low* response. Why, after this apology, would she respond by calling Cyn a bitch? I automatically edited the careless emails, especially the typo in *you bitch*. There was no ignoring these most recent words, yet what would it mean to contemplate some sort of exoneration of Barrie? If the message was genuine, Cyn had come to think she had caused the woman pain. How could Cyn, my brilliant, straight-thinking Cyn, have been so mistaken or so taken in?

All over again, I searched for a way of writing my child. But how was one to collapse a life of thirty-nine years to the couple hours it takes to read a book – not without ripping out whole dimensions of what one knew, and what one knew was never more than a fraction of the whole. If there was a whole. Parts came together, fissured and broke away again even as others formed, hardened, crumbled, collided, fused. What was any such tale but a sketch from some peculiar angle, filtered and blurred by the artist's agenda and astigmatism.

Indy had asked what we would all do if the lockdown went on and on. Once the children were occupied and happy, I knew what I would do: write on, indefinitely, however unnoticed. For I must always be out of focus, mustn't I – off the radar as an elderly and middle-class academic, racially muddled, an island voice fuzzed by interference from all directions. Able to write only from outside because inside was so concentrated as to defy definition. Nowhere have I ever been inside enough to be an insider.

Disturbed, I rambled out of my study, glancing at the TV, muted but busy with headlines it was better not to read. I flipped channels and encountered deodorant ads of that explicit nature that jarred on me by spelling out and quantifying intimate odours or body fluids. As if one needed all that one's body produced named and blazoned abroad. Flitting from room to room I found the twins sleeping but Mattie's bunk empty. In our room he was curled up with Joel, both asleep among a litter of storybooks, watched over by Bear and his goslings, Wilfred, Gruffalo, Hatchie and Rumpelstiltskin.

What a balm there is in the presence of a sleeping child. If I'd just climbed in, I'd have been soothed to sleep myself. Instead I wandered back into the living room and stared at Australians flooding onto the beaches for a last swim before their expected lockdown. That jolted me – like some short in my thought processes – and I powered off the set, went back to the laptop and withdrew into myself to ponder Mattie. And there I hovered, the thought of him suspended like the fragile nucleus of a single cell fraught with generation, until I recognized that it was not Mattie I needed to think out to begin with, not if I were to make any headway at all. It was not even Cyn.

Searching and listening for Barrie against the silent mayhem of the pandemic I could make out nothing for a long time. I was grossly offended at her calling Cyn a bitch. Or perhaps the word meant less to her?

In the end, what came through it all to me was, mostly, a young woman in baffling distress and incalculable pain. And the grief I had held down for nearly a year, except in my breaking apart before an antique desk – my loss rose up to meet hers, which had manifested itself in such chaos. And when I allowed myself to sense that, a wall of fear and annoyance crumbled and nothing stood between me and her brokenness.

15

CELL

BARRIE PICKED UP ON SOME SOFTENING in my attitude, I suppose, for she called from Sydney eight days later. To enquire about the children, she said after thanking me for my brief (almost, I would say, curt) acknowledgement of her messages. She had asked if the children were well and how we were managing. On the phone she felt me out delicately about how we might keep them out the path of infection and breathed her audible sigh of relief that we could close ourselves in on our own premises with all they might need. After Easter this would include school online, but now they had space to play ball in the open air, pick fruit, sweep leaves, and then come in to eat, read and play cards.

How would she have guessed? Even if she could have supposed the country to be civilized – here, like elsewhere, there was mind-breaking poverty and now unemployment would spread like the contagion itself. In multi-floored apartments, tightly packed families shared common corridors and stairs. Children breathed stale air while squeezing in and out entrances between frustrated loafers drinking and slamming dominoes. Tiny homes huddled on narrow streets along which brave women toiled forth daily for a pound of rice or flour or one roll of toilet paper.

As in other countries, people of our age often lived isolated in rooms at the tops of stairs they could no longer climb down. Some barely peeped out at the world through faded curtains in flats where packaged soup and diabetes medicine were running out. Even the most active might not venture out by route taxi, packed close and inhaling whatever lurked in each other's breath. There, too, were children no different to our three, for custodial grandparents to feed and keep locked up and prevent from dropping out of windows. And here, as in more affluent countries, were luxurious mansions.

"The children work and play as they would anywhere else," I told Barrie. "We keep them home, but busy."

"I know so little about your world," Barrie admitted humbly. She had this amazing voice control, but I caught the inflection of surprise emanating from the usual ignorance of Caribbean life. Still, her acknowledgement cushioned the impact. Besides, not all views from outside were unfounded. Andrea's novel had caught explosive tensions in the society that I pressed from mind.

Yet later, when Joel brought up the topic of Anthea's guardianship, I was less enthused than he expected. "Only because I doubt she'd stay here with the children," I told him, as we cleared the table after Sunday lunch. "Not that she wouldn't devote herself to them, but it wouldn't be *here*. She hasn't any faith in the place or . . . or, it doesn't offer what's important to her. I've no doubt she believes in what she's saying about wanting to give it a try here, but it won't take her through."

Then my analysis ran away with me. "Another scenario below the surface too, eh? She doesn't believe these countries have a future, but risking a few years here will get her current Caribbean experience, perhaps even a university position on her profile."

Joel stared, shocked. "Thought you liked Andrea so much."

"Oh, I love her. But she writes about a Caribbean she felt the need to discard and now knows mainly through foreign news, some on target and some warped. She extrapolates from distant memory and outsider reports. Not invested in the region – but she doesn't know that. She'll do her best for the children and her best is to take them elsewhere. The question before us is – do we want them to be Americans?"

"Where's the harm?" He shrugged. "Well, ideally, maybe no. But the States wasn't always like this and won't be forever. I can think of worse fates."

"Sure. So can I, even though their present government has to be a symptom of some underlying condition. But say that wasn't so – is further relocation best for the children?"

"You're the one extrapolating. You don't like Andrea's book, so she's – what? Unfit as a guardian? She's dissembling?"

"Lord, no. I don't think for a minute she's dishonest. It's a question of different exposure. You bring up a child according to your understanding of the truth, and Andrea's truth is not our truth. But she's the dearest woman, intelligent and caring."

"So where's that leave us?"

"Just . . . I don't know. Trying to stay alive and with-it as long as possible." I set about straightening the dining table chairs with more energy than even I thought it was worth. It was an uncomfortable conversation but not nearly as gruelling as those I was postponing. Meanwhile, I didn't put into words my other hang-up: that all the two of us had gone through recently resulted from atrocity in the outside world unlike anything practised here. Besides, there was that vista of criminal negligence in relation to the virus, officially entrenched negligence.

"So far, we're a lot safer where we are," was all I added.

Joel agreed. "Mind you – set of mad people here mightn't take on the government for long. At least the government's paying attention to the scientists."

For now, innumerable families were locking themselves away like us, biding time doggedly. Inevitably, there was outcry. Pleas echoed through the media, urging the government to send a plane for the unfortunates stranded in Margarita. The Minister of National Security asked again how the plane would get to them when Venezuela had closed its borders. The questions pelted down. Surinam, then? And what about the nationals from that cruise – to Qatar, or was it South Africa? Both? Was it one or two cruises? The ones who had managed to get back as far as Barbados?

We have hundreds of thousands of nationals abroad, the prime minister replied, all over the globe. The muscles of his face tightened as he reined in his temper. However many of them with dual citizenship lived elsewhere, this now seemed a safer place to be. Where to draw the line? With our finite resources we need only let up slightly to be wiped out. So the borders stayed closed and the parallel health care system held. The authorities linked our eighty-nine cases with travel history.

Then, one or two with no known contacts. Oh, Lord God: local spread? Death toll, four.

Curbside shopping only. "Wash hands, my baby. Don't touch the delivery – just reach out the big steel bowl and open the bin for Mama to dump the plastic wrappings." (Good Lord – when did we stop recycling? Sorry, I flung a mental apology to Mother Earth: right now is me or the planet, yes.) "Wait. No orange for you yet, little bird. Wash hands again and spread clean towels."

"Scrubadub," Mattie agreed.

"Water in the bowl, and you get to squirt the soap, thank you. Now off you go to Papa."

My turn. Strip and dump the foam and plastic packaging. (Where *did* the blasted recycle bin go?) Discard outer leaves, slide tomatoes and pimentos into the suds. Scrub oranges first, then potatoes and plantains. Bottom of pawpaw soggy again, oh well. Wipe and set out to dry, such as it is. Lay chives on paper roll. Turn the fan. Hands, *hands* before touching kettle, then boiling water over the drainboard. Can all this be necessary? Stupidness.

But what if it is? Some said no to masks at first, right? Right. Droplets and surfaces. (But ent lettuce have surface?) Non-perishables now. Glass, plastic, cardboard, tins stay put till tomorrow – except these couple we need today, for Clorox wipe. Wait. where's Mattie? OK. Alcohol for the credit card.

All the while, the children policed us and each other: *Papa, Papa, Micah ate a cherry from the ground. Drop shoes outside, Mama. Gargle, Ratbag.*

In the midst of all this, Barrie called again, asking about the children. The pandemic raging between us rendered harmless whatever response I made, and I began, occasionally, to ask about Cyn. Had she seemed to feel settled in Sydney? So we stumbled into conversation that remained stilted by distrust on both sides. Joel knew nothing of it. The implications of holding back from him racked me, but with him I remained quiet on the subject of Barrie even while I drew her out.

Should I have barricaded her out instead?

I turned this over and over in my head while staring blankly at the TV, where the streets of New York yawned in our living room, empty, echoing only with the wailing of ambulances as hospitals overflowed, and now some mayor or governor pleaded for ventilators. A prominent newscaster whose name escaped me lamented lack of action on the national level, which had brought them down to operate like some little developing country. I steupsed and switched back to TV6, where local voices protested as our borders stayed closed. The prime minister said his daughter was in New York and he'd have preferred her safe at home.

"Mama, is it our borders in Australia are closed too, why the plane couldn' bring Cyn 'n' Con, an' what means borders?" Questions close at hand and far away prompted us to search out ways of skirting unpalatable truths. At the same time, prognoses of deaths in the millions set us grappling with surreal figures while beleaguered governors, political commentators, epidemiologists and social activists bickered and pleaded on screen, anchorless. Against political indifference to widescale death sounded individual demands for freedom.

"Proud of my toxic masculinity," a prominent athlete declared himself, contemptuous of protocols. "If the aunties feel threatened, let them stay home." (Did he say *aunties* or *panties*? I couldn't tell.) Entitled to his freedom, he declared.

Words warped into whatever their speakers wanted them to mean. I tried it out on Joel. "No manners, masquerading as freedom of speech; no lockdown, masquerading as freedom of movement; no mask, masquerading as freedom of dress."

"Nope," Joel said. "You're over-intellectualizing again. Just freedom to live at the expense of the rest. Watch."

Arms raised as if in blessing, their president prophesied, "It'll all be over – like magic." His disciples cheered and gave way before the leader shepherding them backwards over the ever-steepening cliff of statistics.

"Like everything turn ole mas over there." Over the phone Francis's voice was unusually hushed.

We drew ourselves in, away from the encroaching shadow of alien madness. But we had our own clowns. I slowed by a fruit stand on the roadside to yearn over plump purple kymet. The vender who wore his mask as a chin-guard tossed his head scornfully when I signalled him to pull it up so I could lower the car window. "I does walk on Covid," he announced. So off I drove, fruitless.

Police cars coasted by on lookout for every sort of gathering from Covid parties to beach limes. Mattie protested. "Francis can come, Papa. The police say no more than five people together, and he'd just make five because I'm only small and I don't count."

"Sorry, Matts. You count." Joel swung him up on his shoulders.

"*And* I'm brave and strong. I'm not afraid to go out," he announced.

"Sometimes braver to stay put," Joel replied. "We need a different type of strong."

The backed-up, enduring kind. Out there, the habitually powerful floundered in denial, refusing to accept that choice had evaporated. It had taken Europe two months longer than Trinidad and Tobago to lock out China, and eventually infections on the eastern coast of North America turned out to have come from Europe rather than directly from China.

"Travellers," I groaned. "Well, we've barred them all out now, even our own."

A look of satisfaction crossed Joel's face. "At least That Woman is off our horizon," he said.

No point remonstrating with him. When I reviewed my household protocols, I could make out the gathering nimbus of paranoia. It was growing harder not to overdo.

"Mama, why Papa doesn't want us to pat Mystique anymore? Is it because of the tiger who got sick in that zoo and so cats and thing can get it? Mystique stays home mostly, like us. I'm sure she's healthy. Sure, sure."

I regarded Mattie sympathetically. "I think so too. But the virus is such a mystery still, and you know it would be just like Philander to pick up Covid and bring it in. Let's give the kitties a few weeks and see how it goes." Even our own backyards spawned day-to-day trivia to negotiate. Our way lay through unknown terrain – for what false step might set off more confusion, what minor thoughtlessness amount to cruelty? Some tracks we can't retrace.

Briefings. The health minister's voice, set soft on bedside manner, urged us to respect the bereaved and hold back questions about suspected cases.

"Papa, what means *case*?"

"Cases are people who don't feel well, son."

Joel's definition turned out to be a luxury not everyone could indulge, as statistics spiked. Graphs tilted abruptly, almost vertical, and by the end of March, boxes of foreign statistics in the right-hand corner of our screens deepened as the boxes for burial in New York stacked up in their wide trench. And it was borne home more and more that so much could have been avoided, but for pig-headed insistence on *choice* – in that word's sprained meaning.

So much could always have been avoided. Alternative routes cut this way and that through my head. What if on the way to the plane, Cyn, or the pilot, or the terrorist (if there was one) . . . Or if it had been the airport shuttle or taxi that had crashed, barely enough to break an arm . . . And then, a shaft through the brain – a choice of my own. What if Barrie could tell me more, now she couldn't get to us? And if I now closed my mind to Barrie's voice? How would I ever know?

But know what? I didn't know. I didn't know what I didn't know.

Which left no option but to listen. Only, should I?

Do the right thing and then sleep, Joel liked to say. But I was not like him. My eyes popped open irrevocably in the wee hours and my brain seethed. And Lord – the sheer beastliness of three a.m. For how could I ever be sure I'd done the right thing? And so, when might I ever sleep again? (Like a dull echo: *Through my most grievous fault*.) I'd lost sight of Cyn's *Promise me*.

Unfulfilled vows gather import and reshape. I can almost see them floating out there, tufts like white silk cotton on the wind, fine shimmering hairs. One drifts clear from the rest and wafts my way. Down and down, gossamer light at first, its delicate shafts spiking, until the distance closes and it gains bulk and speed, looms closer, a massive hunk of shrapnel hurtling in, its jagged edges ablaze.

Amid the screaming and the choking smell of searing skin, I awake sweating, jolted from one nightmare into the next.

—⟩⟨—

Ten minutes sleep doesn't do much for one, especially ten minutes of *that*. I lay in the excruciating silence, straining to hear something, anything. Then from up the road an explosion of barking rose in crescendo until cut off by a cat's prolonged scream. I crushed my hands over my ears until the quiet rushed back, and I lay paralyzed.

So, having no insight into what the right thing might be, locked in by day and, by night, worn out with lying awake and raking my mind for clues, I clutched my mobile the next day and ducked into my study to read and acknowledge Barrie's most recent message. Then the next. I read them silently, one after the next. I found myself answering more frequently, though as briefly and neutrally as I could. I took her calls. I put my foot down regarding her language, which got pretty raw as she went along, and she checked herself.

Any light Cyn might have shed had gone out. In the unrelieved hollowness of separation and my desperation to glimpse something of my child's recent years, I let Barrie's anguish penetrate my suspicion and resentment. I tried to write what I deduced amidst the conflicting emotions that skewered me. But the setting for what I was trying to assemble was blank, and the characters became more unknowable with everything I found out. Cyn had always told us everything, I thought. Now her last nine years seemed blank to me. Hadn't she trusted us after all? Or were her circumstances too troubling for me to bear?

Writing squeezed tighter and tighter into the crevices in my waking hours, and sometimes, even when time allowed, speculation sharpened to pain that forced me to lay aside my reassembling of Cyn. I broke the work by short stints of local news. But the voices grew louder, angrier – impassioned pleas to reopen liquor marts, furious arguments against or in favour of litigation for releasing a well-known talk show host from quarantine although he had tested positive, ongoing outcries over closed borders.

I switched channels from the World Health Organization's protest against US withdrawal of funds only to be faced with Boris, ghastly pale as death warmed over. [But can I write that? Now that writers are advised against calling eyes almond-shaped and skin chocolate and noses Jewish, is *pale* an offensive word for an ill white man? *Bleached* won't do, because he has just enough sense not to have tried that prescription. Perhaps *ashen*? *Washed-out* might do. Poor, drained Boris.] A foremost proponent of herd immunity, he had barely tottered to his feet from under the hooves of the stampede, thanking his medical team again and again for saving his life.

Still, pictures flashed of nurses in Britain facing the pestilence in light surgical masks and robed in garbage bags. Statistics for health workers climbed on while the authorities applauded their bravery. And the virus dodged theorists, mocking hypotheses that if it only killed enough, the rest would stop dying. And creeping, creeping up, numbers for infection and death among black and Hispanic health workers and patients overtook the rest in full view of all the world.

"Do you kinda miss school?" Micah asked Melody in hushed tones, as if wary of blasphemy. "Or what about church, Mama? It would be somewhere to go." The flat voice of someone scraping the bottom of the barrel.

"I remember Sunday School," Mattie put in. "Sunday School was OK."

"All be online soon," I reminded them. But I knew *out* was what they wanted.

Our precautions displaced habits we had taken for granted over generations: no setting off to work or school, no savouring a doubles on the road corner near the vendor, no travel to family in Miami, New York or Toronto, no crowding into a maxi taxi, no liming over a drink, no gathering for a festival, no belting out "How Great Thou Art" side by side in the pew or hugging for the passing of the peace, no arbitrary patting of children who wandered within arm's length. No dropping in on friends. The new place we were beginning to inhabit seemed conjured up by some fevered imagination, and basic routines became tortuous.

"Is Auntie Ena coming back?" Mattie enquired. "*Ever?*"

"So, Ena," I said to her, loudly for her to hear me over the choking, spitting noises on the phone. "How we getting this envelope to you?"

"Mrs Roche, I don't know nah. Like we have to just let that wait likkle, yes. To tell you the truth I fraid taxi. Like how I did radiation and thing."

"Of course you mustn't take taxi. What about Penny?" I asked. "She can't move either then?"

"But after Penny not here. Ent I tell you she went by she brother – what time? Is weeks she outside. Border close, no plane flying. She can't come back. I here by myself and tell you the truth I don't go nowhere."

"All this time? Alone? Ena, how you managing?"

"I go make out, Mrs Roche. I plant what I can – the soil not good. I mind a few fowl and they lay egg. It have a young boy nearby: sometimes I give him a little change and he get me rice, flour, phone card – dem ting. If I pay him he go drive me to make grocery but I too frighten to go out. And you see the set of mask and sanitizer to buy when you have to go about? Too much of expense. I stay by myself and save that money. Too besides, that same boy who I tell you willing to drive me – he self does lime all about. How I will get into car with he?"

"Ena, you could have been staying here. You didn't tell me you were alone. I thought it was the brother in Couva Penny went to see."

"Nah. The boy in Florida send ticket and she say she must go – after she never gone abroad before. She was to go long time, but I wasn't well, so she say this year she going spend two, three week and come back. That is what? Months now. She there outside. Nah, nah. I staying right here, I good. Safe. It come like a quarantine."

A box of groceries along with the cash, Joel and I agreed. But he was between cataracts and not driving. I had no clue of the way, so I called her again for directions. She remained adamant we must not come and that she was right to isolate herself even from us.

"After the money not running away nowhere. I have food, phone, TV, and if I shout the same young boy next door will come one time – I suppose I go wear mask. And how much longer they can keep border close? Penny go come back just now."

The minute she could, I felt sure, straining through the haze of partisan reporting from Florida. I could barely imagine Penny marooned on an extended stay at the edge of a welcoming but already overburdened family. Searching for her mentally on some Miami street, I realized I couldn't picture her face. I'd met her once before but she was real to me only through Ena's passing comments. In the crush of a vast population crisis, a stranded foreigner struggling for transport to a hospital could disappear. Whether such a one lived or died was of limited interest to most people, I discovered unwillingly. News of a sort, but a passing distraction.

News? There was no further news about the crash. Instead, I picked through accusation and rumour in disbelief. Could US officials actually be hijacking personal protective equipment for health workers by seizing goods destined for their own states or for other countries? Piracy, Germany denounced it as the miasma of distrust widened. But hold: even tiny countries. Neighbouring Caribbean islands, contriving wonders of understatement, expressed disappointment at being deprived of masks, ventilators or other equipment they had bought or been gifted.

What to believe, what to dismiss? Lines between truth and deceit faded from official accounts as they had from media chat.

"Joel?" I pointed to an online article.

"Thuggery's taken over." He stomped off to his desk.

Somewhere above the social and moral morass floated a cacophony of voices across states unevenly affected by the pandemic. Among the governors, legislators, economists, mayors, medics and historians on screen, I caught well-known faces I could put no name to. One grimaced, almost hysterically outraged that this state of affairs could have taken place, he said, in the most civilized country the world had ever seen.

That must have been where I nodded off, without even vague awareness of how I found my way to bed.

It was six o'clock and Joel was shouting into his phone. "Andrea! What you mean you don't know how I heard? You don't see it's all over the media? I just got a message congratulating *me!*"

"What about Andrea? She's OK?" I pushed off the sheet that had been trying to strangle me and raced down to his den as he dropped the cell phone back on his work table.

"More than OK. She's just won this hefty literary award and is being invited to speak here, there and yon, either in the postpandemic future or sooner, online." He grinned and enveloped me in a hug. "Guess you're the only one who doesn't like the book. Well, perhaps *we.* I skimmed it and found stuff I couldn't accept either. Just as well we don't make the market."

"I'm glad for her," I said, pleasantly surprised to feel myself wreathed in smiles. For in a personal way I *was* delighted. (I just wasn't glad for the book.)

I set that aside to get the children ready for class with their snacks for break in place, so I could catch the update: *No assembling whatever.* Joel joined me, but I was the one flipping channels. "Like some US states resisting stay-at-home orders while no instruction coming down at national level." I paused and laid down the remote while one governor explained helplessly that he hadn't known before about people who seemed symptom-free carrying the virus. But Joel clutched his head with one hand and felt for the remote with the other. He powered off without a glance at me, though I hadn't been about to argue. Anger was stressful – let alone for him. He pressed his stomach.

"If it were some little place," he said crossly, "the world would write it off as backward beyond remedy or just . . . tell it what to do." But it loomed huge over us. Dementia? Joel grumbled about deferring responsibility for evil. What if a few leaders from the invisible small places of the world had found themselves in charge of the continents, I wondered. Might they have foregone the level of hubris that calls down nemesis, and spared humanity needless mourning?

Some leaders in a scattering of states had exerted themselves early enough to close borders, forbid assemblies or face down bullying bar owners, church leaders, school boards. But in other states the system folded in domino fashion, spawning protocols, such as those to be followed in *hard choices.* Whom to let go. My thoughts got bound up in this chain of euphemism.

The sound of a quick intake of breath turned me to Melody, who was standing very still in the doorway and studying my face. "Did I do something, Mama?"

And I hugged her. "Only kept me sane."

"Did you know I was named after you, *Aria*?" She pronounced my name slowly, deliberately, instantly dispelling the cloud of disquiet that had been thickening round me.

"Yes. And I am so proud and honoured," I replied. "We're practically synonyms."

She laughed and danced around the room in a rare moment of abandon. So by the time I had the children off to bed, I was at peace in the still house.

Just as well, for rage distracts from scrutiny. At my desk I prayed briefly, and then locked the great world out, to fasten on what healing lay in writing. I began putting down what I could to reconstruct those circumstances that had brought Cyn and Connor onto the plane and the children permanently into our lives. Noise was an irritant, even the silent white noise of headlines running under the figures who gesticulated on the screen I passed en route to the kitchen for more ice. Simple muting could not cover up the disruption of all things. I powered off completely.

Outside was quiet. Even earlier there had been no groups of walkers chatting as they went by our gate to be challenged by dogs that set each other off house by house and eventually chorused their disapproval along the road. No cars revving their engines, backfiring or even tooling gently past. Only the sound of birds and, beyond, the faraway surging of the sea we would never have heard ordinarily. In this eerie lull I strained for voices no one else could hear. Francis had sent me flowers and Joel had put them on my desk, but I hadn't watered them and now my open diary was spattered with red petals. The paper wrapping on the van Gogh print crackled loudly as I unwrapped it, took down a map from my wall and hung Cyn's sunflowers above her desk.

How to write her. I hardened myself to strive for the sort of spiky writing that hooks critics. There was this pressure to project unpalatable realities, write confrontationally so as to *sell*. But then deep pitfalls lay in speaking the unspeakable. *Cancel culture* was that term I'd recently tripped over. In the world of letters, silencers point at the writer from all directions, but voice is the last thing I'll relinquish. So, what is it I'm called on to *say*?

"Promise," Cynnie had whispered from the tightly folded paper passed to me through Melody. But how to keep that promise without the confidences I'd have thought she'd share?

I made my notes, manoeuvring little bits and pieces into place – because that was how my mind worked – but the missing parts could only come from Barrie, through my records of one conversation with her after the next. There was no way of seeing but through her eyes, and I reached for what equipment I had in me to adjust the lens. I cranked up what mental machinery I could summon for assembling scattered and fleeting sensations into coherent experience. So tentatively, almost tremulously, I began to piece together Barrie's story, closing my own eyes and listening through the quiet of our seclusion, straining to make her out and, in the process, adopting her voice where I could.

What little she conveyed was utterly at odds with everything I knew of the universe that had been laid out before me from I first opened my eyes on the world.

16

MISCARRYINGS

BARRIE (?)

WHAT MARRIAGE? ME AND CONNOR? YOU mean like the commitment crap? OMG. So OK, cool, it celebrated the thing was official – whatever. But it had always, only, been about the sex. What else?

We fell apart long before I even heard of Cyndra. Earlier, when I got wind of the little slappa in Connor's office, he stood watching – like entertained – while I lost it. "You don't ★★★★ing care if I know?" I screamed.

He leaned on the wall of our bedroom and turned my question over like we were discussing the feelings of a third party. "Well, if you'd mind your business instead of spying on me, you wouldn't know, would you? Or feel whatever you claim to feel." His hands tightened on my arms. "So what about we change that?" He crushed me close and his voice thickened to honey. "You know no one else does anything to me. Who? *That*? You must be mad." His arms tightened so I could hardly breathe. "But that's OK. Mad turns me on." When I made to shove him off, he laughed and said fine – he could find hotter words than *mad* for me.

He blotted out the hurt and fury only for so long. When he let go and took off again, I slid down the wall and crouched a while before finding my way to the bed. I don't know how much time passed.

I dropped into one of those pits that was full of nothing – emptiness, but heavy. Too thick to move through. It congealed in my chest, this certainty that all of it, the whole mess, was my own doing. I'd brought myself to rock bottom, and I lay pinned there wanting never to feel anything ever again.

Out. It churned over and over in my head, not for the first time. No other way in sight but to opt out. Out of all of it.

But I'd been there before. Just like that I shot back up. I threw myself into this whirl of partying, into the thick of the giddiest crowd I could reel in around me. I could hear myself fluent, witty, talking. Outtalking the rest, but what the ★★★★. Nothing mattered but to turn Connor on. Like a craving. (Chocolate? Brandy?) No, more like a frenzy. Getting home before him I'd drop my stuff on the floor and message him to just get there hurry up. "What for?" The smile in his voice infuriated and stroked me. I'd say, just because he was hot AF. Then he'd say, "That's more like it, Firefly."

So I get more wired – like agitated? Like I was outside myself, watching me – off at a tangent, one topic to the next, ricocheting between clubs, shows, dives. That's when Connor pulls away, and it's lights dimming, music fading again, my mind blanking.

But I might duck off. I'd kinda like skim the lip of that void, plunging instead into this buying spree to draw him back in with wild clothes, kinky toys, anything. That could hold him a couple months. But after a while he was messaging me, BBS, evening after evening, and I figured – Hell, not another ★★★★ing recess. Anything to grab his eye, fix it on me alone. The more shocking the better.

I got to messaging him, boasting about exploits I'd never have contemplated, then trying them, however reckless, illegal, forbidden – walking the bridge rail, clinging to the tattooed back of some stranger on motorbike, inhaling whatever new high, flaunting skin under the strobe flash, bragging about it all on Facebook. When he unfriended me, I sent a pic on Instagram – me and friend. That did unleash something, beyond anything I expected. The dark in him shook me, and I was alarmed but lit again, only soon he sunk me with the *BBS* again, and I plunged down once more, deeper than ever.

Sure, you'll find this hard to believe – not about me, I know that. About him.

Connor was not the guy you knew. The charm, yes, but insidious, entrapping. He was this different animal, a species like *you* couldn't imagine. But me? I was always on the lookout for something wild and unpredictable, and when I'd first sighted him across the room, I told my girlfriend, yum – I could just eat that up. And he really was like some exotic food you overpaid for and pigged out on, only to have it rip through you and leave you for dead, scoured dry.

But. Our lives were incredible at first, until this thing about having a child surfaced. After a while we fought, I mean physically fought, cursed each other, smashed what came to hand – the Bombay box side-table, vintage gramophone, oriental lamp (hand painted) and, most disastrous of all, this distressed gilt antique mirror that had been my grandmother's. I broke that, not him. He was furious because it was valuable, like an heirloom, but ★★★★, she'd been *my* grandmother, not his.

A couple months on, things looked up when I agreed to the IVF. Only, after that, the more he talked about *his* family, *his* property, *his* future, the emptier I got. Like there was nothing of value in me but equipment to conceive and bear. When I eventually pushed his baby out, I'd have fulfilled my mission and become redundant. Worthless. He actually said, yeh, sure – my head was hopelessly messed up, so good job my body functioned in ways that mattered.

"I've a mind to be what your type calls a laughing heir," he jibed at me.

And I snapped, "Not a chance! You can't inherit any of this." But I saw it in his eyes. He meant to take over the place my mother left me. After a while I got to be afraid I might make all he said true, so then I told him to ★★★★ off, and to hell with the IVF.

Look. If every goddamn little expletive gets you so worked up, there's no way I can convey the filth he poured out on me, the withering malice of it. Hey, he called down a blight on me for refusing to bear his child, convinced me I was crap, and all that kept me from going over the edge was this thought I clung to that I had to be, *had to be* more than a womb.

When, eventually, I got Connor out my house, he took charge of the embryos. Fine. I signed them over like a shot. I'd never wanted children before he wooed and badgered me into it, and once I got him out, I wanted nothing more to do with him or them. (I *told myself* I wanted nothing more to do with him.)

It was a tweet alerted me that he was after Cyndra, and she seemed enamoured. He plastered their pictures all over Facebook long before he gave in to the divorce. Later it turned out she only knew there'd been a previous marriage and she thought it legally ended; but I only realized that afterwards. Connor had told Cyndra I was *deeply troubled*, and maybe that explained her tripping over her tongue when she called me about the embryos. It took a while to grasp the meat of it – that he'd been urging her to continue the IVF process he'd started with me.

Like, I suppose she deserved some credit. I mean, for refusing to consider it if I objected. But see, I was hung up on the creepiness of her contemplating it at all. Mostly I felt to puke at the idea of Connor bringing up a kid, but how was Cyndra to see that?

When he telephoned spewing abuse, I felt all the more justified in having put her off. Only then, I caught on that he'd get the child he wanted one way or the next. "All it takes is a womb." He said it. "Any womb." Empty talk, sure, but it brought it home to me that a kid had at least a fighting chance with Cyndra.

Resent her? No. Not really, and I never hated her. After a while, in fact, I kinda took to her. She was a battler, you know? And it wasn't to say she was taking anything I wanted. Or so I told myself, when I lay with the pillow over my head straining for the crunch of Connor's step on the stair.

At the time, though, I convinced myself all I wanted was my work. I resisted the black misery that sucked me down every so often, for I had the firm: Barrington Intyre and Associates had been my mother's, and *she* had built it with her father. I'd taken it over as a formidable operation. My mother, Pauline, had been one of the city's top attorneys, and I knew my way about: I'd been Pauline's offside for years.

So I was like totally cool staying married to the office. Besides, since Pauline's death I'd had her house, where Connor and I lived at first. This coastal pad so, you know, ocean view, some of it overlooking the garden too. Lacework balconies and stuff – oh, yes, hell of a spread in what's become an overpriced suburb. So. Valuable – and left to me and then any daughter I might have. He'd hinted and then nagged about me putting it in both our names, but I was never such a bloody ass as to try that on.

When I heard Cyndra and Connor had relocated to L.A. and signed up for IVF at some clinic there, I said good for her and dumped the pair of them out my mind. Then a friend messaged me: *Heard your ex's wife is preggo?* So, great. Nothing I was part of had anything to do with them.

Except, then, Cyndra miscarried. With that her grip on Connor tightened – as he told it. For he started whatsapping me sometimes, to *unburden*, as he put it, and talking like we'd never come apart.

What? I was to, like, cut him off? Sorry. ★★★★ing couldn't.

He'd got to complaining she'd grown needy, clinging, and then he started on about missing what we'd had. That'd been real, he said, true. And didn't I feel it too? Well. Truth? So often I've had to hone my own – like whatever version of events could bring the client off, so I figured he'd be making his *truths* up as he went along. But also, I guessed that if Cyndra was clinging it was to the Connor she had met to begin with, caring, soft spoken, devoted. See, I'd been there before, watched one version of him transition through the next.

Who knew his moves better than I did? That sort of feral grace enticed, captured, monopolized; those liquid eyes drew you in. I remember when I felt it first, this hypnotic, arresting gaze that stirred interest to begin with, but then, a sort of breathless apprehension.

He told me once – one of his moments of reckless bragging – how fear turned him on. Watching it grow, I mean, helpless terror. He said pleading excited him, almost made him crazy. Almost, not quite. He said he had to stay in control to get there. He'd calm and soothe and re-establish confidence so as to watch again that first faint chill of uncertainty, of disbelief displaced by anxiety trembling into panic. That made him crazy. But it was never like that between us, that thing about helpless terror. No, once I got past the initial rawness of discovering what he was, I veered fast from hurt to fury, and I was never afraid.

I should have been. I knew him so much better than most people that I never realized how much more lay hidden. The dazzle blinded one so. For one thing, I never saw that the more I raged at him and the quieter he got, the more malevolent he became.

Don't imagine it was just my bloody blindness. Connor dissembled. Yet – hell, he flaunted too. That hidden side of him was nothing one discovered; he held it down till he was ready to display it.

But right – I get it you can't handle that, so enough. Let's get back to Cyndra.

To begin with, most of what I heard came from Connor.

It was no time at all after the first miscarriage that the second devastated her. Besides, it set Connor harping on the embryos that were there already, while Cyndra kept on playing for more time. I went abroad for weeks and tried to distance myself from it, but Connor's messages and calls kept coming in, full of irritation and resentment towards his wife and steeped with nostalgia for the fun times he'd had with me. I must have kinda wallowed in that, because I found myself shattered when his calls stopped. This sudden silence, unexplained.

I worked out later that he played on some sense of inadequacy the miscarriages brought on. Unlike me, she'd wanted kids and she'd only given up on the idea at the onset of the relationship, for Connor's sake. Then it got urgent. She bargained for a year or two while he pressed what I can only term his indecent proposal to use an existing embryo, then started to feel she was running out of time – for whatever reason. Some sort of disorder, Connor hinted to me, something she didn't want getting in the way permanently. Like she was trying to outstrip it.

Then almost a year afterwards, I heard they had their twins in L.A. Like – Whew! Last chain broken.

—⁄ı∖—

No contact for a couple years, then we meet up accidentally on this beach. They'd moved back to Sydney. Connor introduced me to the children as their aunt, and Cyndra's face was a picture. She obviously considered this an excess of goodwill on his part, but I knew what moved him was spite, pure and simple. Or perhaps he was playing for some high – two competing wives – who knows what went through his sick head?

Why I never cut myself off from them permanently? No explaining it to someone like you. OK, OK. I suppose I still hoped. Connor was a fever in my veins. We had barely met, in the first instance, before I took in a glance, a breath, and he went viral in me. Afterwards despite all the devastation he'd wrought, he remained like some . . . condition that flared up on every encounter. Like ★★★★ing shingles or whatever.

In a while, though, the few friends we still had in common whispered of trouble between the two of them. "Usual problem," one murmured to me, with an arch lift of her so tanned and lotioned shoulder. And perhaps the change in circumstances accounted for Cyndra's allowing me into the children's lives. Right – you find that hard to swallow and I can get why, but she'd no idea how I still felt about him, and by then she saw he wasn't quite what he'd seemed. So perhaps she sensed I hadn't been such a liar after all.

But as for the twins – they took to me right off. They turned out more enchanting than I could possibly have imagined, for I'd had no experience of small children. Like zilch. In no time I got to feeling that time spent with Micah and Melly was time with the only children I was ever likely to have in reach. But then, as this yearning sharpened, I started to rethink. For what prevented me from having my own?

Connor need never be involved, though who knew what he might get up to if I put my mind to it. He'd even hinted in one of those late-night heart-to-heart calls — but all that aside, fertilization could be a simple commercial undertaking, uncomplicated by our history. Perhaps I'd just drop in at the clinic. All that was simply procedural. My mind strayed a bit and played with it. You know? Connor? Not Connor? Anyway — I figured no immediate verdict about him need deflect me right then, one way or the other. I toyed with various scenarios for mere weeks before finalizing my arrangements.

Then, the positive reading. Like, Hallelujah.

I spent those months that followed charged with excitement. Kinda continuous high? On the way to a check-up, I stopped at a news agent and glimpsed a headline: a plane had plunged into the French Alps killing everyone. So I never bought the papers. In the waiting room I didn't spare a glance at the TV. I had like no space for anything bleak in my head. All I could think of was getting to see the baby on the screen in the examination room, and then I thought about visiting the twins afterwards, on my way home.

I was in first-rate shape, up for anything, if I'd still been my old risk-taking self. I mightn't have climbed rocks or gone scuba diving, but I felt normal enough to sail or even club crawl, though of course I didn't. What I most wanted was to curl up as close to Micah and Melly as I could get, playing Go Fish and listening to their chatter. "I'd like our children to be friends," I remember blurting out to Cyndra.

The kids were watching, so I spread my arms and whirled around, and they clapped, laughing. I was ecstatic — I can't describe it: as if every cell in me was aglow, and I could hear my body like music strumming, chords — I don't know — a keyboard rippling, sometimes soft chimes. And when I turned my attention outside myself it was, like, the whole world smelled of lavender.

Stuff would break in, of course. Like on TV. That was when tens of thousands of refugees trekked across Europe in the hope of reaching Germany, or anywhere that might take them. Only, along the way, border after border closed in front them. On one newspaper a father held his toddler and sobbed before a razor-wire fence, and that pierced me — I had to toss the paper aside. Easy to lock thousands of agonized people out your mind when you have your own life — it's automatic, and my baby was safe and well, tumbling under the arms I hugged around myself.

When I dropped in to see them, Connor eyed me kinda menacingly, but I was done with the hate now. I'd got the better of him, hadn't I? With the child I wanted inside me, I felt no attraction even.

A long time before, he'd threatened me, half laughing, that if I messed up the IVF project he'd do me a mischief, but I'd never taken that crap seriously. And now this was my project, mine alone.

I looked past him, at Cyndra, and insisted, "It'll be fine. It has to be." I stroked my belly longingly, and just the thought of the child was like velvet. What the ★★★★ could go wrong?

17

LAUNCHINGS

ALONG THE WAY I'D INTERVENED IN the odd stream of obscenity from Barrie, and, after a flurry of asterisks, deletions or rewordings, I put my foot down. "I don't speak your language," I snapped. "I won't." She resisted me for a while, acknowledging that she was (as she put it) a bit potty-mouthed and that was just how it was, but I said I'd hang up.

Then she groaned. "God. Like daughter, like mother."

Perhaps mention this calling of the Lord's name in vain? No. I reined myself in for the time being to keep her talking, even though her revelations went through and through me. Quite apart from the slew of ex-wife spite, vignettes like those on the miscarriages undid me.

Besides – the absurdities in her tale. Con chatting with her on the phone? Discussing his wife as if she floated on the periphery of this cozy relationship that lingered on between him and Barrie? Not that I doubted Barrie's capacity to play confidante to a husband she'd abandoned. Extrapolating some platonic conversation on Con's side, perhaps? Well, hardly about Cyn's most private circumstances. I saw very well that Barrie was twisting my nerves as she twisted everything.

But more than that got to me – stripping away thick years of insulation I had layered in. I cotched on the edge of the chair holding my belly and hearing again my own voice wailing from a distance. Even against that, I strained for insight into Cyn's trauma, for such it must have been, however Barrie sought to distort it. There was my own experience from my twenties, which no one knew about, least of all Joel. Entering into Cyndra's ordeal reopened the old wound.

Clueless as she must be, what would Barrie do but utterly misread her, and with her, Con? Or was Barrie wilfully distorting things?

How much of the spin was conscious?

See, this woman, this Barrie, should have been a writer. Making it up out of nowhere, contriving characters from thin air – the hardest thing to do, I give her that. Overdone of course, but if I didn't know the originals, she might have taken me in with her mish-mash of exaggeration and delusion. I stuck to it because Cyn's name kept coming up, and with it perhaps a chance of gathering something about those missing years. But *could* anything Barrie said be of use?

Yet the revelation about miscarriages stopped me cold. Oh, Cynnie, couldn't you have told me?

No. She'd opt to spare me for as long as she could keep us safely out of it, package all that was wrong and lock it away. I leaned over my jottings again and spread my fingers on the keyboard, knowing I could scrap as much as I had to from whatever I wrote next. But I had to deliver myself of it now – while my four were all asleep and no one would come to this desk. I had to set it down at least temporarily to account for Cyn's desperation. For how else to contextualize what it meant to bear a child after losing the one before, even in the most blameless of circumstances. And mine had not been blameless – which had convinced me I would never conceive again. Even when a doctor assured me everything was normal, I felt certain inside myself the stone I had become – after what I'd lost and how I lost it.

What a word is *lost*. How easy to stave off the forever in it, to cling to its unspoken promise of something left temporarily out of sight and likely to come to light sometime. That first pregnancy of mine, that baby was not that type of *lost*. It was my doing, that losing – loosing the irreplaceable from my body.

⸺⫻⫻⸺

Joel and I married when we were still early in our graduate programmes, and four months later I was pregnant. At barely twenty-three. So Joel was almost twenty-nine, but still – no money beyond our modest scholarships. I had set my eye on the life I wanted, the life for which I was constituted – or so I saw it. Then the wand signalled *pregnant*.

I suppose I went mad. It helps to think so. At any rate, I left our flat and took the usual route taxi to my parents' house in Princes Town. My mother was out. She'd lived alone since my father's death, and the old house was empty. At first I ran up and down the stairs looking for her, and then — I just ran up and down the stairs. I did that, on and on, till I collapsed.

When she came in and bundled me into the car to take me to the doctor, I said I'd come to tell her I was pregnant and had fallen on the stairs. I made her promise on the way that if anything went wrong, she would never tell Joel. I should have told him first, I said, and for him to hear now, when it would do no good — just say nothing about any baby, I pleaded.

She was aghast at the idea of keeping it from Joel, and I promised to tell him later.

I had the advantage of her, being too ill to argue with. In the end all she told Joel was that I had fallen on the steps and my cramps had come worse than usual, but I'd seen a doctor and needed only stay still a day or so. She set his mind completely at rest, as was her wont.

But nothing could rest mine. When I cried, they gave me medication for the pain and stopped the bleeding, but nothing could numb or staunch the guilt. For I had done it. Consciously. Purposefully. There was nothing mad about me, even temporarily. I didn't deserve the second chance. Later, when Joel and I were ready for children and none came, I was not surprised. I knew what was gone. I knew I didn't deserve a child. I saw myself, physically, as having blighted my body and, philosophically, spiritually — I don't know — as having wasted some sort of *allocation*.

When Cyn came, safely, easily through a Caesarean, I floated in a state of disbelief. And when everyone congratulated and cooed over me, I thought, *None of you knows what I did, what I am*. But there was Cynnie, perfect in body and mind, so she healed me. Sometimes I thought: I don't deserve her. Then I'd go cold with fear that I might lose her.

When I did, only last year, there was that instant of recognition, that glimpse of myself tearing up and down the old staircase, and I thought, I did this too, in some way. Only, reason insisted that was not how the physical world operated, and my own faith didn't accommodate a spiteful God. I told myself it was my persistent guilt making that connection. But say what? In the final analysis I'd lost my child. Again. Gone.

My *gone* is bigger than your *gone*, I told Barrie in my mind before I inclined my ear to her once more. At least she spoke sympathetically of Cyn, but — since nothing inhibited her maligning Connor — I could only suppose that was to keep my attention.

So. Barrie. How much if anything was true? What to keep in the record and how?

I'd have to tone her down, I thought, leaning my forehead on my fingertips. If I were ever to put her in a book, I'd have to dilute her or no one would swallow it. Or were there enough unconscionable people about to render her convincing? Mind you, I'd encountered characters in real life so bizarre they were hard to believe in even when they were in my face. For now, I'd just get down what I could.

"You know," Joel's voice broke in softly on me from the doorway, "now I've read Andrea's book properly, I see what you mean. But I also find her writing so engaging, the pictures so sharp. Not surprised it's doing well."

"How well?" I asked, minimizing my screen. "Any new development?"

"Besides the prize? I forwarded her last message with details of the award and about all the kudos. You didn't see it?"

"Right." I clicked on it, staring again at the announcement of the first prize. "Lovely."

I interrogated myself. What exactly worried me about Andrea's novel? Could it be that it had drawn more attention than mine? Ye olde sour grapes? I stared that in the eye, then relaxed. No. Her book had seized attention by feeding foreign notions of the Caribbean in ways that set off little shivers of recognition outside our region – a frisson I thought augmented some deep-set sense of superiority in the metropolitan world, made it possible for readers abroad to claim knowledge of us without ever having looked. It didn't have to be like that. I spun my mind through all I'd read from the Caribbean diaspora that shed direct rather than refracted light.

"I called her again," Joel added. "She's thinking of applying to one of the UWI campuses – and this could be the one. She had to check. Do you know of some post in Caribbean Criticism that also calls for a published creative writer? Ought to stand a chance. Says she's being recognized by Caribbeanists everywhere – UK, Canada, US – everywhere: *a fresh new voice speaking for the region* and all that. She's on lists for Best Reads and – hear this – One Hundred Most Influential Voices in prose fiction of the twenty-first century. There are YouTube interviews, podcasts, you name it. Hold on: here is it. Ha! *Fifty most important authors in world literature today.*"

"Aunt Drea's coming to *live* here?" Micah surprised us with his usual lightning processing of overheard snippets.

"Who knows?" Joel held out his tablet with the shot of the book cover. "We're talking about this book she wrote. Lots of people like it."

"I'm happy for her," I said. And I was. I wanted the children to know her better. I'd seen the post advertised for our campus, and I'd be delighted if the university went through with its searches and selected her. Only, recent stringency would be nothing compared to the financial crunch likely to follow on the pandemic. Vacant posts might well be frozen. Besides, when would she ever fly in? At best she'd be teaching online. I felt a wave of disappointment in advance at Andrea's chance to move here dematerializing.

But alongside that rose another counteracting wave of disquiet about the literary world appraising the Caribbean from outside. Still. Even deciding what was Caribbean. Then I ran through Andrea's claim, trying to be fair. Caribbean ancestry – check. Caribbean birth – check. Caribbean upbringing – for a good while. How much Caribbeanness was Caribbean enough for me? Well. Andrea certainly *could* write, and, hey, she was a good, good woman. Let's keep a grip, I thought. I hoped she'd get the post when . . . *if* things opened up.

As Joel and Micah set off in search of the others, it occurred to me that it was the *if* I found most disorienting. That future veiled a world hard to divine in the present climate of huge nations in discord. How united *was* the United States if it were true that states were bidding against each other for life-saving supplies and dodging federal agents who were outbidding and confiscating goods they might have provided in the first place? How much more organized had the United Kingdom been to begin with? And what did my fictions or Andrea's matter when reality was in convulsions?

Then, too, apart from the vista of a virtual dimension swallowing up all others, when would a metropolitan or local venue emerge for Andrea's launch? There was no conjuring up the civilized and civilizing launch of a novel to an audience of critics, artists, booksellers, readers generally – celebrants of intellectual labour gathered for the purpose. So with an odd combination of relief and regret, I closed *that* book gently, for the time being, to turn back to Barrie.

Cyndra wasn't a bad little thing, she'd said.

Tossed in to appease me, yes. Yet she must see she wouldn't change my view of Cyn however hard she worked to vilify Connor. So why *that* particular character assassination? What was in it for her? Or was it all an unmotivated psychotic rant?

Next, I couldn't envision wife and ex cozying up. Not on Cyn's watch. Of course, if Barrie got ill . . . Cynnie's soft heart . . . Only – dropped off children at Barrie's house? Surely not. I pondered the Cyn I knew, cautious and pragmatic. Hadn't she seen through Barrie? Whatever compassion I occasionally mustered for Barrie, I *saw* her still. As unreliable a narrator as one could get, I concluded before turning back to her testimony.

Just then, at my study door, there came a little muttering followed by two tentative knocks, and the twins peeked in. "I told him no, but he's not listening," Melody announced quickly.

Startled, I glanced at the window, because locked in as we were, Joel and I often lost track of the time of day.

"But why? Just a little walk," Micah insisted. "Nobody's on the road. Nobody. You can come watch us, Mama. And we'll cross it if we meet anyone – the way they say they do it now in England."

I shook my head apologetically. "Because you may bring home the virus," I said. "You may meet someone who sneezes near you or pat some dear little dog someone has been hugging and coughing on."

"Children hardly get sick," Micah objected.

"But they pass it on," Melody said. "Older people who get it can die."

At that Micah dried up, but he was clearly unconvinced.

When they went back outside, I heard him arguing with Melody. "Only if the old people are sick anyway," he said. "Mama and Papa are strong."

"Well, Mama has heart and Papa has sugar."

"Oho. I thought they were OK when you said the wheat and thing didn' matter."

I sent them to the porch to wait on a snack, while I drew out the frozen package I had hoarded for just such a time, nuked its contents briefly, and popped a tray into the toaster oven.

Twenty minutes later, when I set the plate on the porch table – and "Samosas?" – Micah tossed aside the cards and threw me a look glowing with adoration.

"How? When you got those?"

"A month or two ago when I foresaw the future. Listen," I said. "It's true the risk is extra high for Papa and me. But even children can get ill, and a few die if they have other disorders. Remember it attacks your lungs." I waited for that to sink in, but they watched me, clueless, and I had to spell it out. "Mattie is asthmatic."

They froze, the two of them. "Mattie could die?" Micah whispered.

"Don't even let's talk about it, and certainly not to him," I said, "because he doesn't have to. Once we all stay home. Quiet as mice."

"No one goes out, nothing comes in," Micah breathed, and Melody nodded sagely.

"One day there'll be medicine to cure and a vaccine to prevent it," I said. "For now, we have to keep ourselves entertained at home. Each one of us has to think hard about how to have fun right here."

Melody said tentatively, "Francis phoned. He said he wanted to get us a puppy if it was OK with you."

"Perfect," I said at once. Then I froze. "Wait. I'm sorry, chickens. Sorry, let me think."

"Why not, Mama?"

"When you get a puppy, you have to take him up and down for shots; there's food to buy and stuff to get so as to be ready for him. It's extra moving around and . . . and shopping . . . You see I already stocked up so as not to go out much now, and I didn't know to buy kibble –" I could hear my voice crack. They huddled close then, petting and comforting me. "I guess I could get kibble curbside," I added nervously. "But how to bring in a workman to mesh the gate, how. . ."

"Afterwards," Melody said. "OK, afterwards, right?"

And I nodded, wordless. I wasn't even sure anymore what that word might mean: *afterwards*.

"At least you have space outside to play." I found my voice. "You have food – not just to keep you alive – you even have samosas now and then. What if you had plain boiled rice and nothing else? People do. What if we lived in a crowded house with no yard outside, and everyone around us ill, so we had to stay in our one room and keep the doors and windows shut all day, all night?"

⁓⫶⁓

"I can't believe how understanding they are," I told Joel that night. Especially since adults in the wider society were beginning to act up, the loudest voices often the least deserving. One pastor demanded an exorbitant handout from the government, against the spreading want as salaries shrank or vanished altogether. Then – distractions from the simply restless.

Francis had told us how police stopped cars whose drivers claimed to be taking food for elderly parents, and searched trunks, sending home young people in beachwear with coolers full of beer. The government even had to reduce opening hours of hardware stores. "And is not wire sparking or bust pipe," Francis said. "Nah. They browsing house paint and barbecue pit. Still, it have enough people with sense to keep they tail home. We going make it, man."

Would that answer if the virus kept burgeoning on our doorstep? I felt less and less able to resist mounting resentment as the US president tweeted his followers to liberate what states they could from shutdown. But soon leaders in the United Kingdom and Canada were resisting pressure to lift shutdowns, their eyes on the likelihood of further waves. Outside, there was no consensus to guide us.

I foresaw us, restrictions relaxed, venturing out masked and gloved. The children would go back to school. Should we be masked when they came home . . .?

The phone rang before I could think that through, and it was Gabrielle, crying with the news that Jackie's son had died. No, she didn't know what had taken him to New York. And it had seemed a mild case before he collapsed. "He couldn't breathe. And . . . and other stuff." Gabriel couldn't go on.

But he was young, I protested. Not forty-five.

"Covid, though," she said. "Only with these strange clots no one can explain."

No one understood any of it. We must stay in, perhaps indefinitely. And Jackie had lost her child; he had died alone in the ambulance awaiting admission to a hospital too overwhelmed to accept him, where he would have died anyway. And I could not go to see Jackie, who had been my friend for over sixty years, or even talk to her on WhatsApp, because she didn't have a smart phone. The landline was the old type in the living room, and she couldn't raise from her bed, Gabrielle said.

"What, Mama?" Micah leaned over and twisted his head to see my face, because I was bent double.

"My friend's son died and I can't visit her."

He put his arms round me and said, "No one goes out. Nothing comes in."

I held onto him to prevent myself from going under.

For Jackie's loss brought it home. This initial containment here could hardly last. After a lull must come a surge, a spike. Twists, unforeseeable as the virus mutated, growing swifter and fiercer. For wasn't that what plagues did?

The phone again, and it was Francis asking if it wasn't time to collect curbside for us again, but we couldn't impose on him indefinitely and I'd filled the form already. I set out for the supermarket, driving for the first time in weeks, registering potholes that had widened and accepting there'd be no money to fix them for a while.

Back home I spent the hour washing fruit and vegetables, and disinfecting bottles and cans. It was already difficult to contemplate eating anything that other hands had touched unless it was something we could cook or scrub. Might that mean growing lettuce? I began working through how we'd acquire plants. Meanwhile I sliced off the little knob at the bottom of the head as I'd seen on YouTube, and I called Mattie to plant it in any flowerpot that had gone empty on the porch.

Their online classes over, Micah and Melody hurried down the back step to tear down palm branches and directed Mattie to help build a shelter outside. They declared their intention to live in the backyard forever. Only then I noticed the haze, Saharan dust blanketing the horizon and even the San Fernando Hill. We had to gather inside and seal it out, for Mattie. When he insisted on bringing in his *pet lettuce*, I realized that even if it ever did take root and grow, he'd never let us eat it.

By then I was spending hours devising games, printing pictures to colour or cut out, and providing for them blocks, cushions, books and rolls of toilet paper to build edifices. I would write only at night – Barrie's story as far as I could make it out. It could never be Cyn's till I unravelled truth from venom in the tangle of Barrie's ravings.

That night I returned to my desk, which accommodated my legs better than Cynnie's did, and my concentration must have lapsed. Something broke in, and for a while I could not work it out. Then I pinned it down. The new stillness of our evenings was torn every so often by voices raised farther along the road – probably in the house patronized by the Toyota lady whom Joel called Parker, the woman who left her car just past our gate before making her way uphill.

Joel poked his face around the door. "Heard that?"

"They're getting worse," I told him. "Locked together day and night now."

And after the late news, a wail of anguish rose from the same house up the road, followed by a crash. "Oh God, oh God, ohGodohGod." Her voice. A door slamming, being pounded. She bawled, "Help me!"

I grabbed the phone.

"What?" I hadn't seen Joel nodding off on the couch, and now he jumped, startling me.

"You don't hear? I'm calling police. I not waiting for him to kill her."

"Didn't hear a thing." He stared at me. Then a crash again in the distance.

The woman's voice. Screaming.

Joel grabbed the keys and opened up the front door then the wrought iron, and the mask slipped from his fingers as he went racing for the gate. Before I could follow with it, he was across the road and up outside their gate. Slamming his fist on the bell.

"Stop this!" he yelled. "We calling police."

Silence instantly.

By now I was out in our front yard holding the mask up foolishly, and I heard the woman's voice raised. "Is OK. I just knock down something and I was upset. Was a wedding present."

"Well, the gentleman will explain that to the police," Joel shouted and turned away. The gate to that house slid open behind him after he left, and when he was about to cross the road back to our side, the man caught up with him. By now I was back up on our porch, but I could see and hear them clearly. The man grabbed at Joel's arm from behind, *touched* him.

"Wait. Oh Gooosh, boy. Hold on. I wouldn't like you to misunderstand, nah."

But Joel shook him off and crossed without looking back. "The only people you need to satisfy with your explanation is the police." He slammed our gate behind him as I went in ahead and started up the stairs.

Moments later I heard him locking up, but then, before he could have got his shoes off, he was on the downstairs phone, loud and clear.

"OK, OK," he snapped. "I hear you. Sorry about you job and all of it. But you see this business tonight? Not again. Next time I wouldn' tell you nothing. You will just hear the siren." A pause. "Nah. I don't need no drink outside my house. Everything I need right here." He slammed the receiver in its cradle.

"Papa?" Melody's voice husky with sleep. "What's going on?"

Then Mattie. "Is it bandits?"

"No. It's fine. Go back to sleep."

"But you sounded angry." She was awed. "Who was that?"

Afterwards, back at my desk, what with all Joel's fuming about the neighbours and my trying to keep the details from the children, it took a while before I could pick up what I'd been assembling. I was unsettled by events playing out only yards away from us, but I was determined not to be deflected from getting to the bottom of whatever had taken place in Sydney.

I was beginning to think Barrie a brilliant girl in breakdown brought on by heart-rending distress. I couldn't say I found her likeable, or even tolerable. Any sympathy she stirred got swallowed up promptly by distaste. And, OK, trepidation, for she seemed this mess of imagined horrors, in her state of mind likely to do untold damage. She had to be kept away from the children, at least for now. *Needs help though*, I noted. [*Help*. Word for a hand under the elbow, friendly advice, light medication, shock treatment. Needs help. Don't we all?]

I must have been worrying it for hours, slowly coming to the conclusion that we might never be able to completely resolve Mattie's unrest, or indeed that of the twins, without confronting the anguish of this woman whose connection with them couldn't be dismissed, and whose life was ripped apart.

In trying to reach into whatever turmoil the children might be suppressing, I tripped over something else left undone. Counselling. Lord. We'd let that slip. We'd made a follow-up appointment with Dr Mohammed for the week following The Day of the Container. That excitement and Barrie's calls afterwards had put it from our minds. Then the lockdown. By now, though, there must be some sort of a Zoom thing. It jarred, but I knew I must work it out.

Then, outside, an explosion of noise along the street: dogs barking furiously gate by gate, voices laughing, so I rushed to the window to see what had shattered the silence this time.

Impossible. *Fools* walking together, close-close on the road in their pretty tights, swinging stylish water bottles and chatting in each other's faces — as if they couldn't exercise in their own yards. For these were not people without space of their own: these were spoilt babies. Theirs was a whole separate disease, this failure of imagination that blocked basic information from making an impression on the brain. Theirs was a disorder so widespread it sequestered the smaller, thinking population in shrinking pockets of hyperawareness where we might just waste away in isolation.

In disgust I gathered up laptop and notes from my desk and plonked them back on Cyn's as if that would settle things down. Only, the walkers had revealed it was five-thirty. I'd worked through the night — which was bad for me. Irresponsible. Well, five minutes more then.

Only, the most intransigent problem was that the more divergent Barrie's behaviour appeared, the more wounded she showed herself to be and the more quietly convincing her tone became. And even as her humanity grew more compelling, somehow, independently of that, the emerging tale progressed mechanically, almost pitilessly, cogwheels meshing with whatever information already projected here and there in my mind.

So. Pursue this account through, at least over the next few nights. Reading Barrie, let alone writing her, was unhinging. Only, having turned her on, I found it impossible now to turn her off.

18

TREBLE DAMAGES

BARRIE (?)

VAGUELY I RECALL PAIN, SHARPENING. BLINDING, rending pain. Then the screaming. Freezing corridors with brilliant lights rushed by and attendants in scrubs raced alongside the gurney. Wheels whooshing beneath me. Voices, indistinct. Cyndra's face floated above me, eyes spilling over, then she was beyond reach, glimpsed through glass. Connor's face though – his eyes conveyed nothing. I searched them, and nothing. The hollowness of the empty-hearted, I think, now it comes back to me. I remember this sense of falling, falling into an icy void.

I had no idea how long I was out, but Cyndra was there when I opened my eyes. She held Mattie close to me as I recovered. The sweetness of him, the smell of his skin and rhythmic rise and fall of his belly. Aah, Mattie. "You'll be fine," Cyndra whispered. Later, when the television screens were full of terror attacks on Paris, Cyndra switched it off. "Life," she insisted. "We celebrate life."

I could sense it beyond the lingering nightmare. "Life." I repeated it after her, lacing my fingers through Mattie's curls.

"We'll be fine," Cyndra kept repeating.

But we weren't fine. Even when I felt better physically, other sensations persisted – an awareness of rushing cold and the terror that everything I had ever craved might be slipping away.

Barely after I recovered and got back to my office, I found someone had been spreading filth about me. Then, a break-in at home and my desk ransacked. I figured Connor might still have some bunch of old keys, and I changed the locks. I told Cyndra nothing. Don't stir, I thought.

Leave their marriage to work if it can because – you know – the children. And besides, Cyndra. She'd been good to me for no reason I could see.

Not that I saw so much of her or the children anymore.

Sometimes, though, she managed to bring them over and leave them while she ran a quick errand. The old house lit up with their faces, with silly songs, the thud of play dough thumped into shape, daring acrobatics and wild, noisy games. I can close my eyes and hear it: laughter bubbling up through the cracks between the floorboards and up the rusty pipes, percolating through every crevice.

But these tantalizing shafts of well-being could never last. Connor insisted the twins were dirty when they came home; I kept a nasty house and he wouldn't have them rolling in it. Cyndra assured me I was welcome to come to their house, but I understood – only when he was out. Now there was no dropping them off when she had to shop or chase off to the hospital for an emergency. That meant less of Mattie too, because he adored the twins and I hadn't the heart to tear him away. Besides, there was just the one sitter to watch over the three children together.

So I saw less of them and plunged down into the usual abyss, unable to work, bathe, or swallow solid food. Or leave the house or sleep for more than half an hour at a time. Looking back, I can see myself tightening my knees to my chest and squeezing myself smaller and smaller as if I could make myself disappear. Solve everything once and for all.

One night I messaged Cyndra, "Morituri te salutamus." Then I passed out under the heavy desk that had been my mother's.

That was how Cyndra found me, and she must have been telephoning insistently for some time before she gave up and drove over, because a phone somewhere above my head had nagged on and on. Then someone was dragging me out between the thick oak legs of Pauline's desk and screaming for help. I knew when Cyndra left me on the car seat where the gardener she'd called in helped set me down and when Cyndra went back to lock the house. I think I stayed exactly as they had placed me while she drove to the hospital. Later, after the doctor in Emergency agreed to release me, I curled up tight on the backseat while she took me to her house.

"Someone has to get her back on her feet," I caught that stubborn inflection to her voice. I picked up Connor's expression of loathing as he set down my legs, and I closed my eyes again, hearing a muted crackle as Cyn spread plastic on a bed. I believe she and the twins were rolling me onto it when I passed out.

I remember, first, light curtains fluttering at the window. I think they had small flowers embroidered here and there, for shadows floated over me and the white-white cloth shimmered all around as the breeze took the fabric. I drifted in and out of consciousness, and when I woke up properly I was on a soft sheet, in clean pyjamas, feeling just bathed. Melly was sitting on the floor beside the bed, turning the pages of a book with turrets on the cover and Rapunzel letting down her hair.

"You're going to share my tower," Melly announced, "and I'll make you better."

And she meant it. They put her in Micah's room, but she and Micah would come in when Cyndra was around. They pretended reading, between bickering over me, and they blackmailed me into eating and swallowing medicine.

But after a while I began to sense I'd outstayed my welcome. It seemed the linen on the twin beds was never changed, the room not cleaned. I dragged a mop and bucket and did it myself – only reasonable while I was sleeping there, after all. But I thought, wouldn't they at least ensure the room that was normally their little girl's stayed clean? Suddenly I took it in – the unsanitary conditions in the whole house. Face basins and toilets, God. I wore slippers into the shower.

After a while I worked out the source of strange squeals and scuttling overhead. In the bathroom a pipe ran up to the ceiling into an opening that was for some reason too wide for it. Perhaps some moulding had fallen off. But, anyway, I was sitting on the toilet when a scampering overhead turned my eyes up in time to see a huge rat racing down. Then it stopped, locked eyes with me, glittering black eyes, and then chased up again, leaving its long bare tail hanging down through the gap. Squirming.

How could anyone, let alone a doctor, live like that? But it was the thought of the children that freaked me out, the twins at home in this, eating and sleeping in it. Whatever I said to Cyndra (for I kept clear of Connor) she regarded me blankly. Was it that she didn't see? Smell? Was it that if I were well enough to talk about cleaning I must be in shape to go on home?

One day I thought – to hell with tiptoeing round this. I grabbed Cyndra's hand and tugged her into the room loaned me by Melly. "Look."

I pointed to the bed. "Don't you see the rat crap on the sheet? You don't smell the urine, from clear outside the goddamn room? I don't know how you draw breath. What about the children? You don't ★★★★ing care if they end up with leptospirosis?"

"I'll have to consult Con," she said. So quietly, her face a blank.

When he came in, she asked me to tell him what the trouble was while she got out fresh sheets. I wasn't about to tell him anything, but I was so wound up now I couldn't stop talking anyway.

He said perhaps Cyndra might understand at last what he'd been trying to tell her.

Silently she shook out the fresh sheets, and they billowed over the bed. It was dreamlike, the pastels drifting against the brilliant whiteness of the background fabric. But of course the mattress was gross. I tried to calm myself with the thought of this glimmer of clean cloth between it and my body, between it and Melly's body when I'd left, but I could not have looked convinced. I was squeezing my arms tight against myself so as not to touch anything, and he was pointing, pointing at me, his forefinger like a gun at my temple.

"Have you got it at last?" he shouted at Cyndra.

She didn't answer. So much was in her face – shock, disbelief, bewilderment – but she had nothing to say. She looked too busy processing alternative explanations for what was going on. Then, tentatively, she wondered aloud whether my medication was OK, or whether there could have been some mixup at the chemist's.

And that was when I knew. Connor had been replacing pills my doctor had prescribed.

"This can't be right," Cyndra was saying.

And how was I to distinguish between the effects of whatever he had planted in the dispenser and my actual circumstances. I could see, feel, smell it all, the nastiness. Cyndra went in search of the dispenser but it was empty, and Connor brought out the last bag he had picked up from the chemist. She scrutinized every vial.

"This looks absolutely fine," she told him. "What could the explanation be?"

I left the room urgently. It was impossible to swallow my saliva, and I found myself having to spit frequently. Although that made no difference to the condition of the room, I tried, as a matter of principle, to keep it near to a wall.

Well into the night I heard them talking in low voices in the hall outside my room. "This isn't from anything on her prescription," Cyndra insisted. My ear hurt, jammed against the door. "It's like — I don't know — a bad trip. Like a psychotic reaction. From Ecstasy or something."

"No, it's not like a psychotic reaction. It's psychosis," he snapped. "The woman is stone mad, and you bring her into the same house with our children. I'm not taking it a minute longer."

I knew now I had to get as far from them as possible, so I stuffed a few items in a pillowcase and stormed out to the kitchen. "Open this door." I pounded on the back door to the driveway, and he came striding out with his keys.

"Good riddance," Connor muttered at me in the doorway as I passed by him, his lips drawn back and eyes narrowed, tightening his face to an expression more vicious than I had seen before, and I wondered how he had ever been alluring.

"You're in your pyjamas, for God's sake," Cyndra shouted at me, but as she came after to drive me home, he turned to her, changed again: the meanness vanished, swept aside by a sort of tired compassion.

"Just drop her at the house and come straight back, Cyn," he said. "Don't go inside with her. Promise now, or I'll worry about you."

"I promise," she said. But she looked back and forth between us, confused.

I stopped all medication and slept little over the next couple weeks. But at least the tension of his house wore off, and I could prepare to get back to work. Now and then the walls closed in, the ceiling lowered, dripping muck, but I held on to the thought of Barrington Intyre and Associates. Once I got to the office I could perform, so no one guessed what I went through outside the office, inside my head. I was a different person at work, my true self.

With the children forbidden to come to me, though, home shrivelled to a safe place for the night, a stop to bathe and change clothes. The office, having never had anything to do with the children, remained unspoiled. But home, stripped of them, was denuded, violated. Yes, occasionally I met them by chance with Cyndra or Connor, but it was no good. They twitched restlessly through the brief encounter and then they were gone.

"Listen," I said to Cyn when I called on her office phone so my number wouldn't register on her mobile. "You're doing them no good, sheltering them in this state of denial about their father. He's a menace," I told her. "You need to protect them from him."

That turned out to be the last straw, because of course she clung to her own vision of him and, worse, must have relayed the conversation. Things never recovered afterwards. I plowed on through months of Connor's unrelenting malice, and eventually I telephoned him and perhaps said more than I should. I know now that I should have expected what came next.

The next day Connor stormed into my office, slammed the door and leaned over my desk, threatening to force me into an institution for good if I didn't turn myself in for treatment. I shoved the chair back from the desk and came round to face him, for I was almost his height and wouldn't have him looming over me. Treatment? Me?

"Because *you're* psychotic?" I demanded.

"Stop it," he said, managing to look hurt and misunderstood – he did that so well. "We've been good to you beyond belief."

"Well beyond," I agreed. "Spread scandal about me right here in my own firm, enveloped me in nastiness in your house. Drugged me. I'd have steered clear of you if it hadn't been for the children."

"Only, all that pseudo-maternal crap has come in so late." Then he shocked me by locking his arms around me and tugging me close, kissing me bruisingly while I struggled. He whispered, "We could've kept the fireworks going in that mansion your mother left you, but I can enjoy it without you in the long run. For now, I've a roof over my head *and* a restraining order. Come near my children and I'll see you put away." I could feel him laughing silently. "And the sooner the better." As he thrust me from him, I struggled, whacking my head against the filing cabinet.

If only I could have pretended after that, I might have been able to ride it out. But it was his lies. Inconceivable, mind-blowing lies. Subtly, untraceably, he began poisoning my employees' minds. So there I was – my authority in the firm undermined and the future hazy. Micah and Melody seemed uncertain about me now on those rare occasions when I saw them – almost frightened. That was why, when I worked out that Connor was arranging to get rid of me, I set out to protect myself.

No, not paranoia: common sense. When you're under attack by something irrational, you don't pause to debate with it, you fight it off. I gathered from a client that it was easy enough to get a gun, and I saw it was imperative – not for the sake of my own life, but for the children.

With me gone, who would be on hand to warn or support Cyndra? He would end up with absolute and permanent control. You could get a handgun on the grey market, I discovered. Not outright illegal – a firearm that should have been surrendered years ago, perhaps, once its owner died. But it turned out not to be as simple as my client had made out. At least, not for me.

So, no gun.

What I had to do was prep parts of the house where I might be cornered. I phoned Cyndra and warned her to get away with the children, as far from him as she could. "You gotta go back home. Get back to Trinidad," I told her. It was going to blow up – it had to. She was going to hear the talk that had already started. She wouldn't put up with it and he wouldn't back down. He wasn't going to just let her go. I knew him better than anyone else.

Needless to say, he distorted everything he heard I'd said. He squeezed and wrung my life into a tale of his own invention – until the men came for me and hauled me away. Locked me up. That was the first time. But soon as I got out, I told her again. *Get yourself and the children back where you belong.*

Up to then, she'd believed him – that I was mentally deranged, no more to it than that. But now she knew he was playing around. She'd found him out on at least that level. So I got it out of her that she'd warned him she would take the children and go if it didn't stop. That was when I told her he would kill her if he believed she was going to leave.

Well, naturally Cyndra insisted he would never hurt her. She stared at me in shock, and I realized it was compassion that stopped her from cutting me off. She was a doctor and I was ill: I saw that in her face. The idea of a man as gentle as Connor being a threat was outrageous. I tried to ram it home that she must get as far away as she could. This made no sense, she argued. Gently. She always spoke softly to me. The thing to do was to sort things out right where she was, Cyndra said. He'd only follow her anyway. As he should.

But I knew better. "He's not going to Trinidad," I told her. "Believe me. You say he'll be off to Vienna for two weeks. This course, as he calls it – but you know better. Be ready. The minute he goes, get yourself and the children on the plane. Drop them in your parents' hands and double back. While you're gone I'll pack up all I can of your stuff for shipment.

The instant you're back, you put it in your parents' names rather than your own and send it off. Then, straight back on the plane. You can be gone again days before he gets back and there'll be nothing he can do."

"Aha? You see this endless hauling and pulling? I not able," Cyndra said, indistinctly – more like she was talking to herself. "One thing I know for sure – I done with that." But I could see I was getting through to her. She was wavering. She muttered, "My father would say – Do like Hannibal. Find a way out or make one." I know she told you they both had jobs lined up for them in the Caribbean. I know she told the twins she was moving to get away from me. I'm the one who advised her what the story had to be.

For in the end it came down to my plan. She wasn't about to put up with blatant infidelity, but she wouldn't have it out with him in front the children. When she learnt the worst of it, she let me call in packers and get stuff crated up while she was doing the turnaround in Trinidad, and when she got back to Sydney she sent off the shipment. I dropped her at the airport and helped her find the right gate, then sat to finish my coffee. I was walking towards the door of the departure area when I came face to face with Connor.

He'd got back early, seen half the house stripped bare and a kettle on the kitchen table still warm. He tore out and headed for the airport, making phone calls all along the way. He confronted me in the departure lounge, and I was so shattered about the finality of Cyndra's move and the children gone that when I saw him I could hardly take it in – that he was there.

He'd already phoned the police, going on about his bloody restraining order, and called the hospital for help regarding a psychiatric emergency. He had me on record as potentially dangerous, and now he told them I had terrorized his wife into taking his children out of the country. He couldn't have known the kids had gone before.

But I found all that out later. When I caught sight of him, I turned around and darted across the hall weaving between shocked travellers and their confused families and friends, bewildered faces ducking away as I dodged airport officials trying to head me off. But I had no chance against the three hefty officers that appeared from every side. They converged and ★★★★ing dragged me off. When I managed to glance back, Connor was gone.

He must have bought his ticket immediately, because I was in the van when her message came through that she had seen him board the plane. He took his seat in the row behind, then convinced the woman beside Cyndra, in the middle of the row, to exchange with him for a window seat. From the bathroom Cyndra sent me this hasty message that he'd told her neither of them would be going to Trinidad. Knowing him I realized that when they stopped for her connection, he'd make a turnaround and ★★★★ing bring her back to Sydney alive or dead.

The man beside me in the van snatched my phone and I never saw it again. Nothing further came to me from the outside world for weeks.

The hospital walls pressed in on me. The ceiling crushed down. I couldn't fling up my arms to stave it off because they were strapped tight to these metal bars along the sides of the mattress. I couldn't bring up my knees because my ankles were bound as well, each lashed to its corner at the foot of the bed. Another patient said a member of my staff came enquiring for me, and I was torn between shame at being discovered in such a place and yearning to see a face I could bear to look at. But the authorities would not allow me to see anyone until I was more composed.

For a time I fought them. I screamed at Connor, then for Mattie. Eventually I cried and cried for Cyndra. Then I gave in. I wanted only to get out. While I pretended to have resigned myself, the days and nights slid into and through each other until I lost count of how long I had been there, how long since I had seen or held the children. After a while they said my family was welcome to visit, but who was there? Once he had brought Cyndra back, she would never have found a way of avoiding him so as to find me. And what of the children? Where were they? Had he got them sent back to Sydney?

I waited for mail from Cyndra, for relayed telephone messages, anything. I gave her number and email contact to the doctor assigned to me, to the orderlies and nurses on my block. My sister, I told them. Tell her where I am and ask her to send a message – any message, I pleaded. They said there was no response, and I didn't believe they'd tried. I know now they may have.

Years seemed to pass, but I knew at the time it might only be months, even weeks. When they released me it was on condition that I report in regularly, and the driver took me to a flat in a lightly supervised hostel they approved for convalescents, a sort of halfway house.

I waited just inside the door without taking in anything about the room. As soon as I heard the van that had dropped me pull away, I shot out and slammed the door behind me. Then I flagged down a taxi to the house I had packed up for Cyndra.

It was exactly the same as we had left it but for the dilapidation that sets in so quickly when a place is abandoned. The curtains half open at the window seemed familiar after I stared past the mould. Next door, a car I vaguely recognized stood in the garage. So I walked across and enquired.

Yes, they said. Wasn't it sad?

That was how I learned about the crash. Since Cyndra had nodded to them from the other side of the fence before getting into the taxi with the children, they had seen no one but me, packing up. Some people said she had come back, but no one knew when. Perhaps Connor did come home before going to meet his wife for the flight, they said, for the records showed he was on the plane. They heard nothing until . . . it had all happened. They watched my face as the inevitable thought of murder-suicide played across my mind, but then they told me how the newsflash had shattered the morning. They recounted what they knew and how much no one knew, speaking softly as to an overexcited child or a dying friend, and they asked how I could possibly not have heard. "Where were you?" they whispered.

And the guilt that weighed on me: I'd goaded Cyndra into snatching them all away for good. She'd never have done it if I hadn't convinced her he wouldn't follow.

Weeks later it was, while I was struggling to resume work and floundering in the backlog, that I gathered enough information to track the paperwork and gain access to a record of passengers. Only then did I see with my own eyes that Connor really had been on the plane.

I felt a storm of conflicting reactions. I had loved him once as fiercely as I'd come to hate him and . . . and yes, grief – that I'd lost him in so many ways – it slammed down on me. And there was Cyndra, who'd deserved none of this but – so it seemed to me sometimes – she'd brought it all down by giving in to him over and over. But I needed her now as I'd never needed anyone. Still, Mattie was alive, and Micah and Melody, orphaned as they were – all of them more mine now than anyone else's. My own. So relief surged up alongside the heartache and I struggled in these conflicting currents for – I don't know – weeks, before finding my feet and working out how to contact the children.

Now, nine months since the crash, and four or five since my first call to Trinidad, I've spoken repeatedly with their grandmother. Yet I've been feeling myself sink again into the loss and isolation. Before this I was suspicious of all doctors, especially after the hell Connor had thrown me into. But this time, of my own volition, I sought out a doctor of my choice. I came to the conclusion I had to get a grip on myself if I was ever to act in the best interest of the children.

Making contact months ago had been straightforward. I thought it out of the question that two old people on a backward island should keep these three children — all the family I had on earth. But in March a few words with their grandmother, there on the phone in the bedroom of that Tobago hotel — that brief conversation made me rethink. I found no reason to consider her senile, but, more than that, something . . . resonated. What if I had been right about the twins having grown afraid of me. And then, Mattie confused. Mattie was better now, she said but, before . . . *distraught*, that was the word she used.

I began to second guess how much I understood of what had gone before. Then what took hold of me was Cyndra's willingness — well, perhaps not willingness — but her acceptance of the need to take them as far away as she could. Perhaps from me, as much as from Connor. And I was shaken.

Literally. An unfamiliar sensation made me stare down at my hands, and they were trembling. For the first time I wondered what to do. It was only weeks before that I'd booked the most convenient flight I could get — to Tobago — from which to reach Trinidad and take charge of the children. I'd planned to collect Mattie before, then decided not to separate them. Besides, I did not then have all the paperwork I would eventually gather. At the same time, one country after the next was locking down, and who knew how long it would take me to complete a legal process in Trinidad. Also — perhaps the medication was kicking in — there was the danger of bringing them back to Sydney on a series of flights.

I was frantic. After trying to reach them by phone, I picked up that message from Cyndra's mother. She had Cyndra's voice, begging me not to unsettle Mattie, and that familiarity of her tone, accent, mannerisms of speech shook me. It came to me there, by the hotel landline in Tobago, that before doing anything I must get myself in condition to make a sound decision.

Sitting on that plane back to Sydney, hours of it, forced me to think and rethink. Before leaving home, I'd seen someone and got a prescription to help me sit still all that way, and what might have been a gruelling trip there and back turned, ironically, into an opportunity for thinking things through. The medication calmed me and cleared my mind.

I was still certain I could go back for them anytime the virus died off, and I knew I must have them. This wasn't a hunger that would pass. Only, then, as I began to see the world in sharper focus, I grasped what the pandemic meant. With borders closed and airlines down, the whole worldwide mess, I wouldn't get near to them again for . . . I didn't know how long. And I wanted them, so being kept away was like I'd been tied up, and I could have chewed off my own arm to tear loose and find them.

And in that instant of craving, their absence struck me again with a force that set my flesh throbbing. For I had driven Cyndra away not only to shield the children from Connor's influence (though I wanted that, more than I can say), and not only to punish him for all the suffering he had unleashed on me (though I wanted that as well), but because I wanted him left behind. Free. I'd fought him off but never torn him out of me.

And when that came to me, a dizziness swept me as if everything beneath my feet had given way, and I was not in my apartment any longer but back in the St Mary of the Cross MacKillop Medical Sanctuary. MacMed, the staff said. Only, the sacrilegious called it MacKillop Paddock. I was back there where I had been months or years earlier when time was fluid, contracting or expanding limitlessly. And as I recognized that instant in MacMed, I relived the jolt that had gone through me. Was that the shock treatment? Strapped in as I was, I heard a man yell words I could not catch, foreign perhaps, or distorted somehow. I don't know. But on the flight home, looking back, I remembered the world tilting, and I cried out. A flight attendant's tray clattered down, and I was suddenly part of the crash, screams all around and cases sliding, the plane plummeting, a roar and flash, then nothing. Metal shards and blazing fragments plunged into the sea, the water seething. *I'm here, Connor*, I screamed.

I fell apart again, as I had that time in MacMed, only now my arms were not strapped down. I sat in my seat on that plane home, burying my face in my hands while the flight attendant held me, and I sobbed, "Oh God, why wasn't I there?"

When we landed in Sydney, I had calmed enough to deplane without help but was shaken to the core. I got home and stayed in bed for two days. Then, I took a taxi – I didn't trust myself to drive – and consulted the same doctor I'd found I could trust. I agreed to continue with his prescription, although in the past I'd always given up quickly on medication or rejected it outright, especially after Connor messed with those pills. Now I was intent on reclaiming my life, for the children's sake.

I also kept contact with the airline and followed up on the matter of damages. I called Cyndra's mother again and we kept up a connection. Meanwhile I continued consultation with the doctor:

"You spoke of their father." Dr Nguyen tilted back his head and contemplated me in a relaxed, almost impersonal manner. "Who was that?"

That ****ed me off. Hadn't he been listening? What was I paying him for? "I've told you everything I can think of about my ex-husband, Connor."

"Aah, and Melody and Micah were his." I'd said all that. I'd explained about the process for claiming compensation from the airline, for care of the children. What didn't he ****ing understand? "You claimed for all three children, then?"

"Obviously."

"But Mattie's father. Who was he?" Dr Nguyen's voice continued, gouging it out. "What was the name of Mattie's father? Was it Connor or was it a more recent lover, or some anonymous sperm donor? All done through the clinic? For, if so, why did the airline acknowledge proof of Connor's *three* children? Who was Mattie's father?"

"Connor." How many times must I tell you?

"Then who is Mattie's mother – who actually gave birth to him?"

He ripped open my mind and forced me to look past the raw lips of the wound, deep inside the crimson seeping core of it, and there was Cyndra four years ago, holding a healthy boy with one arm and supporting me with the other while my clothes clung to me, soaked, and she was smeared with blood too. She held me while I clutched my belly in both hands, the pain unbearable.

Afterwards, when I woke up and reached for Mattie, she kept hold of him. But Connor — I thought in the dazed way one does coming out of anesthetic — it's Connor you must keep them from before he assumes his real shape and eats their hearts.

Nguyen asked why I thought that, and I heard myself wailing, "He devoured mine." Yet when he asked how I felt about Connor now, I couldn't bring myself to say.

From the doctor's office I returned to my barren apartment, and, after a couple days, to my own desk at Barrington Intyre and Associates. All the time I worked frantically through my head to figure out what to do about the children. The compulsion to fly back to the Caribbean was almost overwhelming, but there was no way in. Borders were closed tight. and in between, one country after another plague-ridden.

Dr Nguyen advised me to check into a home or hostel nearby, and I went along with a facility he recommended, a restful place to sort through my thoughts.

My office was closed because of the pandemic, and I wanted to involve myself in something utterly different from anything I'd done before. I did what work there was for the facility in which I stayed, and registered online for a programme I thought might grip my mind. Once since doing that I've opened my laptop to write the children, but then rethought it. I'm still considering how to go forward.

19

DISTANCINGS

✧

I TORE MYSELF AWAY FROM BARRIE'S version of things and hurried off on a long-postponed visit to the bathroom. While I sat there, I reached back for a notepad I kept with a pen in a Ziploc bag on the tank. Afterwards I stuck for a while holding the lever down after the flushing finished, almost unaware of where I was. I assessed Barrie as a narrator again and found her even harder to trust, though it was impossible not to plow on.

I forced my mind back to earlier parts of her story. Cyn's house then. Cyn who had – if she had any disorder – a phobia for dirt. I shifted my thoughts from Barrie to the children. Careless like other kids, dropping things about – towels, peanut shells, slippers. But they washed their hands, scuffed shoes on the doormat, dropped tissue in the toilet. Flushed the toilet. They hadn't learnt that in a nasty house. Even if I hadn't known Cyn, that was clear enough.

Was Barrie mad or malicious?

Good God. I rubbed my forehead, trying to get her in focus again, this persistently metamorphosing organism, and it came to me once more that she inhabited a different world to any I could draw up in my mind, just as if she were some alien life form beamed in from an unknown planet or an age of which nothing else was known. And then, she had been there all the time, remote and unseen, before this breakout of unlikely events had cast her in our path.

The enormity of it surfaced in my mind – what had been unfolding behind the calm face of our child as we chatted on Skype. She and Connor would have gone to work with their usual professional serenity so none of their colleagues could guess what they were up against in their domestic lives. And there was Barrie, sedately advising her clients on the law in between viciously slandering her ex-husband and shopping, quietly on the grey market, for a gun.

The workplace, the supermarket, social gatherings. This was what unnerved me: the feeling that from now on, everywhere, I might see faces composed to project one version of reality over another. And if the time came when I might go again to the department for mail, or even exchange bows in passing the peace on a Sunday morning, or bump elbows with Jackie – there I would be, juggling normals.

I cried and cried for Cyndra, she'd said. Cyn deserved none of this, according to Barrie. Yet, to Cyn's mysterious apology (*I never knew, Barrie. Can you ever forgive me?*), she'd replied, *you bitch.*

A feeling of contamination crept over me, and before I knew what I was about I was under the shower, hot water steaming down as I scrubbed and scrubbed compulsively even while reminding myself to get back and shut down the laptop before grabbing what sleep I could.

A mistake.

~/|\~

I returned to Cyn's desk and found Joel sitting there, his face blank, turned up to the sunflower print that seemed suddenly fraught with unpleasant associations I could not pause to work out. In his left hand he twirled my green ink pen.

"Where," he asked, in a tone so grim as to be unrecognizable, "did all this come from?" He flicked his fingers at the screen while staring at me incredulously. "You mean you've been in touch with that monster? Made and maintained a connection with someone intent on taking the children, someone who would happily have shot their father? Who drove Cyn and her husband from their home onto that plane, drove them to their death?"

His reading my work had never bothered me. We riffled among papers on each other's desks quite freely. We'd always skimmed each other's writing. What floored me was the view he held up.

"This is just so you can weave her lies into stories –"

"How can you think that for an instant –?"

"– some make-believe world is . . . is what it's for, this endless chat and message and *connection,* this encouraging contact? Drawing into our space a proven danger to Cyn's children? Something grown into a mental disaster hanging over Mattie?" His voice broke off, his face contorted as he drew breath to go on. "Are you *mad*?"

"She has so many faces, voices, selves; why do you assume her true self is the worst of them?" I protested, hearing, even as I spoke, the lameness of it.

"I don't," Joel whispered. "I say she's all of them including the worst that we know of and a lot we don't. Her *self* is legion." He stared at me in disbelief then got up and backed away, and when he turned to walk out the room I felt it was because he couldn't bear to breathe the same air. Or perhaps, if he stayed, he might explode in a way that could end in one of my attacks, with the children to raise in close confines and the pestilence stalking outside.

We had never clashed like this before – disagreed, of course, from time to time, but never had there been an outburst of fury and rejection such as he was now clearly holding down.

I went after him. "If you would hear what I have to say . . ."

"Not now. I won't hear it. I can't look at you." But then he did look at me. Searchingly, as if he were trying to place me. After a long time he whispered, "I don't know you."

And in that instant it was all changed inside, as it had changed outside over the last weeks – the house, my very flesh. At the idea of having trivialized Cyn's death or endangered the children I felt tainted to the soul . . . *done those things I ought not to have done and no health in me.*

⇁⁄ι∖⇁

I'd sat at my desk trying to work through my thoughts, but I got nowhere, so an hour later I went to join him in the dining room. We had to get the twins' books, stationery and tablets in place for class before streaming began and to lay snacks for break near at hand. For a few moments we leaned against opposite walls of the room, staring at the entrails of our marriage strewn between us, knowing we soon had to stuff them back out of sight for the sake of the children. We would get the three of them ready for a normal day, in a situation where everything, *everything*, was abnormal.

In the kitchen, we yanked small cartons of apple juice from the fridge for lunch kits, and flung together peanut butter sandwiches, plantain chips and bright orange portugals that left the smell of citrus rind clinging to my fingers. Three heaps, so things could feel familiar and reinforce the sense of being at school. For Mattie we'd take turns to reproduce some elements of kindergarten in between unstructured play.

"But suppose Mattie *was* Barrie's child. Wouldn't it be important to know whether he was hers or Cyn's?" I persisted recklessly.

He stopped sawing off the edges from the sandwiches. "How could you doubt he's Cyn's?" Even as his fingers wafted my uncertainty away, his lips tightened, and then came a barrage of other questions. "Even so, how could that help Mattie? How could your 'knowing' that help him? How can't you see that woman must be totally eradicated from their lives? You mean a person of your intellect doesn't grasp she can't be . . . *let in* for an instant? That the merest possibility of her in their range *cannot* be entertained? You've shut your eye to what she is and shifted it off to this, this . . . whatever you've made up. You've let yourself lose track of *the children*."

I turned away leaving the lunch kits to him and found my way slowly upstairs, back to my study. I must have sat there for an hour and a half, I don't know. I lost direction, doing nothing but trying to think, and failing. A dark place*, because the straightforward pathway had been lost.*

When he came in, his eyes – deeply shadowed as they always were when he was disturbed – wandered blindly over the desk and scattered papers. He had got the twins in front their screens and left Mattie painting.

"This, this knitting of tales or trying to . . . reassemble what was a horrifying presence in the life of our child, our dead child. And these children – are they . . . resources for your next story?"

"No. Lord, no. What would possess you to . . .?" My voice dried up, because he gave no sign of hearing.

He stared at me as if I had morphed into something unforeseen and disquieting. Then he actually worded it. "What have you become?"

I backed away, blindly. Only the moulding of the door frame under my fingertips, a graze from that little brass hook on the wall where a picture had fallen off and, especially, the slight indentation in a floorboard underfoot led me effortlessly to our room. And dumbly: wordless to explain – even to myself.

What had brought me here? My longing to recapture something

of Cyn? But so much more. Yet I could not fully account to him for conversing with Barrie, even as I wanted to explain. (It might even have helped me penetrate her testimony.) The reasons I could give could not come together into anything he would deem rational. From the surge and tumble of impressions now, I couldn't word what had seemed compelling and still faintly echoed in me. I struggled to recapture why I'd allowed her my ear. It wasn't only Cyn's *Promise me*, because Cyn would never have set such a request on par with the children's welfare. And what hope had I of working it out? Whatever Cyn had eventually decided to tell us about Barrie was forever lost in the corrupt file.

We went through that day and the next few speaking little to each other, only of the children's needs. Melody asked whether I was ill, and I heard her checking with Joel too. "It's not her heart or anything?" At nights we crawled under the covers in a silence so thick it stifled thought.

I needed air, space to retrieve whatever had prompted me and to track logical connections I had not articulated or crystallized but discerned subconsciously and followed. I wanted to explain myself – to understand myself, even – but needed time to ferret out of my brain what had prompted my compassion for this tormented woman, threatening as she well might be.

On the bedside table my phone chimed an incoming email, and my fingers responded automatically. It was junk, but before that was a message I had missed from Isaac that his examiners had reported and the oral was scheduled. Some remote part of me breathed relief, for it was accomplished scholarship, I knew. I tried to sidetrack my current perplexity by calling to mind his most impressive arguments – a diversion where comfort was impossible. But my thoughts were too churned up for anything to take shape.

Distracted by this weird inability to think, as if recent demands on my brain had resulted in an overload or electrical short, I ran my hands among the clothes in my cupboard and dragged out a suitcase. I let it drop, for how was I to do that – drive off and find a hotel in which to work through my mind alone – when he had the three of them to take care of? And what hotel? And, once out, how to return without exposing them all? I would stay out, opening myself to infection. All of a piece anyway – an ICU bed or my own at home, shut out of Joel's heart. Just slow terminal suffering in isolation.

Presumably marriages don't end like that? I tried to think. People quarrel for years – which would be cold comfort if it applied to us. For the first time it came to me that I couldn't breathe amid such contention. While it lasted I'd have to get out, or suffocate.

I tried my study again, unable to pick up the work lying on Cyn's desk, fumbling over miscellany in my head. What light there was slanted in between the drapes with the bamboo pattern but illuminated nothing.

It closed in on me, a sense of iron-barred gates slamming all around and heavy bolts sliding in place with echoing finality. Then almost at once these sensations evaporated to sudden and complete emptiness, suspension in a void. The thought of even temporarily separating myself – not only from him (he clearly wanted nothing to do with me for now) but from the children and, oddly, I realized, Melody in particular – made my legs give way, and I knew I must lie down. I found my way to the room and felt for the bedpost, feet melting and hands slackened. I slid down, rather than collapsing all at once on the hardwood floor.

Curls of black ash clung to two books that had slipped behind the bed, and white dust filmed the base of the standing lamp on the side. I turned my eyes away. That must have been gathering for weeks. Ena getting older too. The prospect of disorder intensifying around me on every dimension undid me further.

How to proceed? I was paralyzed. The days ahead wound as trackless as the ones that had brought me here. As dizziness intensified to nausea, I knew I was on the verge of passing out, and it occurred to me, hazily, that perhaps the ultimate solution was at hand. He would forever blame himself, though.

So much for the inclination to embrace delivery from a disintegrating life. I willed myself to rest for a few moments, then pressed up onto my knees and, finding myself in position anyway, sent up a couple incoherent phrases. I dragged my legs onto the bed as well and tugged the sheet over my ears, drawing my knees up tight towards my chin.

Just as *she* had described, it came to me. Perhaps little distinguished any of us but ways in which others could bear to read us. Which if any of us is *un*troubled?

But that brought me uncomfortably close to Joel's reading of me now. It led nowhere I could bear to contemplate, so I turned to those elusive reasons for attending to Barrie as she shape-shifted through impressions that had floated in fitfully – childish formulations perhaps: bad Barrie, mad Barrie, sad Barrie. Not just somebody's aunt, but once somebody's wife, perhaps somebody's mother – and in an odd, distorted way, Cyn's sister. Once, even, somebody's baby. Bright, sparkling, promising, loving. Unravelling. When did she begin to come apart?

Had it begun in childhood before her parents' eyes? Who was left now to care about her? My fingers crawled of their own accord for the tablet beside my bed, to make a note or two. Even as I sighed over Joel's fury – justified, no doubt – a couple sentences on Barrie's anguish found their way out, unfastening my will from his in one anarchic onslaught of fingers on the keyboard. Because I was right, too, however illogical that was. Illogical? Alternatives floated up readily: irrational, specious, contradictory, invalid, irreconcilable, incongruous, unreasonable, perverse, absurd. So many they seemed to be everywhere – they drifted over me, coating then smothering all else.

I became conscious of my fingers cramped on the tablet but could not summon the will to release them as I contemplated the wasteland – my life (for days? weeks? Who knew how long?) without Joel's spurts of talk, however monosyllabic. Yes. I had done a stupid, stupid thing. I must be getting foolish in old age, losing it after all. *I fear I am not in my rightful mind.*

I must have slept, for I came to when Joel sank onto the edge of the bed, beside me, and unlocked my fingers so as to set the tablet aside. He said, "If she isn't his mother, she *can't* just take him, though he'll ask about her, and . . . I guess we must be able to answer. Suppose I see that."

The few words after days of near silence seemed almost unreal, and his face was gaunt, tragic. I still drifted somehow unmoored from what was going on, and too drained to pick up a hint of sparkle, a potential for return to my life. I tried to respond and nothing came, my mouth and tongue parched, thought and feeling dried up. He perched motionless on the edge of the mattress as we studied each other before he went on.

"If evidence emerges that she is his mother, we must prove her unfit, so we have to know all we can. Either way, Mattie will want to know about her. Better shape she gets into, easier it will be for him to deal with the subject of . . . this woman . . . in the long run. When the world gets back to normal. Or whatever." After a long silence he picked up the thread again. "They'll all ask eventually. May even see this so-called aunt as all they have left of their father."

I regarded him, waiting.

"But I can never have anything to do with her," he said. After a pause, he muttered, "You'll do what you think right anyway." Then, "I know you're not doing it for yourself."

Exhaustedly I dragged myself up against the pillows. "She mustn't come near them," I agreed at once. Then I hesitated, but it had to come out. "She's devastated —"

I stopped, because he was looking at me with an expression of intense attention but seemed elsewhere. Confused.

"What is it?" I shrugged off the unaccustomed lethargy and grabbed his shoulders. "Something else has happened." But he stared wordlessly at me. "What?" I insisted.

"Walters." One word, then he just sat there.

"Are you going to tell me?"

"Dead. They say an accident. Car shot off the edge of Lady Young Highway at a corner, and down the precipice. Minutes after three this morning."

"You think . . . someone . . . from one of those cases he reported on? Or — Joel, not the police?"

Head tilted, he shot that sidelong glance that was really a foray into his own thoughts. "Suspect he just packed it in. His state of mind . . ." He paused. "He'd been sent home on leave. They were worried about him. He couldn't stand being in it, and he didn't know how to be out of it let alone locked in at home. Service this evening — yes, right away: he was Muslim. I didn't know. Didn't know anything personal — except the mess inside his head. I won't go — well, of course one can't, no assembling — and even if I could there's too much unresolved here anyway." His tall spare frame seemed to cave in. "Mattie. I couldn't give him up and see him separated from the others. Much less let them all go."

"Me neither. I wish I could say something, be easier to live with. I wish I could . . . could . . ." I broke off helplessly.

"Find the words?" Dry humour in a humourless situation.

"Do you ever wish," I asked, "that you *could* control me?"

He fanned it away, denying or dodging the question — I could not tell. "*Burn but her books*," he murmured, entangling our fingers. Then he seemed to cave again. "But Mattie."

I squeezed his hands and brought him back. "Joel, everything suggests that Barrie lost her own baby and fixated on Mattie. And that Cyn conceived and gave birth to him, like Micah and Melody. She did the whole process – what we know of it – in L.A., while Barry and Con had worked with a clinic in Sydney. Everything suggests – only, nothing's documented."

"I never doubted the three were wholly Cyn's – not for a moment." That startled me. Then I remembered how much I had kept from him. "But where to find proof regarding Mattie?" He pushed towards me the tall glass of melting ice and water that he had at some point rested nearby. "What do we really know about Mattie's birth? Have you thought Cyn might have conceived him naturally?"

I gaped at him. It had never entered my mind since the first notification from the clinic. Yet I had read that sometimes happened, later, after an earlier successful IVF conception and delivery.

"You recall anything Cyn told us about him as a baby?" he probed as we made our way downstairs.

"You and Cyn wrote each other," I reminded him. "You would still have her letters somewhere, though she wouldn't have written about the birth till a bit after. You'd never have thrown those away. I talked to her on Skype. I've nothing in black and white."

"But the details of the birth – she'd have told you more." We were in the kitchen by then, and Joel leaned over the microwave to press the old louvre windows closed against the whirling grey filaments that the dry season wind was forcing into the house through every crevice. "Wait. Wasn't he unusually delicate? But why is it we don't know more?"

"Early," I reminded him, switching on the kettle again. "He came early, and it was emergency surgery, some blood pressure spike she had. By the time we heard, she was fine, and the baby was in an incubator but doing well. So I guess there were no scary details to lodge in our minds. It's stayed vague in mine. Or – you think she never passed on much of what had happened?"

"She said the preemie diapers were like boats on him. Remember that?"

"Mattie was a seven-month baby." Other details bobbed back disconnected. They had come to us in fragments anyway, as afterthoughts, because by the time we heard them they were no longer relevant. "A hospital would have a record – if we could work out what hospital."

"Francis said we should have gone to them," Joel reflected. "Insisted Cyn must need us. But by then Cyn and Connor said all was well. Francis wasn't comfortable for some reason. Can you remember why?" I couldn't. But by then a silence had yawned, till he said, "Thy face."

"What's wrong with it?"

"*As a book where men might read strange matters.*"

And I said, "I suppose I have to pass on to you a question or two about Francis."

Perhaps not a good time. But when would a good time come? By then we were sitting on the porch with tea. Not a car passed, and without the distant hum of traffic on the highway, we could hear the sea swish in and out. I tried to look beyond the house opposite – such a lowering colour.

"Here's the thing," I said, and began disentangling the contrary skeins that might be part of that tapestry we called Francis.

⌇

"Don't be offended by Ena telling me this thing now," I warned him. "I had to bleed it out of her."

"But why?"

"Why what?"

"Why bleed it out?" I stared at him until he said, "OK, OK. I suppose if it were true we would have to know."

"You're certain it isn't?"

"Ena's a wonderful woman. But *Francis*? We've known him all his life. Nah!" Then as an afterthought, "And why wouldn't there have been so much as a hint before this? How long you had this in your head?"

"Mmm," I returned. Francis would be out of contact with the children for a while anyway. "Well. We have more compelling dilemmas, I'll say that." I tried to suppress a surge of irritation: it wasn't as if he had never hidden anything himself.

⌇

His father was the one who let *that* out – unintentionally, for by then the old man had lost control. Words just slid from him. All his life a quiet, uncommunicative man, he unravelled into the tremulous, fretful, at times garrulous condition that let slip momentous secrets so easily I wondered how he had kept them in, year in, year out, this stoic trapped in protracted tragedy.

He lived with us towards the end, when his mind was coming undone, demons from the past stalking him. I found myself holding him, my arms locked around his shoulders, rocking and whispering comfort without deciphering the agonized jumble of confidences. But as more and more of these hitherto unspoken terrors found their way out, they pooled in my head. And gradually, as I thought the jumbled utterances over, there emerged a sort of order in which they might be intelligible.

"She." (*She* was always Andrea.) "She could never listen. Warned her that man had nothing in him." He called a name, but I lost it at once in the long, fluting complaint. "Come home two o'clock morning – her face, oh God. Her feet swell too. Blood on her skirt. Walk barefoot from I don't know where. Pouring rain, soak to her skin. Shivering and barefoot. I call her brother. Then, he now." (*He* was always Patrick, Andrea's brother, Francis's father.)

"Like he go mad. He leave his wife and baby son home. Search high and low and find this man. I had beg the boy don't go after him. Ent I know he temper? But Andrea. When he see her face, you see. How it swell you couldn't recognize who. Her nose take weeks, must be months to set. He find this man, he say when he see *his* face he don't know what happen he can't stop. He go berserk. Is me he run to. Who else but his father he would run to?

"But like I seize up. I couldn'. Couldn' move.

"Who to call but Joel. Married a while back and saving for some project – house he building to rent out, he tell me. I done see Andrea face, and from her brother gone I get to realize what coming for this man who . . . attack her. And when I watch. Nah, nah, nah. I watch and oh God I couldn' – and I feel it. A thud. In my head. And this thing like my hand can't lift, my mouth – I can't move my tongue. When Joel reach in the hospital he bend over me talking quiet-quiet so the doctor and them can't hear him. He say, 'Don't worry, Dad, I going to sort it out.'

"Joel draw out every cent he save. He buy ticket and bribe police. That time I in hospital with the stroke. Joel get he brother on the plane, out the country. Cover it up. All he save to build house gone in this thing.

He sister-in-law refuse to follow her husband and she stay here with the baby, Francis. Joel support them too. Joel do it all or I would see my young son in jail or hang.

"I don't see the boy again. But at least I never had to see he in jail. Joel take a loan and pay for Andrea to have the surgery. Joel make sure Francis finish school. Joel. The one son leave to me."

—⁘—

Oh yes. Joel had his own untold snatches of story that could only be assembled through speculation, that might in some instances be his father's effort to put together a bearable past. The old man's wonderings and wanderings contrived – at least in part – the legend that was Joel. Whatever the true full version though, Joel was a good, good man. Nothing imaginary about that part.

I pushed this mesh of uncertainties aside when Joel said, "What do we really have to go on regarding Matts?"

So later, when the children settled in front the TV, we went to my study and set forth our printouts of the documents we had from Cyn alongside my notes on what I'd learnt of Barrie. Still nothing concrete to account for Mattie. By the time Mattie entered the picture, Cyn's files were chaotic.

Apart from her few careful records of exchanges with Barrie, whatever files we found from after Mattie's birth were randomly jammed into one folder or the other. It seemed like surface turbulence, this incoherence of papers about Cyn's recent years. Joel thought back to Melody's account and extrapolated: perhaps Cyn and Connor had dropped everything outside their jobs and the children's needs as more and more energy was swallowed up in responding to one distraction after the other from Barrie. I thought of Cyn's almost compulsive orderliness, not just the physical tidiness that drove me but her mental rigour and meticulousness. And I closed my eyes and massaged my forehead. When I opened them and looked up at Joel, his were swimming.

We had never been able to open that *B* file. Even in this we remained excluded from what Cyn wanted us to know. Still, one of the documents from Cyn's desk had addresses and contact numbers, including those of a couple hospitals and a home for assisted living. Barrie's mobile number, which I had, wouldn't show us exactly where she was now. So I compared Cyn's record of phone numbers to the notes I had used to reconstruct Barrie's story. At least we might locate her, even if Joel refused to speak to her. It was next morning before Joel agreed to call St Mary of the Cross. We must wait for night again, to catch Sydney office hours, and put our mundane questions out across a planet in turmoil of lockdowns, protests, and ranting politicians.

"Mama," Micah's voice suddenly, choking with outrage. "Is it true about the birds from the Wild Fowl Trust?"

"What birds?"

"That people are stealing them? To eat?"

"*What?* I don't know anything about that. Where you got that?"

"Someone on TV *said*. He had a picture of a man holding up a duck."

Mattie chimed in, "It's neck was all floppy."

"I was thinking to take a drive down to the bridge," Joel butt in with supreme disregard for the topic. "If nobody's around I want to get out the car and see whether I can glimpse any caimans." He set off jingling car keys, the three clamouring behind him.

"That was brilliant," I told him a couple hours after their return. We were watching the Covid melodrama playing out on TV, from the safety of our side of the glass, screened from the disease that might yet take hold around us, and from metropolitan nations that seemed to have come unhinged across the planet. But also, Joel reminded me, from a madwoman on the other side of the world.

We both jumped, almost superstitiously, when the phone jangled, but it was Cecile, desperate for an ear. "My nephew and all pick up Covid," she said. "The one in Tampa. After they all refuse to wear mask. And he take it home – some sort of reunion they was having, not that they bother contact me, but I wasn't going anyway. So, girl, I have to say this thing somehow –" Her voice broke, and I waited on tenterhooks to hear the rest.

Her brother had died. "Not Preston?" I said in disbelief.

"Preston, yes. And he son, the same nephew, have a stroke." Yes, of course, she insisted, I would remember him because he was the same age as Shelley and Francis and that set. Anyway, they were the only ones she was in touch with, and it was weird because now, Cecile said, she didn't know how many were left. A set of them came down with it. No, of course she couldn't ask the nephew – after he couldn' talk. Is stroke he had. She only know because somebody say they hear they niece talking about this thing they see on Facebook.

Who? No, girl. Right now nobody know where Charlene. Shelley reach back to Toronto, though, and say she trying to pick up with Charlene. She say don't worry – Charlene go land on she feet.

I listened to Cecile for fifty minutes, putting in barely a word, because there was nothing else I could do for her, and by the end of it she had calmed into the odd reminiscence about school days and it seemed safe to let her go.

Afterwards, Joel and I called the hospital in Sydney. No, said the woman who answered. They had no one by the name of Intyre or Firaki, nor did their protocols permit them to divulge whether she had ever been a patient.

Joel pounced on this: "Which means she was." But I thought denial of information might be a standard response.

Then I recalled the doctor Barrie had mentioned. Nguyen seemed an unusual name. I'd heard it only once before Barrie mentioned it – an author. But it turned out to be too common in that part of the world for us to track on our own. When we called St Mary of the Cross again, though, the receptionist gave us a contact number for a small private facility through which we might reach a Dr Nguyen, a psychiatrist.

"Not that he'll be able to reveal anything," I said to Joel.

"Only finding out where she is, eh?" He glanced at me as I turned from my notes back to the phone.

I ignored him, snatched up the receiver and dialled, as he leaned over to put the call on speaker.

"The director is out and the secretary on extended leave," said the woman who picked up the call. "Overseas? 868 is Trinidad and Tobago, isn't it? Barrie Intyre speaking."

I dropped the phone as if it were a scorpion.

Joel and I argued for half an hour in whispers – as if she might hear us – Joel going on about calls leaving a record of our phone numbers.

"You're raving," I said gently. "She knows where we are anyway. A couple months ago you were the one who said she was stalking us by phone." He nodded, unnerved, his hands flexing, agitated. "Look," I said, "Tell me exactly what's on your mind, in case you're right."

"I think this is the new Game, and Barrie's *It.*" Only, then, he spread his palms in resignation, looking heartbreakingly weary, and we tried the number again.

She answered on the first ring as if she'd been sitting by the phone. "I'm glad you called back."

I should have recognized that cultured, measured voice from the outset, but it sounded marginally more upbeat, or at least less stricken than on previous conversations.

"I wasn't sure you would. How'd you find me?" A lull on our side, and she continued more diffidently. "I've been out of touch, I know. Certain . . . circumstances threw me. I shut down completely before I could begin thinking my way forward. I'm even considering selling my practice. You find me here because, well, the house was quieter than I could bear, and this place (something between a nursing home and a hostel) is almost empty, what with everyone over sixty relocated. Here in the office on my own I've been sorting out legal issues that have dogged them for an age."

I hesitated so as to give Joel a chance to talk, but mulishly he kept his mouth shut.

She asked, "So. Are the children OK?"

"Won't be discussing them with you," Joel whipped back, then continued more evenly. "I wish you well – at least, trying to . . . but we . . . I can't."

In the shocked silence that followed, it came to me she was unprepared for any voice but mine. Then she said, "Cyndra's dad?"

"Could you put us through to whoever's in charge?"

I swung the phone away from his reach and said, "Barrie, a word with the director first please. Then I'll get back to you. OK?"

Joel glowered at the receiver resentfully.

"Well." Barrie's voice wavered. "To be honest I'm going to have a word with her first. Then I'll put you through. But I've been desperate for news of the children. You know I have the home number, and I haven't tried for months. I haven't intruded recently."

"That was a threat," Joel mouthed. Clamping his hand over the mouthpiece, he almost knocked it from my fingers. "You don't see?"

"Hello? Are you there?" At a grunt from Joel, she continued. "Right, I thought we'd got disconnected again. Look, I'm trying not to unsettle them. Truly. Can't you just let me know? It's not as if I'm demanding to speak to them."

"Sorry," Joel mumbled, not sounding sorry at all. "Not able to talk about them . . . with you."

There was a sigh. "OK. When I've said my piece to the director, I'll WhatsApp the home's Skype contact. It's an old-fashioned place. I'll have her look out for your call about this time tomorrow. But please know – as hard as this must be for you to believe – we do have one goal in common: what's best for the children. Bye, for now."

The connection went dead, and Joel and I regarded each other warily. So smooth. Bright. Melody had quoted her father as saying *a gifted lawyer.* So, Joel concluded now, adept at pressing buttons. At least we knew where she was for the time being – safely on the other side of a world in which physical connections were in ruin, and also settled for a while in a place where she might receive care. Still, we did not know yet who or what she was.

But that could be said too of others. I leaned my head back and studied the ceiling as my mind whirled through the other imponderables of our lives. Was the Francis we knew real? Was there some other twisted version underneath or side by side or intermittent? Was he deranged or plain unrighteous? Or misunderstood? So many people who look whole turn out to be seriously damaged; so many of those who wreak havoc to be grievously wounded. I came down to the age-old dilemma: where does incapacity or illness end and responsibility begin?

I became aware of Joel regarding me distrustfully. "What's going through your head? You're not going to call her back and comfort her after I leave the room, or anything?"

"*What?*"

"Well, I don't know." But the tension was easing out of him somehow. "You realize," Joel threw out, "I've lived in mortal fear for months that you may take it into your head to re-employ Tinsel?"

So, trivia. He was coming around.

As if on cue, Tinsel dropped by to visit us next morning. More cheery than usual, I thought.

"But I can't let you in, Tinsel." It was provoking, having to explain the obvious. It occurred to me that over the past weeks I had become an angrier person. I modulated my voice. "We staying quiet here till they work out a vaccine."

"*Dat*? Nah, Ms Roach. I wouldn't advise you tek dat, nah. They ent go ketch me with dat." She reached through the bars to take hold of the bolt.

"Tinsel, we lockdown like the prime minister say." I stood a good three metres back from the gate with the late-morning heat shimmering up around me from the asphalt driveway.

"And you go listen to he? Well, OK if you don't want let me in. But, Ms Roach, I say you and I so alike you not going hold me no grudge." She radiated the sunniest of smiles. "Look – I take me time and make amchar for you and Ena." She hung a bag with the two bottles of fiery appetizer on the gate and pushed her face against the bars. "But I have to talk quiet because I don't want anyone to hear my business, not even Ena. What you say? She not here? Well, *if* you say so. Anyway, I did really want to tell you, as how me husband come back home and we make up, we decide to have a prayers and renew we vow an dem. I dream something and it win, so as I get the little change I say is to hold a prayers. He say he done wi all dem stupidness he did use to carry on. Hmm, I don't need to tell you, right?"

I shifted across to the grass, getting a palm between me and the sun, and she walked along to the side of the gate nearest by, clutching bar after bar.

"Even though nobody could know how much trouble I see. I never get a chance to tell you how that night I come outta hospital – that same time I did sick and you fire me? All right, all right, we wouldn't call it that. But that time when I come outta hospital and gone home by myself – because nobody come for me with no car – I get home and *he* car park up right there. And I gone inside and the place in one mess and nothing not there in the fridge, and I hearing a set of noise in the bedroom and I go in. And when I *do so* I see he and a woman in me bed. The bed *I* buy. And I bawl out, and what I bawl I can't say to you, Ms Roach, but I well cuss he tail and he jump out the bed naked and box me down.

"Like I must be hit me head; how long I lie there I can't tell you. But when I get up it quiet-quiet and the place in the same mess, or *wuss*, and nothing to eat. I haul dem sheet off the bed and pelt them through the door and I lie down on the mattress just so and I sleep like I dead. Next day I clean up the place and I walk little by little till I reach a parlour and buy a soup. And I don't see he again for mustbe three month.

"Is then he come back crying he sorry and he want to make up. If you see how he cry. I say, dat good. Well, I make he beg me. He well beg me. And I say, 'We go see, nah.' And he study beg me take him back till I say, 'And is so you go treat you wife?'

"Well, he boil right down like bhagee and he tell me we go do the vow again. And I say, very well. So I just come to let you know you invite and to gi you the postcard."

Joel had been watching me from the doorway. "What now?" he demanded when I dropped off my shoes at the door to go in search of my purse.

"More money," I groaned, and held up my palm. "Don't start. I need to get her from in front the house, and if a re-wedding present is what it takes, so be it."

⌐ᴧ⌐

Tinsel had barely detached herself from the gate and headed back up the road before Joel called to me from the porch upstairs, holding out the phone. I nipped up the steps.

"Some Mrs Hamilton," he mouthed. But I shook my head. I couldn't fit in anymore, especially as I was coming around to Joel's reading of Francis.

A man might be slack, Joel had said, untrustworthy as far as women were concerned, without being capable of physical brutality. The spoilt-child type might even bluster a bit so as to get his own way. But the evidence of years had shown us nothing but Francis's affection for the two of us and for Cyn, and now for her children. Never a sign of callousness, let alone cruelty. "He adored Cynnie," Joel reminded me. "Was unfailingly gentle."

She was like a baby sister to him, though, I thought – five years younger. "Was his father like that, with Andrea?" I could inflect my voice with innocence when I liked, but he glanced back at me, startled. "I thought you'd said Patrick and Andrea were particularly close," I added.

Joel returned some incomprehensible sounds, and I let it go. I had rarely even met Patrick, and what did I know of him? Judge not, I concluded.

Still, I warned Joel that I wasn't ever leaving the children alone with Francis. Just *because*.

He shrugged. "The Arabs have a saying: Trust in Allah, but tie your camel." He jumped as a weird yowl rose up outside the window directly behind him, but it was only Philander crooning to Mystique.

20

SPLIT IMAGE

—⁀ノ⋀⌐—

I RECALLED HIS FATHER WHISPERING TO ME, "The boy must never come back here. Never, never. I can't fly, so I wouldn't see him again." Now and then a phone call. Or Joel would set up Skype so they could peer at each other. The old man ran shaking fingers over his son's face on the screen.

Andrea wrote him often, and I was the one who read her letters to him in later years, but they made no mention of that night.

Once I saw my father-in-law raise his lips to Joel's ear with a loud whisper. "And that other thing. Nothing come of that?"

"Nor ever will. Shh. Do not torment yourself."

I looked up to see Joel assessing me. "Don't torment yourself," I said gently but a little absently, because I had got to wondering how far back he had read in my notes.

"It's late, but when last did we have a glass of shiraz?" he wondered.

"Aah. Well bethought."

Perhaps we all have conditions, it occurred to me as I reached out the glasses. Some deadly, some not. Who knows what festers in the row behind us? Poor Walters, eh?

The phone distracted me, and it took some seconds to recognize Jackie's voice, thin and tremulous. After a few minutes she asked for Joel. She and Gabrielle had sent half their money ahead to Edmonton, and the question was what to do now her son was gone. And, yes, her daughter wanted them to come to her instead, but when? The future of travel – you know. By the time that conversation ended, Joel and I settled for cocoa instead of wine.

—⁀⋀⌐—

After trying most of the following day we failed to make our Skype connection to the director who ran the facility where we'd located Barrie in Sydney. By afternoon, WhatsApp brought in Andrea.

"Did you get it?" she asked. "I sent a signed copy a little while back."

"Of course," I said, thanking her enthusiastically while feeling vile about not having called at once.

"You probably haven't had time to look at it yet." Under the laughter her voice was wistful.

"You crazy? I pounced on it one-time and couldn't put it down." I scoured my mind for my next pronouncement as she waited anxiously.

"What did you like about it?" she prompted me.

"Your language. And, well, it was poignant. You know? This child's anger. Not limited or, I should say, narrowed to just one particular setting – don't you know? But an all-encompassing rage at being left behind and locked in." I felt around hastily in my head. "And at the sheer misguidedness of adults. A universal child, an archetypal trauma." What the hell was I saying?

But she seemed moved. "I'd never thought of it that way myself," she said. "I was even afraid of it being too insular for the international audience – for the reader who knows nothing of the Caribbean. But I suppose it's in my blood, so it had to come through."

"Mmm," I said. "Yet do you know the chapters that really blew me away were those set in that immigrant community. You lived in that area for a few years, didn't you? Aah, and came and went since? So it's an aunt you have there. Really? Still alive and strong? Contact as regular as that?" Her rousing sketch of Aunt Margie gave way to another lull. "So," I continued, "have you started the next?" It was the question everyone asked me, so I snatched at it.

Once she'd explained the type of material she might need next, I led her off to the prospect of her moving to the Caribbean, at least for a while, when travel became possible again. And that discussion prospered because I was genuinely eager about it. "You really mean it, don't you?" I asked. "Taking a position here if you can get it."

"Yo, girl. Can't wait."

While she spoke, though, I couldn't help wondering whether she still thought we should move out – from a country that had so far proved itself capable of keeping its roughly two thousand square miles relatively untouched by the virus to another, perhaps the one on our doorstep, which in my flustered state of mind seemed to be over three and a half million square miles of chaos.

Just as well I never brought it up. Who knew how long we would control the infection more successfully than our better-equipped neighbours. Sometime there'd be a vaccine and there must spring up dizzards enough to be more afraid of it than of the virus. After suppressing this first wave, our lockdown would end. And I could see it – one set of jokers tumbling out to celebrate: jump an' wave, misbehave. Winin' up on each other. Or they'd throw one big bram for the family, or tek a few for that in a rumshop, or cram up in a church to praise the Lord or share the touch. Why should I suppose that because we were riding it out now, we wouldn't mess up next time – especially since most people didn't conceive of a *next time*.

What did I know anyway? My angle on the rest of the world pivoted on whatever came to me as newsworthy from foreign media. Abroad, as here, pockets of the spectacular took over the field of vision, blotting from awareness vast areas of normalcy.

"I suppose the same thing happens to us looking out at them as happens to them looking in at us," I remarked to Joel after Andrea's call.

"You think?" He sounded too weary to engage with me in an exploration of what made news.

"Except we're not wired to measure everything beyond our shores against ourselves as, you know, we-the-normal." I stopped and regarded him anxiously. "Is that unkind?"

"Don't think you can be." He groaned and stretched. "Tired already, though. Why?"

The children both sapped and enlivened us. In the balance the reward outweighed the demand. We agreed our bodies felt as though the day we'd come through had been beset with meetings and crises in the workplace. Yet once we kept our minds on the children or on our work, we were buoyed up.

Still, here we were fixed in place while the world barely beyond our borders seemed hurtling to ruin. The White House churned out policies sublimely contemptuous of expert advice on the pandemic. As denialism took hold, cracks had opened up in the bedrock of common belief, shared by millions inside and outside their country, regarding everything from superior health care to human rights. It was hard not to stare at the screen, yet also hard not to flinch and turn our eyes away from what now seemed bared naked before the world – a deep-laid bully mentality.

"No drinking a glass of wine against that," Joel complained, and we powered off the set and got out to the porch.

In the human stillness, the natural world throbbed more vibrant, the crickets shriller. Earlier I had thought the quits merrier and grackles more daring. Now something swooped close before darting off – perhaps to the poui, Joel theorized. The sky dimmed fast and little moved in it but a billow of flittering shadows from the direction of the hill.

A notification chimed, and I saw it was one of those messages that had been delayed somehow. Not important. But before that was another I had never seen, although it was dated over a week ago. It was a voice message from Walters, and I stepped into the bathroom to hear it.

"Mrs Roche, I don't like to disturb you but I need to talk to Joel. I wouldn't be long, I don't mean to take up his time, only right now it have no one else it make sense to talk to. You could ask him to give me a call? When he can."

"Joel?"

"Aha?"

I thought again, and all I said was, "You look so, so tired. Come to bed."

"Just finishing my drink. You don't want yours?"

I returned to the porch, and it was later, when we were turning inside, that Isaac called. He'd wondered how I could possibly bear being locked up, he said, and then he realized I'd have just climbed into my laptop and taken shelter there. But call him at once, he added, for anything I needed. That lifted me – that the younger lot should remember and pause to phone. But even that welcome attention couldn't unfasten the new unease that crept up and clung.

Had the notification of Walters' message chimed eight or nine days ago, and had I just ignored it? As I brooded, the notion gathered weight and dug its claws deeper into bruised tissue. How could it help to saddle Joel with this? But how could I withhold it?

I remember Joel saying a couple weeks before, "I wonder if I need to talk to this boy in person."

"Stick with the phone," I'd said. "We're in lockdown for a reason."

Now I said, "Joel?"

"Yup?"

"Sleep well, love." I figured I might never sleep again.

⟶⟋⟨⟵

Most of the night, though, I thought about the lockdown. Survival. Children to bring through.

As long as the borders locked tight and kept out non-nationals and nationals alike, we were relatively safe, but the time must come for even the smallest fissure. Conscience and compassion demanded it – to permit a trickle from the thousands of our own people now trapped on the wrong side of the cordon. For otherwise how were Penny and countless others to live through weeks turning to months? Yet the new cases of infection they'd inevitably bring would undermine resolve, set off rumour and send out ripples of suspicion. I could foresee growing impatience with masks, and whispers about community spread feeding an escalating distrust of everyone from government ministers to Venezuelan refugees. Then the glance of panic at a hay fever sniffle, at the clearing of a throat from a cracker crumb gone wrong way down, at fingers passed over the temple on a hot day where all days are hot.

Fed up, people would say. All we needed was an instance or two of selfish abandon and here too persons would vanish into statistics. Enough people set on carrying on *as normal* would render us abnormal as anywhere else. Abroad in what called itself the developed world the poor, the black, the elderly died in greater numbers and died alone, but what might be *our* profile of abnormality? And an election was sidling up. Still, *one night at a time*. I kept repeating that to myself against the replay of Walters' message in my head.

⟶⟋⟨⟵

Eraly next morning, Skype being unavailable, we made easy contact by WhatsApp with the director of the facility where Barry had self-isolated. We stayed with audio only, for better reception.

Mrs McGregor explained that Barrie's disorder was controlled. "I understand it to be mild end of the range anyway," she said. "True – stress can make things worse, and if she drank or did drugs, who knows where that would end. But she's disciplined, and with the medication she operates like anyone else."

"What disorder would that be?" Joel asked directly.

"Well, that would be private, wouldn't it?" She proceeded more cautiously. "I'd prefer not to infringe. Maybe I've said too much. And remember I administrate: I'm not a doctor. The point is that from what she's told me she's come incredibly far. And such a lovely, caring person." The director took off again on an enthusiastic account of Barrie's tireless pro bono work.

"Right. A veritable Mother Teresa." Joel's voice rumbled loud and clear in the background, and I heard the swift intake of breath from the other end of the line.

Hurriedly I thanked Mrs McGregor for her time and asked to speak to Barrie. Joel eyed me suspiciously, and I turned my back.

Barrie came on the line and said, "You need to know I've no immediate plan to take the children from you. Not only because I can't – what with borders closed and Covid rampant – but because I've talked to you and can tell they're in able hands. If they're better off with you, I won't disturb them whatever right I have."

"What right?" I blurted out.

"I can send documentation if you like, but it doesn't matter. For now, be assured I'm not coming for them, even when this madness lets up."

When I rang off, Joel said, "For now."

I sat searching his face, my heart breaking for him. "You're still afraid of Barrie," I said, running my forefinger down his cheek.

"Aren't you?"

"Y-yes. But. I don't want it to blind me." After a while I added, tentatively, "She loves them, at any rate."

Flick of fingers. "I don't know that."

"I believe she's trying," I insisted.

"No doubt. Question is – trying what? Didn't you hear she's not seriously ill? It's a guise. This woman is accustomed to playing nice while scheming. Benefit of the doubt? What doubt? Compassion could blind you more than fear – *listen* to me." He grabbed my arms urgently as if I were about to slide over a cliff. "You're able to think two contradictory thoughts at the same time – fine for analyzing a play or verse, so you're sensitive to . . . nuance or whatever. This is a dangerous woman. And the situation is . . . is *real*."

He was right about me. I had always been able to read contradictory information from a text and arrive at opposing conclusions in the same instant. The problem, as it crystallized in my brain, was his distinction between what was real and what was imaginary when we knew nothing except by hearsay and speculation. Besides – and this was what his mind locked out – Barrie's pain was unequivocally and inarguably real.

Still, who or what she was eluded us.

And beyond her there materialized another issue. It occurred to me a couple hours later, while tugging off chicken skin and scrutinizing the little hollows in and between bones for unwanted leavings of lung or kidney: we had lost sight of our initial problem, one so nebulous we had never kept focus on it. That was not knowing any other connection Connor may have had. We'd recognized from the start that – Cyn being what she was – he'd be a decent man himself, a fine man. Strong, too, or he'd never have attracted her. But the little direct experience we had of him included nothing that threw light on his ex-wife – and we could hardly cross-examine the children to find out what he might have had to say about her. Nor had we a clue to connect him with anyone else.

"Tell us about your folks, Con," I'd said one rainy evening on the first visit. We were settled in the living room with both of them, and with Francis sprawled on the floor, cushions beneath his neck and shoulder and a couple under his knees. The room was cozy with the sound of rain against the windows and the smell of hot cocoa.

"Well. Not much to tell. Parents gone years now." Con bumped his forehead on Cyn's, and his face lit up as it turned back to us. "Guess that leaves you guys."

Francis piped up, "This is where you're supposed to say, 'Aww'."

"Wish I'd met them," Cyn reflected.

Con grinned. "You'd have been a revelation to them. They were just a quiet, traditional couple, no pretensions. Not expectations really. They had nothing, but they did their best with it balancing the day and night jobs while I was a kid. I went off to school. Then it was college. By the time I was old enough to understand them I was away, and they weren't writers so we never kept in touch as we should. Then they were gone." He paused and shot Joel and me an apologetic glance. "It wasn't like you two and Cyn. I wish now we'd been closer."

We didn't want to prolong memories shadowed by regret, and Cyn must have felt it too. She sprang up saying she'd get a cup for herself after all. But he swept three fingers down her arm and told her to sit still while he made it and another half cup for himself. He glanced at me.

"And for you? With your dreadful creamer?"

Cynnie's husband had been a matter of fervent interest from the outset, but then we met and our anxiety evaporated. With it went our curiosity, swept aside in a sense of having known him for years. Now that he was permanently beyond reach, he'd become indistinct again, a sketch rendered by scattered memory and hearsay. Whose hearsay, though, my mind insisted as it revved up later, in the wee hours. I dropped off again but the question popped back up midmorning when I was out in the front yard.

What with the twins working online and Joel and Mattie washing up in the kitchen, I was quite alone. I paused over the usual chores of spraying the gate and postbox, and then passing Lysol over door handles. Stepping carefully over five pairs of shoes turned sole-up outside the door for the light film of spray to dry, I closed the grille door only, lest I forget the shoes outside.

"Don't you ever stop?" Joel called down from the landing at the top of the front steps. "And when last you drank water?"

"See how slow I am? Tinsel would have cleaned downstairs in half the time I take," I said. I could hear him on the steps and met him halfway.

"Don't think about it," he begged.

"She means no harm," I insisted. "Well, not most of the time."

"Famous last words." He scowled at me.

I shrugged. "No intention of bickering with you over Tinsel." I patted his face. "You're too cute and nice."

I made my exit in good order.

—⟩⟨—

Half an hour later I leaned against the wrought-iron bars before peeling off gloves and thought of Con again. Whose hearsay? Cyn was trustworthy but had said little; Barrie had outpoured a barrage of spite.

I registered more than a slight discomfort about some details. For one thing I couldn't excuse Con for deceiving Cyn about his marital status, however certain he had been about the divorce. And that idea of her bearing the embryos from Barrie's old IVF treatment was . . . well, *weird* was the only word I could come up with. But aren't there kinks in all of us?

So much more jarring to think of Barrie. And why had she insisted Connor wouldn't follow Cyn to Trinidad, only to show herself up as mistaken. And then to tell me about it. Odd to have betrayed that failure in judgement in the midst of her whole diatribe of self-justification. It didn't fit. Still, if Mrs McGregor were to be believed about the mildness of Barrie's disorder, how delusional was she rather than cold-bloodedly mischievous?

Joel's time-consuming enquiry to the airline had eventually confirmed that Connor's passage was not booked through to Trinidad. "It was Sydney – LA – Sydney, booked same day as the flight." He stared at me, stunned, and despite all Barrie had told me, I was shaken too.

"And why wouldn't Con have come straight here?" I argued. "If Barrie's story is all a lie, why fly only part of the way – and the greater part at that? OK. Say they had problems in the marriage, and he wasn't ready to relocate. Once he got as far as buying the ticket out, wouldn't he want to come at least briefly, to see the children till they could work things out?"

"Apart from the cost of the entire airfare?" Joel objected. "Question rests on the belief that Barrie has a truthful bone in her body. The man may have boarded for the shorter run so as to persuade his wife to come back to him. That is, if they had any problem at all, and we have only Barrie to thank for that idea. He could even have had a meeting coming up in L.A. and planned to come on to us a week later. Look," Joel continued, "we may never see eye to eye on the woman, but at least we must agree on how to operate regarding her."

I nodded, convinced we must move forward together on that front. Yet none of this stopped my thoughts racing in other directions, nor the feelers I kept putting out for whatever other information I could muster. It was harum-scarum, like a student scrunting online for pilferable essay parts.

Now, on my way through the dining room, I felt around in my mind for reasons why people I knew left the islands, some rarely to return: Cyn pursuing specialization in her field then marrying at such a distance, Andrea putting behind her an unutterable violation, Jackie and Gabriel – if they ever did leave – escaping self-incarceration. None of them quite ruled out a visit home. Well, Patrick. I knew why he couldn't come back, and why Francis had grown up without his father. Joel's father had clung to me and whispered, *The boy called me. It was me he called. But I could only call Joel. What to do, what to do? All that blood.*

At the sink I paused in the process of washing and filling the two humidifiers, one in Mattie's room for the first half of his night and one in ours for the rest.

How did the old man know about the blood? I wondered for the first time. I'd thought *the boy* had run to him. Home to him. I hadn't thought of Papa Roche being there, having gone to the place where it happened. Was he confused when he told me? Remembering more than he had actually seen?

I don't know whether the beating kill this man or whether it was the lick he lick his head on the sink when he fall or what. Pretty specific for him to dream up. I stared at my sink wondering why two men locked in fatal struggle were in the kitchen. Or was it the bathroom? *I couldn't look, I could never stand the sight of blood and now, now my son in this thing. He can never come home. How he go come back here? Poor child, poor child. He was never like Joel. A good boy but not able to govern himself. Well. He must be learn control now, I suppose. All the years I want to see his face.* The old man had held my arm, hard, bony fingers biting into my flesh, and he sobbed.

Sometimes Joel would organize for a Skype call, and I'd say, "I'll leave you guys to talk." Always his father broke down in tears. At first, before there was Skype, I had asked whether the phone calls to Patrick made sense when they left Papa Roche so distraught.

Joel said, "But so then the old fellow would never get to talk to his son." And I used to wonder: How come the little brute can't buy a ticket and come visit his father? When I worked out the answer, I stopped asking questions.

Papa Roche's fingers clenched on my arm, his tears running, dripping, his fingers sliding on them. Again and again it comes at me, one way or the next: love and what passes for it can be so ravaging.

But here we were, Joel and me, skirting some topics but for the most part back to the mind to mind on the porch or, before sleep, warm and tightly enfolded on one edge or other of the now redundantly spacious king-size. We were back to Joel propping up his head on awakening and staring incredulously at me. Again life extended promise, not only of laughter and warmth but of confidence in at least half an hour per day of intelligent adult conversation. Yet he was as freaked out by Barrie as ever and inclined to slide into all his reasons for distrust soon after he sat up in the morning.

"Even though she's going along with us keeping the children?" I asked.

"For now," he said, the light leaving his eyes as he looked down whatever tortuous path he glimpsed into the future. "Perhaps she does love them – after her fashion. If and when she comes after them – and I still believe there's a chance of that – she'd want them in good shape."

"You make her sound like a witch overseeing the fattening," I objected, and his lips twisted in distaste. I'd wanted him to smile but had overdone the facetiousness. (Only worked when he did it.) "Sorry," I put in, then added edgily, "You think I'm not frightened too?"

"Not enough. Look, she's moved from the *divide the living child in two* stance to the *mother thereof*. Only ratifies her claim." That was unanswerable, especially as my brain seethed with other irritants – the disinfecting and scrubbing, the tyranny of hand washing, the multiplying yet unyielding borders that tightened around me at every turn. Then shafts of horrific awareness. How I had failed to reach out, time after time.

～✦～

I was forearm deep in lather when Ena called to enquire how we were doing, then beat around the bush a little before unburdening. Tinsel had been phoning and badgering her to come and witness the renewal of vows regardless of the ban on any sort of assembly, insisting no one could get sick by attending prayers.

"Mrs Roche, I was wondering whether you would feel *how* if I just cut this Tinself off completely. Like I can't handle she at all again."

I managed to get out, hearing my voice husky with fatigue, "For God's sake block her blasted number."

I had had the call on speaker while drying hands, so when I returned to my study for a glance at my printer, there was Joel waiting in the doorway.

"Case in point," he said. "Never entertain a mischievous or spiteful entity." Which took him straight back to Barrie, and he plonked down the cup of coffee he had brought to my study for a break from the papers mounting up on his own desk.

Perhaps Melody hadn't heard him as she walked past my door? She'd kept her face straight instead of glancing in. She occupied a part of my mind that churned all the time. She looked self-contained and calm yet not relaxed. I felt convinced she wanted to be nowhere else, yet that she missed her mother too much to speak of her or to mention her father either. I'd never seen her cry. At times her eyes went tragic, without welling over. Melody carried herself as if her heart would shatter into splinters of ice before she afforded herself one tear.

I tore my thoughts from her while I had Joel sitting still. "To get back to Tinsel," I told him. "I can't help wondering how she will live. It's day by day for her."

"Apart from re-wedding presents? She might postpone expenditure on the prayers," he suggested. Then he added, "I know I know. Have Kevin get something to her, and we send him a cheque? But *after* the prayers."

Guilty and helpless as we felt about the plight of thousands we could barely envision, there seemed no key to reaching beyond the lines we had marked out. We could summon neither strength nor time to do more than keep cloistered in our own small corner. True the numbers of cases and deaths globally nowhere approached those of the Spanish Flu, let alone the Bubonic. But this was early days – however end-of-the-world it seemed already. Under criminal mismanagement and befuddling, foreign statistics for unemployment lengthened with food lines and processions of coffins.

"Could just as easily have happened here," Joel remarked, and I dashed an imaginary red line under his use of tense.

"Still might," I pointed out.

Pervasive ignorance and helplessness in even the wealthiest and most powerful countries had swept the world backwards and unmoored the future. "Can you believe it?" I asked. "Science drowned out by mumbo-jumbo about scamdemic?"

As indiscipline took over the world stage, Joel turned up his palms. "Watch," he said. "Jab Molassie blowing the whistle."

"To get a money," I agreed. "Demons inhabiting political platforms, like they're on a Carnival stage in our savannah. You could hear them shouting, *Pay the devil.*"

"Yanking their chains and beating blue bat wings," he concluded.

Where the virus still raged, or had waned and begun to build again, world leaders pushed forward plans for opening up willy-nilly. In the bacchanal, the huge neighbour so many of us had viewed as a benefactor shapeshifted into a growing threat.

And here? Next move? I swept the diary aside, suddenly unable to follow a basic schedule. Never before had I realized how disparate emergencies could multiply and fill one's mind to bursting without displacing each other, nor how the mundane could expand to squeeze aside the momentous. Here I was searching out pockets of time to write between frantic cooking and continuous cleaning – countertops and door handles, fallen mangos, floors, light switches, chicken parts, electric fans, books, toilets, children. Little chores non-stop exerted continuous pressure while the real griefs and dangers ran amok.

Sometimes nothing steadied me but compulsive tidying. But as easily, that stressed me out. Months ago I'd stored away ornaments and pictures to reduce the number of objects I would be driven to straighten, wipe or put back in place. Now I looked around, the unornamented surfaces of tables and cabinets bared my life, stripped my present of mementos, of testimony to a memorable past with excursions in the great world.

The phone rang, and Joel picked it up. He got it on speaker so I could hear Francis too.

Charlene and the baby were back with Shelley, safe in Toronto. Francis had found out from some chat group. Charlene had applied for refugee status so as to stay in Canada.

"Any lie she can dream up," Francis spluttered, "even if she have to make me out to be a monster and the whole island in a state of savagery." Tu'n the whole ting upside down. "You know what?" he added, "Let she go. She say I send her away with not a rag to her back, so I send to tell her come take what you want. She don't even have to come to the house since I am such a beast. I packing it up and bringing it by my uncle and them, for her to collect at any such time."

Charlene's stuff? All her clothes? Here? For her to come and collect? From off a plane?

But what plane could come in? I steupsed and retreated to the porch with a knife and two bowls, one with potatoes, one for peel. The call ended, and Joel followed me carrying the third bowl, water for the peeled potatoes.

Then the phone again. Isaac.

"Prof, hear nah. What you ask is absolutely no trouble. Nothing you could ask can be a trouble. I know the area well – I had an uncle down that way. What's the lady's name? Ena? Watch me. When I phone tomorrow you just put the package down outside your gate and go back in. We could wave. No probs. Lockdown? Borders? Nah! My horizons are limitless. You don't know is *Dr* Isaac Barrow you talking to or what?"

I passed the phone to Joel so he could give Isaac directions to Ena's house. Then we returned to the potatoes.

"Who's Isaac?" asked Melody, Micah close behind.

While I explained about graduate students, Micah waited impatiently. Then he asked, "You think Auntie Ena will make a pone and send?"

"Pone, pone," Mattie shouted, jumping around till he collided with a house plant and went down howling in the midst of upturned fern and shattered clay pot. I comforted him while Joel swept up, then herded them off to bed.

"I'm not tired," Micah protested.

"We are," I said.

Back on the porch we pushed the potatoes aside and sank into our chairs thankfully with our glasses. Bats reeled giddily in a triumphal dance against the gathering night. Nature, dislocated over the ages, was everywhere retaking its own space – gently sometimes, in a modest billow of butterflies forgotten since childhood, or a bold venturing forth of wildlife from forest into backyards. But also, across the planet over the past few years, the physical world had been striking back, vengefully – ripping human habitations apart in mega storms and scouring floods, unleashing famine to creep over scorched earth so gaunt-faced, wide-staring children, eyes like bottomless pools, squatted in swirling dust under the sun or flapping shreds of desiccated shelters. The earth was spawning superbugs, loosing novel viruses to sweep continents, setting limbs afire with fever and rashes, mouths agape for air.

I can't breathe.

I glanced back to ensure the children had stayed put in their rooms. Right behind our heads on a screen in the living room it was playing again, the repetition unbearable as it was essential. Only the night before, the unrelenting knee to a black man's neck by a Minneapolis policeman had brought into full view in sitting rooms across the world the murderous undercurrents of American culture. As the officer suitably named Chauvin chatted unconcerned, hand in pocket, millions worldwide watched Forde gasp his last, over and over. "I can't watch," I'd told Joel, "or even listen." He got up and clicked it off before coming back out.

"Health care, equal opportunity – what again?" Joel asked now. "Left to tempt us, I mean?"

"Well, some sense of security. Military strength and organization, I guess."

"Who knows?" He stared out at the horizon, head rocking side to side. "One day they might have to cozy up with the Taliban to fight terror. Of course there's always big buddy, Putin."

I hit him with a cushion, for I knew he was only trying to turn off the horror, then I raised the cushion to blot eyes and cheeks. Assumptions that had undergirded our lives were unfastening one by one under the barrage of images, but the images themselves, in their inhumanity, skewered us. And so many following each other unrelentingly. Troubles – *not single spies but in battalions.*

From however far away, the onslaught on reason struck home. A US governor had gesticulated about the effect of lockdowns on the economy, and he'd demanded sacrifice. Of course people will die, he acknowledged forthrightly. It was time to be honest with the population. Business could not resume otherwise, so it was time to accept that and move forward. People, I thought. Us again. I pushed the scene from my thoughts and resolutely rested my eyes on the sea.

Andrea, are you listening? If we'd moved, we'd be the sacrifice. Brown, elderly, dispensable – no longer part of the workforce and contributing to the economy, but a drain on it, all memory of what we'd given struck from the accounts. Invisible, relegated to the grey area of humanity, an acceptable offering. Around us here the role of the elderly remained so intrinsic I had never noticed how missing it might be from other frames of thought. Leave our tiny nook for refuge out in the great world? Not bloody likely.

Andrea? Bless her heart, but I'd be beefing up my exercise routine so as to live as long as it took. To the important places outside we might be shadows beyond the pale – at best, rarely manifest; at worst, expendable.

"Well, I'm damn well real," I said, "and here to stay."

I hadn't realized I was saying it aloud, and jumped when Joel said, "What?"

By the next day, though, I realized determination was not all that surged up. More and more I registered anger, what had been a relatively rare sensation for me, welling, corroding. Rebukes on world news, which compared idiotic government in great nations to *little banana republics*, strewed insult upon those small countries that had conducted themselves with exemplary grace so far. So much metropolitan farseness. But quickly the irritation faded into the grey-blue expanse or sea and sky that parted on the horizon of dusty pale hills. Once again it lapped gently on my mind – a safety in islands.

Yet here, too, yawned gulfs that might wash us down. Joel said, "It all hinges on parents who can't stay home from work, can't take the child along, can't leave him with grandparents.

"Right." Contemplating all that would come unlodged with that deep-set strut in Caribbean life, my vague but ever-circling anxieties hooked one image after the next. "Sometime, some desperate mother's going to pack one off to school with a runny nose or drag her along to work. But besides, some workman clinging feverishly to the job will deliver school lunches." And unleash contagion, I added mentally.

For it had begun to flit in as tattered impressions of sheer tiredness – carelessly flung out scraps of ridicule, sullenness or plain unconcern about protocols. Erratic, dizzy flights of illogic about some inevitable cosmic adjustment that would bring the virus in line. So the problem would go away: Poof.

The phone jangled, not distracting so much as intensifying this creeping sense of dread. Don't answer it, I begged myself, reaching for the receiver nevertheless. It was Tinsel calling to thank me for the envelope she get through Mr What-him-name. She asked in surprise whether we was still *inside*.

"All dem lockdown and mask is one waste," she went on. "Like none of them in charge know what they doing. Who they think have time for them? Watch. I walk in Massy and they take me temperature. Is normal-normal. What I wearing mask for to walk round? I do it to keep the peace, but is not to say it make sense."

I let it go. No point arguing with the surrender to synecdoche and generalization that was rampant now.

"You see the pressure I take when my business close?" On screen a bar owner emitted a prolonged steups into the mike a reporter held up to him. "I entitle to de-stress and if I feel to chill with a couple pardner on my own premises I'se a big man. Government what? We know what the hell we doing so let them get out we face. Who don't like to party could stay home." It went with a swagger but was despair tricked out as brazenness. So much harder to hold oneself down than to shrug off the suffering one might bring on others.

That was when I saw it. I'd been as blind as those abroad who had been irritating me steadily for months, for I had not thought this of *us*. Disappointment sparked anger again, and deepened sadness.

"Let them go ahead," I fumed, as Joel switched from the local channels to BBC. I flagged it all away. "You see us? You and I could work and shop from home, feed, entertain – for God's sake even educate the children, without putting a toe out for two years."

I'd left the living room and flounced back to my desk before I heard myself. The mindlessness of limers outside kept me locked up, yes, but those it threatened most fearfully were the vast majority who could not hide home or lay in supplies – thousands I'd dismissed in a mental flourish. I was party to that very creeping syndrome of indifference that had repulsed me. The inward glimpse shook me so that when the phone rang again I dived for it thankfully.

Ena's voice. "I get the package, Mrs Roche. I can't tell you how glad. I don't go nowhere now and not even the little good-for-nothing boy to call on since police take him up housing that set of illegal vennies."

I asked after her granddaughter.

"Penny? Mrs Roche when I tell you. Penny still in Florida – no, how she could come back and border still close? But at least she OK now. You mean I don't talk to you so long? You never know I get to hear Penny and all did have Covid? But it wasn't bad. Not like how people say. Like was just a little flu for true and she get better one time. Her brother's mother-in-law though – that lady well sick. Like she mightn't make it."

When I expressed relief that she was being careful, she continued.

"Well, I here quiet-quiet. But Mrs Roche – don't mind I tell Mr Roche not to send Francis with nothing for me. I didn't mean to make you find someone else, you know – I good right here. But what you send is a great help, thank you. And later Penny will come. The virus will done. Ent it must over sometime? Then we go catch up."

As I hung up, I strained again to recall Penny's face.

There we were – not only indolent and self-serving as a country, not so far removed from the arrogant and heartless on other shores. And I personally, as much as anyone else. The shame suffused me, intensifying prickles of fear that broke out as stories began to emerge about more cases around us than we had thought.

"They say what we saw as our relatively controlled situation was a delusion," I told Joel later. "What you think?"

"The deluge might be at hand," he answered, calmly sharpening a pencil.

Unless Francis was right and such reports amounted to politically motivated scaremongering. Who was to know? Every step was on unstable ground.

"What's a deluge, Papa?" Mattie asked.

Unrest? Here? Lying in the two-thirty dark, I recalled the tremor of anxiety in Meera's voice when we'd spoken earlier.

"The crime, girl. Is getting overbearing. Don' mind this is a gated community I fraid to open my door after dark. And people can't go out an work so it's real pressure. Where it will end?"

I had felt safe in the townhouse, but perhaps she was right. If I could be so infected with anger, what of those with nothing to prompt hope? And what use could I be to them?

When I closed my eyes, glimpses of children flitted in. Little strangers circled, trudged after or ducked away. Small indistinct figures sheltered in an abandoned ruin, a barrel, packing case or tottering lean-to. They hid from frustrated teachers, abusive fathers, exhausted mothers, and offered themselves to any employer who would toss them money or a meal, or who would charge them with some errand and equip them with brand-name shoes or a gun.

What was the word *pandemic* to them – as they rifled through garbage? What protocols for handwashing could a child observe if the nearest tap was half an hour's walk away from the last patch of grass where he had squatted to relieve himself. If these children fell sick they would die. It was the way of the world in which they knew they could change nothing. A girl of roughly Melody's height took form, stared straight at me and announced bitterly, *I'm not your imaginary friend. You're not my friend, and you're the one who's imaginary.*

Right. Shut that down. Joel was properly asleep, so I crept out of the blasted bed. The more we locked infection out, the deeper it penetrated the mind.

I turned on all the lights in the living room and took a cup of chamomile to my rocker. The hardest thing to take in was widespread blindness to the solution before all eyes. *Of course* it was straightforward, but science had no name for it and there was no legislating that most basic of laws, to protect every other life as one's own. Nothing else could shatter the chain of transmission, but the odds were stacked against it. Perhaps love was a concept too clichéd to take seriously. And through my fault as well. My most grievous . . .

I drifted fitfully in and out of sleep till daybreak, when the cushion slipped from my neck. I woke up with nothing to buffer me from the sharp outlines of the new real. Life resolved into concentric circles with the five of us at the core, most of the world outside and Covid circling our shores for a way in, while Barrie haunted the margins of awareness.

You bitch, she'd said to Cyn. My Cyn.

⸙

All that day the children bickered and whined. I had grown afraid of weekends. School, even online, conferred a backbone on the day, made it stable. Saturdays were sliding into a shapeless mess.

Joel saved the day by assembling wrought-iron chairs around an old blanket spread on the ground outside, and I hauled out a shower curtain for a roof.

"It's too low, though," Micah said, and Joel pointed to a shovel.

"Dig!" He bent for a corner of the blanket and flung it aside.

Lowering the floor kept them occupied for hours, and the hosing down afterwards topped off the afternoon as though turning water on the three of them cleansed both of us as well.

Joel and I got ready for bed that night in better spirits than we had known for months.

Yet still he was obsessed. "Is there *no* way to prove she isn't Mattie's mother?" he demanded as he took his p.m. pills. Yet again, his tone projected the question as a breakthrough enquiry never voiced before.

The house was still sealed against Saharan dust that had hazed our sunsets for weeks and elided the border of land and sea across the gulf. For a week the hills had shown through only sporadically. So although Mattie and the others were in bed, we hadn't bothered to settle ourselves on the porch. Beyond, in all directions, played out the outbreakdystopiaapocalypsehorror movie no one could turn off, because we were all inside it. So we took our glasses to our quiet bedroom in the still house on our noiseless street, and we moved into each other's thoughts by way of what Joel had long ago teasingly entitled the nightly symposium.

Originally it had been a time for assembling and assessing facts, suppositions and intentions. Then, over the past months it had turned into harassed exchanges under bombardment. Now in the calm we somehow contrived there had come about something in the atmosphere or in my brain, a sort of mental texture, tinder dry and waiting only for a spark. Something I could not identify propelled me off the bed to our own files of recent correspondence – as if now that the two of us were back in sync, our minds must be sharper and clearer than before.

I snatched up my tablet and flipped through recent notes on Barrie until they threw up a phrase or two that had lain like embers barely alive beneath other incoherent refuse – Cyn had been holding Mattie when Barrie, washed in blood, doubled over clutching her own belly.

"There has to be a record," I whispered. "Barrie definitely miscarried. Mattie wasn't the child she conceived through the IVF."

"Entirely Cyn's, the three of them. Never doubted it," Joel said. Then, "Yet how, if only two eggs fertilized?"

I caught my breath. As if sleepwalking, I made my way to his cupboard and rummaged through to a box of photographs. Then I got into the gallery on my phone. For Joel I scrolled through photo after photo of Mattie held alongside two prints of Micah at roughly the same age. Not for nothing did Micah seem to regard Mattie as if he were looking back at his younger self, while Mattie clearly projected Micah as his future. Like time-sensitive mirrors, Francis had observed, chuckling.

Leaning across Joel to his bedside table, I snatched up our file on the IVF clinic. "Two eggs harvested and fertilized, two embryos implanted together."

"Of course," he said. "Brother and sister."

"Fraternal twins," I agreed, "from separate fertilized eggs, Micah and Melody. But Micah was from one that had already divided."

He locked eyes with me. "That second embryo from the divided egg, thawed and implanted years later. Mattie."

I leaned in, touching my forehead to his. "Mattie – Micah's identical twin, four years younger."

We fell silent, trying it out on our brains again and again. By then I could hardly look at Joel – I was so mortified to acknowledge even those faint doubts I had let that wretched woman seed in my mind. Ill, I tried to remind myself, yet according to Mrs McGregor *only mildly delusional*.

"I don't see how you can ever forgive me," I whispered.

"What you talking about?"

"You know very well how angry you were. Yes you do – you locked me out." I choked but forced myself on. "And we . . . we breathe the same air."

"We do more than that," he objected, but gently. "We mingle minds." I cast him a glance of accusation and he conceded, "Mostly. Mind's a big place. Couple mysteries linger on – so what? Ask."

"Ask what?"

"Whatever."

"There's nothing I need to ask now. I know who you are. I've not always been that forthcoming either."

His arms stayed clasped around me as the most recent wave of conflicting sensations ebbed and relief took over. For we knew our children too. Whatever unlikely plan had occurred to Con in his desperation to have a family, he had given in to Cyn's persuasion in the end. Not only were Micah and Melody theirs alone: so was Mattie. It swirled over me like seawater, warm, cleansing and buoyant: Barrie had no part in any of them.

21

IN PRINT

Dear Mom,
   I hope you don't mind, but I imagine you as Cyndra spoke of you, and these days I think of Cyndra a great deal.

I PUT DOWN THE LID OF THE LAPTOP, but Barrie's greeting – weeks after I dismissed any claim she might have to the children – burns on as if freshly branded on my brain. Of course I *mind*. The single person who should call me that is gone, because *you* imagined her children were yours and her husband a monster, and so you pushed her onto that plane. How dare you presume that my concern, superficial and soppy as concern can possibly be – I see that now – could make your calling me *Mom* anything but revolting?

Micah saunters past my open door holding one hand closed behind his back and wearing a look of saintliness that bodes ill. But I don't bother about it, for I know now that he will do no hurt. Not like Barrie. There's nothing of Barrie in him.

Another thought penetrates that thick fog of umbrage, a shaft of light, I suppose, allied with another alternative plane of knowledge – the seer dimension of the elderly. As our physical vision wears out, there snaps in, hopefully, lenses of tolerance and even empathy. Might there yet be something genuine in Barrie's opening gambit, perhaps a yearning to call someone Mom again, just once.

Or is it to contrive in me an answering hunger – to be called Mom again, *once* more?

No. If she has to address me at all, she must call me Aria. Better than Joel getting wind of her calling me Mom. Even once. Here, people call you Moms, Tants, Nani – out of respect, they say, but often I think to acknowledge your age (and sometimes just when you could have done without the reminder). But Barrie calling me Mom was . . . (I searched: *different*? No. *Distorted*? Not the word. The one I wanted wasn't one thrown about anymore. No longer politically correct. How could I be scrummaging around for a word? Has it come to that?) . . . a *deformation*.

How? How could Barrie calling me Mom deform the word? *Deform*. I unwrap it: "bend, mar, warp, deface, mutilate, vandalize". I pick up an odour of some agenda. What lies under Barrie's choice of address?

As usual, hard to determine. Wheedling? A plea for adoption? A strategy for forgiveness fraught with self-recrimination, underlain by implied apology? A cry fuelled by desperation that is real enough but aimed at penetrating my heart, inveigling herself into my trust, under my skin. I can only shake my head: she remains illegible.

Not only hard to read but to transcribe. Or re-scribe. Besides, she'd slid further and further from mind as the children settled – the twins signed up for online taekwondo and Mattie in an art club on Zoom. Around us there crop up challenges enough without Barrie's dramatics.

I am raw with the exposure ongoing at so many levels. Now, barely a year from Cyn's phone call and with the anniversary of the crash approaching, the country is testing the first stages of unlocking, and coming out is so much more trying than going in. The terror of a wrong move unnerves me. Surrounded by uncertainties and conflicting advice, I find myself continually bracing for collision between hope and distrust. Every new bit of information seems suspect.

Only – my contradictory impulses as usual: surely I must glean all I can – even from Barrie. I stopped messaging once we verified she could make no claim to the children. Even Mattie rarely mentions her. But suppose some jot of truth is forthcoming at last, never mind the metallic taste of dread on my tongue.

> . . . *and these days I think of Cyndra a great deal.*
>
> *Having heard nothing from you for a while I'm addressing this and leaving it up to you to decide when, and if, you judge it safe for me to be in touch with the children or even for you to talk to them about me.*

How she *writes* isn't how she talks or messages.

> *Right now I only want to set straight a record that is so convoluted I may*

still have it wrong, although I do believe I am on my way along a clear path at last. Was I disturbed, as they said? Such a misleading word, according to Cyndra, such a tool for evasion. Nothing and no one external dropped in to muddy or set off shock waves in my thinking. Whatever evil came in, I suppose I invited it, even lured it. More likely, something unfastened inside. I can't account for how exactly I came undone.

So can some part of this chaos recur? I honestly can't promise that it won't. But this much I can say: right now I'm well enough to discern choices. Most important to me is the choice between inflicting my issues on the children or enabling them to grow up safely, even if that means far away from me.

Yes, I was off course for a while, for one spell after the next. First the break with Connor. Understand — he was like a chemical to my brain, a high I couldn't pass up however far I crashed afterwards. I had to have more, more, however poisonous. Except later, when I too was expecting. Then I found I could withstand what I knew was polluting, and I first began to see Cyndra as completely distinct from him.

I went into labour prematurely just as she had, shortly after her. Only, I lost mine. It happened late in the pregnancy. I was alone, and if Cyndra had not come the instant I called her, I'd have died. She pulled me through, and that was not the only time. But after that, every time I saw Mattie, the craving got so intense it consumed me. I suppose some lingering, chronic but subconscious resentment of Cyndra flared and I fixated on him. I lactated, betraying my need to mother him in the two telltale wet patches. But he was so delicate, at the first so poised on the edge of disaster, that Cyn was extra-protective, and I found myself excluded. Unbearably.

(Barrie-of-a-thousand-voices. Not a cuss word yet. Still refined and courteous. Perhaps the medication?)

Now, I want Mattie to know he will be my little boy for always, but he is Cyndra's child as much as Micah and Melly are. Your evidence is their birth certificates (virtual copies attached, as Cyndra left a few digital documents with me for safekeeping) as well as whatever records her clinic agrees to release.

Except — what contradicts this is their DNA, which is in your hands to check for yourself, along with further information the clinic may provide. After miscarrying a second time, Cyndra succumbed to Connor's insistence. He arranged for the Sydney clinic to transfer the embryos to L.A., and she gave birth to the twins. (Scans of correspondence attached.)

It slams through me – this bald disclosure. After months of haunting supposition, I had rationalized my terrors into a sort of prowling unquiet. Even this I'd recently dismissed. But now here it is. Actual data to shatter my painfully engineered peace of mind. Reaching for a chip of ice, I encounter only tepid water in the glass and pass my wet fingers over my brow, sagging back helplessly in Cyn's chair.

Barrie's off-hand revelation reverberates while I read on.

At first I thought she'd done it on her own. But later, when I lost my baby and the doctors said I could never have another, she whispered to me that I had three; they were mine and hers equally, and no one could ever take that away from either of us. We were bound to each other from that moment, Cyndra and I. "Joined at the womb," she said gently, touching my cheek. "But Connor mustn't know I told you."

"Yo." I grabbed her hand. "We get to be twins, kinda."

It came back, that message, just as I had received it: *"Yo bitch."*

Aha, instead of *you bitch*, as I'd edited it, Barrie's response to Cyn expressed affirmation. Was almost . . . a salute. *You were absolutely right all along. But I never knew, Barrie. Can you ever forgive me?*

Yo, bitch.

So, they had come to terms.

By then Cyndra had come to see Connor as she never had before. Earlier, a few years after the twins were born, when Connor was insisting on another child, making wild threats to pay some woman, any woman, to have it for him, Cyndra had given in again. But only because Connor insisted he could legally get custody of the twins. He convinced her he'd take them from her if she refused. Nothing I said could shake her fear this. So then, on my advice, she got him to sign an agreement on their equal custody of their children once she gave birth to a third child.

What was he after? All I can think is that my mother's will left everything to me and, should I die or be declared incompetent, to any daughter or daughters of my body. The child would be overseen by her guardian if she came into the property as a minor. But right – I can't prove his motive, so no more on that. The point is Cyndra's marriage was rocky even before the ultrasound revealed she was pregnant with another boy. After that, she let fall there'd been flareups of insufferable behaviour from Connor, and he'd sworn to keep the children if she left. Meanwhile, he'd always played for their affection, especially Melly's.

Cyndra hid this side of Connor from the children, but how long could she have kept that up? I honour her memory for that patience when I first knew her and for her generosity later — but especially for her iron will in the long run. But — and forgive me saying this when it must give you pain — I've come to think the children best off as they are, protected from the knowledge of what their father was.

If you find it possible to speak of me, please tell Mattie I made a terrible mistake when I was too ill to see what was best for him. Tell them all as little about their father as you can. He fastened on Cyndra as he had on me. Like a hook-and-eye — on clothes but also a line of verse I read in school: "a fish hook, an open eye". As I relive them, my connections with Cyndra and Connor fasten and rend at once.

I shall never get over it — that but for me, the children's mother (in that word's truest sense) would be alive. I can never express how wretchedly sorry I am, how tortured by regret. Yet, if they'd stayed, it would have ended in greater tragedy for the three of them. I can only say I've suffered too. Much of me, so entangled with both Cyndra and Connor, went down with them.

After learning of the crash, I passed into these dreary wanderings through a past that trapped and muddled me, and somewhere in the murk I applied for compensation from the airline as Connor's ex-wife and the children's biological mother. If they grant anything, I'll put it in trust for the children. I'd think they deserve substantial damages in their own right, and can work with you on that. At the time my only thought was to take them back and raise them as my own. Now I see clearly I was wrong.

All this has moved me to make another change: I've enrolled in a Master's programme in Child Law. I suppose after what has happened this may ring false, but I feel impelled to do something of value. (I've even volunteered for the human testing phase of vaccines they're trialling here.)

Still, I'm torn by conflicting highs and lows, ecstatic that the children were not on the plane but alive and well somewhere, proud of how far I've come, dismal because of everything I lost, angry at my part in the devastation. Fortunately, the medication helps me hold on.

If the children choose never to see me again, I'll understand. Why would they want to? I know I ought never have charge of them. But in case they ever need me, I intend to be in charge of myself.

Looking back over what I've written, I wonder if addressing you as Mom at the beginning of this letter caused you pain. I apologize but won't go back and change that, because you have something that commands it.

What, pray tell?

I think it is authority, steeped with compassion. Whatever. It will take the children through. Just tell them that now, as far as possible, I'm learning to be whole and that with your help they must do the same.

The mother thereof, Joel had warned. A persuasive posture.

A moment, a few moments to sift it all. For still it does not sit well. She is still set on vilifying Connor against not only the limited evidence of my own eyes but Cyn's vision as she relayed it to the end. Why, though?

One thing I must ask you not to tell them. I've postponed answering the question you emailed me a fortnight ago at 3 am (your time). But I see I must address it. Cyndra put that same question to me, and my answer was what persuaded her onto the plane: What made me sure Connor wouldn't follow her to Trinidad?

I passed on to her what he told me when I warned Cyndra against having his children. When his torrent of abuse dried up, I let him know I had recorded all he'd said on my phone and sent it to my own lawyer for safekeeping. "I taught that one a lesson," was what he said. Those were his words.

There had been some girl he came upon when he and Cyndra visited you in Trinidad – a domestic servant at some friend's house, I suppose. She led him on at first, then got panicky and began avoiding him. But by then he was obsessed with her. He spent a fortune on phone calls even after returning to Sydney, and when she stopped taking the calls, he went back – actually flew back to Trinidad. Not a soul knew except some friend there who told him he was "nuts", but this man, Francis, agreed to set up the meeting for him.

Only now the girl found this was way too weird. She ducked every possible encounter. He'd given her a fancy phone with Firaki as the first contact saved on it, but now she blocked calls and messages from him. Eventually she figured she'd have to end it personally.

And that was when, in his words, he "let her have it". He inveigled her into a last quiet meeting "to say goodbye". Tears overflowed, scalding my cheeks. *His buddy, some official in the police force or national security there, got him out and hushed it up. There was a whisper or two, but that went nowhere. From then on, though, this same friend cut all connection with him. One thing liking one's little fun, he wrote in a message Connor actually showed me, but Connor was much too rich for his stomach. He'd done all he could, this guy said, and not for Connor. This Francis said he'd done no more for his uncle than his uncle had done for him (or his father – whoever), but he didn't want to hear from Connor Firaki ever again. In any case, Connor wasn't returning to Trinidad lest some link with the old case came to light.*

Of course, none of this must ever get back to the children, not a whisper. I only pass it on because you have insisted. And I trust you.
Barrie

The images bombard me. Jasmine, Jasmine. A smashing.

I feel myself coming apart. No, these things don't, *don't*. Not to quiet, everyday . . . not to us . . . And then, through a haze – *Francis*.

Francis must have cleaned up after him. Had he washed clothes Connor left, later burning them in that half-drum in his backyard? Shoes would have required more effort. I could envision the white Nike mottled with browning spatter marks. Whether Francis threw them in the sea or chopped them small and distributed them between bags of garbage over the next weeks, nothing ever came of that.

I rested my head on the desk, forcing myself to stop gulping air, to breath slowly and push back the flood of unwanted images.

22

MEASURES OF IMMUNITY

—⁄↑⬞—

REAL LIFE MUTATES MORE RADICALLY THAN any contrived narrative. At times like this it is hard even to grasp a pen, let alone force my fingers over the keys. At least there is the delete button, a godsend.

No, the children can never know. And thank God Joel's acid reflux is letting up at last, for I could never clean this all away on my own. As Francis did Connor's mess.

But if I keep Barrie's counsel, she will remain a monster in their eyes, and where's the justice of that? Whom to absolve? Barrie? Connor? For a moment I squeeze my eyes shut – *a plague on both your houses.*

What choice really? It comes back to me, asking Mattie's teacher months ago whether the child was afraid of Barrie. She had said no: his friend would protect him. But she could not say from whom, and Mattie did not seem to know himself. Only now had a window opened on the unthinkable. Could this have been what Cyn tried getting to me through the *B* file?

Joel's voice cuts across it all: "Tell Mama I'm gone to the ATM. Coming straight back." And Melody answers, "Be safe, Papa."

A question is forming in my head when, almost immediately, I hear the phone and see Tinsel's name. I want to ignore it, but it comes back to mind how I missed Walters' message . . . and what followed. Suppose the woman is in trouble?

"Ms Roach, I could give you a day's work this week. Not tomorrow, because I not feeling so right. Nah, is a fresh cold and I believe my pressure raise. Another two, three days? No? So when to come then?"

I urge her to see a doctor but promise to call. When she rings off, I search back to that shadow of a query she interrupted. *"Be safe,"* Melody told Joel.

Everyone says that now. But last year when Cyn was getting into the taxi for the airport, Melody called, "Love you, Mom. Be safe." That was before Covid. What was in the child's head?

There are so many lockdowns, so many pestilences. When something flies howling in from the out-there, all we can bring to bear on it is what we can find inside of our humanity – and that changes day by day. It must. Bit by bit I find I must replace some part of me with something more viable for the latest circumstances, construct myself anew fragment by fragment, distinct from the original (if ever there was one), to form the novel mosaic I am becoming. Now and then a dark horse, though.

Behold a pale horse and his name that sat on him . . . My fingers tighten on my most recent wad of notes, destined for the shredder. The printed manuscript so far shows nothing of Barrie's latest revelation.

Why did Connor tell her about Jasmine? I've read of merciless characters who exult in the damage they've caused and seem wired to brag of it. A way of flaunting their power, I suppose – showing themselves off as untouchable. Mostly, I suppose he told her his secret as a kind of threat. She'd know the kind of man she was messing with.

How to keep my promise to Cyn, then, without betraying those flaws in her judgement we never suspected? Failings that even now I find hard to believe. To write Cynnie, how much to reveal and how to make up for what I must conceal? If I shred all I feel I must, what will be left of her story?

Lines. Where to draw them? I cannot even keep any permanent record of Jasmine's last words to me as they come back:

"Mrs Roche, I sorry but I wouldn't be able to work again. I need to get home. Oh God, I just speak to my mother and she say come right *now*. Things not good. You know sometimes you think is just a small thing you pick up somewhere and then it turn bad? So bad. I never expect anything like this and my mother in one state. Please, I can't talk bout it, is nothing you would even want to know, I so sorry – I have to just go stay with my mother."

This current file of Cyn's story remains on the laptop for now, only because it is my rule to keep every note and draft until publication. But I'll leave nothing on paper even temporarily. Meanwhile, I shall edit the version that goes forward, scouring it to ensure nothing slips through that can hurt the children. Let every detail regarding Connor die with him. Yet he persists in my brain, lifting his glass to touch mine. *Blood*, he says, his voice caressing.

When my breathing settles and the cold sweat passes, no other symptoms follow. I heard the car drive back in so I compose my face to take my sanitized version of Barrie's message in search of Joel. I read it purged of that mode of address he would find inflammatory and stop short of her final disclosure – but only until this evening on the porch. For now, Joel says, "Mmm," three fingers of his right hand dispensing with her as he turns away with a remote in the left, content that the pandemic has walled her off for the time being and in that sense made us safer – what he outlandishly terms The Pangolin Solution.

"Where does that leave us?" That small voice I hardly recognize as my own halts him in the doorway, and he turns but shrugs as if there is no room for doubt. Only, his eyes gleam, and I feel myself lighting up. I answer my own question with another. *"With mirth and laughter?"*

"Yup."

I laugh and drag the A/C remote from his fingers, so as to press the one for the TV in his hand instead.

"Will work better," he agrees.

So it will.

He adds that Francis has promised the children a pup if I have no objection, a chocolate Lab that he will source and deliver when the government eases the stay-home order in a few weeks. Francis told him there was nothing he wouldn't do for Cyn's three. "Of course, nothing can replace their mother," he said, then added, "and of course Connor – he was . . . like no one else I've met. But you see where these children plant now? Solid."

I raise my face to the light and warmth of discovery that the two of us are growing younger in their midst.

In the morning Melody will assemble us to make a new list, including kibble and wire mesh. More work. But. Leave all this for an apartment in some great city?

An hour or two later, here are Joel and the three of them – like four children together, evening and dawn having so much in common, I suppose – sucking up juice and wolfing corn chips.

"Plastic straws to recycle bin," I remind them. "Can't let all that slip again."

"Con's salsa would be good with these," Micah remarks, crunching noisily, and Mattie says, "Yeh."

Melody lays aside her bowl as if she's lost the taste for them. And I see her all over again for the first time.

The five of us will bring each other through this, and, yes, sometimes I go back to stare into the chaos that has been Barrie and feel myself being pulled in, with a sickening clench in my stomach, as if I gave her birth and am responsible for her. Then I grasp at the belief that she has steadied on one of these versions of herself and may maintain her perch; and the vertigo passes. For there is Francis too, however distinct from the man we seemed to know for decades, still recognizable. I detect in him strong traits I can continue to believe in. My affection for him surges up alongside the anxieties that do not fully dissipate. Connor, as I have come to fathom him, I purge from conversation and script, though he remains a stain on my reflections about possible and impossible narrative. And I am changed – beyond the possibility of ever again contriving to don my mask as quiet member of the literati into whose ordered existence melodrama does not intrude.

But I give thanks for the healing technology of stringing events together in meaningful ways. I tap the sides of the manuscript beside me to discipline the pages into a flawless block, marking on the newly copied file those passages I must delete before printing.

Now, the nearer I write my way to anyone, the more contradiction I encounter. Completely as we loved Cynnie, how much of the story she asked of me can I produce from the little I've discovered of her? And how much less have we worked out from our intimations of Barrie? Or Francis? The list goes on. *Melody.* I search my brain to word what she makes me feel. Perhaps *alignment*.

I make a note in my diary of the job reference for Isaac, of an invited article for December and of a reading to deliver in July – against the noise of the four rolling around on the living room floor, Joel more raucous than the rest, with the TV muted for a White House update.

A shriek of laughter pierces the quiet and shade of my room, and lights the future – so much to look forward to and to find out. For look what Mattie told us just this morning.

"This is my desk Cyn made," he said.

"What you mean, *made*?" He'd startled me, and my voice, louder than I intended, brought them all around Mattie and me, crouched over the sandy coloured table busy with smiling creatures.

"Oh yes," Micah said. "I remember her doing it. She spread stuff on the dining table that's mine now and rested it on top to paint."

"She started with this one," said Melody, leaning over and stroking one of the animals, the smallest and liveliest of them. It was the wallaby with the little joey in its pouch. Cyn had caught its energy, bounding along. "The day before we got on the plane, she kinda patted it and said it was her best self-portrait yet."

"'s mine." Mattie rounded off the story, and Joel patted his head.

After they wandered off, it took me a while to tear my eyes away from that wallaby, to compose myself as far as I was able. For I have not assembled my *self* on my own. Now that these preliminary sketches of my characters mesh into the not-book of them all, the most I can swear to so far is that together they have made me up.